Also by Isabella League

Fiction:

The Jongleur

This page intentionally
left blank

Land of the Firebird

A Fantasy Novel
by
Isabella League

HELENENTHAL BOOKS

FIRST EDITION

10 9 8 7 6 5 4 3 2 1

ISBN 978-1-888071-18-4

Artwork by E.E. Coad
Layout & Design by Gregory S. Coad

Dedication

For my husband — whose love, support and hard work have made these books a reality and not just a dream.

Prologue

The Extreme Northern Pacific Ocean, Autumn 1831

He was cold.

He had never imagined it possible to feel this cold. At his home, far to the south, one could see snow peaks in the mountains, but the temperature, on the whole, seldom fell below true freezing, and a padded, quilted jacket was sufficient to keep out the chill.

But now, with borrowed felt boots under fur-lined leather on his feet, a great-coat of heavy fur and a hat of the same material pulled well down over his ears and even fur-lined mittens, he was cold clear through, cold from inside out, as if he could never possibly ever be warm again. His teeth were chattering and long shudders shook his thin frame.

He stood on the deck of an anchored ship, her deck and surfaces shrouded in ice, for last night there had been a brief, but violent episode of snow, mingled with an icy rain. He was waiting, staring out at a gray sea covered in whitecaps, and at a most inhospitable shore. Snowflakes drifted down from an equally gray sky – this in spite of the fact that it was only early October, as these people he had accompanied here reckoned it.

Only a little to the north of this place lay the Bering Sea and the Arctic Circle.

They had not allowed him to go with them ashore, citing his age and the fact that he was unused to the climate. He was not deceived – they did not want him to see what they were going to do. This expedition had been presented to him as an opportunity to learn, to add to his knowledge about the subject he had studied all his life – dracophilology – the study of dragons.

But almost from the time they had left his native China he had become suspicious that these Russians were not what they seemed and that they had a deeply secret ulterior motive.

In his homeland the men from Russia were called "foreign devils". And devils they had proved to be. In spite of his scholarly curiosity he had not wanted to visit this cold, barren land of Siberia. But they had cajoled and bullied him and had last presented him with an Edict from his own Emperor, commanding that he give every bit of cooperation to these representatives of the Czar of all the Russias, lest there be a regrettable incident between the two great countries that shared a border. He dared not refuse.

And now here he was, waiting for he knew not what, with a sick feeling of dread on top of the bone-chilling cold. They had gone off this morning, after picking his brain for all he knew of the habits of dragons, not listening to his protests that he knew but little of the dragons here in this cold wasteland – no one in the world knew much about them. He was familiar with what had been written about the other types of dragons in the world – indeed, he had correspondence with other dracophilologists from wherever dragons were found and thus knew of the habits of dragons in the Americas, Scandinavia, Australia and the British Isles, as well as China, Japan, and Siam, even of the few known of in the largely unexplored African Continent.

They had left him here with the Captain and the crew of this very modern steam vessel, *The Sea of Azov*. None of them spoke a language he understood – they had no Chinese nor did he speak Russian. He spoke English with his so-called colleagues. He had learned that language in order to correspond more easily with his *true* colleagues of draco-philology Most books on the subject seemed to be in English, for the Americans had been the first to begin formally studying dragons. He had deep doubts that any of his present companions were even University Professors as they claimed.

The shore was as gray as the sea, shrouded in the veil of falling snow, with a bitter wind that sent particles of the icy precipitation into his face, stinging what little was exposed to the frigid air. It was a cold, harsh land, par-ticularly to someone more used to fertile green valleys.

Lost in the misery of cold he failed to hear the oars in the water and was startled when, over the side rail, appeared a bulky figure.

It was Dmitriov, the man who claimed to share his profession – even though it had become apparent that he was as ignorant as a child on the subject.

The Russian shouted something in his own language, which produced an immediate reaction amongst the Captain and crew – orders were barked, the crew ran to obey – it looked as if they were about to get underway.

Dmitriov turned and reached back downwards over the railing. He took a canvas wrapped bundle from someone below. He turned back to the deck and caught sight of the man so bundled in furs.

"Oh, it's you, Quong," he said in English, with a chuckle, "Have you been out here all this time? It was not necessary for you to wait for us!"

The ship gave a lurch beneath their feet as two more men climbed on board. The anchor was weighed and beneath their feet the engine started up, feeding off the steam that had been building since the three Russians had gone ashore.

"What have you there?" Dr. Quong Lee queried, through chapped lips and clacking teeth.

Dmitriov grinned, his teeth white in his immense black beard. "A rare prize, Quong!" He was a burly man who appeared even bigger in his heavy fur great-coat. The cold did not seem to bother him at all.

He pulled back the canvas cover to reveal a ovoid object of crystal, streaked with silver. Within it appeared to be a tiny form – one that Dr. Quong recognized immediately.

What had they done? Dr. Quong thought in horror. Was this why they had needed his knowledge? Whatever were they going to do with this? What ever they meant to do – it was not going to be good!

They had stolen a dragon's egg!

1

Tragedy at Trinity

Trinity University, Dublin, Ireland
End of Michaelmas Term, December 1831

The voices came clearly through the slightly ajar door.

"How much prep did old Stillfield give you for the Christmas Hols?"

"Oh, not awfully much," answered another. "Some reading…" the voice faded as they passed down the corridor.

Old Stillfield? thought the inadvertent listener. *Old* Stillfield?

He would be thirty on his next birthday.

Professor Simon Stillfield, *Magus Magistra*, Master of Wizardly Arts and Fellow of Trinity University, Doctor of Dracophilology (earned at Harvard University in America) and Master Druid, paused in stuffing end of term papers into his bulging briefcase.

In all fairness, most of his students, almost all of them junior freshmen (first years), were only seventeen or eighteen. To them thirty must seem ancient beyond belief.

But Simon was more used to people looking at him and saying in disbelief "You're far and away too young to have done all of that!" For in addition to his multiple degrees, he was the author of no less than six books on the study of dragons, and a recognized authority on the subject. He looked far too youthful, with his pale flyaway hair like thistledown and slender height. In an effort to look older he had once tried to grow a beard but his sister Noelle had kindly told him that it looked like some disgusting form of face fungus.

And he still lived at home with his parents and siblings.

It was high time that he established a home and family of his own, before he became too old and set in his ways. There were many old bachelors here at University who had let the chance for love and family pass them by. Simon did not want to be one of them. This had been much on his mind lately. But he was curiously reluctant to make a commitment to the young lady he had been seeing for a while now. With a start he realized that it had been nearly a year that they had attended concerts and lectures together. She was his acknowledged partner at all social occasions. And this length of time was considering a suitable courtship, usually followed by marriage.

The young lady in question was Birgit Comedon, attractive and intelligent and the daughter of a professor of Gaelic literature here at University. Birgit was very pretty with great masses of copper hair, a trim waist, green eyes and a lively air. It was a most suitable match. But she was non-magical. She had very little magical talent and no interest in it.

With the example of his adopted parents before him – a union of magic and souls, Simon had hoped for more. He felt at the most some affection for Birgit, not the passion he saw between his parents. He wanted to be married – he longed for a home and a wife and children but he had met no one who stirred him deeply. He seemed to be drifting into marriage with Birgit and what she had said yester eve confirmed that she had been thinking that way as well.

They had attended a lecture on ancient Irish architecture. Birgit was very 'blue" and prized intellectual ability over most other things. On the way back to her home they had discussed architecture and Birgit had begun talking about what kind of house they would have when they were married.

He had not as yet offered for her. But lately he had begun to feel as if he *would* offer for her whether or not he really wanted to do so – and more and more he was having doubts. She expected it; all of their friends expected it. He was not certain how his parents felt about it, for they had chosen not to interfere with his decisions and had not made their opinions of Birgit as a daughter-in-law known to him. They were always cordial to her, of course. One of his sisters, Noelle, liked Birgit very well. His other sister, Holly, did not like her that well, but Holly liked very few people, for she was shy and diffident. Stuart, Simon's brother had not made his thoughts on her known.

The door to the classroom suddenly opened and Janus, Simon's familiar, came in. She had run an errand for him and was now ready to go home. The day had been a long one and the air itself was cold — for Dublin — and damp with fog. Several people had speculated on snow falling.

Janus was a good-sized money cat, black and white and orange, with a face cut vertically in half by equal parts of black and orange. This had caused Simon to name her Janus for the Roman two-faced god, when she had come to him as a kitten almost twenty-one years ago. For an ordinary cat twenty was a great age. But familiars lived for the life span of their Witch or Wizard. It was thought that being in the company of Wizards and Witches, and therefore in the presence of the practice of magic, extended their lives.

"Are you ready to go home?" she now asked somewhat plaintively. She had had a litter of kittens recently and could only imagine what deviltry they had committed while she was at University with her Wizard. Holly had promised to watch them, but Janus knew that Holly would begin practicing her pianoforte music and completely forget about the kittens. Very soon the kittens would go to their chosen Witches and Wizards. Janus was very glad of it. They had exhausted her. She had decided that this would be her last litter.

"I just have to fit a few more papers in here," said Simon, undertaking that task.

"Shall I call Lakota?" Janus leaped to the windowsill, to call to the dragon who waited to take them home.

Before she could do so quick footsteps were heard and one of the Ancient Languages professors, Sean Ó Briain, who Simon knew slightly, burst into he classroom.

He looked pale and sick. "Professor Stillfield!" he said, gulping. "They were sending me to tell you! Professor Delamar needs you! "Tis horrible, it is!"

"Has something happened to my father?" Simon demanded sharply, instantly afraid.

"No, 'tis being one of his students! But Professor Delamar is much upset!" Ó Briain said.

Simon picked up his briefcase. "Tell me as we go," he ordered and ushered the other out in to the hall, activating the spell that locked the classroom door.

"Ye'll be knowing Rupert Henshaw?" Ó Briain asked as they began walking quickly down the corridor to the staircase.

Simon grimaced. No one in Trinity did not know the arrogant young heir to an English Viscount. He had cut a wide swathe through University — drinking, carousing and cutting up pranks. He had been on the verge of expulsion many times. He was charming. always contrite, and what was worse, brilliant. But he refused to apply himself and was noted for being a disruptive influence in any class he took. Simon had taught him in a Basic Dracophilology course and found him impossible. Henshaw was certain, always, that he knew more than did his professors. His class work failed to endorse this delusion.

"He dematerialized without taking care of the protocols and came out in a wall!" Ó Briain shuddered visibly, looking as if he might be ill.

"My God!" said Simon. There was no need to ask if Henshaw was dead; no one could survive that.

Simon's adopted father, Professor René Delamar, taught, amongst other things, dematerialization. The protocols for safety were very strict. Undergraduates were never to   attempt dematerialization outside the classroom and strict control was kept over each step of the process. One could not dematerialize without having a firm picture of where one was going, or else a tragedy like this was inevitable.

"Was he drunk?" Simon asked.

"That's what they're saying," Ó Briain said miserably.

It was stressed to the undergraduates that drinking to excess and magic were a bad mixture. A Wizard needed all his wits about him. This did not mean one could never have a pint with one's chums at the pub, but when one was serious about working magic it was best to have a clear head. And to dematerialize, probably the most difficult and exacting of magics, while drunk, was criminal stupidity.

Simon's classroom was on the third floor, while his father's was two flights of stairs down. Simon's long legs covered these effortlessly while the much shorter Ó Briain struggled to keep up. Janus followed them, mewing distressfully.

There was a crowd of students and even some professors in the hall outside the classroom, all talking in lowered but excited voices. They made way for Simon, for Séan Ó Briain, showing a surprising aggressiveness, pushed his way through the press of bodies, ordering them to make way.

His father would be alone for the moment, Simon knew, for his closest friend, Diarmait Mag Uidhir, who also taught part-time here at Trinity, was at the Tara Druidry that day, where his duties as second to the Arch Druid, Conchobar Ó Cléirigh, kept him most of the time.

"The Chancellor is on his way," someone called out as Simon and Seam passed through the crowd. It was highly likely that the head of the University would be accompanied by the Dean of the College of magic.

"I'll be leaving ye here," said Sean as they stopped in front of the closed door.

"Thank you for coming to tell me," Simon said and then tapped briefly on the door. It was not locked and he opened it and slipped inside when there was no response, Janus right on his heels.

Simon's father was seated at his desk, his head in his hands. His familiar, Beau, was rubbing himself over and over on his Wizard's hands and arms.

Simon felt a brief spurt of anger. What had happened was entirely Henshaw's own fault. But Simon knew his father too well. He would blame himself for the tragedy, thinking that he ought to have known that Henshaw was capable of such idiocy and kept a closer watch on him.

"Papa," Simon said, going up to the desk. The old name slipped out – in these latter years Simon had begun to use the more adult "Father " and "Mother". But it seemed more natural some-how to use the nursery names in this time of crisis.

Professor Delamar did not raise his head. But when Simon dropped his hand on his father's shoulder the older man put his hand over it.

They stayed that way for a long moment until René let go of Simon's hand and raised his head saying huskily, "They have told you, no? How could he do such a thing, Simon? After all we have tried to teach him? And look how it has ended. How am I to face his parents I do not know!" He was much distressed .

Simon seated himself on the corner of the desk. "It is in no way your fault, Papa. Henshaw was drunk – he ought to have known better." Simon thought of how Henshaw had behaved in his Basic Dracophilology class a year ago. The young idiot had been scorched by going too close to a just hatched dragonet. He had been repeatedly warned that a dragonet was full of gas and had an empty stomach when first out of the shell and that the resulting belching could mean a ten foot long flame, But Henshaw disobeyed, got too close and was burnt for his pains. *He always though that he knew better than anyone else and never profited from his mistakes.* Simon now thought.

"I should have known," said René bitterly. "I should have kept watch, knowing what he was..."

"He should have never been allowed in this class," Simon interrupted. But both he and his father knew that the professors had very little say over who took their classes. The Chancellor had the last word on that. A student with a rich, influential father was unlikely to be denied, particularly if that father was holding out the gift of a new laboratory upon his son's successful graduation.

René rubbed his eyes. He suddenly looked much older to Simon, even though he was not yet fifty. He had changed very little in the nearly twenty-one years Simon had been his son. There was silver in his mahogany hair, and a few more lines on his face, but since he not only practiced magic, which resulted in extended age and youthful looks, but he had the blood of the *Sidhe*, the Shining Ones, who were immortal.

"I must meet with the Chancellor," he said tiredly. "Will you go home, Simon, and tell them?"

"I'll be glad to," Once again he laid a comforting hand on his father's shoulder. "Shall I send Lakota back for you?"

René shook his head. *"Mais non* – I know that you have the dragon-ball practice. Send Cerridwen." Cerridwen was the family dragon – a Welsh Red.

"I doubt that we will have practice this afternoon. I daresay it will be cancelled," Simon said. "No one will be in the mood for it after this."

There came a brisk knock on the door.

"That will be the Chancellor." Simon rose from his perch and gathered Janus up in his arms where she at once went to his shoulder He put his briefcase under one arm.

Janus's brother Beau, usually so full of opinions, said nothing, but continued to rub his head on his Wizard, over and over again. As Simon took leave of his parent René gathered the black and white cat up in his arms and held him up to his face, where Beau at once began patting him with his paws and making little cat sounds of sympathy.

"Beau will help him," said Janus confidently as they briefly greeted the Chancellor and went through the crowd and headed back towards the stairs at the end of the long hall.

"My mother will help him even more," said Simon.

When they were back upstairs Simon unlocked his classroom and fetched his flying suit from the cloak rack behind the door. After donning the flying suit he wound a long knitted muffler in the Trinity colours — two stripes of blue, with a white stripe between, this in turn bisected by red — around his neck. This had been knit by his sister Holly and had been a gift for his last birthday this past September.

Janus hopped onto his shoulder again and they went at once downstairs, where a small door opened onto the Campanile, the great green swathe that surrounded the buildings of the College and University.

Here were a number of dragons waiting for their employers. Many people at the University and College lived well outside Dublin and with the speed of dragon flight could easily live in the suburbs and work in Dublin.

But Lakota, Simon's dragon friend, was not an employee. He and Simon were bonded in a way unique to the British Isles.

For Lakota was not a British dragon. Amidst the reds, coppers, bronzes, browns, blacks and greens of native dragons, his cerulean blue hide stood out like a beacon. His scales were tinged with opal and his horns were dark blue, larger than those of most British breeds, and striated with strands of opal. His legs were longer and slimmer than those of the British dragons. and his wings were opal as well. He had exceptionally large eyes and they were blue. Most British dragons had eyes of amber. Lakota had another different

15

feature – a ruff behind his head that became extended when he was angry or happy – it gave him the look of wearing an Elizabethan collar. He had only small ridges on his back and tail, making his harness a bit difficult to fit. He had five talons to the other dragon's three and these talons, too, were opal. In Britain his breed was known as an American Opal, but in his native America he was a Colorado Opal.

He had been one of a large cache of eggs found in the Colorado area in America. These eggs had been stolen from their keepers, the Lakota Sioux people, and discovered and rescued by a young American physician, Andrew Eaton Pierce, in 1826. Grateful to the young doctor, the Sioux had given him five eggs. As he already had a dragon, he offered the eggs to his old Professor, John Wycliffe, at Harvard University in Boston, Massachusetts. As it happened, Wycliffe had taught Simon when Simon had attended Harvard several years earlier. Wycliffe had written at once to offer an egg to Simon, who eagerly accepted. Carefully magiced to be kept warm, it had been brought by swift packet to Ireland.

Americans treated their dragons differently than did those in the British Isles. Dragons, from the moment of birth, were bonded in a special closeness to one person, rather than being employed by a family or the Royal Mail or a transport service, which were some of the professions open to dragons. In America dragon and rider were employed as a team, their unique bond making them very valuable. Simon was the first person in the British Isles to be so bonded with a dragon. He could not imagine life without Lakota – the dragon was his best friend and they loved one another as if they were brothers. Lakota was an immense help in the Dracophilology classes and was paid a salary by the University.

Lakota, with the long sight of all dragons, saw Simon at once and gracefully trotted up to him and Janus. Most dragons, while graceful in the air, were rather lumbering on the ground, but Lakota's longer legs gave him an advantage.

The blue dragon now looked distressed, his ruff drooping. "I heard what happened," he said. He had a distinct American accent that five years in Ireland had not abated. Dragons absorbed their language skills while in the shell and his early exposure had been to Americans. "I'm so sorry. Is your father all right?"

"He blames himself," said Simon shortly. Lakota dropped down on his forelegs so that Simon could tuck his briefcase into the carry sack of Lakota's chest harness. Lakota was, at five, still growing, but the rate had slowed down a great deal. He was not a big dragon, being only twenty-five feet long, and slender compared to a Highland Dhu or a Cornish Copper, but he was very strong and fit.

"Henshaw was stupid," said Lakota, who had very decided opinions of his own. "Even your father can't teach people not to be stupid." Then he added abruptly, "Dragon-ball practice was cancelled."

Dragon-ball was a sport that Simon had learned in America, where there were not only professional teams, but University teams as well. Simon would never forget his first dragon-ball match – the traditional Harvard/Yale game. It had been exciting beyond belief – the dragons darting about in the sky, the riders with their long mallets striking the ball into the goal poles high in the air. The dragons were allowed to make goals, too, and played with keen enthusiasm. Simon's letters home had inspired Stuart to try dragon-ball with some of his friends and by the time Simon returned from America it was all the rage, particularly amongst the dragons, who spread it all over the Isles. Now most Universities had a team and Trinity was to meet Oxford for the very first collegiate match this spring in Trinity term. Lakota was particularly good at dragon-ball – he was fast and could turn in mid-air as easily as other dragons could fly in a straight line.

After Simon and Janus mounted and secured the safety straps – Janus rode inside Simon's flying suit, curled against his chest – Lakota launched himself into the air and headed in a westerly direction. Nearly ten years ago Simon's parents had built a house in the countryside when their Dublin home became too small for a growing family. It was a large, roomy house for a family with four children and frequent guests. A Wizard's Tower stood at each corner. It was a pleasant, light-filled house, comfortable and welcoming, and filled with music and laughter, set amongst extensive gardens and protected by old trees.

Lakota's wings, which with no effort on his part sent them along at a fast clip, soon had them back at the family home, which was called Amberwell. It was named for the Faerie well that had been discovered on the property. An optical illusion made the bowl of the well look as if it was lined with amber.

Lakota circled down and landed in the spacious dragon pen near the stables. Cerridwen was there, munching on a leg of mutton. She looked up and called out a greeting as Lakota landed.

"Everyone's home!" she announced and then noted the absence of someone important. "Why, where is Professor René?" Dragons loved learning and Cerridwen was very proud to work for a University family.

Briefly, Simon explained what had happened and she was much distressed. She at once said she would fly to Dublin and fetch René home. Simon advised here to finish her meal first, for no doubt his father would be a long time with the Chan-cellor.

He then unharnessed Lakota so the dragon could have a good roll in the sand and deposited the harness in the tack room. There was a rack there for flying suits as well. Janus went ahead to the house, concerned about her kittens, while Simon went to see his horse, Eluin, and took an apple from a barrel in the tack room. Eluin was an Elvensteed, a gift from Oberon when Simon came of age. She was a beautiful fiery creature and kept herself amused (and the grooms bemused) when Simon was at University by changing her appearance. Today she was a chestnut with four white stockings and a white blaze. She greeted Simon affectionately and he promised here a good run that evening.

He then went onto the house where he was instantly let in by the butler, Fearghail, a man who might have served as an illustration for the ideal butler.

"Good afternoon, Dr. Simon," he said, taking Simon's hat and muffler. As a PhD from Harvard Simon was entitled to be addressed as Doctor, but no one outside University, save the butler, a stickler for protocol, ever did so.

He also was the only one who called Simon's parents by their titles – the Marquis and March-ioness of Keir.

"Where is my mother, Fearghail?" Simon asked.

"Her ladyship is in her sitting room," the butler informed him.

Simon was glad to hear it. His mother's sitting room was a quiet, private place to tell her the news.

He mounted the curving stair that led to the first floor. Halfway up he bumped into his brother, Stuart.

"Stuart!" he exclaimed joyfully. "When did you get back from Edinburgh?"

"Just this moment," his sibling answered. Stuart was nearly as tall as Simon, with his father's mahogany hair and his mother's violet eyes. He was a very good-looking young man and young ladies had been casting out lures to him for years. He gave them little attention for he was in training to become a Wizard Healer at the premier medical school in the British Isles – the University at Edinburgh in Scotland. It had been his first term and he had done brilliantly. His grandfather, the Duke of Chenevix, disapproved of the eventual heir to the Dukedom becoming a physician, but his family had known ever since Stuart's magical aura had manifested itself as brilliant green that he would be drawn to healing.

Stuart now said with a slight frown, "What is this I hear in Dublin? I stopped there briefly for some Christmas shopping and it was all over town that one of Papa's students dematerialized inside a wall?"

"Rupert Henshaw," Simon said.

Stuart made a face. He had heard about Henshaw in letters from his father and from his brother. "How is Papa taking it?"

"Badly – he blames himself," said Simon on a sigh. "I left him meeting with the Chancellor. Did you tell Mama?"

Stuart shook his head. "I've just arrived – you just missed the transport dragon leaving." He bent down from the stair and gave Simon a hug. "I'm glad to be home! I loved Edinburgh but there's no place like home! I've so much to tell you!"

"Come up to my Tower later and we'll crack a bottle and have a long cose," Simon suggested.

"Done!" Stuart grinned. "Now that I'm old enough to have a drink and not have Nurse come scolding after me!"

They separated and Simon went on up to his mother's sitting room.

The door stood open invitingly. Simon entered quietly, enjoying the sight of his mother embroidering before the fire.

He had first met her when he was eight. She had been his stepmother then, newly widowed, and they took to each other at once. His real mother had died at his birth and he had been little acquainted with his real father, a serving soldier in the Peninsula. He had been a rather lonely and neglected child, living with elderly, ill, grand-parents and cousins who tormented him. The coming of Lady Diana Stillfield into his life was as sunshine illuminating a dark cloud. Simon had always dreamed of a true family where he was wanted and loved. And when she married René Delamar, who had been Simon's tutor, his family was complete. They had formally adopted him – he was entitled to call himself Stillfield–Delamar — and had always treated him as their own child, even when children of their union had arrived. Simon had been delighted to have a brother and two sisters. He felt cocooned in the love and warmth of a family. Perhaps this was one reason why he was so reluctant to strike out on his own.

Lady Diana was still slim and youthful – she was an accomplished Witch and her dark hair and violet eyes showed little sign of aging. There were a few silver strands in her hair and she was not quite as slim as she had been before bearing a son and a set of twin girls, but she was still counted a beauty in Dublin society.

Simon said softly, "Mama, am I disturbing you?"

She looked up, a smile lighting her face. "Simon! You never disturb me!" she said in pleasure, putting aside her embroidery. She held out her hands to him. He crossed the room in two swift strides and bent over her to give her a kiss.

"Come, sit beside me and tell me about your day. I am surprised to see you this early – did you not have dragon-ball practice this afternoon?" She patted the sofa cushions invitingly.

"It was cancelled. Something happened today that I must tell you about." He took her hands in his and quickly told her of the tragedy.

20

She was shocked and said at once, "My poor René – he will blame himself for this! Simon, do you go belowstairs and tell Fearghail to show your father up here to me at once. And please ask Clíodna to bring a tea tray for two. Cook made almond macaroons today – his favorites."

Looking at the love and concern on her face Simon was much struck and wondered suddenly if Birgit would react the same if he had a serious problem with one of his students. She seemed bored, he sometimes thought, by his talking of his classes and studies.

He gave his mother another kiss and left the room to do as she asked.

After talking to the butler and to the maid who would take the tea tray above stairs, he went in search of his sisters.

As he had expected, Holly was in the music room at the pianoforte. She was a fine musician – she was teased by Stuart that she spent every waking moment at the pianoforte.

The music room was large and faced south with wide French doors looking out on a now rather desolate garden. In summer it was a riot of colour but now the last of the summer flowers were long gone and it was rather dull and mono-chromatic in tone.

The room was big enough for a considerable gathering, and contained, besides Holly's pianoforte, music stands, a harp, and storage for sheet music and other instruments. Simon's parents were musical – his father played the violin and the flute, his mother, as well as playing the pianoforte, had a rich contralto singing voice. Many of their friends played diverse instruments so that most dinner parties turned into musical evenings with everything from the pianoforte to traditional Irish instruments. Simon himself, having been gifted with a hammered dulcimer on his ninth birthday, had become a dab hand at it. Stuart was accomplished upon the Uilleann pipes and Noelle, like her mother, sang. Simon much enjoyed the evenings of music, singing and dancing.

In a family of tall people Holly was small. She was very fair with sherry coloured eye like her grandmother Lucie, Duchess of Chenevix.

21

To her eternal despair, she was slightly plump. She was very shy and only felt comfortable with her family and with people she knew very well, such as the Mag Uidhirs and their large brood of children. She had been sent to Miss Minchin's School for the Daughters of Gentlemen Wizards, where her mother had studied, but it had been such a nightmare for her that she had been allowed to come home where familiar surroundings soothed here lacerated sensibilities and she cold be taught by a governess.

Her sister Noelle, however, had loved school and would leave it with some regrets, although she was looking forward to her come-out in two years' time in London. But Holly dreaded this event.

To Simon's surprise, Noelle was in the music room with Holly. She and Holly were not identical twins – in looks as well as personality they were totally different. Noelle was tall, slender and graceful, with curling dark hair and light grey eyes. She was outgoing and flirtatious. At the age of fifteen – sixteen in a few days' time – she was quite the young lady. She seemed years older than Holly. At this moment in time her primary interest was in clothing and attending as many parties as here parents allowed. She thought it terribly unfair that not yet being out prevented her from more parties than just those sanctioned for the very young. But she attended more than many of her friends, for their parents had always allowed the girls to be as social as possible, rather than keeping them locked in the school room.

Now Noelle jumped up from the low sofa she had been sitting on. "Simon! We heard the news! What exactly happened?"

Holly turned around on the piano bench. "How is Papa taking it?" she asked, here eyes clouded in anxiety.

He told them what he knew, which, he realized, was but the bare facts.

The girls took the news characteristically. Holly was concerned for their father and sorrowful that someone had died. Noelle was more apt to mourn the loss of a handsome and charming young man from Dublin society. They talked about it for a few minutes and then Noelle gasped and said "Simon, I nearly forgot! You have a visitor! He is up in your Tower!"

22

"Fearghail didn't tell me –" Simon began, but Noelle interrupted him.

"Fearghail doesn't know about him. I met him on the steps when I was returning from shopping and when he told me he wanted to see you I took him around through the conservatory and up to the Tower. He's the funniest little man – he's wearing an immense fur coat and a tall fur hat as if he expected a snowstorm! His English isn't very good and when he saw Cerridwen from the window of the Tower I thought that he would faint with fright! I made him some tea and biscuits from your supplies and offered to sit with him but he said he would prefer to wait alone," Noelle finished breathlessly. "He gave me his name but I cannot remember it – it was foreign. It might have been Popoff or something like that."

Who could this be? Simon was in correspondence with Dracophilologists all over the world and many had visited him, but most had written or scryed and had asked if their visit would be convenient. And the name Popoff, or something like it, did not sound at all familiar.

"I'll go right up," he said with a sigh. It had been a long day – the last day of term was always hectic – and add to that today's tragedy. He really had no desire to entertain a stranger. He wanted a ride on Eluin, a bath, his dinner, a visit with Stuart and then bed in that order.

But Amberwell was famous for its hospitality and Simon did not like to be rude to a colleague (although what kind of Dracophilologist would be frightened at the sight of a common Welsh Red?) so he left his sisters and went up to his Tower in search of Mr., or more probably, Professor Popoff.

23

2

A Visitor From Far Away

Simon was tired and in no mood to entertain a visitor who probably wanted to talk dragons far into the night. When Dracophilologists got together with one another who shared their interest, they tended to become garrulous.

He took the stairs of the winding staircase two at a time up to his Tower. Perhaps he could talk Professor Popoff into returning in the morning, although good manners demanded that the Professor be asked to take his dinner with them. Why hadn't Noelle obtained the man's visiting card? It would help a great deal if Simon only knew what his proper name was.

When he at last reached the top of the stairs he tapped briefly on the oaken door and then entered.

Simon's Tower was that of a typical English Wizard. The walls were lined with bookcases, home not only to volumes of arcane lore, but to the herbs and esoteric ingredients a Wizard used in his spells. There was an armillary and a telescope. There were several sturdy work tables, laden with beakers and laboratory equipment. Storage cabinets held candles and crystals and Simon's scry bowl stood on a tall three legged table.. There were also several comfortable arm chairs, a sofa, and a drinks table with silver tray, crystal glassware and well-filled bottles of sherry, port, Madeira and *uisce beatha*, Irish whiskey.

Simon found his visitor staring out the window towards the dragon pen which was illuminated by mage lights. He wore a look of horrified fascination and murmured to himself in a language that Simon did not understand.

He was indeed a small man, as Noelle had said. He would barely come up to Simon's shoulder. He had a round, rather heavy face and was a trifle stout. His hair, what there was left of it, was dark and sprinkled with grey. He wore a huge drooping mustache, which with his large dark eyes gave him a look of abject melancholy. On a chair close by lay a huge pile of fur – a coat and hat. These garments were much

24

more suited to the winters Simon remembered in Boston, not the milder climate of Dublin. The visitor was clad in a dark frock coat, dark pantaloons and heavy boots. *Perhaps he thought Dublin is near the Arctic circle,* Simon thought in some amusement.

"You wanted to see me, sir?" he said aloud "I am Simon Stillfield."

The little man whirled about, looking startled. But he soon recovered. With a short jerky bow, clicking his heels together, he said: "Dmitry Sergievich Pozharsky. You are famous Dragon – Dragon – " he looked at Simon worriedly. "Dragon – ?"

"Dracophilologist," Simon supplied, wondering how Noelle had heard "Popoff" in this man's name And whatever he was, he was not a Dracophilologist, not given his reaction to the two dragons below and the fact that he could not even pronounce 'Dracophilologist', the term universally accepted for those who had made the study of dragons their life's work. Simon's curiosity rose.

"Pray have a seat, Mr. Pozharsky," said Simon. "What may I do for you?"

"Is *Count* Pozharsky," his visitor said, almost apologetically.

"Excuse me, Count," Simon said, equally apologetically, waving the Count to the most comfortable chair in the room. He offered sherry and it was accepted. It disappeared down the Count's throat in one gulp.

"Is good," he pronounced, holding out his glass for another drink. "Is not *wodka*, but is good." He disposed of this second glass just as fast as he had the first. Simon winced. A good sherry was meant to be sipped.

"How may I help you, Count?" Simon asked again, ignoring the Count's soulful glances at the bottle of sherry.

"I come from Mother Russia, from Czar. We need to help – no, is not right, we need dragons – no, have dragons!"

Watching his struggles with English, Simon was sympathetic. He had read somewhere that the upper classes in Russia spoke French in preference to their native tongue. He now said in that language, "Would you rather speak French, Count? My father is half French and I am completely fluent."

The Count's face lit up and his melancholy face lightened for a moment. "Ah, yes!" he exclaimed in French. "I am indeed thrilled to find that you speak a civilized tongue, *M'sieur*! My briefing at the Court indicated that the English never bother to learn any language save their own."

This was rather insulting but Simon, slowly sipping his sherry, let it pass. His curiosity was far too great.

"When our late Czar, Alexander, was in England during the Peace celebrations after the conflict with Bonaparte, he was much impressed with your Dragon Post. We would like to implement such a service in Russia. But we have no idea how to set about it and our current Czar, Nicholas, thought that we should consult an acknowledged expert."

"But there are naught but Ice dragons in Russia," said Simon, frowning slightly. "I have been unable to find any extensive literature on them – what little there is comes from China – and every indication is that they are both ferocious and feral. Scarcely prospects for carrying the mail!"

"But you are a Wizard, also, *non*?" the Count said eagerly. "We have few Wizards in Russia and they know little of dragons. There is a spell for taming dragons?"

"There is," Simon admitted, "They use it in New Spain to enslave full grown dragons. It is a cruel and totally barbaric practice! Dragons are meant to be free. It is much better to have a willing dragon."

"You have two dragons, I see," said the Count. "They are bespelled?"

"Of course not," answered Simon shortly. "The Welsh Red, Cerridwen, is employed by my family as a transport dragon. Lakota, the American Opal, is bonded to me. I find the very idea of bespelling dragons totally repulsive!"

"This red dragon is *paid* to work for you?" The Count's slim eyebrows, a startling contrast to his huge mustache, went up to what remained of his hairline.

"All dragons are paid for the work they do," Simon told him. "They are sentient creatures, not our slaves. In America they are considered citizens and male dragons can even vote."

"Everyone knows Americans are crazy," the Count waved his hand dismissively. "But we wish you to come to

Russia and help us set up our own Dragon Post – the Czar will make it well worth your while. He can be a very generous man. I can imagine that a professor does not make much money. The Czar is fond of learning and holds educators in high esteem. And St Petersburg is the most beautiful city on earth! There are lovely women, balls, song and dance every night!"

Simon was not tempted. Russia was a long ways away. His life was here in Dublin. "I must turn down your generous offer, Count," he said with no regret. "My commitments to the University will not allow me to leave – not in the middle of the school year."

The Count argued with him a few minutes more, dropping broad hints at the munificent sum that the grateful Czar would bestow on him and how superior the society was in St Petersburg – Simon would be lionized and invited to all of the best homes.

But Simon was adamant. He did not wish to leave Dublin at this time, not when his personal life was so uncertain. And he had sincere doubts that Ice Dragons, according to what he had read, could ever be successfully tamed to carry the Imperial Mail. As far as he knew, there were no other dragon breeds in Russia. When the European dragons, proscribed as evil by the Catholic church in 938, had fled the Continent they had gone north, west and south rather than east.

Politely, Simon asked the Count to dinner, but Pozharsky had arranged to dine at the Russian Embassy. Since Ireland was a sovereign nation, aligned to Britain under a loose commonwealth of the Six nations of the British Isles – Ireland, England, Scotland, Wales, Cornwall and the Isle of Man, she was entitled to her own embassies from around the world.

The Count continued to entreat Simon to come to Russia, but when it became apparent that Simon would not be swayed, the Count said that he must take his leave. He then pressed his card on Simon. "If you change your mind, *M'sieur*, I will be at the embassy for a few weeks, for there is no ship that sails for Norway until mid January. I shall go over land from there, as the Baltic sea will be well iced by then."

27

Then the Count inquired abruptly, "Is it always this warm in December?"

"Warm?" Simon blinked in surprise. "This is considered very cold for Dublin!"

"A strange country," said the Count, shrugging,

While the Count watched in amazement, Simon scryed a hackney company in Dublin who promised a hack there within the hour. The Count flatly refused to let Lakota or Cerridwen fly him into Dublin. It was obvious that he thought he would end up as a dragon treat. While waiting for the hack Simon gave the Count yet more sherry and sweet biscuits and listened to interminable stories about the Court, St Petersburg society and the superiority of everything Russian. The Count finished the bottle with no signs of impairment, walking just as steadily and bowing just as stiffly as he had when Simon first met him.

When he had finally seen the Count off Simon went upstairs to his room. The dressing bell had just rung and it was time to change for dinner. And he had hoped to have a bath before the meal.

He almost threw the Count's card in the fire. He could not conceive under what circumstances he might ever need it.

But something stayed his hand and he put the card instead, in a small drawer of his desk, where he kept such things.

There were but the four of them at dinner – Holly and Noelle, Stuart and Simon. Their parents had ordered a tray in their sitting room. His siblings were concerned about this but, as Simon told them, it was probably the best thing. "Mama will make Papa realize that what happened is not his fault and could not have been prevented."

"Will Papa lose his position at University?" asked Holly. Since there was no lack of money in the family they did not have to be concerned about the loss of income should the worst happen and their father was unemployed. But it would be a tragedy nonetheless, for all of them knew that their father loved teaching and would be bereft indeed if he could not practice his profession.

"It's too early to say," said Simon, "It depends upon the Chancellor and probably upon Henshaw's father – if he is the vindictive sort –"

"An investigation will vindicate Papa!" said Stuart hotly. "Even I heard that Henshaw was more than three parts drunk! Any booby knows you do not dematerialize when you're bosky!"

"How will they have a funeral?" said Noelle suddenly. "If he is in a wall –"

"There are spells that Forensic Wizards know that will release the body from the wall," Simon explained shortly. He had read of it – it was a terrible and exacting process and the body that was recovered was barely recognizable as human. But he was not about to sully his sisters' ears with a description of this.

Holly was looking pale. "Please, may we talk of something else? This is making me feel ill just thinking about it!"

Simon smiled at her and Stuart reached across the table and patted her hand. "Let's have Simon tell us of his visitor!" he suggested.

Holly smiled back at her brothers. Noelle looked disappointed. Simon suspected that Noelle had a bloodthirsty streak. She was the least magical one in the family and had not done well in her magical studies at Miss Minchin's. In spite of her lack of talent she was interested in reading about black magicians, and spells gone wrong.

As Fearghail supervised the changing of the courses Simon entertained his siblings with a description of the Count and his strange pro-position.

"Did he really think you would just drop everything and go to Russia in the dead of winter?" Stuart asked in amazement as the footman, Connor, put a plate of salmon covered in dill sauce in front of him. "Thank you, Connor," The Delamar children had all been trained to appreciate and be thoughtful of the servants.

"But I am a poorly paid professor and must needs leap at the chance to gild my coffers!" Simon informed them.

This invoked an explosion of laughter from the other three. Simon was quite well off. His books made a good amount of money and in addition, when he was nineteen, a godmother of who he had been unaware had died and left him her entire not inconsiderable fortune, making him independently wealthy, able to command all the elegancies of life.

When the laughter had subsided Stuart said thoughtfully, "If the late Czar was so impressed with the Royal Dragon Post why did they wait until now, some sixteen years later, to implement this plan? It seems dashed smoky to me."

Simon shrugged. He had no intention of going to Russia. He was not overly concerned with the whys and wherefores of Count Pozharsky's proposal. In the next few years time there was to be mounted an expedition, still in the planning stage, to China to study the fascinating Oriental dragons, which were both like and unlike their Western counterparts. This was to be sponsored by the Royal Society and Simon had already committed himself to the journey. Since Siberia, the home of the Ice Dragons, was so near to China, he would investigate them at that time.

The topic soon changed – the girls wanted ideas on what would make the best Christmas gifts for their parents and the discussion became rather heated before Fearghail and the two footmen cleared away the remains of dinner.

It was difficult to get out of bed the next morning. It had turned into a late night. Simon had indeed taken Eluin for a run – the Elvensteed could see in the dark as well as a cat and there was little danger of a spill in even a full gallop. Simon got his longed-for bath and then Stuart, with several bottles of ale and a plate of sandwiches, had joined him in the Tower and they talked until nearly one AM. When Simon at last collapsed into bed he fell at once into a deep, dreamless sleep.

He awoke shortly before nine. feeling somewhat disoriented. It always took some getting used to, this free time between terms when one's life was not ruled by the tyranny of the clock. The day lay before him, all his own, to do with as he liked. But what he wanted to do most urgently, was talk to his father and find out what the Chancellor had said. He had put the odd visitor from the previous evening out of his mind. He expected never to see Count Pozharsky again.

30

Accordingly he shaved himself and dressed, with the help of his valet, Sanders, who had been with him since he was a boy. Simon was hoping that he was not the only one that had overslept and that he would find most of the family at the breakfast table.

He was in luck. Stuart and both of their parents were still at breakfast. Dimly, he could hear a pianoforte – that meant Holly was already practicing. Noelle, Stuart informed his brother as Simon slid into his place, was still abed, getting her beauty sleep.

As Simon greeted his parents he looked anxiously at his father. René looked a trifle fine-drawn and weary this morning but the awful haunted look that Simon had noticed in his eyes yesterday afternoon was gone. Mama had worked her magic on him. Once again, Simon wondered if Birgit would supply him with the same love and support that was so obvious between his parents – the same kind that he would want to give to her if they were to marry. And once again, he had his doubts.

"What has the Chancellor decided , Papa?" he asked, helping himself to eggs, kippers, ham and grilled tomatoes. They dined quite informally in the morning.

"There is to be the investigation and he has decided that the dematerialization class shall be suspended until at least the autumn of next year," René answered with a sigh. There was a good amount of food on his plate but it was quite obvious he had only picked at it.

Stuart frowned and then protested, "But that's as if you are admitting to being at fault, Papa!"

"I have not the heart to go on with teaching it," said René sadly.

"Even at Tara?" queried Simon, for René taught this subject at the Druidry also,

"Yes, and I shall tell Conchobar so this morning."

"We had an early scry from the Mag Uidhirs –" put in Diana. "We are to go there for a nuncheon with them and the Ó Cléirighs, to discuss what has happened."

"And this afternoon Henshaw's parents will be arriving from England," said René on a sigh. "I do not know what I might say to them, for surely they will be angry and full of hate."

31

"If their precious son hadn't been full of beer, I'll go bail this never would have happened." Stuart rather viciously stabbed at the last piece of ham on the Wedgwood platter.

René put a hand over his eyes and Simon and his mother exchanged looks of concern.

"Come my dear," said Diana gently. "We have several hours before we must needs go to Tara. I think you had ought to lay down – you slept very ill last night.'

Her husband was nothing loathe, and allowed him to lead him back upstairs to the sanctuary of their rooms.

"Papa is taking this very hard," Stuart said with a frown. "I wish there was something we could do."

Simon knew that there really was nothing they could do. The tragedy had to be played out to its conclusion and most of it was not going to be pleasant. The only thing they could do for their father was to offer him their love and support.

Simon was then struck by a part of the house hold that was missing. "Where are the cats?" he asked. Usually at breakfast the room and the space beneath the table was full of feline familiars. The house at the moment contained Simon's Janus. René's Beau, Diana's Rascal, Stuart's Dr. Foster, and Holly's Allegra, and Janus's four kittens. The kittens were known as One, Two, Three and Four, for they would get their real names when they went to their Witches or Wizards.

"The kittens have gone missing. All of the cats are out searching for them. The dragons are too. I said I'd help as soon as I ate my breakfast," Stuart answered, pushing back his chair. "Are you going to eat that last muffin?"

Simon shook his head. He watched as Stuart crammed the last muffin in his mouth. Stuart had single handedly cleaned most of the plates on the table . Simon could remember eating like that, but now the thought of it made him slightly queasy.

"Did anyone think to ask Eluin if she had seen them?" Simon asked. The Elvensteed was usually aware of every-thing happening on the estate.

Stuart nodded. "She hasn't seen them. No one has. I hope the little fluff-balls are not in trouble again. I don't think Janus has ever had such a litter so ripe for mischief!"

The four kittens had already had to be rescued from the well, from the hayloft, from a bull in a neighbors' field, been stuck up a chimney, and found in amongst the good china and crystal in the Plate room. How they got in there no one knew, for it was kept locked and was still locked when they were found.

The kittens were eventually found – stuck up a tree near the succession house. They were afraid of climbing down and perhaps falling through the glass roof below them. They mewed most distressingly until Lakota stood up against the tree with Simon on his back and the kittens, scolded by their mother, allowed Simon to pluck them off one by one. Such was their fear that they had rammed their little claws deep into the bark of the tree and Simon had to employ a minor releasing spell to free them.

"Whew!" said Stuart, who had helped in the operation by soothing the rest of the felines who were milling about his feet, worried about the kittens. He took the kittens one at a time as Simon handed them down, to give to their worried and angry mother. She boxed their ears with a firm paw and then rapidly licked them, scolding all the while.

"Shall we go into Dublin?" Stuart asked his brother as Simon swung down from Lakota's back. "When I was in the bookshop yesterday Jonas told me that they've got in a brand new shipment of arcane books and novels. I haven't finished my Christmas shopping as yet. Perhaps we might even get up a scratch team for a little dragon-ball!" he added hopefully.

Simon agreed to this plan – Lakota, he thought, would too, for the blue dragon dearly loved a good dragon-ball match.

But the dragon said rather hesitantly, "That sounds fine, Stuart. But I have to talk to Simon about something first. It's urgent."

"Don't worry – I'll take the furry horde back to the house and feed everyone. When you're ready I'll be in the kitchen," Stuart said cheerfully and allowed the kittens to climb up to his shoulders.

It was a bright but cold day and Lakota was as blue as the sky above. His face, normally smiling and good-natured was now frowning. Simon's heart sank. Whatever was wrong?

Lakota seemed a little hesitant at first and then said quickly, "I over heard something you ought to know, Simon. I wasn't eavesdropping; I couldn't help but overhear. I have been trying to decide if I should tell you or not. But I think you ought to know."

"What is it?" Simon asked in no little tre-pidation.

"At the beginning of the week I was waiting for you on the Campanile when Birgit and a friend of hers came by. They were talking loudly and I swear I wasn't trying to listen in –"

"I know you weren't, Lakota." Simon interrupted. Dragons had incredible hearing as well as eyesight like a hawk's.

"She doesn't like dragons, Simon. She wants you to stop working with dragons and teach something respectable! I can't repeat what she said – it hurt my feelings. She said that she could make you give up your dragon studies – and me! Could she do that?" he added worriedly.

Simon was instantly infuriated. In fact he couldn't recall ever being so angry. Expect him to give up his life's work, which he loved, to suit her notions of respectability? And she thought that he would be weak-willed enough to let her reorder his life?

He had been aware that she did not like flying – many people had a fear of heights or became dragon-sick in the air, but he had not been aware that she actually disliked dragons. Some people did, Simon was aware, although he did not understand it in the least.

Lakota noticed the look on his face, and said, "I'm sorry –"

"Don't be sorry," Simon interrupted. "This is just what I needed to hear to help me make up my mind. If it had not been for Henshaw and now this I probably would have married her. But now I know it's impossible!"

Lakota said simply, "I'm glad. I don't think you would have been happy with her. And what's more, I think your parents will be glad as well."

Simon suddenly felt as if he wanted to be far, far away from everything and everyone, especially Birgit. Where could he go that was new and different, where he would see neither Birgit nor all of the people who no doubt expected

34

them to be married? He immediately thought of the Count. "Lakota, do you know anything about Russia?" he asked his dragon friend.

3

A Countess Below Stairs

St Petersburg, Russia, May 1832

She was dreaming again of Mikhailovskoe.

In the dream it was high summer. The estate was set in acres of woodland, with no near neighbors. She had just come from swimming in the river and was walking up through the village to the house The fields were ripe with wheat, rye and barley. As she walked down the street of the village, the serfs called out greetings to her. She could she so clearly the *izbas,* the log homes of the serfs, lining the road on each side, framed by birch trees. Each *izba* was decorated with beautiful carvings and bright colours. In her fancy, she could even feel a warm breeze on her face and the dirt of the road under her bare feet. The scent of the birch and fir woods was rich, as was the scent from hay making.

But when she reached her home, everything changed. Where had stood the house, made of wood and decorated with a multitude of onion domes, stood a smoking ruin.

"Father! Sacha!" she screamed, running to the edge of the vast green lawn, only to be brought up short by the sight of her cousin Evgeny, clad in his Hussar uniform of red jacket and elk-skin breeches. A mocking smile lit his face. "Your father is dead," he said cruelly. As she began to sob, he went on, "Your family is ruined. You will have to beg for your bread. You will never be happy again!"

And Countess Tatiana Ivanova Kustodieva awoke with a shudder.

And, alas, her dream was all too true.

She lay in an attic, dusty and dreary. She slept on the floor, on a rude mattress beneath a ragged blanket that was inadequate in the winter, for no comfortable tiled stove warmed the room. They had to make do with the heat that drifted up from the floor below. The other furnishings of the room were a screen to wash and dress behind, a warped bureau with a cracked mirror and a washstand and commode. Nails pounded into the wall served as a clothes press.

Tatiana shared the room with her brother Alexander, who was twelve years of age to her twenty–six. He was the child of her father's second marriage, whose mother, like her own, had not survived his birth. He was very dear to her, as was the other occupant of the room, Vron, the sleek black cat who was now curled against her. As she stirred on the straw mattress Vron raised his head and looked at her. inquiringly. Sometimes she fancied that he could almost talk to her – he looked so intelligent, and listened so intently to what she had to say.

"Tatya? Are you awake? It's gone cockcrow," her brother whispered from his mattress. "It's time –"

Tatya sighed. "Yes, Sacha, I know – time to get up!" She threw off the blanket and rose from the floor. Beside her, Vron yawned and stretched. He would be able to go back to sleep later, but for Tatya and Sacha, a long, busy day of service to their aunt, uncle and cousins was just beginning.

As their aunt, Ekaterina Feodorova Rostova, never ceased to remind them, she had given them a home when their father had been disgraced and ruined. It was the least they could do to show their gratitude for her magnanimity – to make themselves useful. Her aunt's definition of make themselves useful was more like that of unpaid servants.

The Rostov family consisted of Ekaterina, her husband, Yuri Pavlovich, daughters Olga and Natalya and Evgeny, their son, the oldest, who fortunately did not live at home, but in one of the many barracks in St Petersburg with his regiment of Hussars. Tatya cordially disliked her aunt, uncle and Olga and Natalya, but she hated and feared Evgeny. He was in little at home, for he held his relatives in contempt. This was much to Tatya's relief. He looked at her in a way that filled her with terror.

They were not a pleasant or loving family. Aunt Ekaterina thought of little but her social position and getting her daughters suitably married. Natalya and Olga were occupied only with finery and *beaux*. They had little conversation besides cascades of headache inducing giggling. Uncle Yuri was hen-pecked by his spouse and browbeaten by his superiors at his civil service position. As a result he was a domestic tyrant with the servants, who felt his birch whip frequently. This included Sacha and Tatya.

And it was a bleak household as well. There were very few books – sometimes Tatya wondered if her aunt and cousins could actually read. The rooms kept to impress company were the only rooms that were decorated with pictures or flowers.

The Rostovs lived on the remains of the family fortune and what Yuri earned at his civil service appointment. Since, in Russia, the estate was split evenly between all the sons (once the daughters were provided for) what had once been a considerable holding of land and serfs had dwindled in just a few generations to very little. Yuri Pavlovich had been cursed with ancestors who had bred prolific amounts of sons – he himself had five brothers. Ekaterina had been forced to make reductions in the household and over the course of nearly twenty-five years this had become a religion to her. She squeezed a *kopek* so tight that it burst under the strain. She brought serfs up from the small estate they still held and put them to work in their St Petersburg home, rather than hire expensive city-trained servants. Luba Efremova, a good plain Russian cook, was forced to learn French cuisine, so that no one would know that the Rostovs could not afford a French chef as was fashionable.

The serf girls had proved unsuitable as maids for Natalya and Olga, so, by default, Tatya served as maid to her cousins, in addition to anything else her aunt could think of her to do. Sacha did everything from cleaning boots to cleaning the stables with old Mikhail, the super-annuated coachman.

To Ekaterina's disgust the serfs had brought with them all the old superstitions of the countryside. Luba put out a meal each night for the *domovoi,* the house spirit, who could bring bad luck to the house if he chose. Old Mikhail believed in the *dvorovoi*, the yard spirit, who could take a dislike to the colour of a horse or cow and then harass the stock as a punishment. Mikhail had refused to drive a troika team of grey Orlovs Ekaterina had obtained quite cheaply, for the *dvorovoi* did not like the colour grey.

And most annoying was the behavior of the serfs about the old fashioned bath house. To Ekaterina the bath house was an affront – but her spouse had been adamant about this one thing – he wanted his traditional Russian bath house with its steam bath and bundle of birch twigs for scouring the body.

The serfs were fanatic about leaving the second bath of the day for the *bannik*, the bathhouse spirit. They became hysterical if someone tried to take a bath at night, for this would insult the *bannik* and he would send for the *cherti*, demons who would then punish the person who dared to bathe at night. *Cherti* even stole children!

Privately Tatya thought that even the *cherti* would balk at stealing Olga and Natalya. Her cousins were past childhood now, being sixteen and eighteen respectively, but even when they were younger the *cherti* would not have wanted them

Tatya and Sacha had now lived with their relatives for nearly seven years, ever since their father, Count Ivan Petrorvich Kustodiev, had been sentenced to fifteen years of hard labor in the camps of Siberia. He would not be returning, for in addition to the labor sentence he had been banished to Siberia for life. His children had no idea if he was alive or dead. If a letter had ever arrived about him or from him, Tatya was certain that her aunt would have destroyed it, for Aunt Ekaterina was terribly afraid that someone would find out that Count Ivan was related to them. He was not her brother, but her brother-in-law, her half-sister, Tatya's mother, married to him so briefly. At first Ekaterina had been reluctant to take the children of a condemned criminal into her home, but the thought of free service soon overcame her scruples. As she had no intention of allowing either of them out on society, no one would ever know of their presence.

For Count Ivan, a charming, improvident man who fancied himself a poet, had become involved with the Decembrists in 1825 and had incurred the wrath of Czar Nicholas.

Tatya had never understood her father's involvement. He was not political, but he was easily led and she could only suppose that he had been talked into it by one of his many friends – friends who somehow melted away when he was arrested.

The Decembrists had believed that Constantine, the late Alexander's eldest surviving brother, ought to be the next Czar. When the news had come of Alexander's death Constantine was in Warsaw and Nicholas was unsure of what to do. He wanted to be Czar and he had Alexander's promise that he and not Constantine, would wear the crown. But to the people, Constantine, the elder, was the true successor.
Nicholas at once swore allegiance to his brother and urged everyone else to do so.

But Constantine did not want to be Czar. After a spate of messages to each other, each one swearing allegiance to his brother, Nicholas received news from Taganrog of a conspiracy that began with a group of aristocratic young army officers. Their aims were a constitutional monarchy among other things. After a fiasco in which the insurgents gathered in St Petersburg's Senate Square, over five hundred were arrested and out of them five were executed and one hundred and twenty three were punished by Nicholas. Among them was Tatya's father.

And every thing they owned had vanished, Tatya knew not how. In what seemed but overnight their comfortable fortune had dissipated. Mik-hailovskoe was no longer theirs. The State money lender, the Lombard, took a great deal of it. It was as if anyone her father had ever known had put in a claim to his property. Count Ivan had been open handed and generous to his friends and they paid him back by stealing from his children, who were left penniless and homeless.

It was totally different life that they were thrown into at the Rostovs'. Sacha bore it better than did Tatya, for he was only five when his father was arrested and their lives changed forever. But Tatya was wild with grief and fought bitterly against her new life. She was used to a happy life, filled with the leisurely times at Mikhailovskoe. Her father had not cared for life in St Petersburg – even in the depths of winter they were to be found at Mikhailovskoe, the house filled with constant guests: army officers, ballerinas, singers and musicians and the intelligentsia. Conversations were stimulating and thought-provoking – there were books to read, impromptu theatricals, music and dancing each day more interesting than the last.

40

And now each day was naught but work and more work, work of a stultifying dullness. Perhaps if she had never known any other life she could have better borne it.

After a period of heart-breaking rebellion and many birch switches broken over her back by her uncle (for impertinence, disrespect, and failure to be grateful — among other failings) she came at last to a sort of dull resignation. Now she lived only to see Sacha somehow escape and make a better life for himself. She would accomplish this somehow — although she had no idea how she could make this come about.

Today would be no different. She had to maid her cousins, then go to market for fresh food, dependent on what fancy dishes her aunt ordered. Old Luba would be grumbling — she hated French cookery and could not see why a Russian family could not eat good Russian food. Like most of the serfs she spoke but little French and Aunt Ekaterina spoke little else. To speak Russian was "*mauvais ton*" and this to Ekaterina was the ultimate sin. Tatya spent a great deal of her time translating Ekaterina's orders to the serfs. Ekaterina was completely fluent in Russian but she refused to soil her tongue with the language of the serfs as she called it.

Before breakfast, which for Tatya and Sacha was a simple bowl of *kasha* – boiled buckwheat – Sacha went to the stables and Tatya brought wood upstairs to feed the stoves of her cousins and that of her aunt and uncle. Small tiled stoves kept their rooms cozy. As it would never do for a manservant to enter the rooms of a lady, this job fell to Tatya. Pavel, one of the footmen, had stacked the wood up for her and she made a mental note to thank him.

The Rostov home was typical of St Petersburg. It was of wood, long and low, with many large windows. Several wings, unseen from the street were in the back and there was a spacious courtyard in which the wooden steam bath house stood. The rooms were spacious, and due to Ekaterina's parsimony, somewhat under furnished – except for the public rooms. Which were there to impress visitors.

The morning passed quickly for Tatya. Her cousins took their usual lengthy time deciding what to wear out of their over-full wardrobes. Surprisingly, their rooms were sparsely furnished with a wardrobe, a bed, dressing tables and sanitary facilities. Ekaterina declared that they could have well-furnished rooms when they were married and their husbands were footing the bill. No one saw their rooms. Their clothes, however, were for display.

Natalya and Olga looked much alike. They were short, inclined to be pudgy (for they liked *bon-bons* all too well), with round faces, blue eyes and faded blonde hair that Tatya, with the aid of sugar water, had to transform into bunches of ringlets daily. They were back and forth to each other's rooms, giggling and talking about the officers and gentlemen they had danced with at last night's ball as Tatya dressed them.

Lacing up their corsets was the hardest part, for they barely fit into their small waisted gowns without a good corset tightly laced. The current fashion for wide *gigot* sleeves, sloping shoulders and a small waisted bell skirt gave them the illusion of slimness, but they complained bitterly as they were laced up. Careful choice of styles, colours and jewelry made them more attractive than they actually were.

In contrast to her cousins Tatya was a little brown bird. She was of medium height, rather thin, brown of hair and eyes with a heart- shaped face. Her slightly slanted eyes were her best feature, a warm golden amber in colour, while her hair had gold highlights if she spent a good deal of time out in the sun. Her skin, rather than fashionably pale, was golden in tone. Aunt Ekaterina said slightingly that there must be Tatar blood on her father's side of the family.

Her overall impression of browness was worsened by the drab brown dresses that Ekaterina thought suitable. They were a mockery of the current style, with subdued sleeves and high to the neck, rather than showing the expanse of skin that the dropped shoulders allowed. These gowns were bare of an ornamentation – no lace collars or cuffs, or pin tucking or embroidery was allowed. The buttons were bone, dyed to match the plain gown. Even the serfs wore bright embroidered skirts and blouses in their favorite blues and reds. Tatya felt a complete nonentity in these clothes. And that of course, was Ekaterina's objective.

Once she had her cousins dressed (and had a throbbing headache from their piercing, shrieking laughter) Tatya went below stairs to attend her aunt. Here she was given a shopping list and a purse of money inadequate to pay for the items on the list. She was nevertheless expected to bargain and shop carefully in order to bring home everything on the list. There would be no excuses accepted if she did not accomplish this nearly impossible task.

Pausing in the kitchen to grab her shawl (it, too, was brown) Tatya set out for the market. She hoped the fresh air would help her headache. If she could see Sacha about she usually took him with her. But today he was not in evidence and she went by herself.

Passing down the street she was surprised to see her Uncle Yuri heading towards the house. Whatever was he doing coming home at this time of day? From the scowl on his face and the irritated way he swung his cane it was not for a happy reason. Tatya was suddenly glad she had to go to the market. It did not do to get into Uncle's way when he was in a mood like this.

"We are to do what?" Ekaterina shrieked

Yuri winced. His wife had a particularly piercing voice when she was enraged. Her sharp-featured face became suffused with red and her lank blonde hair seemed to frizz around her head. Her lathe-thin figure grew stiff with indignation.

"We are to give house room to an English Wizard and his dragon," Yuri repeated.

"Why us?" Ekaterina demanded. "Why should we be put in danger of being eaten by a dragon or changed into toads by a Wizard? Why did you not tell them no, Yuri Pavlovich?"

"Ekaterina, they promised me advancement to the eighth rank if I would do this!" Yuri said defensively.

In Russian society there was a system of ranking for every subject. Peasants were tied to the land. Merchants remained merchants. And the nobility and the gentry were obliged to enter state service, either in the military or civil service. Everyone was recognized as belonging to one of these estates. This system had been established by Peter the Great,

43

who had hoped it would award and bring to the forefront those of merit. The rankings, or *tchinn*, were fourteen in all, with fourteen being the lowest. One could move upwards with incredible quickness.

Yuri had been sent to the school at Czarskoe Selo for the training of those "destined for high rank in the State." Therefore when he graduated and received his posting as an Undersecretary in the Foreign Office his official ranking was at the tenth rank. When one achieved the eighth rank, one was automatically 'noble'. Pedigreed and noble title counted for little in Russia if one did not have a suitable state ranking. There was a saying: *"Chin, chai* and *shchi...* rank, tea and cabbage soup.... are our gods."

Yuri had remained at the tenth rank for his entire career. He was not well-liked and was neither efficient or brilliant at his job. Ekaterina had been frustrated for years by this circumstance. When she had married him she had been certain that he would advance to noble rank very shortly and when he had not she had become voluble on the subject of his lack of ambition and his superiors' stupidity.

Now she paused in her shrieking and looked very thoughtful. "Eighth rank – just like that? They have *promised* this?"

"They showed me an order signed by the Czar himself that I would be granted eighth rank after the Wizard has gone."

"After – it couldn't be before?" she said sharply. "How long must we house this menace?"

Yuri spread his hands. "They don't know." He explained to her about setting up a postal service with dragons.

Ekaterina could not believe that the English used dragons as mail carriers. "They must be fools!" she remarked scathingly. "Our serfs will be consulting the old women Witches for charms to protect them. For this once they can do so with my blessing."

"There is an entertainment allowance as well," Yuri informed her. "My superiors want us to make a good impression – everything is to be of the finest."

Ekaterina's eyes lit with greed. Perhaps having an unwanted, probably dangerous guest would not be such a bad thing!

4

Preparing To Depart

In the end it proved impossible for Simon to leave Ireland before the end of Trinity term in May. The Chancellor insisted that he finish out the school year. His dragon-ball team mates were adamant — they could not defeat Oxford without him and Lakota. (And they did beat Oxford – 17 to 10).

When he first informed his family that he was to go to Russia, they insisted on his waiting until the weather was improved. He, and particularly Lakota, were not used to the extreme cold found in Russia.

Although dragons did not feel changes in temperature the way humans did, it was far, far colder than anything Lakota was accustomed to, since he had lived in the mild Irish climate since he was hatched.

Unfortunately this wait precipitated a violent quarrel with Birgit. She was incensed when she learned that he was to go to Russia and would probably be gone all of the summer. What began as a fit of pique that she would be without an escort for the height of the social season ended in a vituperative argument in which it came out that she was planning a summer wedding. When Simon pointed out that he had not yet offered for her, she became hostile and offensive and tallied everything he had ever done that she did not like – it was quite a lengthy list. In the end he was forced to tell her that he had no intention of offering for her; that they would not suit. She did not remain to hear his reasons, departing with the admonition that she would not wait for him. "I don't expect you to do so," Simon said quietly. He had kept an admirable hold on his temper throughout the argument. With this she had stormed from the Dublin tea shop where they had met.

The circumstances of this altercation made Simon all the more anxious to leave Ireland. He felt as if everyone had something to say about it and that mostly things he would have preferred not to hear – save his parents. They were non-

45

judgmental and accepted his decision. He was never more glad to have their loving support.

He was happy to have remained for one reason – his father had had a difficult time since the death of Henshaw. Henshaw's father, the Viscount Froxe, was eager to blame someone for the tragedy. The Chancellor stood by René, saying that the evidence was inescapable. No less than twenty undergraduates and several barmen had testified that Henshaw was completely drunken and had ignored anyone who had attempted to dissuade him from trying to dematerialize in such a condition. The Chancellor also pointed out to the Viscount that it was at his own insistence that his son had been in the dematerialization class at all. Young Henshaw had not been recommended for it as were most other students. The prestige of being able to dematerialize was great – not everyone was able to do it. The Viscount had wanted that prestige for his son.

In the end, René had not lost his position, but he did not wish to begin teaching the subject again any time soon. In the over twenty years he had been instructing students in dematerialization a death had never happened, either at Trinity or at the Tara Druidry. René was both surprised and grateful that the Chancellor had taken his part against the Viscount. He might not have felt so if he knew the true circumstances. The Chancellor well knew upon which side his bread was buttered. Weighing the value of the Viscount against the wrath of the Duke of Chenevix, a very powerful gentleman indeed (who, unbeknownst to his son, had written a very nasty letter to the Chancellor) the head of University knew to which gentleman he had ought to pay heed.

But René had been low and depressed ever since the death of his pupil and only as the spring advanced showed signs of returning to his old self.

There had been an argument about Lakota going to Russia. Count Pozharsky did not see the need for his presence. But Simon pointed out that if he was to work with foreign dragons, Lakota would be of immense help. All dragons around the world spoke the same Dragon tongue. Although Simon could understand Dragon, he could not speak it, for draconic vocal chords were different than those of humans. Dragons had very low tones and gutturals in it that a human could not reproduce. At length the Count gave in – for Simon refused to go without his dragon friend.

Once it became apparent that Simon would really leave, he began to receive all sorts of advice and gifts from people. Much of the advice was foolish, for as it turned out people were very ill-informed about Russia. Count Pozharsky was slightly more helpful before he left for Russia in mid-January (he claimed that he was called home and could not wait). He gave Simon several books on Russia, its people, customs and climate. They were, of course, in Russian but Trinity had a bespelled translation table that allowed the reader to study any foreign book in his native language. His great uncle the Marquis of Lyonshall, who was married to René's grandmother Ninon, sent a marvelous gift that they had just developed – a traveling Wizard's laboratory. It was filled with the herbs and the essential ingredients a Wizard might need in his work. There were vials of mermaid's tears, bat wool, a mummified finny snake, eye of newt, a piece of unicorn horn, and many others. By magic, this collapsed into a flat package which, with the tap of a wand, turned again into a bulging satchel.

His parents gave him a journal that was bespelled to appear blank should any unauthorized person attempt to read it. Best of all, one could use any ink or any pen in it. Stuart's gift was a copy of *Emergency Magical Healing for the Amateur*. Stuart had been told in Edinburgh that Russian physicians were few and ill-trained and none of them had any Healing magic. The girls gave Simon the medical supplies that were listed in the book, as well as mufflers and mittens for him and a long be-tasseled scarf for Lakota. The dragon delighted in this and could hardly be dissuaded to take it off. The Duke of Chenevix sent a generous letter of credit.

The time drew near, faster than could be thought possible, for their departure. Janus was to accompany them – she was Simon's familiar after all. Unlike Simon, she had very little packing, but Holly had knit her a little coat and boots, in case that Russia was even colder than the Count's books had stated.

The day before they were to depart Simon was in his Tower, doing a last minute check to make certain that nothing that they would need had been left behind. In

47

addition to clothing – Count Pozharsky had advised him to bring two complete sets of evening dress, for St Petersburg delighted in balls and entertainments – there were magical supplies and camping supplies. They would be sleeping out at night on the journey. Simon was just checking on these last when a knock came at the door. He opened it to find Fearghail, looking somewhat startled, standing there.

"If you please, Dr. Simon, you've a visitor!" he said. "A very special visitor!" He stepped back and announced "His Majesty, Oberon, High King of Faerie!" in thrilling tones.

Ever since Simon was quite young he had been familiar with the Elfin King. His family was accounted "Elf friends" and they had been visited by Oberon, his Queen, Tatania, and various members of their Court. The family had spent time in the Hollow Hills as well.

But the Elf King never failed to cast those who saw him into awe, even dressed as an ordinary English gentleman in dark knee-length frock coat, light trousers, a striped waist coat, silk top hat and walking stick. His usually shoulder length dark hair was fashionably short. Oberon delighted in tricking himself out like this. But nothing could diminish his sheer presence and personal beauty. Whatever he wore, he shone with the light of the *Sidhe,* the Shining Ones.

Now he came forward as Simon bowed deeply. "You do me great honor, Sire," Simon said.

Oberon sometimes wasted little time on ceremony. Now he said rather abruptly, "I understand that you are to journey to Russia."

Simon did not waste any time in trying to ascertain how Oberon had learned of his journey far away in the Hollow Hills of England. He did not even ask how the Elf King had journeyed to Ireland. It was probably not on a dragon or on the ferry, that was certain. Both the Elf King's knowledge of outside events and how he traveled so quickly from place to place were mysteries. One did not question the *Sidhe.*

Simon offered the Elf King a seat and a glass of port, of which he know Oberon to be quite fond.

When they were comfortably situated and Oberon had had a sip of his beverage Simon waited for Oberon to state the object of his visit. One could not hurry an Elf. Being immortal they saw no need for haste.

48

Janus came trotting into the room. All of the cats adored Elves and the feeling was mutual. Oberon welcomed her in to his lap, and then said, "I wonder if you might undertake a commission for me whilst you are in Russia?" as he stroked Janus, much to her delight.

Simon indicated his willingness to do so.

Oberon smiled at him and said, "Wait until you find out what it is, young Simon! I wish that you will try and find any of my people that might be in Russia. With the Continent between us and the Cold Iron employed by the armies of the Inquisition we lost touch with them many years ago. With the recent discovery of Elves in America I have hopes that our people fled to the East as well almost a thousand years ago. We have legends that it is so, but no contact. I will give you a mark of my favor that will tell the others that you are an Elf friend."

With this said, he reached out and touched Simon on the forehead between his brows.

Simon felt a sharp tingling which rapidly cooled.

Oberon handed him a mirror, which he seemed to have been carrying in his breast pocket. "To anyone who does not have Othersight," the Elf King said, "it will look as if you have a small light mark on your forehead. Use your Othersight and look at it now."

Simon did so and saw a glorious golden star on his brow.

"Any Elf will recognize that – I hope, even after all these years of separation. And you will find this useful as well, for it will make you completely fluent in Russian. I would hope that those of our race still speak the Elven tongue – and you are a scholar of that, I know, but one never knows," Oberon said. "I will give my favor to Janus and Lakota as well." Saying so, he reached down and touched Janus. She meowed at the slight tingle and then Simon saw the same star appear on her.

"In addition, my Queen and her ladies prepared these for you." Suddenly Oberon held a medium sized package. Wrapped in silver paper, it was light and not bulky.

Carefully, Simon unwrapped the package and found it to contain five hooded, quilted Elfin cloaks. Each had a brooch pinned to it of exquisite enameled leaves. "We have

Foreseen that you will have need of these. They are woven of spider silk and lined with hummingbird feathers. You will find that they will conform themselves to fit anyone and are warmer than anything human made. They are also water-proof and will hide you from your enemies."

Then Oberon produced another package, this one wrapped in leaves. "Journey bread." Oberon passed the package to Simon.

"Thank you, Sire!" said Simon fervently. "This is generosity indeed!" Simon knew well the many virtues of Elfin journey bread. It was delicious, satisfied the worst hunger pangs with just a small piece and never became stale but always remained fresh and wholesome. He had never been able to ascertain what was in it, however. It tasted of all sorts of good things and looked as if there were some type of fruit baked into it but what he could not tell.

Simon did not make the mistake of becoming overly grateful. The Elves admired gratitude properly expressed but frowned on excessive thank-yous. They hated sycophants.

"I shall wish you good journey, then, and pay my respects to your parents before I go. I shall visit Lakota as I leave." Oberon put Janus carefully on the floor and stood up. Simon envied the Elf King, for no matter how many cats he had in his lap there was never any cat hair on his clothing. Even a Wizard could not manage that.

When he had escorted Oberon to the door, Simon carefully packed away the Elfin gifts.

He thought of the task Oberon had set him – to find Elves in Russia – that would mean a visit to a heavily wooded area, for Elves were not at all urban. He must ask his hosts (some people called Rostov) where the largest forest might be. Simon had received several letters, all in French, from Count Pozharsky, the last containing detailed instructions as to how to enter St Petersburg and directions to the Rostov home, which, the Count pointed out, had a large, sunny courtyard suitable for Lakota.

Tomorrow morning they would leave, bright and early. Stuart and Noelle had arrived from their schools yesterday, for they had not wanted Simon to leave without their being able to say goodbye.

And Simon was now beginning to feel excited about the coming trip. He had been visited by both the Royal Society and the Foreign Office, both of whom wanted him to observe and learn as much as possible about the vast, mysterious country to the East.

The trip was no longer just an escape from the situation with Birgit. It was an opportunity to see new things and perhaps add to the body of draconic knowledge. He could hardly wait.

It was late when Sacha finally was released by old Mikhail. They had groomed the horses until they shone and then washed both the *troika* and the family *droshky*. Sacha thought it was rather odd to be spending so much time on the *troika*, the sleigh, as it would not be used until the snow began to fly again, but Mikhail explained that everything must be in spotless condition, according to the Master. As they cleaned the tack, Mikhail had told Sacha that they were to have a very important guest. Since Mikhail had been with the Rostovs since he was a boy, he was a privileged family retainer and had no trouble at all finding out just who and what this special guest was. Sacha's big blue eyes grew rounder and rounder as he listened to Mikhail and he had to be reminded by the old coachman to keep soaping the leather.

Sacha did not look much like his half-sister. He was a sturdy, well-grown boy with thick blonde hair that hung down over his eyes. He had a snub nose, a rather square face and what his aunt called a cheeky smile. He had a sunny, cheerful nature and wasted little time regretting the vanished life at Mikhailovskoe. For one thing, he could scarcely remember it, or his father. His temper was equable and while his sister despaired of his becoming more than a stable hand, he quite liked working with old Mikhail and the others in the stable. He loved horses and being strong and big for his age did not find the work onerous. He took each day as it came and did not worry about the future as his sister did. But he loved Tatya dearly – like her he did not like his aunt, uncle and cousins, especially Evgeny, who mistreated the horses. Sacha tried his best to please Tatya, even to the point of sitting up over a flickering stub of a candle and learning whatever schooling she could impart to him without the help of many books. What few they had were in poor condition, taken from the old no longer used schoolroom.

Old Mikhail had filled Sacha with all of the legends of Russia. Sacha firmly believed in the yard and house spirits and the *bannik* in the bath house. Mikhail had told the boy tales of Grandfather Frost, the Snow Maiden, the Firebird, and the *Rusalka* that dwelled in the lakes and ponds and drowned the unwary young men who were foolish enough to fall in love with her. He heard tales of bear and wolf hunts, of serf revels and festivals that made him long to live in the country. Nothing like that ever happened here. Other than church on Sundays and the Holy days and a trip to the food market with Tatya there was very little going on, save when Uncle Yuri lost his temper and took out the birch switch or Evgeny descended on them, usually to demand money.

When the long afternoon had finally ended and Sacha was free to go, he was big with news and could hardly wait to see Tatya. He had to stop in the kitchen first, for his stomach made it known that the noon meal had been a long time ago.

Old Luba, with whom he was a great favorite, smiled toothlessly at him and gave him a bowl of *borscht* and a stack of dark bread and a cup of strong tea. There was even butter for the bread, which was a treat that did not often come his way. Sacha made short work of this and after thanking Luba, made his way upstairs to the top of the house.

He opened the door to their room carefully in case she was sleeping. He hoped that she was awake for he had such news!

To his horror she was on her mattress, but not asleep. She was crying.

"Tatya!" he exclaimed, falling to his knees beside the mattress. "What is it? Did Uncle beat you again?" His hands clenched into fists. One day when he was big enough he was going to take that birch switch and let uncle have a taste of it.

"No," came an exhausted whisper. "I am so tired. Sacha! This morning was laundry day and there were all sorts of extra things to wash and wring out. Then aunt had Masha and I clean the guest room. We scrubbed it from top to bottom – even the ceiling! And then the bed had to be aired and the mattress turned and the furniture polished...and then we are

52

to do the rest of the house by the end of the week! We worked tonight until we could no longer see...."

"It is the same in the stables," said Sacha. "Tomorrow we are to clean the yard and the bath house."

"We are to have some important visitor," Tatya said tiredly. "I only hope that it is not Evgeny or one of his dissolute friends."

Sacha could contain his news no longer. "It isn't Evgeny!" he burst out. "Tatya, it's a Wizard! A real Wizard! And he is bringing his dragon!"

"What?" Tatya sat up, dislodging Vron who had been asleep on her chest. "Sacha, you can't be serious! Wizards don't really exist except in folk tales!"

"They do exist! Mikhail has told me! He actually saw a Wizard once when he was a young man. Mikhail says there aren't as many as there used to be. They now live in the mountains and in the depths of the forest, like Baba Yaga, although she's really a Witch. This is a *foreign* Wizard who is coming. He's going to do something for the Czar. And he's staying her with us, *and* his dragon."

Tatya was puzzled as to why a foreign Wizard would stay with the Rostov family. It was a conundrum to her why anyone would stay with the Rostovs. Certainly the Wizard wouldn't enjoy it, unless he enjoyed being toadied to by her aunt. Aunt was sickening when she got within speaking distance of even a minor notable. And if this foreign Wizard had the Czar's ear – aunt would be all over him.

"I can hardly wait to see them!" Sacha was enthusing." Mikhail says that Wizards are very tall, and wear fancy caftans studded with jewels! He will probably have a great black beard and look fierce and dangerous! And the dragon – Mikhail told me about them too – they breathe ice and glitter and have cold eyes like a snake – you can't look into them or you'll freeze solid! And they have huge teeth! They eat people!"

Tatya felt a chill of fear. "Sacha, you are not to go near these creatures! Do you understand me?" Her voice was very hard and cold.

"But, Tatya, I just want to *look* -" the boy pleaded.

"No!" she said firmly. "If these creatures are real they are dreadfully dangerous! I do not want you eaten by a dragon or turned into something awful by a bad-tempered Wizard! Promise me you will stay well away from them!"

Sacha sighed. He felt much put a upon. Women! They always spoiled all the fun.

Nevertheless, he said, on a sigh, and somewhat sullenly, "I promise, Tatya. I will try to keep out of their way."

Tatya lay down again after telling Sacha to seek his bed as well. Morning would come all too early.

But why did they have to entertain a Wizard, of all things? *And* a dragon! Tatya could see no good coming from this, not at all.

But Sacha lay awake for a long time after soft breathing told him his sister had fallen asleep. Somehow he would get close to these exciting guests. He wanted to see the dragon, perhaps even touch it. And he wanted to talk to the Wizard. How did one become a Wizard anyway? He would not rest until he had seen them both and had his questions answered.

5

Journey And Arrival

It was a bright end of May morning when Simon, Lakota and Janus left for Russia. The entire household had assembled on the lawn to bid them good bye, complete with last minute advice and cautions. There were tears and hugs for all of them, and admonitions to be sure and write often. No one was certain whether or not Simon would be able to scry over such a long distance and over several bodies of water. Druids had perfected the art of scrying over water some years earlier, but very long distances were difficult, if not impossible. Simon had been unable to scry home when he was in America.

The route had been carefully planned to spare Lakota having to fly any long distance over the ocean. This was always difficult, for a dragon needed firestone to ingest and mingle with his flight gasses. Even a large dragon such as a Highland Dhu could not carry much firestone – it was heavy and awkward. No good spell had as yet been devised to make it easier to carry. At one point during the long flight over the North Sea Lakota would have to bend his neck back and take firestone from Simon. This was always a difficult task. No dragon had yet been able to fly across the Atlantic – special large, barge-type ships transported the few dragons that did cross.

Due to the stranglehold the Inquisition had upon the continent of Europe they could not fly over any of the continental nations. If they had to land for some reason they would be at the mercy of the Army of the Inquisition and would not escape with their lives. Magic was forbidden there, as were dragons. Even Janus would be put to death, as the Inquisition saw a talking familiar as unnatural and a tool of the Devil.

Fortunately the Scandinavian countries took a broader view and welcomed Wizards and dragons. There were several dragon breeds indigenous to Scandinavia and magical persons as well. Simon had been in communication with several shamans and even a fellow Dracophilologist to arrange for more firestone and food supplies for their journey. In Sweden they were to spend a night with an eminent Dracophilologist, Professor Lars Svensen, who was eager to see Lakota. The Scandinavian dragons were largely feral, and had little contact with man. Professor Svensen, who had always had to study the dragons of his country whilst hiding in a blind and downwind, was in ecstasy at the thought of talking to a dragon and seeing it up close.

Lakota, who with dragon instinct and a feeling for mileage and land masses that would be the envy of any cartographer, had carefully planned the flight.

The first leg of the journey would be to the Isle of Man, and from there to Ravenglass in Westmorlanshire in England. Then they would head north to Scotland, flying the length of that country to John O'Groats. At each stop they would take on more firestone and Lakota would eat as much as he could before the day's flight.

From John O'Groats they would fly to the Shetland Islands and from there (probably the hardest part of the trip) over the North Sea to Bergen in Norway.

That would be easier on Lakota, for after taking on more firestone in Bergen, he could easily fly to Upsaala in Sweden and their visit with Professor Svensen. From there they would fly over the Gulf of Bothmia that separated Sweden from Finland and then on to St Petersburg. Lakota estimated five days for the journey. It would be leisurely. There was no need for haste.

Simon left the details in Lakota's capable talons. No one knew better that a dragon his own capabilities for flight and how far he could go in a day's travel.

Simon had sent a communication to Count Pozharsky, telling him their time of arrival. Mail between the British Isles and Russia was so slow that he thought they might actually arrive before the letter. Simon had been appalled when he found out how long a journey it was by ship or overland. He was too used to the quickness of dragon-back travel. When he had gone to America, the journey seemed interminable, even though the ship was speeded along by the Wind Wizard on board.

After a last round of hugs and crying on the part of the girls, Simon tucked Janus into the front of his flying suit. The six passenger saddle did not have what was known as a 'familiar basket' attached as Janus preferred to travel inside Simon's flying suit.

He climbed onto Lakota's back, securing the flight straps. To a chorus of 'goodbyes', 'safe journeys' and *bon voyage'*. Lakota leaped into the air and spread his powerful wings, spiraling them up into the air effortlessly.

In no time at all it seemed they were out over the Irish Sea. Looking down, Simon could see the dragon's shadow racing along beneath them.

Many of the creatures who inhabited the Irish Sea called out greetings as they passed. Simon saw some mermaids sunning them selves on the back of a whale who sent up a tall waterspout as they flew over. A sea serpent bellowed at them and as they drew near to the Isle of Man, sea horses, half fish and half horse, began to leap up out of the waves.

On Man Simon paid his respects to the Arch Druid of Man, Douglas Ramey. They had a nuncheon there: Janus enjoying fresh fish and Lakota feasting on half a cow, cooked to tender perfection with mushrooms and wine. Simon remembered how astonished he had been to learn, when as a boy, he found out that dragons preferred their food cooked and were quite fussy about the way it was done, as well.

Lakota was quite certain that he fly to John O' Groats by nightfall and so it proved.

The next few days went swiftly. They had good weather over the cold, grey North Sea and the transfer of firestone went as well as they could expect, with only a little of it dropping into the sea below them. All the same they were glad to reach Bergen, where a Norse shaman awaited them. Since there were no facilities for dragons as there were in England, they would be sleeping out of doors in a large clearing. Much was made of Lakota and Simon teased him about getting a swelled head before their journey ended.

The visit with Professor Svensen went very well – Simon was given a copy of Svensen's new book, *On the Dragons of Scandinavia*, and the two Dracophilologists and the dragon talked long into the night. Professor Svensen was able to talk to Lakota to his heart's content.

Another day saw them over Finland. Lakota had been flying low, so that they might see as much of the country as possible. The immense forests of firs reminded Simon of the trip he had made to Canada whilst in America. Lakota's shadow frightened an enormous herd of reindeer, several of whom took flight into the air. "That mist be the type of reindeer that is used at the North Pole!" Lakota shouted back at Simon as they slowly glided over the tundra.

And the next day they drew close to their goal. It was a grey day – both sea and sky looked cold and bleak, even though it was nearly June.

In one of his innumerable letters of instruction Count Pozharsky had informed Simon that he must, without fail, first visit the island fortress of Kronstadt where he would present his passport and go through customs.

The fortress was located on the island of Kotlin in the Gulf of Finland in the Baltic Sea. Its aspect was not welcoming – it was made of granite, giving an overwhelming impression of both cold and austerity. Its foundation was underwater. It dated from the time of Peter the Great and was surrounded by a forest of masts, which was mainly, as Simon found out later, the ships of the Imperial Navy. Locked in ice for six to eight months of the year, the fleet stayed in the Baltic. In the three months of summer the ships served as training vessels for the cadets of the Navy.

There were a certain number of merchant ships of both Russian and foreign registry and a thriving shipyard at Kronstadt.

Simon had been assured by the Count that there would be an adequate place for Lakota to land at the fortress. This proved to be the roof, and as Lakota spiraled down to land – and it would be a tight space for him – Simon was amazed to see people pointing to the sky and running away, screaming, as the dragon drew nearer, even the soldiers abandoning their posts and throwing down their guns as they fled. Had the Count not warned anyone of their coming?

Lakota turned his head to look at Simon. "Whatever is wrong?" he asked, puzzled.

"I don't think they've ever seen a dragon before," said Simon dryly.

As they came closer to the roof Simon could hear someone yelling "*Nyet*! *Nyet*! There is no danger!" He saw Count Pozharsky on the roof, flapping his arms and screaming at the soldiers, who paid him no attention but kept running.

Then someone began firing a gun at Lakota and a bullet sailed close by Simon's head.

This was not an auspicious beginning to their visit! The bullets bounced harmlessly off the shield that Simon quickly cast over them with his wand.

The fact that his bullets appeared to be doing no good at all so frightened the shooter that he, too, ran off.

When Lakota landed neatly in the small space, there was no one to greet them save Count Pozharsky, who looked pale with apprehension, and stood well away from the dragon. Simon had to give him credit – the Count was a brave man – he was obviously terrified but he stood his ground. Sweat stood out in great beads on his high forehead and his hands were visibly trembling. Simon hoped that the Count would not faint before he was able to convince the others that there was no danger.

Lakota was a friendly soul and he looked straight at the Count and said, in French, "Hello! Are you Count Pozharsky?"

"*Blagdos Christos*!" the Count crossed himself. "It talks!"

"I am not an *it*!" said Lakota indignantly.

"Lakota – HE –is fluent in several languages," Simon said as he undid the safety straps and slid down off the blue dragon. Lakota crouched close to the ground so that Simon could easily dismount.

"Has it eaten recently?" The Count asked fearfully.

Lakota rolled his expressive eyes and exchanged glances with Simon. "They weren't this stupid in Norway or Sweden!" the dragon said disgustedly in Gaelic. They had decided to use this language when they wished to talk privately. As a further precaution, it had been decided not to reveal Oberon's gift of the Russian language.

The front of Simon's flying suit began to stir in a most alarming fashion – at least to the Count. Janus poked her head out and she said on a huge yawn, "Are we there yet?"

Count Pozharsky came as close to fainting as anyone Simon had ever seen. Simon had explained that his familiar would be coming with him and that both the dragon and the cat understood speech and could talk, *He obviously didn't really read my letters*! Simon thought in exasperation. .

When the Count had recovered a bit (although he kept glancing nervously at Lakota and even seemed to regard Janus as a threat to his continued good health) he had to begin coaxing the soldiers and then the Customs officials back onto the roof. Simon tried to be patient – he remembered when he had first seen a dragon at eight and was frightened that it would eat him because his horrid cousins had misinformed him about dragons – but he was far more used to the British Isles and America where dragons were a normal part of daily life and no one was ever afraid of them. He was well aware that in some countries dragons were regarded as evil – particularly the countries of the Inquisition – but could not conceive of such a thing himself. Dragons were friendly, kind and helpful and never ate people, horses or pets.

It took an hour of talking on the Count's part before the first brave souls ventured back up on the roof. Lakota made himself as small as possible to look less intimidating. Simon suggested that the Count stand next to Lakota or even put a hand on his foreleg, but this the Count could not bring himself to do. In the end, Pozharsky threatened the soldiers and the Customs Officials with the Czar's displeasure should he be told of their cowardly behavior and their failure to obey him, Dmitry Sergievich Pozharsky, a high ranking official in the Foreign Office. This brought them out, but they were careful to remain a very long distance from Lakota.

Simon had gone through Customs in America and even in Britain when he had returned from a year abroad, but he had never imagined such a convoluted, tedious process as he was subjected to here in Russia.

His passport was given the most minute scrutiny, as if they suspected it to be false. He was obliged to answered dozens of questions – many of which he considered impertinent and irrelevant. Why did it matter what his grandmother's maiden name was? And why did they want to know where he had gone to school and what subjects he taught at Trinity? All of this involved lengthy explanation on his part, for none of them had ever heard of a Druidry, Dracophilology or seemed to be able to comprehend the fact that one attended Uni-versity to get a baccalaureate in Wizardly studies.

No sooner than this was cleared up than the questions about Lakota began. How long had he owned this dragon? They were appalled that he had not brought the bill of sale with him. In vain did Simon try to explain that he did not 'own' Lakota. But the dragon was an animal, they argued. Animals had to have owners!

Lakota resolved this by suddenly sitting up and announcing in French, in a loud voice "You people are a pack of idiots!" Like his friend Lakota had been keeping a hold on his temper only with the greatest effort.

This almost caused another exodus from the roof, but the Count managed to stop it by screaming "This man is a guest of the Czar!"

Simon obtained a poor impression of the Czar and his powers – everyone seemed to be terrified just at the mention of his title. He must be a tyrant. Simon's liaison from the British Foreign Office, Algernon Bryce-Smith, had hinted as much.

They let the question of who owned Lakota drop, rather reluctantly, and then demanded that Simon pay a surety of 100,000 *rubles* against the possibility of Lakota's eating anyone or damaging any property. This caused Lakota's ruff to flare up and steam trickled from his nostrils.

At this Simon completely lost his temper and declared his intentions of returning home at once. He demanded the return of his passport and when the Customs Comptroller declined to give it back, Simon put out his hand and called it to him with magic. The passport left the Comptroller's clutching hands and shot across to Simon, who then tucked it into the breast pocket of his flying suit

"I've had quite enough of this!" Simon snapped at Pozharsky. "We've been kept on this cold roof for over three hours now! I've done my best to answer all of your intrusive questions but this is outside of enough! Lakota is not a danger to anyone – nor will he destroy property! Once again, although I have completely given up hope of anyone here understanding this, dragons do not eat people!"

The Count looked at him wide-eyed and rather wildly. Looking around at the others Simon could see the looks of awe and fear on their faces. What the devil was wrong with them?

Then he realized – they had never seen magic performed – even such a simple thing as a calling.

The Count swallowed visibly and then said in a shaking voice. "Please, please, *M'sieur*, the Czar will not require a surety – I have been authorized to negotiate... there is no need for violence! Please, you must stay and help us!"

Violence? Simon thought wryly . If they considered that little act violence, he wondered how they would react to seeing the Duel Arcane?

He allowed himself to be persuaded. They had all looked forward to this trip and what they might learn. Both the Royal Society and the Foreign Office would be disappointed as well.

After his minor display of power the balance of the process was finished swiftly. But Simon noticed as he finally climbed abroad Lakota for the seventeen mile flight into St Petersburg, that they were no longer just afraid of the dragon – they were afraid of him as well.

Sacha had been excited all day. The Wizard and his dragon were to arrive today. By now it was all over the house just what kind of guest was expected and most of the household was in a state of fascination tinged with fear. The other two grooms, Grisha and Igor, had talked of little else for days, as had the footmen, Pavel and Boris, and the maids, Masha and Ilenka. Mikhail and Luba found themselves the center of attention, for both remembered the old tales and recounted them with relish to an attentive audience. Sacha himself had caused a sensation when he rummaged in the old nursery and found a long discarded children's book with illustrations of a Wizard who captured young girls – Princesses – and turned them into swans.

The Wizard in this book looked exactly as Mikhail had described him – a very tall man with an immense black beard and thick black brows drawn in a frown. He wore fantastic robes covered in jewels, a tall fur hat and a staff lit at the top with rays of light.

The traditional separation of house and yard servants was forgotten as they all crowded around the kitchen table to peer eagerly at the pictures. Only Tatya was not truly interested. All she cared about, as far as the Wizard and the dragon was concerned, was keeping Sacha away from them. She placed no great dependence on Sacha's reluctantly given promise. He was nearly thirteen and starting to fancy himself grown-up, too old for petticoat government. Mikhail was far more an influence on him now than she was. She knew that Sacha loved her, but his developing independence and curiosity, she was very afraid, would be too much for him. She was much worried, for she could not keep an eye on him every moment. She had far too many duties of her own. And when she spoke to Mikhail about keeping Sacha from the vicinity of danger, he dismissed her fears with a explosive laugh. A little adventure would do the boy good! Why, at Sacha's age he had already killed several enormous wolves and a gigantic bear, as well as wrestled with a *Rusalka,* seen a Wizard, and once, even caught a glimpse of a Firebird in the cherry orchard of his old home. Sacha needed adventures to become a man. Tatya could find no one who shared her disquiet and resolved to keep Sacha as close to her as she could, but she was afraid this would prove nearly impossible

In the end, Sacha was granted his wish and was the first to see the Wizard and the dragon.

He was raking the yard of the stable when the sun came out from behind a cloud. Eagerly, Sacha looked up to see if the sky was clearing, for Mikhail had promised that he could exercise one of the saddle horses if the weather cleared.

What he saw was even better than clearing skies.

Outlined by the sun so that it sparkled of opals, a great blue winged figure descended down from the sky in lazy spirals. It glided like a sea gull, winds outstretched and rigid.

Sacha dropped the broom with a thud, his mouth hanging open in astonishment. It was beautiful! But it was nothing like he had imagined. Mikhail said dragons were white and sparkled like crystal. This one was definitely blue and although large, was smaller than Sacha had imagined. It had a long neck and tail – which Mikhail had said it would but it did not have spikes on its back, nor great talons that could rip a man to shreds.

And then Sacha noticed someone was riding the dragon! This was beyond anything Sacha had been able to fantasize. To actually ride a dragon – to be up in the air! At once, Sacha knew that he wanted to ride on a dragon. He would not be afraid!

Who was riding the dragon? Sacha did not think it was the Wizard – the Wizard, he was certain, would arrive at their door in a decorated *droshky* , pulled by six black horse who probably breathed fire. Indeed, they had all thought that the dragon would be chained to the *droshky*, kept under control by many spells. No one had imagined this magnificent flight.

As Sacha watched the dragon circled down further and disappeared behind an ell of the house that concealed the courtyard. And with no hesitation at all Sacha abandoned his task and ran towards the house. He was not going to miss a chance to see this dragon close up!

6

First Impressions

Sacha ran so fast that he was completely out of breath by the time he had rounded the back of the house and got to the courtyard. He wanted to see the dragon come down onto the ground. Did it land like a bird?

In contrast to a great deal of the people in St Petersburg who preferred to live in one of the many large apartments available, the Rostovs had their own house. It was large and spacious, as many upper class Russian homes were, but Ekaterina thought it old, unfashionable and inconvenient. However, it was rent-free, as it had been in the family since Yuri's grandfather's time. True, it was not in the most fashionable part of town, but it was a charming home nonetheless. It was surrounded by trees and had a fine prospect of the distant Neva. There were several small gardens – which were tended by the grooms and Sacha, as Ekaterina could not see the expense of a gardener, who would have little to do but kick his heels in the winter. The citrus trees and other plants in the tiny orangerie were tended by the maids.

A sparse hedge lay between the courtyard and a flower garden, Sacha crouched behind this, carefully parting the branches so that he might see without being seen.

To his delight he had a perfect view of the dragon. He had missed the landing, but as he watched, it folded its wings and crouched down, allowing the rider to slip of its back. Sacha noticed that the rider dismounted onto one of the dragon's forelegs and from there to the ground. The rider wore a strange outfit that seemed to be made of all leather and wore a brightly coloured striped scarf, and a helmet-like hat, also of leather, with huge spectacles atop it. The dragon, too, wore a scarf in the same colours. It also wore an elaborate harness with a net on its breast that was full of what Sacha decided was baggage.

The dragon was even more beautiful up close. It had deer-like ears, blue horns, and large eyes. It did not look mean at all, as Mikhail had said. If Sacha had to describe its expression, he would have said it had a friendly, interested look about it.

And then it spoke. Sacha nearly fell over backwards in surprise. He could not comprehend what it said, for it spoke a language he could not understand – Russian and French were the only languages he knew. Mikhail had not said that dragons could talk! Perhaps it was speaking dragon language?

As Sacha watched the rider said something back to the dragon and they both laughed. This laughter decided Sacha – Tatya was wrong about the dragon – it was friendly and nothing was going to stop him from becoming acquainted with it. It did have very large teeth, but Sacha was not about to let that deter him.

The rider pulled off his helmet and Sacha was surprised all over again. If this was the Wizard, he was not what they had expected. He had no black beard or fierce mien. He was quite young for one thing and his hair was lighter than Sacha's own. He was tall and slim, and when he slipped out of the leather suit Sacha could see no jeweled caftan, but a black coat and light trousers such as uncle wore. It was very disappointing!

Sacha heard voices approaching, most of them agitated, including the high, shrill tones of Aunt Ekaterina. Sacha crept backwards until he could stand up without being seen. If he was caught here he would get a taste of uncle's birch switch and what was worse, be lectured at by Ekaterina, who would punctuate her talk with strikes on his head with one of her heelless slippers or her fan as she complained about his ingratitude.

But he was not unhappy. He had seen the dragon and would have much to relate in the stables that afternoon.

Simon and Lakota had not been impressed by their first glimpse of the city from the air. A dull-hued sea had lapped on a barren shore. As they flew up the Gulf they could see the low, wet marshes of Ingra which seemed to stretch to a flat wavering line, the only mark of the difference between sky and sea. There were a few clumps of birch in a grey, mossy, peat landscape, melancholy in the extreme.

66

But as they drew nearer the city the sun burst through the clouds and lit up the many golden domes and spires that marked an immense amount of churches and palaces. The city was heavily treed and in this time of year there were many flowers.

And water – everywhere was water; a winding river that Simon knew from the maps Pozharsky had sent, was the Neva. They later learned that Saint Petersburg was built on the many islands of the Neva delta, and therefore was not only a city of the river, but also one of many canals and bridges. It was often called 'the Venice of the North'.

Given the reaction of the people at the fortress, Simon had instructed Lakota to remain relatively high so that they would not cause a general panic. Even from this distance they could see the colourful throngs on the streets – peoples from all over the world. With the aid of his telescope Simon could see Chinese, Arabs, and Africans, to name a few, all in their national dress. And there were many he could not identify. Lakota. with his long dragon sight, could see them all clearly without artificial means.

This second impression was much more favorable. The streets were wide and the buildings handsome, many of them qualifying for the word 'magnificent'. Simon looked forward to exploring it.

They found the Rostov home with little trouble. Simon had asked that a blue banner be put on the roof and to his amazement this had been done. Lakota was able to land with little difficulty in a courtyard, which was quite large. Many of the courtyards in St Petersburg were able to hold an entire cavalry regiment – this was not on that scale, but it was large enough for Lakota to be comfortable in.

As soon as Simon had dismounted, Lakota looked around him. There was a small wooden hut in the courtyard, and the dragon noticed that the house was made of wood as well. "I shall have to be very careful about sneezing!" he remarked to Simon.

"If they ever see you flame there will be mass fainting!" said Simon with a laugh. He was recovering his customary good humor – flying always put him in a good mood.

67

With his acute senses Lakota was conscious of being spied upon, but he did not sense any evil intent. But there was someone behind that hedge. He started to mention it to Simon (although Lakota knew that Simon would have noticed it as well) when he heard a large group of nervously chattering people approaching from the house. They both turned to face the oncoming company. Simon had set Janus on the ground as well, and she immediately began to wash and groom her fur, ruffled from her travels.

The approaching collection of people was headed by a timid Yuri – Ekaterina had pushed him out in front of her, saying that he was the host and therefore should be the first person to talk to the Wizard. Behind Ekaterina were two of Yuri's superiors from the Foreign Office, Vaslav Ilyich Glasunov and Sergei Aleksandrovich Evreihov, neither of whom showed any more courage in approaching a dragon than did Yuri. Even further behind this group was a handful of the servants – Pavel and Boris, and Masha, who was the braver and more curious of the maids. Ilenka was hiding in a closet. At the tail end of the procession was Luba. She felt that at her age she had nothing to lose. If it was her fate to be eaten by a dragon, then it was as God and the Czar willed.

Yuri stopped within twenty feet of the creature and executed a stuff, quick bow, bobbing upright as fast as he could so that he could keep an eye on the beast. He was doubtful that he could run fast enough to escape those jaws. Unlike Sacha he saw no friendliness in Lakota's face, only a desire to eat him.

Lakota in fact was rather depressed. He was open and companionable by nature and to have all of these people afraid of him was lowering to his spirits. Like most dragons, he liked to talk to people and was used to Dublin where, when he was waiting for Simon on the Campanile, he struck up all sorts of conversations with the passers-by. He was accustomed to giving children rides, speaking with students and professors and answering questions about his American origins. Even the non-magical inhabitants felt no compunction in coming right up to him and talking. Very often he was offered dragon treats, which were sold everywhere. It was most enjoyable and he was beginning to be afraid that this sojourn in Russia was going to be very lonely, for Simon would not be able to be with him every moment.

Simon could feel the dragons' depression – and see it , too, for Lakota's ruff, a sure indication of his feelings, drooped sadly. His eyes also looked hurt and rather lost. Simon had no idea how he could help – he could not cast a blanket spell over all of St Petersburg to cure their fear. He could not even use a calming spell on the members of the Rostov household without their permission. The rules of Wizardry were strict. Except in self defense or defending another person from harm, a Wizard was not allowed to cast a spell on an unsuspecting person. Even a Wizard Healer had to ask for permission for treatment of a sick person from that person or a member of his or her family, in order to cast a Healing spell.

Yuri, shoved by Ekaterina in the small of the back as she crouched down behind him, stumbled forward and said in halting English "You are Wizard?"

"Perhaps it would be easier if we spoke French?" Simon suggested in that language. At the look of relief that spread itself over Yuri's features Simon was glad that he made the proposal. It would make it far more straightforward than having to supply English words or both of them becoming thoroughly confused.

Introductions were made with much bowing and compliments, but all the Russians stayed well back from Lakota, all of them eyeing him askance, nervously looking as if they might flee any moment. Lakota had crouched down on the pavement of the courtyard. his wigs folded tight against his body and his tail and legs tucked under him, rather like a cat. Janus had sat down beside her dragon friend. She too, knew why he was depressed and thought the people were idiots. Why a *dog* was more dangerous than a dragon! And they probably had their house filled with dogs! This also showed bad taste in Janus's view.

Ekaterina, like Sacha, was much surprised at Simon's appearance. He seemed much too young and non-threatening to be a dangerous Wizard. He looked like any young gentleman that she might see about St Petersburg. And her discerning eye told her that by the cut of his clothes, he was probably very well-off. Every thing was slightly foreign in cut – for Russian gentlemen followed the more extravagant

French fashion, while Simon's clothes came from Bond Street and were of a more conservative cut. But Ekaterina could estimate to the last *ruble* what they had cost and it was not cheap, of that she was certain. He was rather good-looking as well, she thought, consideringly. She won-dered if he had a wife. She would be willing to marry one of her daughters to a *cherti*, providing the demon had enough money.

Therefore, in spite of the proximity of the dragon, she pasted a large smile on her face, peering over Yuri's shoulder.

After unharnessing the dragon and arranging for the luggage to be taken up to his room, Simon asked that Lakota be provided with a tub of water. He then allowed himself to be borne off into the house, casting a rueful glance back over his shoulder at the dragon. He hoped that his request had been honored and that he had been given a room overlooking the courtyard. He wanted easy access to Lakota.

Pavel, at a brusque command from Yuri, ran off to the stables to order a tub of water. The servants, of course, had not been introduced to the Wizard. Pavel was eager to tell of what he had seen.

Janus remained with the dragon. "So far, I am not impressed," she remarked as soon as the people had disappeared into the house. "They all seem to be stupid beyond belief. Imagine being terrified of a dragon!" She sniffed loudly and drew herself up, wrapping her tail around her. No one had taken any notice of her. "I think that I may stay with you, Lakota, rather than share Simon's room. I don't think I can stomach those people – I don't see how he can! They probably like *dogs*!"

Pavel was disappointed, for Sacha had been before him with a description of the dragon and the Wizard. When the request for water was made, Grisha and Igor sprang forward eagerly. A tub was fetched, and scrubbed clean. There was a pump, usable all year round, for it was in the well-heated bath house, in the courtyard.

"Come, Sacha," said Mikhail to his young helper. "We shall all go and see this beast." Mikhail had been skeptical when Sacha told him the dragon was blue. Obviously it was not a real dragon.

No one was certain how old Mikhail was. He had been called "Old Mikhail" for a score of years. His once dark beard was grey and white and growing sparse. His face was a mass of wrinkles, particularly around his deep-set dark eyes set under thick, heavy brows. He still had a full head of hair, which hung to his shoulders. His strong hands were now gnarled and his back a little bent – he had been a bear of a man in his youth. But he still had a commanding presence – Igor and Grisha were rather in awe of him. He was considered one of the best coachmen in Saint Petersburg, with either *troika* or *droshky* No one had any trouble believing that he had hunted and killed the enormous fierce wolves of the forest, or killed a giant bear with his bare hands.

He had always been kind to Sacha. He firmly believed that it was wrong that the young master, as he called Sacha privately, served in the stables. But That Woman had no notion as how to treat her betters. This feeling extended to Tatya as well. Neither of them should be doing what they were – they were nobility, not servants. He made certain that the other servants treated Sacha and Tatya with respect.

Mikhail led the way to the courtyard. with Sacha at his side. Grisha and Igor followed with the tub. The two grooms were eager to see the strange creature but were fearful as well.

Mikhail had no fear. He had seen many strange things in his time, for he had first served Yuri's grandfather, Vassily Petrovich Rostov, a gentleman who could not stay in one place for very long without becoming restless. In his service, Mikhail had been to nearly every part of Russia, from the steppes of Central Asia to the Black Sea and even to Siberia. It was in Siberia that he had seen a Wizard. And it was in Siberia that he listened to tales of Ice dragons. It had been his dearest wish to see one, but he had never been so fortunate as to have his wish granted.

That was why he was certain that this creature could not be a dragon. People who had actually seen dragons had told him their tales, and Sacha's description did not match any of those stories he had heard so long ago.

When they at last reached the courtyard Mikhail was forced to revise his opinion. In spite of the odd colour, that was definitely a dragon.

Lakota looked up with interest as they came. He was thirsty and was glad that Simon had thought of this – Simon was always thoughtful of his needs. Lakota hoped that they could find a source for cream here – for he dearly loved a drink of cream mixed with honey. He had had a very large meal of reindeer in Finland – which he had found gamy and tough. Dragons ordinarily ate a large meal of meat every two to three days and Lakota did not anticipate needing a meal for a day or so. He remembered ruefully Count Pozharsky asking "Has it eaten recently?"

Two of the people approaching him did not seem afraid – an old man and a boy. Lakota liked children and like all dragons he had reverence for the wisdom of old age. He had learned quite a bit about history by talking to old sailors and soldiers in Dublin, where there were retirement homes for both branches of the service.

And behind then were two young men bearing a tub. They set this down, rather far away and then after surreptitious glances at Lakota, hurried away to the wooden building in the courtyard.

"Well, these two look as if they might have more sense than the rest of them!" said Janus, *sotto voce*. She yawned and closed her eyes, ready to go back to sleep.

Lakota certainly hoped so. He was at first a bit reluctant to speak to them, remembering the reaction of both Count Pozharsky and the others at Kronstadt. But he would never make any friends if he did not make an effort to greet them properly.

So he sat up a little and put on his friendliest face. "Hello!" he said in French. "I'm very pleased to met you!" And then he bowed.

"I told you!" Sacha said excitedly to Mikhail. "It can talk!"

Lakota sighed. Why did all of these people assume he was an *it*? It was difficult to tell the sex of a dragon, but Lakota fancied that he looked quite masculine.

Mikhail could speak and understand French better than most of the serfs, mainly due to his long association with Vassily Petrovich. "You are not like our Siberian Ice dragons," he said, looking right at Lakota.

72

"I'm an American dragon," Lakota explained, "but I now live in Ireland with my friend Simon. My name is Lakota. May I know your names, please?"

Sacha, trembling with excitement, performed the introductions. This was the best thing that had ever happened to him!

With extreme politeness Mikhail asked many questions of Lakota, who obligingly did such things as spreading his wings and standing up to his full height. He did this for Simon's students (and was well paid for doing so by Trinity) and did not object to being a sort of living textbook. He explained what it was like for dragons and people in the British Isles and America and than asked rather wistfully, "Why is everyone else here so afraid of me?"

By this time Igor and Grisha had filled the tub with water and stood back away from the dragon and Mikhail and Sacha (they had moved closer ands closer as they talked). Neither one of the grooms spoke much French, but it was apparent to them that the dragon was not about to eat them. "Probably Mikhail has tamed it," Igor whispered to Grisha.

"We never see dragons here," Sacha offered "or Wizards either. Are you certain that your master is truly a Wizard? He doesn't look like a Wizard."

"What is a Wizard supposed to look like? In my country a Wizard looks just like any one else. And Simon is not my master – he is my friend," Lakota answered.

Mikhail, who felt his age the most when obliged to stand for long periods of time, now sat down on the ground. The sun had warmed it enough so that it was comfortable. Sacha sank down beside him. Grisha and Igor remained standing, ready to flee if the dragon should suddenly become hungry.

They continued to ask questions of Lakota and he answered as best he could. He in turn asked questions of them. He was very happy – it looked as if he would make some new friends after all.

Inside the house things were not going as well. Simon had already decided that he disliked his hostess – she was an insufferable woman, a toad-eater as the Duke of Chenevix would have said. She practically threw her two giggling daughters at him. They were rather stupid, very silly girls who became bores within ten minutes. And Simon's host was both afraid of his wife's sharp tongue and a tyrant to the servants.

The two gentlemen from the Foreign office were soon joined by Count Pozharsky, who was obviously their superior. Not having the advantage of dragon flight he had had to take a slower method to return from Kronstadt – a boat. A whispered conversation followed in rapid Russian, which, to his delight, Simon followed perfectly. Bless Oberon and his gift!

The Count, with much exaggeration, informed Glasunov and Evreihov of what had happened on the roof of the fortress. This caused them to look at Simon out of the corner of their eyes.

A cold collation had been laid out in the dining room and Simon helped himself to cold meat, fruit and bread and pretended not to hear what they were discussing. He paid little heed to a lengthy story from Yuri who was informing his guest of how his grandfather had won this house in a game of cards with a Grand Duke – a Romanov Grand Duke no less, one of the Czar's own family.

Simon also overheard why he was quartered with the Rostovs. No one else in the Foreign Office had wanted a Wizard in their home, much less a dragon. Rostov, the most under of Under Secretaries, had been bribed into taking in the visiting Wizard.

At long last Pozharsky finished his whispered conference with his underlings and joined Simon at the buffet. Yuri he dismissed with a wave of his hand and politely inquired if Simon found everything to his liking.

Simon had been shown first to an upstairs room that indeed looked out over the courtyard. It was a large comfortable room with a soft featherbed, and more than adequate storage for his belongings. He answered in the affirmative and waited for the Count to come to the point, for he was obviously bursting with news.

"We will be providing you with a guide to the City," he informed Simon as he piled a plate high with food. "Naturally you will wish to see as much as is possible while you are here. We have chosen a young officer of good family who is not only

74

completely familiar with St Petersburg, but has the *entré* to all of the best homes as well, for you will no doubt receive many, many invitations. Indeed, the Princess Troblenka gives a *soirée* tomorrow evening – she extends her invitation to you and would be much obliged if you would graciously condescend to attend."

Simon indicated his willingness to attend the Princess's *soirée* – he was not fond of such entertainments, especially when he would know no one there save the Count, but he could see little help for it.

"And of course, we shall begin straight away with our Postal project," the Count continued. With this he looked quickly around the room and then leaning forward confidingly, he whispered, "We have found an egg – a dragon egg! And we would be much obliged if you could look at it as soon as possible!"

7

Dragons' Egg

Much to Simon's disappointment the Count refused to bring the egg to a place where Lakota could see it as well. For reasons of security, the Count kept repeating, the egg must remain where it was. In vain did Simon protest that Lakota could be on immense help – he could actually talk to the egg.

The following morning Simon was conveyed to a location that he was not allowed to see. He was shuttled into a carriage with drawn blinds and taken by a roundabout route to an unnamed location, and hurried from the carriage into a building. He asked the Count rather sarcastically if they wanted him to wear a blindfold, but the Count stared at him blankly, not understanding.

Simon had put together one of his 'egg kits' as Lakota called them. This consisted of measuring tools, a sketchbook, warm wraps, among other things, and the prize of the collection – one of the newly invented stethoscopes, a hollow tube through which he could listen to the dragonet's movements, heart rate and breathing. Long study had enabled Simon to know exactly what a healthy developing dragonet should sound like and how much it should be moving. With a powerful mage light he could candle the egg and the outline of the dragonet and see the little heart beating. If the egg was quite new he would check for the presence of a single yoke and could calculate how long before incubation would begin. These people, of course, knew nothing about dragon eggs and they could not answer his questions. They were even reluctant to tell him where and how they had obtained it.

It was a fairly large building that they entered and they seemed to go down endless corridors as well as up three sets of steep stairs. It was a regular rabbit warren – and it reminded Simon of Chenevix Duchis in Dorsetshire, which had been added on to, indiscriminately, since the Norman Conquest. They passed by many closed doors. No one poked their heads out as would have happened in any government building in Ireland. It was as if no one had any curiosity,

Simon thought and then realized that they had probably been ordered, on pain of the Czar's displeasure, not to exhibit this normal human trait.

At long last they came to the very end of a corridor where the Count unlooked a little door and ushered Simon inside. He locked the door after himself. Simon though all this excessive secrecy was ridiculous.

Within a few moments there was a tap on the door and the Count unlocked it again and admitted Glasunov and Evreihov, the two gentlemen Simon had met the day before. Once again the Count locked the door.

"Where is the egg?" Simon inquired, for the room had only a bare topped desk, a filing cabinet and several chairs and the ubiquitous tiled stove. The louvered blinds were drawn as well and a single oil lamp did little to illuminate the room. The floor was bare and the walls unadorned, save for a large map of the Empire.

For his answer, Evreihov went to the filing cabinet and pulled out a canvas wrapped bundle.

Simon almost groaned aloud. Criminal to treat an egg so! Stuffed in a filing cabinet!

"Put it on the desk," he ordered, and took an egg cradle out of his kit. This cradle enabled the egg to sit on its larger end, which was the best position for the developing dragonet. In the wild, dragon mothers laid the egg in sand, so that the sand could be piled around the egg to hold it upright.

Evreihov, a short, small man with thin fair hair and a perpetually worried expression, handled the egg as if it were poisoned. Simon ended in taking it from him and placing it in the egg cradle.

The first step was to candle the egg and find out if it were still dormant. Simon took a moment to study it. It was an egg unlike any other he had ever seen, It was white, with silver streaks throughout it and almost translucent near the small end. In Simon's experience, the egg colour always indicated the colour of the dragonet inside. Lakota's egg had been as blue as he now was, and streaked with opal.

Simon was also concerned about how cool the egg was – even in dormant stage an egg should never be cooler than 55 degrees Fahrenheit or 12 degrees Celsius. The longer the egg was stored at these temperatures, the longer it would take to hatch. And if the temperature should fall much below these guidelines the dragonet would never incubate and the spark of life that was the dragonet would die.

Without thinking of the effect it would have on the watchers, Simon cast a large mage light behind the egg.

There was a concentrated gasp – exactly as if they had rehearsed it, Simon thought – and all three of them backed away, crossing themselves and muttering prayers.

Simon looked at them with exasperation. Glasunov, tall and as thin as a reed with rather pinched features, was the worst affected – he looked as if he wanted to jump out the window to get away – which would not have been a good idea as they were on the third floor. The other two had wide, terrified eyes.

"If you gentlemen are going to faint every time I perform a simple act of magic, we shall never get anything done," Simon said.

"Simple?" said Evreihov, swallowing heavily. "It is a miracle!"

"Or the work of *cherti*!" muttered Glasunov, edging closer to the window.

Simon decided wisely to ignore them and tipped the egg towards the mage light.

The egg *had* started to incubate. He could see a definite dragonet in there. It should have been moving in response to the egg being handled, but it seemed feeble. Simon grabbed his stethoscope and bent over the egg, with one end of the instrument to his ear.

The heart beat was slow and sluggish, and the breathing shallow. Simon knew exactly what was wrong – the egg was cold and only quick action would save the dragonet.

"This egg must be warmed as soon as possible!" he snapped. "I can magic it for a bit, but it needs an incubator."

They all looked at him blankly and he realized that they had no idea what he was talking about.

"The egg has to be kept at 99.5 Fahrenheit or 35.5 Celsius, in order for it to develop properly and hatch. We need something like a brooder for chickens – to keep the egg warm." As he was trying to explain to them, he wrapped the egg in the warm cloths he had brought and cast a small warming spell on them. Fortunately they couldn't see that.

It took some little while to explain what was needed. The three of them had probably never even see a chicken brooder. That was something only serfs knew about.

Finally the Count sent Glasunov out to fetch a carpenter and in a while later a cheerful serf appeared with wood and a tool box and made a 10" by 14" box with a removable lid to Simon's directions, translated by the Count. The tiled stove in the corner was fired up and Simon placed the box on top of it with the egg on the cradle inside it. The egg was now warm from magic and when Simon checked the dragonet's heart rate it was stronger and its breathing better. It was a great relief – he hated to lose a dragonet and it looked as if this one would make it after all. If he could just convince these people to keep it warm!

In America Simon had learned a very useful spell, created by the research facility in the Department of Dracophilology at Columbia University. It was a spell that kept an incubator at a steady heat – just the proper heat for a dragonet to thrive in – for high heat was just as bad for the egg – it could actually cook and kill the dragonet.

The dragon parents would take turns to heat the sand around the egg with their flames, knowing exactly by instinct how much to heat it. In America and in the British Isles there were incubatories, that were available for orphaned eggs or for dragon parents with large families or a profession that kept them away from the eggs too long. These were staffed by well-trained personnel.

Ideally, Simon would have liked to take the egg with him so that he and Lakota could care for it, but the merest suggestion of this idea brought a firm denial from the Count. The egg must remain where it was.

Once again, Simon was exasperated by what he saw as idiotic stubbornness. He abhorred all of this secrecy and could not imagine why it was so.

He had to explain how to care for the egg to a serf that was dragged in from somewhere. The stove must not go out, nor be piled too high with wood. Sand should be fetched to pile around the egg. And the serf, Savva, must talk to the egg.

"TALK to the egg!" exclaimed the Count, in scorn. "What nonsense is this?"

"That is how dragons learn human speech," Simon explained. "By the time it hatches it will be able to speak to us and be understood. In fact, unless Savva can speak French as well as Russian, it would be a good idea for someone who speaks French to talk to it as well, perhaps even read to it."

By the expression on the Count's face he thought this the most ridiculous thing he had ever heard. But he sighed and said, "I suppose you know what you are talking about," and then went on to say that he would arrange for someone to do this.

"How long before it hatches?" he wanted to know next.

"There is no way of telling," said Simon ."Every breed has a different incubation time and I am not familiar with Ice dragons. Lakota took four months to hatch. Welsh Reds take two months, while a Highland Dhu or a Cornish Copper can take up to a year. Some Oriental breeds can take up to a thousand years to hatch. They spend all of their time in the shell, learning, for from the moment of incubation the greatest scholars in China read to them."

The Count looked dismayed at this information. "But we will know when it is going to hatch?"

"When the egg is completely hard to the touch," Simon said. "This egg is not ready yet – it is still somewhat soft. I should like to come every day and check upon it."

The Count looked dubious, as if this was an impossible request. But in the end he agreed.

Simon wondered if the same measure of secrecy would be made every day – the closed carriage, the quick trip into the building so that he had no time to see any landmarks – he did not enlighten the Count as to the fact that by leaving an indiscernible trail of magic, only able to be seen by himself, Simon could easily find his way here again, even without a guide.

After making certain that the egg was warm enough Simon did a quick sketch with careful measurements and a written description. He showed Savva how to use the curved thermometer that could measure the temperature of the shell. Then Simon was returned by the same covert method to the Rostov household.

He went at once to the courtyard, bypassing the house, so that he could tell Lakota about the egg. The dragon had been bitterly disappointed that he had not been allowed to go and talk to the egg. He had always worked closely with Simon whenever an egg came into their possession and felt left out and more than a little insulted.

Fortunately Sacha had shown up again. Mikhail had given him the task of sweeping the courtyard and filling the pit dug for Lakota's latrine with lime, and Sacha did this eagerly. He could talk to the dragon as he swept the court yard.

To Sacha everything the dragon said about himself, the Wizard or life in Ireland was wonderful. It was beyond anything he had ever imagined – so different from what he knew that he felt as if it were some sort of Faerie tale, like Perrault's stories that Tatya told him when he was little – *Cinderella*, or *La Belle au bois dormant*.

And to Lakota it was amazing that Sacha knew naught about dragons, magic or the ways of Wizards. Lakota was used to living in a society that accepted magic and the presence of dragons as a part of life. Personally, he thought life without magic would be intolerable. But he found the differences interesting.

Sacha also made the acquaintance of Janus and was shocked that a cat could talk. Janus had to explain what a familiar did and why it was necessary for her to talk. Sacha wanted to know if Vron could talk to him if he were a Wizard.

"Probably not," said Janus. "We chose our Wizards as kittens and learn to talk then. And most familiars have at least one familiar as a parent. My father was a familiar although my mother was not."

Janus was interested to hear that there was another cat in residence. And a Tom at that! Sacha had told her that the cat's name, Vron, meant crow, for his black coat. Janus had always a weakness for black Toms.

It was in the midst of this interesting conversation that Simon came back. Sacha leaped up from where he had been sitting on the ground near Lakota and Janus and began to wield his broom energetically.

Lakota greeted Simon enthusiastically. "I've made a friend! This is Sacha, who works in the stable here."

"Hello, Sacha," said Simon cheerfully. He had decided on the way back to be amused by the silly secrecy of the Russians, rather than let it annoy him. "It's good of you to talk with Lakota – he likes nothing better than making new friends."

Sacha bobbed his head in a little bow and said, "I like to talk to him too."

"I'd like to hear what happened this morning," said Lakota. "But for now could I have an oil bath? I'm so itchy!"

Dragons needed frequent oiling, for their scales could dry out and cause itching. This had not been a problem when they were feral, for their scales had become almost rock-like. But nearly a millennia before, when Merlin had changed the dragons to be a partner to man, the great Wizard had made their scales softer, so that a rider would be more comfortable dragon-back and not have to wear a vast amount of padding. Bu this meant the dragon's skin was far more tender and needed frequent oiling. Lakota's last oil bath had been before they left Ireland.

Simon was agreeable to this and briefly disappeared up to his room and returned with a sack full of Lakota's supplies – a large bottle of oil, magiced not to break, several long handled brushes, chamois cloths, a toothbrush (very large-sized) and dragon medications. This included calcium tablets, for dragons were prone to bone disease, most of it caused by a deficiency of calcium. Simon watched Lakota's calcium carefully, making certain that he had a good level of his favorite cream.

Simon had shed his coat and left his silk top hat in his room. He rolled up his sleeves and slipped on a leather apron from the sack. "Would you like to help?" he asked Sacha.

"C-c-could I?" Sacha stammered, thrilled. To be even closer to the dragon, to touch him!

"Certainly," Simon said. Sacha reminded him of himself at an earlier age. Simon had been eight when he became fascinated with dragons and twenty one years had not diminished that fascination. He decided that as soon as Lakota dried off from his oiling and he agreed, they would take Sacha up – Simon well remembered the joy of that very first dragon-back ride.

"What must I do?" Sacha asked rather breathlessly.

"We always start on his back so that the excess oil can drip down and get in to the lower scales. I'll go up first and then help you up." With the brushes and oil bottle under one arm he climbed on to Lakota's foreleg. The dragon lifted his limb up so that Simon could swing over to his back, grabbing one of the small back spikes to steady himself.

"Now you, Sacha," urged Lakota. "Climb up my leg and Simon will help you get on my back."

Sacha was a little nervous, but he climbed onto the outstretched leg. He found it easier than he though for the scales were a little rough and gave good traction. Lakota lifted his leg up and then Simon took his arm and swung him over to the dragon's back.

It seemed a long way off the ground.

"Don't worry – you won't fall – I shan't let you," said Simon reassuringly. "Are you afraid of heights?"

"I don't think so," Sacha answered. "But I've never been up high before." Already he was becoming accustomed to the elevation.

"That's very good," said Simon, "for if you want to fly with us, it's best if you aren't afraid of heights. What do you say, Lakota, shall we take Sacha up?"

Lakota turned his long neck to look at them, "Oh, yes! When I am dry, I'd like nothing better!"

Sacha's bliss was beyond description.

Oiling the dragon should have been hard work, but it was fun, Sacha thought. Lakota thoroughly enjoyed it, wiggling with delight and sighing over how good it felt. He directed then as to where he needed the most attention and obligingly lifted legs and wings and tail so they could reach everywhere.

His wings were beautiful – translucent opal that gleamed in the afternoon sun. Although shaped like a bat's wings, they reminded Sacha more of a butterfly's wings. They seemed too fragile to hold something as large as a dragon aloft . He voiced this thought to Simon, who explained how a dragon flew by the ignition of gasses in his flight cavities and how firestone was necessary to flying.

83

"You know a great deal about dragons," Sacha said. He had not imagined that there was so much to the subjects of dragons.

Simon laughed. "It's my profession – I'm a teacher of Dracophilology at Trinity University in Ireland."

"But you're a Wizard, too?" They were now finishing up Lakota's legs and feet. Lakota held up each foot for them as they progressed around him.

"And a Druid, also," Said Lakota proudly.

"What is a Druid?" Sacha inquired. He found Simon very easy to talk to – not frightening at all. It was what he had imagined having a big brother would be like.

But that question was to remain unanswered for the immediate future. An attention getting cough sounded behind them and all three turned to see a most imposing sight.

A young man, clad on all the glory of the uniform of the Chevalier Guards stood there. He wore white with a red cape and sleeves, high stiff jackboots and a silver helmet crowned by the double eagle. A sword hung by his side which he managed with grace and dexterity as he executed a most elegant bow.

"Professor Stillfield?" he queried in French.

Simon acknowledged his identity, wondering if any-one in Russia actually spoke Russian. Only when they did not wish to be overheard it seemed.

"I am Anatoly Aloyshovich Tcherpnin, Lieutenant in the Chevalier Guards, at your service, I have the honour to be chosen by the Czar himself to be your guide about St Petersburg during your stay." He bowed again.

Feeling it would be the correct thing to do, Simon bowed back and expressed his gratitude. He then introduced Sacha and Lakota, and indicated Janus, who, while Lakota was being oiled, had climbed onto the roof of th bath house and was snoozing in the sun.

The young man – he was only two and twenty – looked taken aback at being introduce to a serf (for that was what Sacha looked) and two animals, but he was very good-natured and bowed to each of them. He did not seem to exhibit the same fear that the other Russians had of Lakota. But he was startled when Lakota bowed back and said he was equally pleased to meet the Lieutenant.

Anatoly Tcherpnin did indeed come from a very good, very old family. His mother was a Princess, vaguely related to the Romanovs, but she could trace her family to the Kievan Prince, Yaroslav the Wise. The Tcherpnins numbered nobility, poets and famous soldiers amongst their ancestors, but were as poor as the proverbial church mice. In their *dacha* near Moscow they lived a simple existence, dining more often than not on cabbage soup and dwelling in the two rooms that actually had furniture left. Anatoly's father, in a burst of enthusiasm for the late Czar Alexander's liberalism, had freed his serfs, so that the 'souls' were not availed to sell and recoup the family fortune. The family, which consisted of Anatoly, his parents, grandmother, two old maiden aunts and five sisters, had sacrificed to send Anatoly to a military academy and from there to the Chevalier Guards, where he was to do his best to advance. But in these peaceful times there was little chance for advancement. He was also to look about him for a wealthy bride, even if she had to be a merchant's daughter.

He had been promised a promotion to Captain for this detail. It seemed an easy one – show this foreign guest about St Petersburg and attend a great many parties. He was relieved of his regular duties and what was even better, given a handsome stipend for his troubles, in addition to his army pay. He was to show the guest the best St Petersburg had to offer.

He had been briefed about the dragon but the sight of it took his breath away. He was not fearful – he had been raised to believe that there were many different and odd things in the world – not all of them immediately understandable.

In appearance he was of middle height with a fine figure – the cut of the Guards uniform gave him a wasp waisted look. He had an open face than more often than not was smiling. His hair was a rich dark brown, while his eyes were very dark, almost black, and they sparkled with good humor. He had a fine military mustache that met with his long side-whiskers giving him a look of wearing a short beard that lef this chin uncovered. He was a fine horseman, a crack shot and a good friend.

Now he inquired if Simon would like to see some of the town this afternoon before they went to the Princess Troblenka's ball.

To his surprise, Simon refused, saying that he had promised Sacha a flight on Lakota.

Anatoly blinked in surprise. This Englishman actually cared about a promise made to a serf! Then it struck him what had been said.

"You're going to ride the dragon? Up in the air?" he said in surprise.

"That's how I got here," Simon said a little dryly.

"*Blagdos Christos*!" Anatoly crossed himself. And then he blurted out, sounding only as old as Sacha, "Might I come too?"

8

Offal

Tatya was exhausted. Since even before the Wizard's arrival she had been run off her feet. Her aunt's demands had been insatiable. New furniture had been purchased from the famous Gamb's furniture shop on the Upper Nevski Prospekt – the ultra-fashionable area where Ekaterina would never dream of going to *actually* spend money. She made a point of being seen there, to give the impression that they *did* shop there, but their shopping baskets, carefully covered, were in reality filled with rags. Tatya did not know of the entertainment allowance from the government or that it was being spent on these items, as well as on new clothing for Ekaterina, Natalya and Olga.

And of course, Tatya, being a superior servant, was given the tasks of caring for and polishing the new furniture as well as hand washing and ironing the multitude of petticoats – all trimmed with exquisite, but difficult to care for, laces – that were necessary to hold the skirts out in the correct shape. Equally delicate 'berthas', the embroidered, beribboned, and lace covered collars that rested on the wide and slopping shoulders of the gowns had to be treated with extreme care. And then there were the *gigot* sleeves – the wide sleeves retained their shape by being stuffed with a pad of goose feathers, which had to be removed every time a gown was worn and then were washed, dried and replaced – all of which tasks fell to Tatya, as Ekaterina would not entrust such a finicking operation to Masha or Ilenka. Tatya's arms, shoulders and back ached from bending over the wash tubs, and wringing out the heavy garments that she washed. Her shoulders ached as well from the irons – some of which were quite substantial. Her hands were rough and chapped.

In the three days since the Wizard's arrival she had not seen him, and had caught only a glimpse of the dragon out of the windows that overlooked the courtyards as she hurried past on her innumerable tasks. She had scarcely had time to talk to Sacha – the press of invitations to the Rostovs had quadrupled and the carriages were called for at all times of the day and night. Sacha was now sleeping out tin the stables so that he might be readily available when horses were needed to be poled-up. At least that was the explanation her brother had given her two days ago when they had seen each other briefly. Tatya did not know that Sacha wanted more opportunities to be near Lakota.

But she was not to remain unenlightened long. Cn the third day after the Wizard's arrival, Tatya actually found time to slip down to the kitchen and have a much needed, restorative cup of tea. Luba always had the *samovar* boiling. Perhaps there would even be some bread left from Luba's morning baking, as Tatya had been so busy preparing her cousins for yet another shopping expedition – this one for bonnets, fans and gloves – that she had not had her breakfast.

Masha, chopping vegetables at the big, much scarred table looked up as Tatya approached. "You look tired." she said sympathetically. She was a broad faced, blonde, girl who wore the usual plait and flowered headscarf of the serf. Her dress was the *ponyova,* a type of skirt made with three lengths of homespun, worn with an embroidered shirt and attached at the waist with a braided cord. Over this she wore an immaculate apron lavishly decorated with calico *appliqué.* For Sundays and holidays she had embroidered garments, made by her own self. Tatya, in her horrid browns, envied Masha the colour and beauty of her simple garments.

"Look, Tatya Ivanova!" Masha indicated a plate on the table, filled with delicious looking treats. "*Pirozhki*! From Filippov's bakery! And they're for us to eat all our own selves!"

Ekaterina did not allow the serfs to address Tatya as 'Countess'. In truth Tatya was glad to have it so – for being called Countess reminded her painfully of her old life.

Now she sat down at the table and eyed the *pirozhki* warily. "If they are from aunt they're probably poisoned," she said.

This bought a laugh from the other two in the kitchen. Luba, in a bright blue *sarafan* with a billowy sleeved blouse, was at the stove stirring a pot, and said, "No, no, they're a gift from our guest – and he bought them for us! There are more

88

than enough for everyone! It is a thank you for how hard we have worked to prepare for his coming."

"Who told him how hard we have worked?" asked Tatya.

Masha tossed her head. "I did! He is a very nice gentleman! I have been taking care of his room and I have talked to him several times." Of all of the indoor serfs she spoke the most French . "He keeps his things tidy and there is no pinching or tickling! He is most respectful and speaks kindly and slowly so that I might understand." To both of the maids it was a relief not to have to deal with someone, like both Yuri and Evgeny, who thought it their right to fondle, kiss and pinch as they pleased. And Evgeny often went beyond fondling.

"The tea is ready," announced Luba and went to the steaming *samovar*, and poured three glasses of tea.

Like everything else in the kitchen the *samovar* and the glasses for tea were poor quality, utilitarian items. The short squat kitchen *samovar* looked nothing like the gilded and ornamented one in the dining room, which fancifully had been designed to resemble the Golden Cockerel of legend. But the kitchen *samovar* worked just as well as its gilded counterpart, the vertical pipe through the center of the urn filled with charcoal kept the water just as hot and the battered teapot in the holder at the top of the pipe brewed the tea just as well.

Tatya gratefully took the chipped glass of tea and took a careful sip. Something was different.

"Luba!" she exclaimed, putting the glass down on the table abruptly. "This isn't –"

"The trash and floor sweepings she buys for us?" the old woman finished for her. "This is her own private stock! She went to a better place to buy tea yesterday and has given us the old tea!" Both Tatya and Masha knew who 'she' was.

Luba reached for a *pirrozhki*. "I like to eat things that I did not have to make!" she announced through a big bite of the delectable treat. "Eat, eat!" she directed the others.

Tatya has scarcely enjoyed one of the *pirozhkis* when Masha said, "I saw Sacha Ivanovich riding the dragon yesterday afternoon and he was very brave –"

89

"You saw *what*?" Tatya's tea glass slipped from suddenly nerveless fingers as she stared at Masha in disbelief. Tea slashed on the table unnoticed as she demanded that Masha repeat herself.

"He was riding the dragon – I saw him when I emptied the dirty wash-water out of doors," Masha said, rather hesitantly. Tatya Ivanova looked so fierce!

"He promised me! He promised me!" Tatya muttered. She then stood up abruptly. "Is the Wizard still in the house?"

"He is up in his room, I think," said Masha. "Everyone else is gone out. Did I do something wrong, Tatya Ivanova?"

Tatya was not angry at Masha and told her so. "My brother gave me his word that he would not go near that beast, nor near the Wizard. And he has not kept his promise."

"Boys!" said Luba."They do not heed their elders – and they are even worse when they grow up to be men!" She had buried four very unsatisfactory husbands.

Without another word Tatya hurried from the room. She was literally shaking from anger. She only wanted to keep him safe – why could he not see that and obey her?

The best way to handle this was to tell this Wizard that he was not to have anything to do with her young brother. She would make it clear to him that Sacha had been forbidden to put himself in harm's way.

She was so angry that she did not even notice where she was going – the way to the guest room passed in a blur.

The door was standing slightly ajar; she rapped on it once and swept in.

Simon had spent a pleasant morning with Anatoly Tcherpnin. They had toured the great Nevski Prospekt that stretched nearly three miles from the Alexander Nevski monastery, which was blue and white in colour, to the golden-spired Admiralty building that over looked the a branch of the river, known as the *Bolskaya* Neva. Near the monastery was a village of wooden houses, carved and painted in the old Russian style in bright reds ad yellows. There were ware-house there as well, filled with goods from almost every part of the world, even America, Anatoly explained, and pointed out with pride, the ironworks there as well. He could arrange for a tour if Simon wished. But Simon, shuddering at the thought of all that Cold Iron, declined this treat.

They saw the Winter market, where sleds and carriages meant for peasants were sold and then strolled on up towards the Admiralty.

The streets were bustling even at a relatively early hour of the morning. It was an international crowd. Anatoly pointed out Circassians, silk clad Bokharians and Persians, Chinese, Ethiopians, Turks, Swedes and people from every country in Europe even Americans – all come to St Petersburg. It nade a colorful, multi-lingual throng.

Anatoly had been amazed that Simon wanted to walk the Nevski Prospekt – Russians much preferred to ride, if not in their own carriage, then in on of the many hacks for hire, driven by coachmen called *Izvozchiki,* of which there were hundreds if not thousands. Anatoly was certain that his guest would cry quits on the long walk and he would be able to cry *"Duva!"* and summon a gaggle of *Izvozchiki*, all vying for their business.

But Simon, raised in the country, was used to long walks and liked to stretch his legs at every opportunity. His only wish was that Lakota could accompany them, for the streets were wide and broad enough for a dragon.

From the Anchikov Bridge to the Admiralty was the most stylish section for shopping, crammed with shops that seemed to offer anything that anyone could ever want. There was Filippov's bakery, which Masha had spoken of so wistfully that very morning. Anatoly was amazed that Simon bought several huge boxes of pastries and had then sent to the Rostov house for the serfs, but held his tongue, as he was not certain whether or not this might be an English custom.

After a visit to a tea shop for a mid-morning repast, Anatoly still being young enough to be hungry most of the time, they had parted, Anatoly to report to his barracks and Simon to be carried off to see the egg. Everything was quite satisfactory there – Savva proved a competent attendant and was singing to the egg when Simon arrived.

He had come back to the Rostovs and decided to write up his journal and then write home. He had several hours before he was to met Anatoly and the Rostovs as well, to attend a military review. Simon was not excited as the others were over this outing – he had seen enough military reviews at home to satisfy him for the balance of his existence, but he did not like to cast a damper on the others' enthusiasm.

After the review it would be time to give Lakota his exercise. Count Pozharsky had promised that a good meal would be delivered to Lakota just about the time when the great cannon at the Peter and Paul Fortress sounded the noon hour. All of three of them had had to get used to the huge boom of the cannon.

Janus was quite happy – she had struck up an acquaintance with Vron, the black Tom, and as they both spoke cat, there was no communication problem.

But Simon was worried about Lakota – he was afraid that the blue dragon was lonely – Sacha had a great deal of work to do and could be with him very little. And the Russians seemed determined to keep him, Simon, entertained. He had been to several balls each night he had been here.

Tonight, once he was alone, he would try to scry. The letter he wrote now would go out in the regular mail pouch from the British Embassy. Simon had been warned that the Russians would try to read any mail, but the Embassy kept a Wizard on staff who magiced every piece of mail so that no one could open it but the one to whom it was addressed. Simon could do this his own self and could imagine the frustration of any of the men in His Majesty's Own Chancery in charge of the State and Security Police, especially those of the Third Section, hated and feared throughout Russia. Its power was such that it made Russia virtually a police state.

He was in the midst of a description of what he had seen that morning when a knock came at the door and a girl he had never seen before slipped in.

By now Simon was well used to the colorful costumes of the serfs. But this girl was a little brown bird, a wren, he thought inconsequently. She was quite small and at first he thought her a child. But another look showed womanly curves, although far less ample than those of Masha.

She wore her gold brown hair in braids wrapped around her head in a coronet. It gave her a little height – Simon estimated if she were standing next to him she might come up to his chin.

She was frowning and her eyes sparkled with anger.

Simon rose courteously when she entered and said in French, "How may I help you, *Mam'selle*?"

"YOU are the great Wizard?" Tatya said in disbelief. He was nothing like they had imagined.

Simon was hard put not to start tearing out his hair in frustration. It had been hard enough at home where everyone thought him too young and now, here in Russia, everyone had obviously been expecting something else. He had heard "*You* are the Wizard?" in tones varying from incredulity to outright scoffing and it had become wearisome.

Now he said somewhat sarcastically, "Yes, *Mam'selle*, I assure you I am the Wizard. Shall I change the bed into a hippogriffe to prove it to you?"

Tatya ignored this. "I am Sacha's sister. I will thank you to leave my brother alone! I forbade him to go near you or that beast of yours and he has disobeyed me! I even heard that he was riding that creature! How dare you put his life in jeopardy!"

Simon was struck at once by the excellence of her French. She did not stop and search for words as did Masha or even Mikhail. But she had the same ridiculous attitude that the rest of the Russians had towards dragons.

"I am sorry that Sacha disobeyed you," he said trying to be reasonable. "Had I known that I would have never taken him up. But he made no mention of being forbidden –"

"Did you never think to ask him?" she cried. "Or are you so lost to all feelings of decency and propriety that you willingly put a little child in danger of his very life?"

"I did not think to ask him, no," Simon admitted . "But at home no one is forbidden to ride a dragon. One only asks permission of the dragon to take a ride. Why, Lakota gives rides to all the children in Dublin –"

"This is not your country – WE do not expose our children to ravening beasts –" she interrupted hotly, her fists clenched and bosom heaving. One part of her mind demanded to know what she thought she was doing, talking to a Wizard in such a fashion, a man who could wave a hand and turn her into a insect that he then might crush beneath his foot.

Simon was beginning to lose his temper. "Sacha was in no danger! Lakota has never eaten a person – no dragon would EVER eat people or horses or pet animals. They only eat the cattle and sheep that are raised for that purpose –".

"What if he had fallen from the dragon's back!" she protested, sounding to Simon's ears a bit hysterical.

He took a deep breath to calm himself and said in the most reasonable tone he could muster, "Sacha was safely strapped onto the harness – no one rides a dragon without a safety harness. Indeed, no dragon would go aloft without his passengers safely strapped in – they are even more fanatical about that than we are! Be reasonable, *Mam'selle*! Sacha was in no danger from falling OR being eaten!"

Since it was a fine, warm day, Simon had opened the large window in his room to let in some fresh air. Suddenly the window was filled with a large blue head and snout.

"Simon," said Lakota plaintively, "They just delivered my food! It's *offal* – intestines, tripe and brains – and not even cooked! I can't eat that!"

Tatya had refrained from screaming only by a supreme effort of will. She pressed a hand to her lips and began to back up away from the creature in the window. She backed up so far that she ran into Simon's bed and fell backwards onto it. She was literally paralyzed with fright and could not seem to move any more. She felt as if she were going to swoon.

Simon had turned to face Lakota and did not see her fall on to the bed. "Of course you can't eat that!" he agreed angrily. "I told that idiot Pozharsky what you required! I daresay there wasn't any cream or honey or grain for you either."

Lakota shook his head and then said, "That girl on the bed looks like Noelle does just before she faints."

Simon spun around to see the little brown girl on the bed put a hand up to her brow. She was pale and trembling, her eyes closed.

The medical kit Stuart had given him was in the top drawer of the ornately carved bureau and Simon hurried across the room to fetch the smelling salts out of it. He then went to the girl's side and propped her up against his shoulder, unstopped the bottle and waved it under her nose.

Her long eyelashes fluttered and she coughed as the pungent fumes from the salts entered her nose.

She awoke just as belligerent as ever. Pushing away from him, she said, "Are you accustomed to accosting young women, and then luring them into your embrace by frightening them almost to death with your beast?"

The hot retort that rose to Simon's lips was never uttered, for Lakota, in a contrite voice said, "Did I frighten you, *Mam'selle*? I am so sorry! I never meant to do so! I am not used to frightening people and I don't like it. Pray forgive me!"

"It talks?" Tatya looked rather wildly at Simon.

Simon gave an exasperated sigh. "Of course he talks! All dragons talk!"

"But, but – he speaks French!" she protested.

"And why shouldn't he – we speak French at home because my father is half French and my grandmother and great grandmother are French as well. In fact, Lakota probably speaks more languages than you do!"

"English, Gaelic, French, Sioux, Spanish, Italian, German and Welsh," Lakota listed proudly. "And we are studying Chinese as well."

"Studying," Tatya repeated weakly.

"Dragons love learning and we will be going to China in a few years time," Simon explained. He rose from the bed and held out a hand to her. "I am not intending to lure you in to my lascivious embrace," he said dryly "but you will find it difficult to rise from a featherbed from your position."

Tatya flushed and accepted his hand. She still eyed Lakota askance.

Simon sighed once again and took her arm. "Come here. I want you to meet Lakota properly." As she protested he said "He will hot eat you! I want you to see that he only wants to be friendly. Lakota, this young lady is Sacha's sister."

"Oh, is she?" said Lakota happily. "Sacha is my friend! I like him a great deal!"

Practically dragging her across the floor, Simon took her over to the blue dragon. She shrank back against Simon, as if he would provide protection.

Simon took her hand in his and laid it on the very tip of Lakota's snout.

At first Tatya was so terrified that she could barely breath. And then she noticed something. "Why, it's like velvet!" she exclaimed at the soft feel of the end of the snout. It felt like a horse's muzzle. Timidly she moved her fingers as Lakota sighed in bliss.

Simon reached into his waistcoat pocket, where he always kept a handful of dragon treats. He unwrapped one and offered it to Tatya. "He loves these."

"Oh, I do!" agreed Lakota, his eyes brightening.

It smelled of honey and ripe grain.

"Do you know how to give a sugar cube to a horse?" Simon asked her. "It's just the same."

Still a little fearfully she stretched out her hand, palm flat with the treat on it.

With the most delicate touch imaginable Lakota took it from her with his forked tongue. He then chewed it briefly and swallowed with a sound of satisfaction. "But I'm still hungry!" he announced.

"I shall have to go and buy you some food," Simon said grimly, "as I cannot trust Pozharsky or his minions to do it. Lieutenant Tcherpnin took me to the Nevski Prospekt this morning and as they seem to sell everything there I am certain that there must be a butcher shop."

"Don't go to the Nevski Prospekt!" said Tatya involuntarily. "You will pay a fortune there!"

"Where do you suggest that I go, *Mam'selle*?" asked Simon, "Remember, I am not familiar with the city."

"The *Gostinny Dvor*, the Merchant's Inn, is near the Nevski Prospekt, but even better, a little further down Sadovaya Street are the *Apraxin Ryook* and the *Shchukin Dvor*, where the peasants and the commoners shop. The prices are much lower."

And to her surprise she found herself saying, "I have to go to the market for my au – mistress. I will take you there and show you the best shops." Unconsciously she had gone back to scratching Lakota's nose.

"Thank you, that would be most obliging," said Simon, rather startled at her change in attitude.

"Before you go you could scratch behind my ears!" said Lakota hopefully.

9

The Bronze Horseman

Tatya collected her shawl and market basket before joining the Wizard on their expedition. She could not imagine what had come over her, to offer to take him to the market. Perhaps he had cast a spell upon her?

He waited for her in the courtyard, with the dragon, who seemed much larger out here than he did when only his head was in the window.

A tub stood on the ground near the dragon and Tatya wrinkled her nose as she drew closer. The meat was old and rank. Little wonder the dragon did not wish to eat it.

She saw the Wizard frowning. He reached inside his breast pocket and withdrew a slender rod which he pointed at the tub of meat. What looked like a violet ribbon shot out the end of the rod and the rancid offal disappeared.

Tatya gasped and dropped her basket.

Both dragon and Wizard looked up at the sound.

"Don't be frightened," Simon said, noting her huge fearful eyes. He bent down and picked up the basket, returning it to her. "As you probably noticed, this meat had gone bad. It would eventually rot away, but it would not be pleasant. I merely made the rotting process a little faster."

"Mikhail would have burned it," Tatya offered, a bit timidly.

"That would have smelled dreadful!" said Lakota. "Not that it didn't *already* smell dreadful," he added.

"And you may be certain that Pozharsky will hear a thing or two from me about this!" Simon promised his dragon friend. "With *Mam'selle's* help –" He paused and looked at Tatya consideringly. "I've just realized – I don't know your name!"

"Nor I yours," she returned.

"That is easily remedied," he said, with a polite bow. "Simon Stillfield at your service, *Mam'selle*. And this is Lakota."

"Tatiana Ivanova Kustodieva." She made a graceful curtsey.

"Tatiana!" said Lakota. "Why, that sounds like the name of our Elf Queen – Tatania."

Tatya was not sure what he meant by an Elf Queen. She was reasonably certain that the Queen of England, the wife of William IV, was called Adelaide. She took every opportunity to read Uncle's discarded news sheets.

"It's a very pretty name," said Simon, smiling at her.

Once again, Tatya was struck by the fact that he did not in the least look like a dangerous Wizard. Evgeny looked far more threatening than did this Englishman. "I am called Tatya," she offered.

"Well, *Mam'selle* Tatya," he said, offering her his arm "Shall we go to the market?"

Tentatively, she put her hand on his arm. "It is a long walk from here," she said. To be offered a gentleman's arm, just as if she were a lady again!

"Then we shall call a hack and ride in comfort – it will be faster as well," Simon suggested.

"Please do go faster," said Lakota wistfully. "I am so hungry!" At this his stomach made a loud noise, and he looked so sheepish that Tatya suddenly lost the last of her fear of him. His expression was so like that of Sacha when he had done something inadvertently rude.

Tatya had quite forgotten what it was to be treated as someone of importance. She was handed carefully in to the carriage, and politely consulted as to the direction they were to take. Simon asked her questions about the places they passed and listened attentively, as if everything she said mattered to him. His questions were intelligent and his comments astute and interesting. When at last the reached the market – too soon – she was handed down and after he paid the *Izvozchik*, she was offered his arm again. It made her feel special; it made her want to cry.

She took him to the *Shchukin Dvor*, where she usually ended in buying the goods her aunt desired. The prices were cheaper here – they were even cheaper at the Haymarket, but Ekaterina was afraid that someone might find out that her goods were purchased at a place mostly frequented by peasants.

The other market that shared space with the *Shchukin Dvor*, the *Apraxin Rynok*, combined with its neighbor to cover some two million square feet. There were over five thousand merchants' stalls. These buildings were so closely packed together that they nearly touched at the top and left only narrow alleys between them. Over the narrow wooden gates at the entrance were suspended icons. More icons and little lamps hung from the wooden arches that went from roof to roof.

The market was dark inside and had a heavy smell. Simon could identify the odors of sauerkraut and leather, amongst others.

Tatya knew where the best meat dealers were to be found and she took Simon at once to a butcher she had dealt with many times and trusted.

The merchant, Pavel Andropovich, greeted her pleasantly by name. He was a short, square man dressed in the blue caftan and blue cap worn by most of the shopkeepers. In excellent French he declared himself pleased to meet such a distinguished guest and stared as he heard the size of the order for meat that Simon placed. When he found out that it was to be repeated every other day, indefinitely, his joy knew no bounds. He even offered to have it cooked when Simon inquired if this could be done. "Bachelor quarters, heh? Your honor must entertain a great deal!" Pavel said cheerfully, thinking that he had discerned the reason why the order was so large.

Simon thought it best, given people's reaction to Lakota, that he not tell the man all of the meat was for a dragon. As he paid Pavel, with little haggling and in gold, he saw Tatya looking disapprovingly at him.

With a last 'thank you' to Pavel, who promised that the finest beef, cooked to tender perfection and seasoned just right, would be delivered to the Rostovs' within the hour, Simon offered his arm again to Tatya.

"What have I done wrong?" he asked her as they walked away from the butcher's.

"That was too much to pay!" she said. "You should have bargained with him further."

"It seemed a very inexpensive price to me," Simon returned. "The meat he showed us was of excellent quality. I would pay about the same in Ireland for first quality meat." Simon had studied the rates of exchange and understood what amount of *rubles* equaled a pound sterling. "I want Lakota to have the best."

"I did not imagine that dragons liked their meat *cooked*." Tatya said.

Simon laughed. "I suppose you imagined him pouncing on a cow tearing it into bloody shreds and gorging himself? Nothing could be further from the truth. Dragons are quite the *gourmets* and extremely fussy about the quality of their food. Only feral dragons actually hunt and kill their food. It would never occur to Lakota to hunt – he expects his food well cooked and served to him."

"It must cost a great deal – feeding a dragon," Tatya said, thinking of the amount he had just spent.

Simon grew sober. "That *is* a problem. Fortunately I can afford it. But there are many people who would be excellent dragon handlers but have not the means to support a dragon. In America, because of a government subsidy, anyone who shows the promise to work with dragons can do so. They pay their loans back by working for the government, with their dragon. I would like to see something like that in the British Isles. It is getting to the point where there are more eggs available than there are people who can support them." He went on to explain to her about his bond with Lakota and the things that dragons did for employment in Britain.

Tatya could not imagine flying on a dragon and to think of it as ordinary! She asked if ladies commonly rode dragons, and was told that indeed they did – his mother and sisters rode both the family dragon, Cerridwen, and had been on Lakota as well.

As Sacha had before her, she thought that Ireland sounded as if one would be living in a constant Faerie story. She said in some surprise that she did not know Wizards had mothers and sisters.

He laughed again. He had a very nice laugh, she thought. "Not only a mother and sisters, but a father and a brother as well and numerous grandparents, and adopted uncles and aunts and cousins."

'Are they all Wizards?" she wanted to know.

"A great many of them, yes." By this time they had come to the dairy sellers and she watched as he ordered a vast quantity of the finest cream. They then went to a grain merchant and she showed him where to get honey.

Her own shopping was quite modest compared to this, and when it was done, it was with some regret that she realized they had no reason not to return to the house.

But the Wizard surprised her. "It has been highly recommended that I see the statue of Peter the Great. Do you know where it is?"

"Everyone knows where it is!" she said. "It is in Senate Square, several blocks from the Winter Palace."

"Would you be so good as to show it to me? And then perhaps we can have some tea." Simon surprised himself. He wanted to prolong this outing. He was enjoying her company. They had talked of all sorts of things as they had walked about the enormous market. She had a quick mind and once she had relaxed, she laughed frequently. And he sensed some mystery about her. He could not make out what her status might be in the Rostov household. From what she had said as they talked he surmised that she had had an excellent education. She could not be a governess, for the daughters of the house were past the age of needing one. She was not a lady's maid, for no lady's maid would go to the market for groceries, considering such beneath her.

"I should really return to the house," she said doubtfully.

"Are you expected back at any special time?" he asked.

"No, but ..."

"Another hour – to look at the statue and have some tea," he said coaxingly, and smiled at her.

That did it. He had a most attractive smile that lit up his whole face and his eyes as well. Tatya allowed herself to be persuaded.

Simon called up another hack and they drove in style to Senate square where the huge statue of Peter faced the Neva.

Again, she was treated like a Princess. He even insisted on carrying her basket for her. She was far more used to the many officers who could not, by law, carry anything so mundane as a basket or a package or who would never dream of carrying a basket for someone who was only a servant.

It was a beautiful day, warm enough so that the brisk breeze coming off the sea was not unwelcome. The sun made diamonds on the water and showed the patina of the equestrian statue.

St Petersburgers were justifiably proud of this statue. It sat atop a huge block of granite that had been mined twelve miles away. It had taken two years to move into place and even after it had been reduced to half its original size it still weighed 1,600 tons. The statue itself had been sculpted by Frenchman Etienne Falconet, (the head done by his pupil, Marthe Callot) who took eleven years to work on it until the final cast in bronze. Tatya told Simon it was familiarly known as 'the Bronze Horseman' and considered one of the finest sculptures in the world. Under the hooves of the rearing horse lay a writhing snake, while Peter's arm seemed to point westward. They admired it from all sides as Tatya told Simon how it had been commissioned by Catherine the Great.

When at last Tatya had exhausted her store of information, they fell silent, content to gaze at the statue and then out over the Neva, reveling in the fresh breeze and ocean tang of the air.

It came to Tatya suddenly that she was happy for the first time in a long while. She could not remember a more enjoyable morning – not since her father had been arrested. It was wonderful to actually have an intelligent conversation again with someone who had a lively mind and an excellent sense of humor. She was far too used to her conversations being limited to orders from her aunt or uncle or to talk with the serfs about work.

And more was to come. They returned to the hack, which Simon had asked to wait for them. He then ordered the *Izvozchik* to drive to a fashionable tea shop on the Nevski Prospekt.

"I can't go there!" she protested.

"Why not?" he asked. "Is it against the law?"

She blushed. "My clothes –"

"I went into a tea shop this morning and saw people in every type of dress imaginable," he told her. "I daresay they would not refuse to serve a lady merely because her dress is a trifle – drab," he added diplomatically. "Please come. I think you will enjoy it."

"I have never had tea on the Nevski Prospekt," she said, her eyes beginning to sparkle. She had heard of the fantastic tea shops there. On the rare occasions when she had money – which was not very often as Ekaterina made her account for every *kopek* spent – she treated herself to tea from a street vendor. On her name day every year, she was given a few *kopeks* by her uncle, who did the same for the serfs, this being a long standing tradition in his family. Then she felt wealthy and would take Sacha with her so they could have tea and *ozsyany kisel*, soft oatmeal, sliced and spread with oil, gingerbread or *pryanki*, little cakes flavored with mint, honey or spices. Sometimes they went to a *chainaya*, a tea shop for ordinary folk, with its colourful sign of a *samovar* surrounded by white tea cups on a blue ground That, to Tatya and Sacha, had been the height of dissipation.

The tea shop on the Nevski Prospekt was beyond anything she could have imagined. On the window was inscribed in bright gold letters: *"Here is sold all sorts of Chinese tea."*

Inside the tea shop it was as if they had stepped in to China itself. Everything was Chinese – from the furniture to the floor covering. Chinese tapestries hung on the wall. Chinese lanterns provided the subdued light. The arrangement of everything was elegant – the shop not only served tea but sold it as well – several hundred varieties of it. These were stacked in beautiful lacquered and enameled boxes – little chests the Chinese called *lansin*. The tea was wrapped in soft paper and encased in lead to preserve the fragrance.

The proprietor of this particular shop, which called Dmitriov's, had indulged his obvious taste for all things Chinese. The decor was based on the colour red (a Russian favorite) with two immense carved golden Chinese dragons hanging from the pagoda like roof. Red silk peony brocade adorned the walls. Shelves lined the back wall, filled with treasures and toys, ranging from porcelain and jade to tea services, wood carvings and ivory and even Chinese papers and wind-up dolls and toys of exquisite workmanship.

A smiling waiter in immaculate white bowed low and inquired in Parisian French if they were there to drink or buy tea.

"Drink tea, if you please," said Simon and the waiter lead them to a secluded table. This was unlike the *chainaya*, where tables were placed in a straight line down the center of the room. Even the tabletop was a work of art, portraying golden dragons on a red background. This art work was covered by a thick sheet of glass.

The waiter handed then a lengthy list of teas available and announced that the pastry of the day was a *gateau millefleur*, or they might have a selection of *zakuski*, which were various little snacks of salted and pickled fish, savories of meat and vegetables and cold salads. Traditionally, these were served before a full meal, but they proved popular with Dmitriov's customers as an accompaniment to the fine tea.

After consulting Tatya Simon ordered the savories and an Imperial tea.

This was served on fine Chinese porcelain, the tea in a beautiful teapot with dragons on it and poured into paper-thin, handleless cups.

"If it wasn't for that idiot Pozharsky, we would have not had this very pleasant morning," said Simon, taking two piping hot savories from the serving tray. "I only wish Lakota had not had to wait for his dinner so long."

Tatya put down her cup, filled with the most fragrant and most delicious tea she had ever drunk. She felt entirely different towards him – she was no longer afraid – in fact, she rather liked him. He needed to be warned.

"You must not talk about the Count Pozharsky like that – someone might hear you," she said in a low voice, casting uneasy glances around the shop as if afraid they might be overheard.

"Why not?" Simon queried. "As far as I am concerned, he *is* an idiot! It would take a good half hour to list all of the idiotic things he has done!"

"He is a very powerful man," Tatya said, lowering her voice.

"He's only an official in the Foreign Office –" Simon began.

Tatya shook her head. "Don't you know? He is in the Third Section – the Secret Police – of the uppermost rank. It is dangerous to criticize or oppose him! Please be careful what you say!"

Simon could only stare at her in consternation.

10

Gemstones and Blackmail

Far away from St Petersburg, to the south and west, lay the *Uralsky Knrebet* mountain range, known to Europeans as the Urals. The Urals were a rich source of minerals such as copper, gold, iron and platinum. There also could be found jasper, porphyry, agate, rhodonite, as well as malachite and lapis lazuli. There, too, were emeralds, topaz and the most beautiful amethysts in the world.

In the forests were fur-bearing animals – sable, ermine, fox, and marten. The forest was also a valuable source of wood. All of these things were an important source of income for the Czar.

Usually the area swarmed with miners, trappers, and woodsmen and those who fished the Kara Sea for grayling, *nelma*, and salmon. But all was now abandoned, the sounds of busy industry and daily life gone; the only sounds left were those of the natural world – the wind in the trees, birdsong and the animals going about their business.

All through the mines, on the edge of the Kara Sea and in the woods lay scattered tools, empty houses, deserted boats and nets and chaos. A traveler to the region would surmise that the former residents had left in a great hurry, due to some disaster. Peering into the houses the traveler would have seen meals left on the tables, personal possessions left behind – clothing, furniture, even toys, lying pathetically on the floors or in the yards of the small houses. Everywhere was the sign of haste.

But the traveler would have seen no cause for this mass exodus. There was no sign of fire, earthquake, cyclone or even pestilence. It was as if they had al decided to leave, *en masse*, for no apparent reason.

High atop the tallest mountain in the Northern or Nether – Polar Urals, sat the reason for the forsaken mountain range.

He was an immense Ice dragon, Volunvoshka by name. He was nearly forty feet long and proportionately tall.

106

His scales were white, overlaid with crystal that glittered in the early summer sun. Each scale was edged with silver, as were his horns and ears. His eyes were pale blue and cold as the ice he was named for. Wings of crystal, edged with silver were folded against his sides. Immense spikes ran from his back to the very tip of his tail, which had a cluster of five deadly looking barbs. More of these barbs were on the joints of his wings. He had long, curved silver talons – three of them – on each of his four feet.

He should have been happy. Single-handedly he had scared off all of the inhabitants of this area, without having to eat a single one of them. In common with most dragons, Volunvoshka did not care for the taste of human flesh. But unlike his draconic peers in other parts of the world, he could and did eat humans if nothing else was available.

But now the great dragon sat on the top of Mount *Narodnaya* and brooded on the iniquities of man.

When he had agreed to do the Wizard Karachev's bidding he had expected to be well-rewarded. The Wizard had promised gold and jewels – that part of the bargain had been fulfilled to the dragon's satisfaction – he had added considerably to his hoard. But he did not like this place he had to guard. It was too warm, unlike his beloved Siberia. In spite of the fact that this range of the Urals held glaciers, it was still uncomfortable for a dragon who usually spent summers near the arctic circle. The temperature was nearly fifty degrees and a warm west wind blew. In his scouting flights over the entire area he had seen a desert just to the south of these mountains – a dry, arid region of steppes. He had been appalled. While other dragons loved dry heat and sand in which to roll and bask, an Ice dragon felt best in the snow and a temperature considerably colder. He also did not like the thick, largely coniferous forests here. There were delicious things to eat – roe deer, reindeer, brown bears, as well as the domesticated animals of the inhabitants, but the forests climbed the sides of the mountains to almost 1,800 feet and provided shelter and cover for the creatures. Volunvoshka had no idea how to hunt in these heavily wooded circumstances. He was used to the open tundra, where nothing could hide or outrun a dragon. He was having to fly farther and farther away to find something to eat. And too often he ended in the southern wastes of Central Asia, where he had learned that the slow moving caravans provided dromedaries and horses that were quite edible. But it was quite warm there and a trip there made him feel miserably ill.

And then had come this morning's bad news. Karachev had promised that he would do something about the tragedy that had come to the Ice dragon colony months ago but so far he had done nothing and time was running out. And this was another reason he had agreed to help Karachev, actually the most important one.

The very thought of this reason infuriated Volunvoshka. He spread his wings and leaped into the air, leaping straight up rather than spiraling as did other breeds of dragons. He would have it out with this Wizard! He would fulfill his promise or he would be dragon fodder!

On the side of Mount *Stredny Baseg* (some 3,000 feet in height) in the Lower Central Urals perched a house. It was actually far too large and commodious to be called by the common name of cabin as were most of the dwellings hereabouts. Siberian spruce climbed the sides of the rather flat-topped mountains. Above this spruce ran a belt of birch and alder. It was in this belt that the house sat.

With difficulty, Volunvoshka landed in front of the house This was another grievance. The Wizard ought to have enlarged a landing area for the use of Volunvoshka and his compatriots. Volunvoshka felt as if he was in a trap the entire time when he had to speak to the Wizard. Due to the trees he could not see above him or around himself with any great degree of ease. Ice dragons had few natural enemies but it was always best to be on guard.

From inside the onion domed house came the sounds of the *balalaika*. Volunvoshka winced. He despised music. He had been glad to terrify the mountain workers into running away for it stopped their infernal singing and playing. Music was deep in the souls of all Russians and they sang at their work; they gathered in large groups when they were not at work and played, sang and danced.

This music was particularly grating to Volunvoshka's ears, for that boy, Illya, played nothing but dirges and melancholy songs. Volunvoshka would have gladly eaten the boy, *balalaika* and all, just to stop him from playing.

108

The Ice dragon let out a bellow, his voice echoing among the mountains. Far off, a bit of the northern glacier avalanched.

Inside the house the *balalaika* ceased abruptly and the outside door flew open.

The Wizard Karachev appeared in the doorway. Vladimir Konstantinovich Karachev was every bit the Wizard of legend. He was tall and broad, with black hair and beard. He wore not a full beard but a close clipped *Henri Quatre* beard, with a mustache, well streaked with grey, for he was nearly fifty. His face was rather sharp featured and his heavy eyebrows always seemed to meet in a frown. He wore red robes, heavily embroidered with gold arcane symbols and bejeweled as well, with topazes and rock crystal, faceted to catch the light. The sleeves of his robe were dagged, lined with cloth of gold and touched the floor. The robe, worn over a red silk shirt, breeches, hose and tall red leather boots, was made high to the neck with a collar that flared out stiffly to frame his face. His head was covered by a close fitting hood that completely covered his hair, ears and neck. It was a costume that might have been worn by an actor playing Mephistopheles in Christopher Marlowe's *Doctor Faustus*. It gave Karachev a diabolical look with which he was well pleased.

Karachev's grey eyes were hard and cold as he looked up at the Ice dragon. "What do you want? I am in the midst of an important conjuration –"

Volunvoshka sneered, his silver lip curling. "You were listening to that damned boy again – I heard the *balalaika*! I wish that you would let me eat him!"

"Music helps my concentration!" the Wizard snapped. "At any rate it is none of your affair. What do you want?"

"I had news from home this morning," the dragon answered. "They have traced the egg – it now resides in St Petersburg."

"And –?" Karachev rose one brow. His tone dismissive and Volunvoshka bridled.

"You gave us your promise, Wizard!" he hissed, lowering his great head so that he stared into the Wizard's eyes. "You swore to us that you would recover the egg that they stole!"

"When the Czar bows to my demands then will be time to have the egg returned," said the Wizard, without flinching at the huge head and tooth-filled maw that was so close to his face.

"That is what you do not understand!" the dragon roared. "There is very little time! What if the egg hatches while the humans have it in their grasp? A dragonet is a wild thing when it emerges from the egg! They will not know how to feed it and will end in killing it! They know nothing of dragons! Nothing! This egg is MINE, Karachev! What am I to tell my mate if it is killed by humans? She does naught but weep as it is!"

"Nonsense!" the Wizard replied. " You are prone to exaggeration –"

Volunvoshka roared again, this time emitting a chill vapor that hung in the air and caused frost to form on Karachev's beard and eyebrows.

The Wizard was again unmoved. He knew that he was in no danger from the dragon. His magic protected him and the dragon well knew that Karachev was perhaps the only way to a return of the egg. He was rather contemptuous of Volunvoshka's insistence on the return of one inconsequential egg. The Ice dragon acted as if his entire race verged on extinction.

The egg had been stolen last year, in the early autumn. The deed had been done cleverly – the thieves had come from the sea, to where Volunvoshka and his mate, Khlebnikova, had made their lair. Khlebnikova loved the mighty surge of the ocean and wished to be near it. Looking back, Volunvoshka was sorry that he had given into her demands and instead insisted that they dwell closer to the rest of the colony.

After the egg had been stolen they found evidence that men had laid in watch for a while, spying upon them and learning when they left the egg for extended periods of time – mostly to eat.

In spite of the fact that the adult Ice dragon preferred the cold, the egg, like every other dragon's egg in the world, had to be kept warm. This was difficult for the Ice dragons, as the climate was harsh and many eggs were lost. They resolved this problem by tunneling to a vent near the earth's core, where it was much warmer. The heat made it uncomfortable for the adults, so that the eggs, of a necessity, were alone much of the time. In a normal colony this was not a problem, for the lairs carved out of earth and rock were numerous, all running into one another – someone was always about, laying eggs, checking eggs, or tending the new hatchlings.

But no one, as yet, shared the new tunnels of Volunvoshka and his mate. It was easy for the human thieves to enter the tunnels when the adults were gone and abscond with the precious burden. They had then taken ships to parts unknown. And of course, none of the dragons could fly any distance over the frigid waters of the North Pacific.

A young adult male, Shishenkov, one of the fastest in the colony, took off after the ship and followed it as best he could from the shore. He was fortunate in seeing it as various ports as the ship beat its way along the Chinese coast, past India and the Cape of Good Hope. It was there that Shishenkov had lost the ship. Overcome by tropical heat he had to give up or die. It had taken him a good while to return to Siberia, where he arrived in very poor condition.

Volunvoshka had at once sent out inquiries to all of the Witches and spirits for news of where the egg had finally ended. And today, finally, word had come.

And now that damned Wizard knew exactly where the egg was and still he refused to do anything about it! When he had contacted the Ice dragons to help him empty the Urals of humans he had promised to find and fetch the egg, as well as enrich the hoards of any dragon that helped him.

Volunvoshka did not understand his plan – it had something to do with forcing the Czar to bow before him and meet with Karachev's demands – but at this point Volunvoshka only wanted the egg back.

Although Volunvoshka argued with the Wizard for a few more minutes it was obvious that the Wizard was barely listening to him.

Volunvoshka seethed with impotent rage. There was nothing he could do to the Wizard. He had tried freezing Karachev (for Ice dragons breathed ice, not fire) – but the Wizard had defrosted himself speedily; with the mocking smile that Volunvoshka found so irritating.

111

With one last exhortation the Ice dragon gave up, and launched himself into the air, peevishly scattering dirt, gravel and dead leaves all over the Wizard's finery.

From inside the house, behind a curtain,Illya Timofeiovich Tairov watched the scene outside. He hoped with a sick hatred that the dragon would one day eat the Wizard, and then he, Illya, would be free. And he could go home to his family – Father and Mother, his two little sisters, Sonia and Irina and older brother Leonid. He would even be glad to see Grandmother Nazdeha, who had, as he thought then, made his life so miserable.

Illya was sixteen years old and had once been the son of a prosperous cloth merchant. He had been expected to follow Leonid into the family business. But he had chafed under the utter boredom of dealing in cloth and placating fussy customers. He liked nothing about the cloth trade – dealing with other merchants for raw materials, consulting with the dyers – the dyes smelled so bad they made him sick! – and worst of all, selling the finished product to the customers. He had come to think of the customers, in his nightmares, as a huge, many armed, many mouthed beast, all of the arms reaching out to envelope him with their demands. To spend the rest of his life thus–- ! It was insupportable.

But his father and brother laughed at his ambitions – he wanted to be a musician. Everyone agreed that he had a professional touch on the *balalaika* and an excellent singing voice as well. He had moved people to tears in their little town south of Moscow. Even the traders who passed through – men who had even been to Moscow and St Petersburg and saw the very best those cities had to offer – called for a song from him whenever they visited Topek.

Illya was a well-grown youth with dark hair and bright green eyes. He had a very stubborn chin and clever hands. He fancied himself ill –used – no one, not even his mother, understood him. His grandmother never left off telling him how easy boys of his generation had it – he had fine clothes and plenty of pocket money thanks to his father's hard work. He did not have to scramble for a living. In her day, he would have been working by now at some physically demanding job instead of being allowed to lounge about the ale house with a group if rowdies who only encouraged his foolish ideas.

One day it became intolerable and he ran away. He left with little but a change of clothing, his beloved *balalaika* and not much money. He was headed for Moscow where he was certain that in very little time he would be rich and famous. How his parents and siblings, his grandmother (and everyone else in the village who had doubted him) would stare when he returned home triumphantly in an enormous *troika*, pulled by prancing Orlovs, complete with servants and himself dressed in the latest fashion and able to dispense largess with an air of nonchalance!

What money he had did not last long and he soon had to take to playing for serfs and other rustics in hedge taverns. Very often his only pay was a meal and a bed on the floor near the fire.

In one of these taverns he had met Karachev.

He had been flattered at first by the older man's interest and appreciation of his talent. He had accepted an invitation to supper and feeling quite grown-up, took a long draught from a flask of 'special' vodka.

It was the last thing he remembered until he woke up with a collar about his neck and was told by Karachev that he was now the Wizard's slave and would do his bidding, which including playing for his 'master' whenever the Wizard desired.

He tried running away from the Wizard. He could only get to a certain distance when terrible pain, centered at his throat and spreading into all parts of his body, brought him to his knees. As much as he tried he could not get the collar off – it seemed to have no buckle or other means of removing it. Under his panicked fingers it was smooth and cold.

He had been enslaved for over a year now. Instead of his well – made European style clothing he wore the baggy trousers and the full sleeved high necked blouse of the peasants, but without the rich embroidery that usually decorated it. His feet were bare and filthy – one of the worst things was being constantly dirty. His hair, once so well tended, was matted and vile, and hung down below his shoulders. Now instead of playing for friends and admirers at the tavern, he cooked and scrubbed and cleaned for Karachev, and played for him as well. He also had had to do many things that made him ill, including disposing of dead and mutilated bodies.

All Illya though about was escaping and going home. To further this end he took every opportunity to spy upon his master, hoping to find out something that could be turned to his advantage and promote his freedom.

He had not understood why they came here to the Urals. Karachev's home was by the Sea of Azov, near Taganrog. Illya had listened to all of the plans made between the dragon and the Wizard, and had come to the conclusion that the Wizard was making demands on the Czar and if these demands were not met, the Wizard would insure that the Urals remained empty of humans – humans who mined and trapped and fished – bringing riches to the Czar – riches necessary to the economy of the country.

How even a powerful Wizard could consort with the fearsome Ice dragon Illya could not figure out. He viewed the cold creature with horrified fascination. There was no doubt about it though – the dragon had terrified the people to flight – they had all gone in less than a week.

When he saw the dragon leave and Karachev began to return to the house, Illya hurriedly took up his place by the tiled stove and took up his *balalaika* again, idly strumming it as the door opened and the Wizard entered.

The house consisted of one great room, littered with books, and tables on which bottles and jars jostled with mortars and pestles. Arcane symbols were inscribed on the floor and Illya had learned, rather painfully, not to step inside them. It was dark, for there were few lamps. Other than cleaning around these tables and doing the washing of both clothing and dishes, Illya was allowed to touch nothing. Sometimes the Wizard had him grind herbs. He also fetched a great deal of water from the well outside, for it seemed a common ingredient in many of the Wizard's experiments.

Illya looked up at the Wizard's entrance, affecting a nonchalance he did not feel. Karachev had caught him spying once and had managed to deliver a painful thrashing without touching him.

"Play," the Wizard said brusquely and seated himself at the table he had left when the dragon bellowed out of doors.

Obediently, Illya struck a chord and began to sing.

Ochy chornia, Ochy iasnia,
Ochy siguchua, Y preecrasnie,
Leash oouidielvas, Patieral pokov,
Y vies meer zabul, Dlia nieya adniy.

As he sang, his fingers skillfully moving over the strings, Illya allowed his mind to drift. One day he would escape, perhaps even have his revenge on the Wizard. He would do whatever it took to gain his freedom. And then he would go home to Topek and gladly become a cloth merchant. His captivity had ended his dreams.

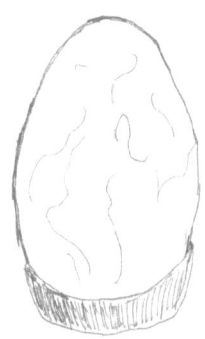

11

Clandestine Operations

Tatya refused to answer any of Simon's questions about the Count. It was as if she were afraid to speak his name out loud.

Simon had nothing but contempt for a society that made its citizens so fearful. In Ireland, one could stand in the middle of the street and hurl epithets at the *Taoiseach* – the Prime Minister – and the only time the Wizard Police would intervene would be if one were blocking traffic. The longer he stayed here, the more conscious he became of an atmosphere of constant surveillance and a severe lack of freedom of speech. He did not care for it in the least.

Obedient to Tatya's wishes, he turned the subject while they finished their tea, and was gratified to see the look of fear leave her eyes. When they were finished he paid the check and purchased several types of tea as gifts for members of his family. He also bought three mechanical toys – one of an exquisite enameled box that opened to display a unfolding peony in a rich pink colour and two Chinese dragons that could be wound up and appeared to fly across the table top. One was black, the other gold, and each bore a tiny Chinese rider complete with robes of silk and a long pigtail. These he had wrapped as gifts. Tatya assumed these were gifts for people back in Ireland, and was completely bewildered when, once they were seated in the hack again, Simon presented her with one of the boxes.

"What is this?" she asked, not taking it from him.

" A thank you gift," he said. "A little memento of the day. And an apology for frightening you."

She shook her head. "I cannot accept it." To her consternation, she felt her throat close up and her eyes fill with tears.

"It's perfectly proper to give you a little something. Even my sister Holly's governess, Miss Prism, who my brother Stuart calls an old battle-axe, would say so!"

She gave him a watery smile, but still did not take the box. "I would not be allowed to keep it. She would see it and take it away. I have no place to hide it and no privacy."

"That is easily remedied," said Simon. He could guess to whom she referred and it did nothing to improve his opinion of Ekaterina Rostova.

He reached into his breast pocket and removed his wand. With this he tapped the box and said "She will not be able to see it."

Tatya blinked. "But I can still see it!" she protested.

"The spell is tuned to you. Other people will see nothing when they look at it. it. The spell is a sort of 'hide in plain sight' conjuration. Now will you accept it?"

She wanted it – even though she knew what it was she desperately wanted the pleasure of opening a present, to actually own something pretty that she could take out and look at with joy. She took it from his hand.

Unwrapping it was sheer enjoyment. The paper was exquisite – a Chinese design of birds and flowers, brightly coloured, and each bird. leaf and petal were edged with gold. A silk ribbon of a beautiful blue was tied around it. These she carefully folded and put aside. She would keep them too , in the little drawer she noticed in the bottom of the peony box.

The peony box was more beautiful than she had thought it was at first. Again and again she opened the box to watch the peony unfold. She could only stammer her thanks.

"You are most welcome," he returned, wondering what sort of life she had, where a little present meant so much to her and she was afraid that it would be taken away from her.

Tatya had been taken back in time. Her father had often gifted her with exquisite toys like this, but not one of those gifts remained to her. What the creditors had not taken, her aunt had. It was not so much the items themselves, but the fact that her father had chosen them for her his own self, and thought of what would please her. They were tokens of his love. For the first time in seven long years someone had thought of what would please her again.

To cover the emotions that swept her and threatened to overcome her, she asked, "Please, what is that thing you used?"

"My wand?" He took it from the pocket to which he had retuned it and held it up so that she might see it.

It was a beautiful thing. It had a silver handle and tip. On the very end of the tip was a magnificent opal. The body of the wand was of wood and intricately carved. Looking at it closer Tatya could see that it was a pattern of dragons in flight, done with amazing skill. The wood was honey coloured and highly polished.

"Do you need that to do every magic?" she asked.

"No, a wand is simply a focus for magical energies. Indeed, using a wand at all is now considered quite old fashioned. Most of my students don't use one – hand and arm gestures are all the thing. Some of them are rather ridiculous!" He smiled, remembering one young man who looked as if he was imitating a wind-mill.

Tatya opened her box again. "This seems to me like magic," she commented.

"That is mechanics, not magic," he returned.

"I thank you again for this," she said, looking down into the box. "I shall treasure this always."

As the carriage drew near the Rostov house Simon was aware that this was no idle promise. She would indeed treasure it always.

Lakota had been more than pleased with the meal that was finally delivered to him. The meat was juicy and tender and had been cooked in some sort of cream sauce with mushrooms and onions. And there was more than enough of it to satisfy the heartiest of draconic appetites.

Sacha met the delivery men and told them where to put their goods. The cream that arrived was put in the ice room beneath the house, where ice cut from the Neva during the winter kept everything cool. Lakota would wait for Simon to return to mix his favorite drink. Rich, ripe grain was delivered also, which Lakota liked for breakfast, mixed with cream and honey and any available fruit. Fruit and honey arrived also – to Lakota's delight the fruit was strawberries.

Luba, busy at the soapstone sink, heard the rattling of carts and the noise of the men as the food was delivered. She could not imagine what was going on. Wiping her hands on a dish towel she went to the window and saw Sacha directing four men wearing butcher's aprons wheeling in a huge tub of something smoking. She saw the dragon, hanging well back while the men delivered the food. When they stepped back he went to the tub at once and began feeding.

To her surprise, the dragon did not gorge on the food, but began to eat daintily, selecting each piece with a long forked tongue and then chewing them thoroughly. He seemed to enjoy it.

Luba had not realized that dragons ate cooked food. And she all at once was insulted – the beast was a guest too – why had she not been asked to cook for it?

She left the kitchen and went out into the courtyard. "Sacha Ivanovich!" she called imperiously.

Both the dragon and the boy looked up at the sound of her voice. Sacha came at once to see what she wanted. "Yes, Luba Efremova?" he asked politely.

"Why was I not asked to cook that meat?" she demanded, hands on hips. "Do you think me too old, or too busy?"

Sacha did not know how to answer this, for he had nothing to do with the ordering of the meat.

Lakota listened in interest. He was glad to find that he understood the old woman perfectly, even though she was speaking in Russian.

"I imagine that Simon did not want to bother you," he said in Russian. "I was very hungry and could not wait."

Luba looked startled for just an instant and then looked up at him. To Lakota's gratification she did not appear frightened of him at all.

"I will cook the meat from now on," she stated. "Do you like good Russian food, dragon?"

"Except for this meat I have never had any," Lakota replied. "But I am very eager to try some!"

Luba came closer and sniffed at the remains of his meal. "I can feed you better than that!" she declared. "I shall make you *blini* and goose cooked in cranberries, and *shchi*..."

"What are those please? *Blini* and *shchi*?" Lakota asked, licking his lips.

"*Blini* are little pancakes smothered in butter and spread with caviar," said Sacha "and *shchi* is cabbage soup."

119

Lakota sighed in bliss. And at the dragon's look of joy the old woman smiled a toothless smile at him. He had made another friend.

It was quite late that evening when Simon returned to the house. He had seen Lakota but briefly that day and heard an account of how Luba had offered to cook for him. That would work out well – Simon made a mental note to pay her for her time and effort and supply her with fuel for the fire as well.

He had accompanied Anatoly and the Rostovs to the promised military review. They had gone to the Field of Mars in Admiralty Place in front of the Winter Palace and send thousands of men in immaculate rows, waiting for the Emperor. There was martial music and the flare of drums and trumpets. Sunlight glinted off polished rifles, gold and silver epaulets, buttons and swords. Colourful pennants of each regiment snapped in the fresh sea breeze. Nicholas rode by as the soldiers presented arms and the spectators uncovered their heads.

"Is he not handsome?" sighed Olga, who was standing beside Simon.

The Czar certainly had a an impressive bearing and sat his horse like a centaur. But Simon thought, when he used his Othersight, that he had never seen a colder face, although he sounded genial enough when he cried "Good day, my lads!" to the soldiers.

But Simon did not like the look of smug satisfaction that appeared on the Czar's face when, like thunder "We thank your Majesty!" burst from the soldiers simultaneously. This was a man who could be ruthless and as chill as artic ice.

Just how ruthless the Czar could be Simon was to find out in the very near future.

The evening continued with a visit to Anatoly's favorite Gypsy restaurant. Simon fell in love with the plaintive Gypsy music of violin and cembalon and the wild dancing.

They finished up the evening at an entertainment at a fine home near the Fontanka Canal. Simon never did learn the name of his host. An open invitation hung over the gateway, written in four languages, inviting everyone 'of decent appearance and behavior' to amuse themselves. There had been refreshments, at least three different bands, dancing, bowling, swings to ride (which Russians adored), a puppet show and to end the evening, fireworks.

But as Simon drove home in a hack – Anatoly having returned to his barracks – he thought again of what Tatya had told him that morning in the tea shop. Everything about this land seemed to make more questions than answers. Why had Pozharsky lied to him about his function in the government? And why, when he had been in Russia nearly a week, had nothing further been done about setting up a Dragon Post? And his concerns about the lack of action were dismissed with a brusque "There is plenty of time." He was told to relax and enjoy himself. They seemed to want to entertain him to death. Why all the secrecy about the egg? He was still hustled in covert fashion back and forth to where it was kept. But most of all he was concerned and mystified about Tatya's revelation. What possible connection could the Secret Police have with dragons?

Anatoly Tcherpnin was feeling guilty and he did not like the feeling. He had thought that escorting the English Wizard about St Petersburg would be a sinecure and perhaps pleasant as well. From the very first moment he had liked Simon – and the dragon. He would never forget his ride on Lakota's back. To be up so high – to see the city from the viewpoint of a sea gull! It was amazing and exciting.

His liking for Simon had grown over the past week. Anatoly felt that they were becoming friends. That made what he had been required to do all the more unpleasant.

From the very first time he had met Simon he had been ordered to write a thorough report on the entire meeting, including what was said and even inferred. He then underwent a grilling by his Colonel and then had another meeting with what he guessed were members of the Secret Police. Then his Colonel met with the Police and while he sat there, went over their reports for conflicting testimony and tried to find inconsistencies in them They read *his* report aloud and picked it to pieces with more and more questions. From the way they spoke to him they were dissatisfied with his reports.

121

They seemed to be looking for something but would not tell him what it was.

When this process was over he felt as limp as a cleaning rag and worn to the bone. He also felt resentful. What did they want? He hated this reporting – it seemed more like spying to him. As far as he could judge the Wizard was not hiding anything, nor did he seem to have an ulterior motive. Nor was he spying upon *them*. He asked no questions about the military or defenses – in fact, he denied a desire to see the various fortresses and defenses in St Petersburg. The Secret Police had been surprised that he had not wanted to tour the iron factory. That had turned out to be a 'test'. Anatoly had been ordered to offer a tour and his superiors spent an hour in speculating why the Englishman had *not* wanted to see the factory.

Many of the questions he was asked Anatoly found incomprehensible. What were the Wizard's political views? When Anatoly explained that they had never discussed politics they were angry with him. They gave him a list of topics he was to discuss.

And he had found it nearly impossible to begin discussing the things they wanted with Simon. Anatoly had an open nature – he was a stranger to subterfuge and began to wonder miserably why they had picked him for this assignment. They wanted a professional spy. But somehow Anatoly did not think that the Wizard could be as easily manipulated as they thought.

And the more he was with Simon, the more he liked him. It seemed like a betrayal of their very new friendship to report on him and try to coerce him into whatever revelations the Secret Police wanted him to make. Anatoly felt as if he was working in the dark and was a traitor as well. He did not know what to do. He could either continue to report on Simon and find whatever it was the Secret Police wanted or he would be disgraced and probably cashiered as well. He lay awake almost every night, wondering what to do.

And on Mount *Narodnaya* the great Ice dragon brooded and thought . Finally he made a decision and with a great bellow, rose into the air, spreading his wings and heading north in the general direction of St Petersburg.

12

Cousin Evgeny

It was barely half after nine the next morning when Tatya was informed by Ilenka that Ekaterina awaited her presence in the private sitting room above stairs. This was delivered with a roll of the maid's eyes and a quick crossing of her breast. "God have mercy," she said, "for the master is there with his birch rods as well."

It was usual for serfs to refer to their master as 'little Father' – a mode of address that extended to the Czar. That no one in the Rostov household used this affectionate form was significant.

Tatya was tired and her nerves on edge. Her cousins had been particularly hard to deal with that morning. They both fancied the same young officer of the Hulans, handsome beyond belief in his blue uniform with red returns and gold. Natalya and Olga had a screaming, hair-pulling fight over which one of them he had paid the most attention. Tatya had had to stop their quarrel and in the process her cheek was grazed and her shoulder wrenched. Her first impulse had been to throw cold water over both of them but she would never have heard the end of that tactic.

She could only suppose that Ekaterina had been awakened by the screaming and blamed her niece for not better controlling the girl's exuberance. And now she was to be punished.

It was so unfair. Why was *she* beaten for *their* misbehavior? For a short while yesterday morning with the English Wizard she had been transported back to the way things had been. And now this morning she was jerked back into brutal reality.

There was no escaping it – if she did not go at once to them, they would come looking for her and the beating would be worse because of her defiance.

Slowly, she dragged herself upstairs and went to the door of her aunt and uncle's suite. She tapped on the door and heard her aunt say, in very nasal French, "*Entrez!*"

Tatya had not been in the private parlour recently and she was stunned by the changes. The furniture was all new – heavily carved in satiny woods and upholstered in the finest silks. The room, as was the fashion, overflowed with greenery and pot plants. Ekaterina had never before followed this fashion, for she considered indoor plants not worth the trouble. There were pictures on the wall and fine porcelain every where. Even the rug was now a glorious Oriental. And the stove had been re-tiled. Tatya had been conscious of workmen and delivery men frequenting the house but she had not realized the extent of the change in parts of the house she seldom saw.

And aunt wore yet another new gown, this one of silk and a-drip with imported French lace. Even Yuri wore a new frock coat, trousers and boots. A diamond tie-pin sparkled in his cravat and his satin waistcoat was lush with white embroidery of silk.

Both wore the oddest expressions on their faces that Tatya had ever seen. Normally when she was called before them, their countenances were severe, disproving, even angry. Although several birch switches lay on the table in front of them, uncle was not swishing one back and forth through the air as he usually did – as if too eager to wait to lay it about her shoulders. They looked almost pleased to see her. What did this mean?

Further surprises were in store.

"Ah, Tatiana Ivanova!" said her uncle pleasantly. "Pray have a seat." He came forward and pulled a chair out for her from its place against the wall.

She could only stare at him as she sat down. She was *never* offered a seat! And he had fetched it for her!

Her aunt smiled at her, showing her large, yellow, horse-like teeth. It was the sort of smile Tatya had always imagined crossed the face of the executioner just before he killed his victims.

"We are informed," Ekaterina said, obviously trying to sound congenial, "that you spent time in the company of the Wizard yesterday. Is that so?"

"Yes, "Tatya answered shortly, her stomach clinching and warning signals going off in her brain.

"We are also informed that he seemed to enjoy your company," Yuri said.

"There is no accounting for taste." Ekaterina waved a dismissive hand.

Were they spying on her? Tatya wondered. And then she realized the Secret Police were probably spying on *him*.

"The Czar would be gratified, we are told, if you were to become 'friendly' with this Wizard and perhaps report to us if he does or says anything that might endanger the state," her uncle explained. "You are the first female he has shown an interest in –"

"Friendly?" Tatya repeated, looking from one to the other of them.

"Stupid girl!" Ekaterina's appearance of amiability vanished. "We wish you to become his mistress! Is that clear enough for you? And if you do not obey us in this matter, you shall feel worse than a birch switch about your shoulders!" She picked up one of the twigs and snapped it in half contemptuously. "If you still prove reluctant there is a cell in the Peter and Paul Fortress awaiting you and probably the *knout* as well. Or perhaps you would be more amenable if your brother were whipped with the *knout*?"

Sacha whipped? Oh no! Tatya shuddered. Those who were whipped by the *knout*, if they lived, were crippled for life. Most died beneath its lash.

What could she do but obey? She realized that these orders had to come from the Secret Police, not from her aunt and uncle. And the Secret Police did not like to be disobeyed. The retaliation was swift and terrible.

She could not know that the Rostovs had been given a vast quantity of *rubles* with which to bribe Tatya should she prove hesitant. Ekaterina could not see giving her niece this money when there were so many other things it could be spent on. Tatya could be coerced in many ways – threats of a beating, short rations or putting her brother at risk.

"You may go now," Ekaterina said when it became apparent that Tatya would not protest. "Be certain and take a bath this afternoon. The English don't like girls reeking of sweat. And I shall give you one of my discarded *negligées*, for I doubt you possess any thing alluring!" she gave a titter of laughter.

125

Tatya had risen to her feet. She had to clutch the back of her chair, for her legs wobbled beneath her. She looked in to their faces for some trace of compassion, or caring that they had just ordered their own blood relative, a lady born and bred, to ruin herself.

But she saw nothing there but smug satisfaction. They cared not one iota for her or her sensibilities.

"Go now, girl!" Ekaterina ordered. "You have work to do! Be sure you go to his room tonight and remember everything he says. Men are often confiding with their bed partners."

Tatya managed to stumble from the room, nauseated and dizzy.

She had always imagined that when she gave herself it would be in love. Once she had dreamed of a bridal. When it had become obvious that no one would marry a dowerless drudge with a traitorous father, she had given up those fantasies. And when the years passed and her world grew narrower, she had put away the dreams of love and romance.

She liked the Wizard – but not in that way. She wanted it to be her own decision, not be forced into it. It was almost a kind of rape.

Worse was to come. As she headed down the stirs she heard voices in the hall. Boris acted as butler and he had just let in some visitors.

Tatya recognized those voices. It was her cousin Evgeny and his horrible friend, Viktor Zukhaarinovich Sumarokov. Sumarokov was in the same regiment of Hussars as was Evgeny and at his side in all of their disreputable and evil doings. Like Evgeny, Viktor Sumarokov was cruel, malicious and dissipated. Evgeny by himself was bad enough but he and Viktor seemed to bring out the absolute worst in one another.

There was only one reason why they had come. No doubt Evgeny had gone down heavily at the gaming tables and was insolvent yet again.

For all the time he spent gambling he never seemed to grasp the principals and remained as poor a practitioner as he had when he first took gaming up at he age of sixteen. For he was rash, prone to anger and easily offended. He would take up any dare, no matter how foolish or risky.

126

Tatya fled. She had been going to use the front stairs, but she ran through the hall and down the back stairs as if the devil himself chased her. Could this day get any worse? And the night was yet to come.

Simon had seen very little of Janus since their arrival. He had asked that she be properly fed, and unlike Lakota, she had dined luxuriously.

But she had spent most of her time with Vron.

Simon was getting dressed to go out with Anatoly again. They were to ride to Czarskoe Selo, some seventeen miles outside the city, where it had been arranged for a tour of the Catherine Palace, the Pavlosk Palace, and the extensive Imperial Gardens, as well as any other sights they had time for. And tonight there would be a Court Ball. Simon had been promised the felicity of an introduction to the Czar and Czarina, since he was a distinguished foreign guest. It was an honour he could have readily bypassed.

As he sat on the edge of his bed pulling on his riding boots, Janus pushed open the slightly ajar door and jumped up on the bed beside him.

She briefly rubbed her head along his arm and said, "I've learned some very interesting things from Vron which you ought to know."

"Oh?" he inquired with interest.

And she proceeded to tell him all she had learned from the black Tom.

Even down in the kitchen they had heard Yuri and Evgeny arguing. Yuri and Ekaterina did not wish to share their new found largesse with their son. Evgeny had a more than handsome allowance in addition to his pay. Many young officers had to exist on far less. Evgeny, they felt, should learn to hold household.

But Evgeny, eyeing the new furnishings and finery, felt that his parents had not come by this excess honestly. He threatened to find out where it was coming from and expose them.

At this threat Yuri was more than a little uneasy. The money had been given to him to entertain the Wizard. So far none of it had gone to that end – it had been spent on

127

furnishings and finery. The one time he had protested to Ekaterina, feeling slightly guilty, she waved his guilt away, saying that surely the Czar did not wish them to appear shabby and old fashioned in front of their guest! Ad were they not hosting a ball in a fortnight in his honour?

Therefore, over Ekaterina's protests, Yuri unlocked his desk and threw a gratifyingly heavy bag of *rubles* at Evgeny. "First that girl and now this!" he grumbled.

"What girl?" asked Evgeny idly, listening to the satisfying clink of gold in the pouch.

"Your cousin," said Yuri, and briefly explained what they had told Tatya to do.

Evgeny and Viktor exchanged looks. This was very interesting.

Evgeny had long marked Tatya as his. The fact that she seemed repulsed by his advances just sweetened the pot, for Evgeny's pleasure was much heightened by terror and pain. He much preferred rape to mutual sharing. It gave him a marvelous feeling of power.

Viktor was just like him. Their exploits with women did not bear repeating, so vile and degraded as they were.

Evgeny was tall, and looked like neither of his parents. Yuri always supposed him to be a throwback to some remote ancestor. He had refined, almost girlish features with wispy blond hair and heavy lidded blue eyes. His poetic looks were spoiled by a thin, cruel mouth and hard eyes. Women found him very attractive for some odd reason.

Like his friend, Viktor was tall and lanky with it. He had brown hair and eyes, and looked so much like a weasel that that was his regimental nickname. His close-set eyes wore a look of cunning and viciousness. Of the two, he was the cleverer, but was quite as depraved as his friend.

Shortly thereafter, they took their leave of Evgeny's parents and started downstairs, swords and spurs jingling.

"I think," said Evgeny with a nasty laugh, "that we should do this Wizard a favor! We should tame the brown filly for him – make certain that she is properly saddle-broke!"

Viktor smiled. It was not a pleasant smile. "A green-broke filly is useless. And I feel like a bit of riding!"

128

Evgeny had hesitated before in taking Tatya – he had been afraid that his parents might cut off his funds if he ruined his cousin. After all, she *was* family. He had contented himself with fondling and grabbing her and forcing kisses upon her. He had enjoyed her fear. But now that they had ordered her to make of herself a whore – he felt himself totally justified in possessing her – and sharing her with Viktor.

Tatya was in the linen room, folding sheets and tablecloths. There was a basket full of her cousin's petticoats to be ironed, and she was heating the flatirons on the stove. The sheets smelled of sun and lavender. Masha had ironed then earlier but had been called into the kitchen by Luba. Tatya felt as if she must keep busy. Therefore she took care of the linens while the irons heated.

Her mind went around and around in circles. Whatever was she to do? How could she go to him and offer herself like a common drab? if she did not either she or Sacha might suffer the *knout*. She feared for herself as much as for Sacha. She had seen a beggar, horribly crippled, once. She had been told had suffered the *knout*. The memory of his terrible injuries had haunted her ever since.

"Well, cousin," came a smooth, mocking voice, "my dear father tells me that you are about to embark on a new career. I always thought you were a whore at heart."

She whirled, dropping a pile of linen on the floor. Evgeny, closely followed by Viktor, was engaged in locking the door. He tossed the key to his disreputable friend, who inserted it in his pocket.

"Good," remarked Viktor, eyeing the pile of linen. "That will serve us well. I never liked fucking on the floor."

Tatya gasped in fright. "You wouldn't dare! My aunt and uncle.."

"Have given me *carte blanche*," Evgeny interrupted. "You should be grateful to me, cousin. Viktor and I have very generously decided to give you a little experience before your assignation with the English Wizard! A man of the world don't care for frightened virgins. When we are done with you, you will be an experienced harlot – much more appealing to a man of jaded tastes!"

"Something about her does not seem right –' said Viktor, studying Tatya so closely that she wanted to scream, but could not. She was like a rabbit, mesmerized by a snake. She could only stare at them, a hand to her throat and heart beating wildly.

"I know what it is!" Viktor said in triumph. "Where is her Russian plait? She's not a proper maiden with her hair bound up around her head! A proper maiden wears her plait down her back!" With this he pulled out his sword and skillfully lifted the pins from her hair. Her two braids tumbled down, almost to her knees. Obscenely, he began to sing an old wedding song, *"The young man with the black curls sits at the table and asks, 'Fair Russian plait, is it really true that you are mine at last?'"*

She could not move. She should fight them, kick and bite. But all she could do was stand there, pleading silently, "Please God, please God!" Her throat was so tight she could not scream as she wanted to.

Not to be outdone by Victor, Evgeny took out his sword as well and with as much skill as his friend, began to cut her gown off her. Again she could not move or scream, her eyes huge and terrified.

"I do believe she's not going to give us any trouble at all," said Evgeny. "A pity. I like it when they scream and fight. It makes the conquest all the sweeter."

"Are we going to get laid or stand here all day discussing it?" Viktor demanded. "Who goes first, you or me?" He was stripping off his tunic as he spoke. Rules required him to be immaculately groomed in public and he feared getting his tunic wrinkled.

"Don't bother with that!" Evgeny grinned as the last of Tatya's clothing fell to the floor. "We can always have her iron it for you – while she's naked and panting for more. I'm feeling generous – you can have her first."

"She's got bigger tits than I thought she'd have," Viktor fumbled at his breeches and advanced on Tatya, shoved her into the pile of linen. "Part those legs!" he ordered, throwing himself on top of her. With brutal hands he pulled her legs apart.

"Please, please," she whimpered. He was so strong!

130

"She's got a nicer body than I could ever see under that drab gown," said Evgeny. "Why don't you show it off, little girl?"

"Who cares about that?" Viktor said carelessly, "Fat or skinny she's just a cunt." He raised himself above the terrified girl and adjusting his breeches with one hand, prepared to take her.

But instead of slamming into Tatya he was flung violently backwards and spread-eagled against he wall. The sword he had discarded on the floor shot upwards and rammed into the ceiling Evgeny's sword joined it and he too was slammed against the wall.

In the doorway stood Simon, white-faced and shaking with anger. From behind him ran Luba, who darted forward with a blanket and covered Tatya with it.

"What have you done?" Evgeny shrieked in rage. "You have no right to interfere, whoever you are!" He hung on the wall with nothing visible holding him there and as much as he struggled, he could not move. Beside him Viktor shrieked impotent curses.

"I have the right of every gentleman to interfere with the rape of an innocent girl!" said Simon grimly. "It is my duty and my privilege to protect this young lady. And if it means killing you two pieces of filth I shall do so."

"I shall cut out your heart on the field of honour!" cried Evgeny.

"Honour?" queried Simon hotly. "How dare you speak of honour after what you tried to do here? And I would not lower myself to meet you! No, I speak of death by magic – which is what holds you against the wall. You shall remain there until I decide to let you go."

"You would not dare kill us! Questions would be asked!" shouted Viktor.

Simon smiled. "Oh, no, there would be no questions asked at all!' he said slowly. "I could arrange it so that no one would remember you existed. It would be as if you had never had been born."

Tatya, wrapped in the blanket and patted in a comforting fashion by Luba (who was muttering invectives against the pair of Hussars) had never seen any one get angry in the way the Wizard did. The people she was accustomed to

131

became red-faced and choleric. They bellowed and shouted. He was white to the lips, and his voice, while not raised in the least, sent a chill down her spine. His eyes were hard with rage as he looked at Evgeny and Viktor.

"Take her some place safe," Simon said over his shoulder to Luba.

Coaxingly, with many love names, Luba got Tatya to her feet. Tatya had to lean heavily on the old woman, for she could not seem to control her legs. Her terror and shame was overwhelming. She could feel an avalanche of tears coming.

As Luba led her down the hall towards the kitchen, Tatya heard Simon say, "I shall leave you there for a while to contemplate your sins. In the meanwhile I shall pen a note to your Colonel. I am certain that he will be shocked to find out your manner of treating a lady."

"She's not a lady – she's a servant!" shrieked Viktor.

"Be quiet!" Simon commanded and suddenly Viktor sounded as if he had been gagged.

Simon turned to go and then thought of something and turned back. "By the bye," he said "I really should tell you that when you finally do come off that wall you both will be completely impotent."

With this he turned and left. As the door close behind him, the crumpled linens rose in the air, shook themselves out and refolded themselves. The irons took themselves from the stove as well.

"Magic!" whispered Evgeny. This simple, homely conjuration frightened him more than a huge thunderclap or explosion might have.

All the same, he wanted revenge. He had been humiliated and cheated out of his cousin's charms. And now he would have to face the censure of his Colonel as well. He would. He vowed have his vengeance against the Wizard. And he would have Tatya as well. And he would hurt her badly. When he finished with her no one would want her ever again.

In the bath house the elderly *bannik* lay steaming himself. The bath house was high, roomy and full of light. To the *bannik's* mind, however, it was in the wrong place. It should have stood on the banks of the Neva, where after a steam as hot as one could stand it (or even hotter than one *could* stand it) one ran out of doors, naked as the day one was born, and plunged into the cold water. And then one had a refreshing scour of the body with birch twigs. Failing the river, one rolled in the snow before scouring.

But in these decadent times one had to make do with a pail of cold water. And it was not very cold most of the time.

The *bannik* was a little, wizened, man-like creature of an all pervading grayness. He wore little besides a pair of baggy trousers, for he spent all of his time steaming in the bath house. When people used the bath house he disappeared. He found it very dull here, for none but Yuri used the bath house. Of course, the master would not share his bath house with serfs – they had to go to the public baths. Ekaterina, in her mania for all things Western, used a tin tub in front of the stove and insisted that the girls do so too.

Yuri was not worth talking to. In many bath houses the resident *bannik* was quite friendly with the members of the family.

But it had become more interesting around here lately. There was a dragon on the yard and a magician in the house. The *bannik*, whose name was Yaroslav, hoped the Wizard would come to the bath house. Long, long ago Yaroslav had known magical people and found them fascinating.

But the Wizard took his bath in a tub, too, or so the *domovoi* had informed him.

Something else had happened today. An inquiry had come, passed along by the house and yard spirits and other *banniks*. A dragon was looking for a lost egg.

It so happened that Yaroslav had over heard two strangers talking about the egg, just outside the bath house. They had mentioned its location. Yaroslav had gladly passed this information along, with his name and direction. The dragon had offered a reward and Yaroslav wanted it. He only hoped that Misha, the yard spirit whom he had entrusted to bear the message, would not take the credit for the information. That was *his* reward!

133

13

Events of an Evening

Simon had been reluctant to go on his outing with Anatoly after what had happened, but Luba insisted he leave. It was better that he not be there when Evgeny and Viktor were finally released by the wall and there was nothing he could do for Tatya. She, Luba, would care for Tatya and guard her from the two Hussars. It would be best for Tatya if she slept away her fear and shame.

Accordingly, Simon gave Luba two herbal blends from Stuart's medical kit – one of soothing, sleep-inducing tea and the other to sprinkle in the bath as a calmative and healer.

In spite of her distrust of any bath besides a Russian steam bath Luba borrowed Ekaterina's tin tub and filled it full of hot water, making liberal use of the herbs the Wizard had given her.

This operation was conducted in Luba's own room, off the kitchen. Tatya had been bundled into Luba's bed, which was a platform (for the cook's bedchamber had once been a store room) made comfortable by the addition of a mattress well stuffed with goose feathers. Luba, no fool, had saved the down of every bird she had ever plucked for the table and had made herself a nice set of mattress and pillows.

With Masha and Ilenka's help Luba readied the water, muttering curses against Evgeny and his friend the entire time. The three women could still hear the Hussars swearing and kicking the wall as they worked.

"Thank the good Lord that the Master and Mistress are still gone out and they cannot hear that noise!" said Ilenka, crossing herself. She looked a great deal like Masha, blonde and well-rounded, but she was shorter and had a shyer, more fearful nature.

"I wish that they could hang up there forever!" declared Masha. She had suffered Evgeny's roving hands and pinching also. "No one deserves it more – Evgeny Yurovich tried his little tricks on me once!" she said, testing the water with a finger.

"What did you do?" Ilenka gasped.

"Kicked him in the balls!" Masha said in satisfaction. "He screamed like a girl!" She lifted her skirts to show red copper-toed boots.

"Heh! Heh!" Luba chortled. She cordially disliked Ekaterina, Yuri and their daughters, but she hated Evgeny. He was evil through and through, as today's events showed all too clearly. To try to rape his own cousin! Luba, of course, did not know what Ekaterina and Yuri had decreed for Tatya.

Tatya, clad in one of Luba's voluminous night gowns. was shivering beneath a pile of quilts on Luba's bed. She cried silently, but great sobs filled every inch of her. She had curled into a little ball and put her hands over her face but nothing seemed to block out the memories of those last few minutes – of the looks on their faces, of the her clothing falling to the ground to expose her to their crude comments, of the pain of being knocked to the floor and her legs pulled apart, of the terror and horror of being almost violated – and of her shame that she had done absolutely nothing to prevent her own rape. She had allowed them to strip her and would have allowed them to take her as well, with nothing but a whimpered plea.

If it had not been for the Wizard... *how* had he known that she was in dire peril? His arrival had been so timely – how had he managed it? Was it magic?

This was a question that was shortly to be answered, for with a short "*mrrpp?*", Vron joined her on Luba's bed and put his furry face up to hers, rubbing lovingly as if he really knew that she needed his solace.

"Oh, Vron!" she sobbed and gathered him into her arms, pressing him against her face and crying into his fur. He had no objections to this treatment, allowing her to cry and use him as a handkerchief, his rumbling purr soothing and loving her.

"You knew I needed you," she wept, holding the warm little body closer.

"Of course he knew," came an unfamiliar voice. "He was the one that came and told us what was happening! You owe Vron your delivery!"

Startled, Tatya looked up to see not the strange woman she expected, but a black and orange cat regarding her from large green eyes. The cat sat at the foot of the bed.

135

"Vron told me and I told Simon," the cat continued. "It was as easy as that. Thank goodness we were in time! We were even able to warn Luba so that she could come with us."

"Y- y- you can talk!" Tatya stammered through her tears.

"How else could I tell Simon?" replied the cat. "Even Wizards can't speak Cat! And as for being able to talk – I am Simon's familiar and all familiars can speak the languages of man. How else would we be of use to our Wizards and Witches?"

Tatya had no idea what a familiar might be. The more she heard about Wizards and magic the less she understood. In some strange fashion, in her present emotional state she was more able to accept the fantastic. Talking cats and men hung on a wall all seemed part of the horrible day she had been having.

Tears still trickling down her face, Tatya said to the cat, "I am very grateful to all of you, and to the Wizard too – if he hadn't come –"

"He only wishes he had known earlier, to prevent ANYTHING happening to you!" said Janus fiercely. "We are both appalled that something like this could happen in a supposedly respectable household! They will be lucky when they come down off that wall, if I don't ask Lakota to incinerate them on the spot! Lakota sends his sympathies, by the bye, as well. We are all shocked and will do anything we can to help. And Vron wants you to know that he loves you and will try better to protect you from now on."

All the sympathy rather overwhelmed Tatya. She could not seem to stop crying and held Vron even tighter against her, saying in Russian that she loved him, too, and thanked him. He purred all the harder and rubbed his face against her cheek.

"You cry it out, my dear," said Janus kindly. "No one needs it more than you do."

Luba came up to the bed. "The bath is ready!" she announced. "Tatya Ivanova, what do you think of this, heh? A talking cat! A talking dragon! And a Wizard! And they're all good! Not like the tales!"

She pulled back the covers and said, "You let old Luba help you into the bath, little cne, and here's your friends to help as well."

The love and concern on the faces of the three serfs made Tatya cry harder and she allowed them to undress her and help her into the tin tub. Ilenka brought her a glass of the herbal tea Simon had provided and saw that she drank every drop.

All over Tatya's body were tiny nicks from the tip of Evgeny's sword. Her shoulder was still sore from the contretemps with her cousins that morning (how long ago that seemed!) and there were huge bruises forming on each thigh from Viktor Sumarakov's brutal hands.

The three serf women seemed to understand that Tatya felt dirtied and besmirched, as if she would never be clean again and would not allow her to do a thing, but scrubbed and cleaned her – even washing her hair. The magiced herbs in the bath did their work and Tatya visibly relaxed, her sobs gradually ceasing, until she lay back, almost asleep, allowing Luba and her helpers to cleanse her. To their amazement the little cuts and the bruises healed as they watched. "Magic!" said Luba in no little satisfaction.

By the time they lifted her from the tub Tatya was sleeping and never felt the towels that patted her dry or the comb Luba drew through her hair. They put her back in Luba's bed.

"Let her sleep," said the old cook. "Sleep is God's gift. If Ekaterina Feodorova asks for her – you send the mistress to me! *I* will deal with her!"

The two cats lay near the sleeping girl to both warm and guard her. Perhaps due to the herbs, or perhaps due to the purring, Tatya slept deeply, untroubled by nightmares.

It was a somewhat distracted Simon that rode out with Anatoly that morning. Simon scarcely notice the well-bred but somewhat restive horse that Anatoly provided, automatically checking the animal's sidling and head tossing.

This did him no disservice in Anatoly's eyes. The Lieutenant was impressed by his new friend's easy horse mastership. Anatoly had borrowed a mount from one of his fellow officers – like his own horse it was a bright chestnut, as all of the officers of the Chevalier Guards were required to ride chestnut horses – and was far from placid. Anatoly was torn between being insulting and asking the Englishman if he were able to control a fractious horse or hoping that what he had read was true and the English were all horse-mad and great riders. Having been thrown on a horse before he could properly walk, Anatoly had great admiration for someone who could manage such an unruly animal, and able to do it when his mind was obviously elsewhere! Anatoly just hoped that his new friend's mind was not occupied by his wondering why Anatoly had been increasingly quiet and withdrawn. It was becoming more and more difficult to behave in the manner proscribed for him by the Secret Police. He hated spying and deceit and he had been able to think of no believable way to introduce the topics of conversation the Secret Police wanted him to discuss. He was torn between his duty to his country and his liking for a new friend.

Simon spoke at last, asking to Anatoly's relief, if the Lieutenant knew Evgeny Rostov.

"Yes, and I wish I didn't!" said Anatoly. "He's a byword in the regiments – a gambler and a womanizer. My Colonel holds him, and the set he runs with, as bad examples!"

"He attempted to rape a young woman in the Rostov household this morning," said Simon, frowning.

"What!" Anatoly was aghast. At home, one of his neighbors routinely offered his male guests a 'bed warmer' but Anatoly's family had condemned such behaviors. Servants, even if they were serfs, were the responsibility of their masters and were not to be used.

"Rostov and one of his cronies –" began Simon

"Probably Sumarokov," Anatoly interrupted, "They're always together – two rotten apples, my Colonel says. Did you stop them?" he asked eagerly. "With magic?"

Simon told him what he had done and Anatoly gave a great shout of laughter, startling his horse who snorted and tossed his head.

"I want to report his conduct," said Simon, when Anatoly had finished laughing. "I threatened to write a note to his Colonel. Is that the way I go about it?"

138

"Better yet – I'll tell my Colonel and he'll see to it," Anatoly suggested. "He won't mind taking Rostov down a peg!"

With this settled Anatoly suggested they work the fidgets out of the horses by letting them have their heads.

As they galloped Simon's mind was still on what might be happening back at the house. Janus would give him a full report, but he wished that he had been able to be of more service to her. He would never forget that brief look he had had of her face beneath that panting lout. Such terror and, mingled with it, hopelessness. Simon's hands tightened on the reins. While he was here, no one would harm her or terrify her again. And before he left for home, he would put magical protections around her that would insure her safety forever.

Simon enjoyed his tour of the enormous Catherine Palace. It was full of treasures and was an architectural gem in its own right, complete with gold cupolas, and gilded statues on gilded balustrades. One beautiful room stretched into another with exquisitely carved doors of linden wood specially treated with heliotrope oil. The Amber room was full of caskets, boxes and chessmen were all of amber as were the honey coloured walls. The mirrored Great Hall was said to be finer than the *Galerie des Glaces* at Versailles. The gallery was two stories high and 180 feet long and blue and white tiled stoves, reaching almost to the ceiling, were at each end. The spaces between the thirteen sets of double windows were filled with mirrors, each mirror surrounded by gilded frames.

They toured the gardens as well, designed with a series of pavilions, and planted in the Dutch fashion with fish canals, bowers and masses of bulbs. Simon paid careful attention, for his mother, a great gardener, would want to hear every detail...

It was after noontime before they had seen everything and they had a late luncheon at a little restaurant much frequented by the officers of Anatoly's regiment. There they met up with some of Anatoly's friends and the afternoon passed agreeably in conversation with them.

Although it had been a pleasant day, Simon's thoughts could not help but stray to Tatya and how she might be feeling. He gave little thought to Evgeny and Viktor. The spell would keep them up on the wall for two hours and then drop them abruptly and, he hoped, painfully, to the floor.

There was to be a Court Ball that evening. When Simon and Anatoly at last separated, it was to go and prepare for that event. But Anatoly would first be required to write his report. The questionings could be put off until tomorrow, for the appearance at the Court Ball was by order of the Czar. But the report must be written.

It was quite late before Tatya woke. Even for these long summer evenings, now rapidly advancing to the endless white nights of midsummer, it was dark. There was one little window, high up in Luba's room, that let in light and air.

For just one moment she was confused, but her stirrings woke Vron, who was still with her and the bright eyes gleaming at her made everything come rushing back.

To her amazement she felt quite extraordinarily well. She was rested and relaxed and had not suffered any nightmares. The bed clothes were untangled and she felt clean and comfortable. She felt almost distanced from the attempted rape, as if it had happened a while before, not this day, and she had been able to cope with it successfully. Was this more magic? If so it was wonderful! She would have expected to be fearful and ashamed when she awoke.

She stretched and yawned, feeling as if she was ready to get up out of bed. And wonder of wonders – she was actually hungry!

She heard one of the cats jump off the bed and a few minutes later Luba appeared,

"You're awake at last!" Luba greeted her. "You've been dreaming for hours."

"What time is it?" Tatya wondered,

"Gone midnight," Luba answered. She held a bundle in her arms and she put this down on the bed. "Here – we've put together a dress for you – it's only a *sarafan* and a blouse, but there was no saving that brown thing you were wearing – it's only good for rags now."

There was a short chemise to wear beneath the bright blue *sarafan*. Tatya let Luba help her dress and braid her long hair. She wanted to ask what had happened to Evgeny

140

and his horrible friend, but something stayed her tongue. Instead she asked, "Has my aunt wanted me?"

"She's been home but an hour this afternoon and was out of here again like a dog with fleas in its tail. There's a Court Ball tonight and even the Wizard is going. I like that Wizard," she added, "he thinks like a Russian." She grinned at Tatya. "It took two hours for those two to come down off the wall and they fell with a bump that shook the house! They slunk out of here like the curs they are!" She gave the *sarafan* a twitch as she pulled it down over Tatya's head. "There! You look a proper Russian maiden – and thanks be to God, you are STILL a maiden! You can some day go to your husband as you should."

"Now, I've food and tea for you. You're to sleep here with me tonight. Masha did the ironing for you and we all cleaned up the linen room – there's no sign of what happened. You can rest easy on that score. We burned your dress so you won't have to look at it."

Tatya turned and hugged the old woman. "Thank you," she said huskily. "I don't know why you're all so good to me,"

"Oh, hush, child! We women have to stick together!" said Luba. "I nearly forgot – there's a package come for you – all wrapped up in silver paper." She reached in her pocket and withdrew a tightly wrapped bundle. "It's not from Evgeny Yurovich, I'm certain! It was delivered by a servant who gave himself such airs!"

It a sprawling hand on the package was written Tatya's name above the direction. Curiously, Tatya opened it and realized at once what it was. It was a *negligee*, as had been promised by her aunt.

"Well, what it is?" asked Luba.

Wordlessly, Tatya shook it out and held it up.

This garment could have never belonged to her aunt. It was black and of the sheerest chiffon fabric imaginable. Two tiny triangles of almost transparent fabric would barely cover the nipples of the breasts, and the rest of the bodice plunged to below the waist from the high waistline and dipped down as far in the back. Strangely, the sleeves were long and full, ending in long cuffs that buttoned tightly

141

almost to the elbow. A card from a *modiste* that catered to courtesans fell to the floor as Tatya held up the garment.

It was a gown for seduction. It was meant for her tryst with the Wizard.

Suddenly, Tatya no longer felt relaxed and refreshed. She felt sick again. Had she escaped with her virginity intact from one man only to lose it to another?

"I can see right through it!" Luba said, picking up a fold and staring at it in amazement. "What kind of a dress is this? Why anyone looking at you could see your chemise!"

"You don't wear a chemise with it," said Tatya emotionlessly. "You're meant to be naked under it."

"That's indecent!" said Luba. "Who would send you such a thing? That Evgeny? I can't imagine him waiting for a woman to put something like this on her back! That one would just as soon tear it off!"

"My aunt sent it," Tatya said. "I am to wear it tonight."

"With nothing beneath it?" Luba said, horrified.

The fact that her aunt had actually gone out and spent money on this erotic night-wear proved to Tatya as very little else could have that Ekaterina was determined that her niece become the Wizard's mistress. She would have to appear before him in this sheer garment (she might as well walk to his door naked) and allow him to take her to bed and complete what Evgeny had started that afternoon. If she did not, both she and Sacha would suffer.

She had no choice at all. And so she told Luba when she informed the old woman of what her aunt expected her to do.

Luba looked at her sadly. Luba was a realist. "I like the Wizard," she said again. "Better him than that Evgeny Yurovich. I think he will treat you with kindness."

Janus had gone up to Simon's rooms to wait for him. Only Vron was present to see and hear what was happening. His understanding of human language was imperfect – what he understood was that Tatya was in a far different mood than when she had first awakened. She had returned to the resignation with which she faced most every day.

"Leave that here." Luba took the negligee from Tatya. "You need food. It will be some time before the Wizard returns

142

from the ball. I have a preparation I will show you how to use – so that you do not become with child from this might's work. May all the curses of Hell fall upon Ekaterina Feodorova!"

14

Snatched!

To please Luba Tatya managed to choke down several mouthfuls of the nice little supper the old woman had prepared for her. But her appetite had fled. Knowing that sometime in the early hours of the morning she would have to go up to the Wizard's room in that shocking *negligee* and lay with him put a lump in her throat that food could barely pass.

It would have been bad enough had she been given one of Ekaterina's discarded *negligées* – they were of satin and silk and lace but at least were not *indecent*. This black gown was a whore's garment. It seemed to underscore what she would be after this night's work – a whore herself. A mistress, who would be discarded after the Wizard's visit. What them would happen to her? Would she be given to Evgeny? Would uncle expect her to sleep with him or would she become an accommodation for male guests? The future appalled her. She had thought her life could not become any worse than it already was. How wrong she had been!

It was after two before they heard the household returning. She had sat in the kitchen with Luba, nursing a cup of tea. She was grateful for the old woman's presence.

It was Luba who helped her from her sarafan, blouse and chemise, and Luba who slid the transparent garment over her head as she stood, naked, shivering in the cool of the early morning. There were tiny ribbons, they found, in the gown to tie and keep the gown in the proper position. The bodice was practically nonexistent and the gown *was* completely sheer.

"It's worse than being naked," was Luba's judgment. "There's something wrong about it – something bad."

Tatya, past even trying to retain her modesty, could only helplessly agree.

At this moment the door was thrust open and Ekaterina, still clad in her ball finery, stood there. She held a little basket full of jars and brushes.

She almost smiled when she saw Tatya. "Here you are! And look at you! It is as good as I thought it would be when I bought it! You have a better figure than I thought – he won't be able to resist you! But why are you hiding down here? I've brought cosmetics – you still look too virginal. You –" she turned to Luba "get a stool. By the time we finish with her he'll be crawling into bed. He'll be pleased to think he needn't sleep alone. He'll probably take you again and again, girl – as far as we know he hasn't had a woman since he has been here." In Ekaterina's experience, no man, meaning her father, brother Maxim, her husband and her son could go more than a day without bedding a female. And the Wizard had been here a week – and who knew how long it had been for him before his arrival? "If you're very sore tomorrow I'll let you stay in bed until eight," she added generously, pushing Tatya down onto the stool Luba brought.

Oblivious to the old woman's mutterings Ekaterina proceeded to make Tatya up, using kohl to outline her eyes and lashes, rouge on her cheeks and lips and powdered silver to brush her eyelids. "They say the French Empress painted her lids silver," she said chattily, as she unbraided Tatya's hair and brushed it hard, until tears of pain came to Tatya's eyes.

She also told Tatya, in some detail, what she could expect from her soon-to-be bed partner. Tatya was not ignorant of the facts of life – she had grown up in the country and seen the farm animals mating – but the way Ekaterina described it made her feel ill – was there no love or tenderness? With one part of her mind she felt sorry for her aunt if that was what she had had to endure from uncle Yuri.

Ekaterina gave a tug on the bodice ribbons, which threatened to spill Tatya's breasts from what little constituted the bodice. Ekaterina even dipped a finger into the rouge pot and rubbed some on each nipple. "Now remember," she said briskly "remember all that he says! And try to act as if you had done this before – men don't like shy virgins, contrary to what the novels say. There!" she leaned back in satisfaction and surveyed the results.

"You've made her look like a whore," said Luba bluntly.

145

"What do you know, old woman?" Ekaterina said scornfully. "She looks like a woman of the world. You must stay all night with him," she directed, turning back to Tatya, "The more times you can encourage him to mount you the chattier he may get. Your uncle be watching. Off you go."

Tatya, feeling like an automaton, stood. Her face felt strange and stiff with the paint aunt had employed. Aunt had also drenched her in chypre, a scant Tatya found cloying and heavy. Was this what it felt like to go to the gallows – this feeling of desperation tinged with resignation? This night would change her life forever. With heavy steps she turned towards the back stairs and began to climb.

Simon had been ready to leave the ball since before midnight.

It was very late in the season for a Court Ball, but there were a number of distinguished foreigners the Czar chose to honour. It was held, as always, in the Nicholas Hall of the imposing Winter Palace. Until nine the guests mingled in the hall, conversing and visiting. At nine precisely the Grand Master of Ceremonies appeared and tapped his cane (embossed with a gold double eagle) three times, loudly, on the shining floor. A sudden hush fell over the crowd.

"Their Imperial Majesties!" he announced. Almost as one, hundreds of people swept into bows or curtseys, gowns rustling and heels clicking. Huge doors opened and there entered the Master and Mistress of the Imperial Households, followed by the Czar and Czarina, great officials of their households, the Czarevich, and the Grand Dukes and Grand Duchesses. The national anthem was played.

The guests then formed themselves into two lines, which left an aisle down the middle. This was the beginning of the grand Polonaise – not a dance but more of a pro-cessional or a march. The orchestra played a majestic air and the Czar led off, giving his hand to a stately Princess. As he preceded down the line, one by one gentlemen detached themselves from the line and in turn offered their hand to a lady. They made a tour of the room and then returned, forming lines again.

Waltzes, quadrilles and mazurkas followed the polonaise. Simon was very glad that his family loved to dance and that he had been well taught, for these Russians had a passion for the dance and did it well.

How Noelle would have loved the gowns – ladies in tarlatan, silk, satin and velvet, taffeta and tulle, in every colour and ablaze with jewels – not just on ears, throats and wrists, but on the ribbons of the gowns and the ruffles of the skirts. Ropes of pearls twisted through hair and diamonds blazed on hair ornaments and hair ribbons.

About eleven the Emperor led the way into another room where tables had been laid for supper. Simon was seated with Count Pozharsky and several Princes and Princesses. The Rostovs had been invited, but they sat in an inconsequential place.

Nor were the Rostovs permitted to be presented to the Czar as Simon was. This happened after supper, when the dancing had begun again. The Czar was very gracious, even inviting (it was more of a command) Simon to bring Lakota to the Square before the Winter Place on the next morning. The Czarevich wished to see a real live dragon.

The Czar spoke as any indulgent father might, but Simon could sense no real warmth in the man. If Nicholas had any of the milk of human kindness in his veins it had long since become frozen into the American confection of ice cream. His eyes were cold and hard and speculative. Simon had the feeling of being measured. He was glad when the Czar turned his attention to others who wished to claim it.

After that, he began to long to leave. The heat was oppressive and there must have been at least one thousand people present. Too crowded for Simon's taste – he much preferred a family party to this stiff formality. But he allowed himself to be presented to various young ladies, all of whom he dutifully danced with. He spent some time with Anatoly and a party of young officers, and saw the Rostov girls giggling their way through a waltz. Again, knowing what was expected of him, he danced with Ekaterina – who talked of nothing but the 'triumph' of her girls dancing with all the young men of all the best – meaning richest – families. Simon danced one dance each – making certain that it was a quadrille and not the more intimate waltz – with Natalya and Olga.

It was an entertainment that had only been interesting for a short while and by the time the Czar and Czarina retired at well after two AM he was more than ready to call it an evening.

He was not to meet Anatoly until the next afternoon for some pleasure boating on a canal with a group of young ladies and officers. Count Pozharsky had again brushed aside his request to know when they would be beginning on the project that had brought him to Russia – the dragon Post. Whatever were they waiting for?

In the meantime, he would get some much needed sleep. The social life here was wearing and if this kept up he would have to order additional evening dress from a Russian tailor as well as several new pair of dancing pumps. Count Pozharsky seemed to feel that Simon should be in alt from this continuous round of entertainment, but in truth, Simon would have much rather spent more evenings with a good book, or with a small party of friends.

It was with relief that Simon finally went to his room, leaving his host and hostess and their hyena-like daughters below stairs. The Rostovs were still excited over the fact that they had been to a Court Ball, which Simon gathered, was a treat that did not often come their way, and the girls had chattered incessantly and brainlessly all the way back from the Winter Palace.

Once in his room he stripped off his evening coat, loosened his cravat and kicked off his shoes. Janus was asleep on his pillow. Simon was eager to learn what had happened to Tatya in his absence, but he decided against wakening the cat – familiars slept more like humans and Janus awoke grumpy. He would have to move her when he got into bed and that would be time enough to hear her report.

He sat down at thee desk and pulled out his journal. He opened it to a fresh page, picked up a pen and, dipping it into the inkwell, began to write.

Simon had been very faithful in keeping this journal. It was already thick with his impressions and accounts of his stay. But if anyone searched his room (and he was certain that someone did so on a regular basis) they would find a blank book and conclude that the English Wizard had neglected his travel diary shamefully. Only Simon, with the right magic, could access the journal.

He liked to write it up at the end of each day when impressions were still fresh in his mind. He could then consult in the next day or so when he wrote lengthy letters home. His letters home took less than a week to arrive because he was allowed to send them home in the Diplomatic pouches that went out every day from the British Embassy. These went by ship to Finland where there had recently been instituted a new diplomatic mail service to the British Isles – hippogriffes through the Scandinavian peninsula and then flying horses over the North Sea. They could carry very little – not even a third of what a dragon could and no packages were allowed, only letters – so the diplomatic pouches were never heavy, thus adding to the speed of the courier service.

Simon recorded that he had asked Anatoly if it was possible to go out into the countryside. If nothing could be done about the Dragon Post, perhaps, Simon thought, he could at least try and fulfill Oberon's commission and find the Russian Elves. It would also be an excellent way for Lakota to stretch his wings – the blue dragon was becoming tired of endless circling over St Petersburg.

At first Simon did not hear the timid scratching at the door. It was only when Janus awoke suddenly with an inquiring "meow?" and yawned loudly that Simon heard the noise.

His first reaction was irritation. Couldn't these people leave him alone? If it was one of the Rostovs, still eager to go over the endless details of the ball– a topic of which Simon had grown very tired – Simon could not answer for his temper.

It was in no good humor that he rose from the desk and went to the door, and threw it open. "What is it now –?" he began, only to stop with a gasp as he saw who was at the door and even more shocking, what she wore – or rather what she *wasn't* wearing.

Being a gentleman, Simon immediately turned around, so that he couldn't see her. "*Mam'selle* Tatya! What are you doing here at this hour of the night and rigged out like a bit of muslin?"

149

That this was a polite term for whore Tatya had little trouble discerning. Nor was she certain how to proceed. Ekaterina had given her the impression that all she had to do was go to him and he would yank her in to the room and take her to bed. Nothing had been said about him keeping her standing in the door and turning his back on her as if he were embarrassed.

Janus said loudly, "Oh, for goodness sake!" She jumped from the bed and grabbed Simon's dressing gown, which lay on the end of the bed, in her mouth. She trotted across the room, dragging this garment behind her. She deposited it at Tatya's feet. "Put this on," she told the young woman "then come in and explain to us what this means."

Tatya was so grateful to the cat that tears filled her eyes yet again. She quickly pulled on the dressing gown – it was a beautiful, warm one of blue quilted silk. It hung in folds around her ankles and the sleeves hung down over her hands, but she could belt it tightly and she was again covered decently.

"You can turn around," Janus said dryly to Simon. The cat, as human as she was at times, had never been able to understand the fuss humans made over nudity, even though they hadn't any fur.

Simon turned and ushered Tatya into the room, first peering out in to the hall to make certain that no one was there. He then pulled out the desk chair for her to sit in.

"*Mam'selle*, what are you doing here and dressed like that?" he asked, perplexed and horrified – although it was rather obvious what she was doing. A sudden thought occurred to him. 'You don't think I expect this of you because I rescued you this afternoon? That would make me no better than those rutting jackasses! You owe me nothing! No gentleman worth his salt would expect *anything* from a lady – much less *this!*"

Tatya could only look at him, her eyes wide and frightened. According to Ekaterina he should have fallen on her like a ravening beast, probably tearing the sheer *negligee* right off. Instead he was asking for an explanation. He showed no sign of wanting to ravish her. Tatya did not know how to answer him.

"It was Janus who guessed the reason. "It was that horrible aunt of yours, wasn't it? This was her idea – it is probably all part and parcel of this endless spying! They probably think you'll confide your secrets to a mistress in pillow talk!" she added in disgust to Simon.

"Was that it?" Simon asked Tatya quite gently.

As tears spilled over Tatya said, "They spied upon us at the market and they thought you were interested in me and since you have not been with a woman since you arrived –" a deep blush ran up from her toes.

Simon went to the wash stand and dipped a clean face cloth in water which he warmed magically. This and a towel he took to Tatya. "Here," he said kindly, "wash that dreadful stuff off your face – your tears have ruined it."

Gratefully, Tatya took the face cloth and scrubbed at her face and lips. She remembered, which caused her to blush again, that her nipples were also heavily rouged, but she could scarcely wash those here.

A sudden thought struck her and she lowered the towel to stare at the other two. "How did you know she was my aunt?"

"Nikita told Vron, who told me," said Janus, hopping back up on the bed and tucking her tail around her.

"Nikita?" Tatya knew of no one in the house named Nikita.

"The *domovoi*," explained Simon.

"The house spirit?" Tatya exclaimed. "But that's just a superstition – there isn't any such thing – is there?" she added doubtfully.

"There certainly is a *domovoi*," said Simon, sitting down on the bed by Janus. "I've spoken with him myself. He knows all about how you, a Countess, are made to be a servant in this household. He considers it a rank injustice but only the sort of thing one could expect from such as your aunt and uncle. My own opinion of them is as low as Nikita's," he said with a grimace

"I'll introduce you to Nikita tomorrow," he went on. "He considers himself your friend and apologizes that he could do nothing to help you this afternoon – but he did come to summon me. He arrived on Vron's heels. Not being corporeal, he could do nothing about your vile cousin."

"You can see this spirit?" Tatya asked in surprise.

"With a simple spell you will be able to see him as well," Simon promised.

Tatya continued to look at him as if he might bite at any minute, only momentarily diverted by the thought of the house spirit. Simon noticed how tightly she clutched the robe about her with one hand as if she was afraid it would be pulled from her at any moment. Mentally, he cursed Ekaterina and Yuri. The poor girl had been nearly brutalized today and now was undergoing another horrifying experience – something that no young woman should ever have to undergo.

"I am more than a little insulted," he said carefully and in a light a tome as possible, "that your relatives think me the sort of man who would take ruthless advantage of a female."

"They think of me as a servant," said Tatya bitterly.

"I was raised to treat *all* women with respect and dignity. If I desire a bed partner, I expect her to desire me as well," said Simon quietly. "It's a mutual agreement – not just because someone sends me a woman – especially one who obviously wants no part of the procedure!"

There was a scratching at the door again but Simon recognized the sound – a cat wanted admittance.

He got up and let in Vron, who was followed by Nikita, the house *domovoi*. With a look at Tatya, Simon quickly cast the spell that would allow her to see Nikita. She gasped as the *domovoi* popped into her sight.

Nikita was no more than three feet tall and dressed in the boots, baggy trousers and high collared shirt favored by the peasants. On his head he wore a flat cap. This he took off and held to his chest as he bowed to Simon. "If your honor pleases," he said in a high sweet voice, with a short jerky bow," I've heard them talking about the young lady here, and think you ought to know what they've planned for both of you."

His rather wizened face was screwed up in distress. He looked much like the leprechauns Simon was familiar with in Ireland. He was of indeterminate age, with kindly features, straggly graying hair and knobby hands that looked as if they had seen much hard work.

In a few brief sentences Nikita informed Simon what he had overheard, of the threats that hung over Tatya and Sacha and of the involvement of the Secret Police.

Simon had thought it was impossible for him to become any angrier. But he felt as if he wanted to first tell them all where to go and then show them how to get there by the most expeditious magical route.

Tatya watched the Wizard's face become white and set, and shrank back in her chair.

"He's not angry with you, dear," said Janus as Vron ran to Tatya and jumped into her lap. "He's angry at what Nikita is telling him. What a completely vile woman your aunt is!" she ended on a long hiss.

"They're watching this room, your honor," said Nikita miserably. "They expect her to stay the night and be taken advantage of Yuri Pavlovich said. There's a spy hole in the wall."

"Oh, that thing!" said Janus on a yawn. "We took care of that the first night we were here. All that they see is Simon writing letters any time they look."

"They can't see me now?" Tatya said in wonder.

"They can only see what Simon wants them to see," Janus answered.

Simon let Nikita out the door, after thanking him for his information.

"Nikita has gone to spy upon your aunt and uncle," Simon told Tatya.

Tatya could not meet his eyes and felt a hot flush staining her cheeks.

"Please don't be embarrassed!" Simon knelt before the chair and took the hand that was not clutching the robe in his. Her little hand was cold and it trembled slightly in his grasp. "There is no need to be frightened of me. I shall not take you to bed or hurt you in any way. I only want to be your friend. On my honour, I shall do my best to protect you. I want you to feel you can come to me if you are in trouble. Do you believe me?"

She could not doubt his sincerity. It was in his face, in his eyes and in his voice. "I believe you," she said at last.

"Good!" he squeezed her hand and then let it go, sitting back on his heels.

153

"Now," he said thoughtfully, "what are we to do about your odious relatives' expectations? If you return to your own room they will think you have failed and most likely punish you."

"Make them think she is pleasing you," Janus suggested slyly. "Throw up an illusion. If you like, I'll provide the proper sounds of a woman in ecstatic passion!"

"I would have to – to *act* as if we were – oh, I couldn't do that!" shuddered Tatya.

"No, no, said Simon soothingly. "I can create an illusion that the person watching will see us in bed together and – enjoying ourselves. But you will sleep in the bed, by yourself, and I will sleep on the floor."

She looked doubtful and he thought he knew what bothered her. "You won't have to see anything. I can bespell the watcher so he sees everything he expects to see."

"Give him an eyeful," said Janus.

Looking from one of them to the other Tatya surprised herself by a sudden urge to giggle. The two conspirators looked like Sacha when he was plotting mischief. Who would have thought this horrid day would have ended in a conspiracy against her aunt and uncle with the help of a brand new friend?

And so it was that Yuri, watching uncomfortably through the peep hole, saw his niece in her transparent gown come to the door, be admitted and swept into the Wizard's bed. What he saw there so aroused him that when it was over he staggered to his own room and awoke Ekaterina for a strenuous session.

Sacha was in a bad mood. He had hoped to go flying with the Wizard this morning but Ekaterina had early called him into the house and demanded that he weed the gardens that very day as they were expecting company to drink tea. Ekaterina had been cross as crabs and walked as if she were in pain. She boxed his ears soundly when he protested.

And he could not find Tatya. She was not in her room or in the kitchen and even Luba refused to say where she was.

The Wizard and the dragon had taken off quite early – they were to do their morning exercise flight and then go to show Lakota to the Czarevich. Sacha could not help feeling rather smug that *he* had done what the Czarevich would more than likely NOT be allowed to do – he had ridden the dragon!

He also smarted under the injustice of Mikhail's taking from him his new possession. Two days ago the Wizard had given him a present – a wind up Chinese dragon with a miniature rider. The Wizard had bespelled this so it actually flew and showed Sacha how to direct it by pointing a finger at it. To Sacha's delight Lakota had received one as well, and they had great fun in the space of an afternoon flying these toys together. But Mikhail had said that Sacha was neglecting his work to play with the dragon – and what was more, encouraging Igor and Grisha it neglect their work as well, watching their antics. He, Mikhail would decide when there was time to play and would release the toy then.

It just wasn't fair! It wasn't as if he spent all his time in play – in fact this was the first real toy Sacha could ever remember owning. He had no memories at all of the time before when they lived with their father and there was time for play. His remembrances were all of endless work. Of course he was thrilled with his new acquisition and wanted to use it and show it off. Mikhail was mean! Sacha savagely pulled up weeds, and a few small plants as well, as he sulkily tended the garden and muttered against the iniquity of it all.

The first hint he had that something was wrong was the horses in the stable. They began screaming in terror and kicking the sides of their stalls. If was as if they sensed or smelled something very frightening. Sacha had wondered earlier why the scent of the dragon had not scared them. The Wizard had explained that Lakota smelt of cinnamon, a scent which horses did not fear.

The next thing Sacha knew, the sun was suddenly gone as if a large dark cloud had covered it and a great wind sprang up, flattening the flowers and grass. Before he could surge to his feet something hard grabbed him around the waist and then bore him aloft as he struggled and began to scream in terror.

A huge silver claw held him in an iron grip.

15

The Next Day

When Tatya awoke she was alone in the room, save for the cats. There was no sign of the Wizard.

She felt as if she had indeed had an excellent night's repose. She wore one of the Wizard's night shirts – too large but far more comfortable for sleeping than that decadent *negligée*.

It had been so long since she slept in a real bed – and now she had been in two different beds in the space of two days.

Tatya sat up amidst the pillows and coverlets, and stretched."Where is he?" she asked Janus. It was amazing how easily one became used to talking animals!

"A command performance for the Czar," said Janus. "The Czarevich wants to see a dragon. Simon was supposed to go to the Winter Palace, but there were many people who were worried about Lakota frightening the horses, so they sent a note and moved the whole thing to the Imperial gardens at the Catherine Palace at Czarskoe Selo. Lakota wanted his exercise before what will probably be a lot of standing about answering questions. So they left quite early," the cat replied. With Vron, she sat at the foot of the bed.

"There's a breakfast tray for you on the desk, and a bath as well. Simon bespelled them both so they will be still nice and hot," Janus continued.

Magic was a wonderful thing, Tatya thought in wonder as she sat down to a hot breakfast of eggs in cream, buttery muffins, *kasha* and crisp bacon. There was fruit as well – strawberries, with a pitcher of thick cream to go over them – the fruit and cream as cold as if they had just come from the ice-room.

She appreciated magic again when she slid into the bath – redolent with fresh herbs and as hot as it had just been drawn. What luxury! She could easily become used to living like this.

156

Janus jumped up on the chair, which Tatya had pulled close to the tin tub to use as a towel rack. "Have you thought what you will tell your aunt when she asks you about last night?" the cat inquired.

Tatya's mood changed at once. "No – I had not –" she admitted.

"I have an idea – if you think you could do it," said the cat. "It would certainly put that horrible hag in her place! She got too much enjoyment out of ruining you!" Her tail lashed angrily, as did Vron's, who had joined her on the chair.

"Tell me," said Tatya.

At first she found what the cat suggested embarrassing beyond belief. And then she began to think of her aunt's reaction and she almost laughed aloud.

"I'll do it!" she finally said, much to Janus' satisfaction. "It will be worth it, just to see the look on her face!"

She did not see Ekaterina until after eight-thirty – for she remembered that Ekaterina had given her permission to stay abed until eight o'clock.

Janus was a marvelous conspirator who thought of everything. She directed Tatya to pour a small vial of blood in the bed on the bottom sheet. "It's bat blood from Simon's Wizard kit," she explained. "I have no doubt that those awful people will check the sheets to see if you lost your virginity and that is the usual sign of it. We want them to believe completely what your uncle saw last night. And if you can play your part equally well – "

Tatya felt that she had no great skill as an actress, but with a little coaxing from Janus, she was ready when the summons finally came from her aunt for Tatya to go to the private parlor.

Ekaterina was in a vile mood. Last night Yuri had come to her room, very late, and insisted on having marital relations no less than three times. Three times in one night! That was disgusting – three times in one week was too much! When he tried for a fourth time and suggested an activity so decadent that she could not believe he would suggest such whore's tricks to his lawful wife – she had got out of bed and, grabbing her hair brush, struck him repeatedly with it until

157

he ran off to his own bed. Where had he gotten ideas like that?

The only redeeming factor was the fact that Tatya had been similarly befouled last night. Ekaterina could not help but look forward to seeing the no doubt weeping and shamed girl. Finally, that arrogant little piece would be put in her place and not give her generous relatives – (who were not obliged to even give her and her pest of a brother house room, much less give them the fine home they had) those looks of her down her aristocratic nose.

From the beginning, Ekaterina had disliked her niece. To begin with, she was the image of Ekaterina's elder half sister Irina, a Countess in her own right, whom everyone seemed to prefer to Ekaterina. Irina had shone in society, and married a wealthy nobleman. When the living image of Irina had been delivered to her Ekaterina had seen it as the hand of God, allowing her to take her revenge for all the snubs and slights, both real and imagined, she had endured over the years as Irina's less pretty, less popular, less loved sister.

Ekaterina had always longed for something that would finally break her niece's spirits and having been raped by a foreigner would have done it. Ekaterina hoped that the Wizard had been rough with Tatya. Ekaterina had not yet talked to Yuri, who had watched the entire process through the spy hole. And Ekaterina was not sure that she was even speaking to Yuri, much less exchanging confidences with him. Last night had been worse than her wedding night.

When Tatya at last appeared before her aunt she entered the room with bowed head. Clad once more in one of her two remaining brown gowns, she curtsied obediently and stood in the middle of the room, eyes down.

She did not look visibly shaken, or upset, or even bruised. Nor did she move as if she had been roughly violated. Ekaterina's voice was sharp as she said "Well, girl, did you please the Wizard? Did he have you?"

To Ekaterina's surprise the face that Tatya raised to hers was glowing. "Oh, yes, aunt!" she said happily. "I cannot thank you enough! I might have else never known such ecstasy! He is a magnificent lover and made love to me again and again! And each time was better than the last! Even the first time – he is so skilled – was incredible! I never felt such

158

feelings before! I am still tingling! I can hardly wait for this afternoon when he returns and I join him in bed again! He wants me to remove my things to his room and sleep with him at every opportunity! I cannot thank you enough! I am so happy!"

Ekaterina's jaw dropped and she looked ad if she had been stupefied. "You – you *liked* it?" she stammered at last.

Remembering Janus's instructions Tatya said, "Like is too mild a word, aunt! I want him to make love to me again and again! I love it! I can barely wait until he is with me once more! It is all I can think about!"

The look on Ekaterina's face was everything that Janus had thought it would be. And there was also – was it? – disappointment.

"Get out!" Ekaterina spat as shock and disappointment turned to rage. "Get out of my sight!"

Tatya curtseyed again. "Yes, aunt. And by the way – he loved the *negligée* – although he thought it too concealing. He's buying me one with less fabric in it!"

Ekaterina shrieked in rage and picking up an empty tea glass that sat on the table before her and threw it at her niece.

Tatya easily dodged this missile and slipped out the door, hearing another piece of porcelain crash on the wall behind her.

She had an urge to burst into hysterics and had to clasp her hands over her mouth so that no laughter escaped. She heard more china or glass breaking as she went down the hall and continued down the stairs to the kitchen.

There she found not only Janus waiting to hear the result of their little ploy, but Luba, Masha and Ilenka as well. She could hardly wait to share her story with them.

Upstairs, Ekaterina could have howled in rage. How dare that girl come in here and declare herself happy about being ruined! She wanted to do it again and again! Ekaterina looked about for something else to throw. Her niece was supposed to be ashamed and fearful. Ekaterina had looked forward to ordering her to sleep with him many times, and reveling in the girl's reluctance. She had pictured Tatya begging, pleading and crying not to have to suffer his

159

attentions again. Ekaterina had even thought of buying further *negligees* – ones that made the black gown look positively prim, and making the girl wear them, making her walk through the house in these skimpy garments and perhaps 'accidentally' having her seen by the menservants. She had looked forward to questioning her niece, making her tell exactly what the Wizard had said, and done to her.

Questioning! Ekaterina did howl – she had completely forgotten the questions the Secret Police had written down for her to ask the girl!

Old Mikhail knew that Sacha was upset with him for confiscating the toy. But he also knew that if the boy were to neglect his work and the Rostovs found out he would be severely punished. Mikhail worried about the boy – and his sister. Yuri was too fond of beating them and Ekaterina, Mikhail was convinced, would do anything she could to harm them. And that Evgeny –! Mikhail had heard of the attempted rape from Luba. He wished he had been there! He would have taken his carriage whip to that scoundrel's hide. It would be worth being sent to Siberia! Mikhail already hated Evgeny for the cruel way he treated horses – a heavy hand on their tender mouths and he used his spurs until their sides ran with blood. To Mikhail's mind, such a one as Evgeny ought to be eliminated. He was sure that Grandfather Vassily would agree with him. An animal breeder would not hesitate to kill a mad, inferior or diseased animal. The same rules ought to apply to humans.

Mikhail sighed. Things were going badly lately and where it would all end he did not know. A fortune teller had told him there were big changes coming and they would not be to the liking of every one.

For now he would attempt to make his peace with the boy. He disliked being on the outs with Sacha, so he decided to tell the boy that he could have his toy that very afternoon.

He walked briskly to the courtyard but almost turned back as the horses suddenly began neighing in fear. But a sudden movement over head made him look up and he gasped when he saw the huge Ice dragon plunging down from high above. He broke into a run, and screamed the boy's name, but the wind raised by the immense wings carried his voice away.

At his age, he could just not run fast enough. He was in time only to catch a piece of parchment that fell from the sky. There were letters on it, written in red. But Mikhail could not read.

Simon had been glad for a change of scene – he, too, had been worried about the effect Lakota would have on the local horses. His scent contained nothing that would frighten a horse, but the sight of him had already frightened a number of horses in the city. Fortunately the damage had been minimal. Lakota was much distressed that he had frightened the horses – he was not used to horses, whom he considered friends, being scared of him.

No horse breeder of any reputation in the British Isles or in America would think of raising horses that were not dragon-broke. Almost from the moment of birth a foal was exposed to dragons. Large horse breeding farms usually employed a dragon just to interact with the foals and it was a common sight to go by the pastures of a horse farm and see a dragon in the pasture with the mares and foals. It was the same with hippogriffs. British and American horses took these creatures for granted and did not think of them as predators. It was strange to both Simon and Lakota to be in a place that was so different and, to their minds, odd.

The Czarevich was thrilled with Lakota, and asked all sorts of questions of both Simon and the dragon. Some other children of the members of the Court had been allowed to join the party. All of them were eager to pet Lakota, talk to him and give him dragon treats. Simon was very glad that he had thought to bring an entire five pound bag of the treats.

None of the parents or nursemaids who had accompanied the children would give permission for their charges to go aloft when Simon suggested it, but they did allow him, at the urging of the Czar himself, to put the children on Lakota's back and walk the dragon about the garden.

"I feel like the pony ride at the Londonderry Fair!" Lakota remarked in Gaelic as they paced carefully around the garden. Simon noticed that many of the mothers present watched with their hearts in their eyes – anxious but trying

161

to hide it, as the Czar's urging was much the same as a command.

Then nothing would do but that Lakota had to put on an aerial display. Simon had brought a ball and he tossed this into the air as Lakota sped after it and caught it, diving from great heights and turning and twisting in the air.

The children shrieked and clapped with delight. When Lakota landed once more, they had to give him more dragon treats, and all pet him at once. One little Grand Duchess even kissed him on the end of the nose.

Lakota was his natural self – friendly, open and obliging. He loved children and it showed. By the time the Czar dismissed them the other parents had visibly relaxed, some of them even rather timidly came up to Simon and thanking him for giving their children such a treat.

It was such a contrast to Dragon Days in the British Isles. Dragon Days had been instituted hundreds of years ago, to acquaint people with the Dragon Post and let them meet dragons. It was really no longer necessary, but it was so popular that it was kept up. It was popular with the dragons, too, who loved meeting new people, giving rides and gorging on dragon treats. There was none of the fear and worry that was common here in Russia. There was scarcely a child in the British Isles, or in America, that had not ridden a dragon by the time he or she was seven years old. Simon reflected that if they ever did create a Dragon Post here there would have to be a great deal of public education. Or perhaps the Czar would just issue an Edict telling his subjects that they were not to be afraid of dragons any more.

Simon was eager to return to the Rostov house. He had to talk to Tatya and they had to decide what she would tell her horrible relatives and what was to be done about the rest of the time he was here – should they keep up the pretence? In the light of day Simon regretted their decision of the night before. He had, in effect, ruined a young lady's reputation. Her relatives, as awful as they were, now thought that Tatya had become his mistress. He could well imagine what his mother, grandmother and great grandmother would say to that!

He was not certain what else he could have done. Nikita was certain that Tatya and perhaps Sacha as well, would have been soundly whipped if her services had been rejected. Nikita was as afraid of the Secret Police as the humans were.

The question still remained – what the devil did the Secret Police want? What secrets was he supposed to impart in pillow talk? What was he supposed to reveal to Anatoly Tcherpnin? Simon had not missed Anatoly's clumsy, shame-faced attempts to talk about matters that really held no interest for either of them. Anatoly, he suspected, was being coerced by the Secret Police as well.

But the question remained like a canker – why? What did they want? What did they hope to find out? What did they think he knew?

Simon had no answers.

It was a pleasant day for flying – a cloudless blue sky and a light breeze. There were excellent conditions for the creation of thermal cells and Lakota was able to glide most of the way back to St Petersburg.

Lakota began to spiral down and then gave a gasp. He turned his head around and said quickly. "Simon – there's something wrong! Tatya and most of the servants are waiting for us and they all look worried and upset!" With his dragon sight, sharper than a hawk's, he could see things hundreds of feet below as clearly as if he stood beside them.

Simon leaned forward in the saddle – he could see about seven ant- sized shapes looking up at them. Something was indeed wrong – it simply wasn't normal for all of those people to be waiting for him so anxiously.

Lakota could not speed up his landing – it wasn't safe to do so – and both Simon, his dragon and the people waiting on the ground thought it took far too long for the blue dragon to glide down and land neatly.

Lakota did not even have time to fold his wings before Tatya ran forward and thrust a piece of parchment at Simon, standing on her tiptoes and leaning against Lakota's leg. All of her fears of him were long gone.

Simon slid onto Lakota's foreleg and bent to take the paper from Tatya.

163

It was in the Cyrillic alphabet. Once again Simon blessed Oberon's foresight in giving them the gift of complete fluency in Russian.

The ink was red and it had been penned by something very sharp, for the paper, a thick brownish parchment, was slightly torn here and there.

Simon read it aloud so that Lakota could hear it.

"Return the egg or the boy dies."

Startled, Simon looked down at Tatya. Sacha?" he asked hurriedly. "When did this happen?"

"Less than an hour ago!" her face was stained with tears. "And my uncle – and the police – will do nothing about it!"

"Well, WE will!" Lakota burst out. "Sacha is our friend!"

"I'll be ready to leave within an hour," said Simon. "If you can get me something of Sacha's an a good map, such as an ordnance map, I can track him down."

"Oh, thank you!" Tatya sobbed, her heart in her eyes.

"Don't worry – we'll find him and get him back if we have to fly to China!" Simon promised.

16

The Theft

Anatoly Tcherpnin had had a rough morning. He had stayed up late that night before, writing his report on the time he had spent with the Wizard. He then had to drag himself from bed at an early hour, after having very little sleep, in order to meet with the Secret Police and his Colonel. They questioned him mercilessly and were thrown into consternation when he repeated Simon's request that he be allowed to go out into the countryside.

"Why does he want to do that?" Zemstov, the elder of the two men from the Third Section demanded. He was a hard-featured, suspicious natured man of about forty. He also had a nasty, devious mind.

Simon had told Anatoly exactly why he wanted to go into the countryside, so Anatoly repeated this. "To look for Elves."

"What is *Elves*?" Zemstov asked, for he had never heard the word. He exchanged looks with his colleague, Matyushin, who shrugged, He did not know what Elves was either.

Matyushin was not the sort, one would think whilst looking at him, to be a very successful member of the Third Section. He was a short, rotund, jovial appearing person but this façade covered a liking for torture and a mind well-suited to spying. It had been his idea to supply Simon with a mistress. Now he said slowly, in a deceptively gentle voice, "Perhaps we should allow this Wizard to look for this *Elves*, whatever it may be. Perhaps this is something we should know about – perhaps it is a threat to Mother Russia. Do you know, Lieutenant, what is *Elves*?"

"No sir," said Anatoly uncomfortably. Simon had not explained. "He did tell me that he has a commission from King Oberon..."

"A king!" said Zemstov sharply. "The English King is called William!"

"The Wizard is actually from Ireland but as I understand it all the countries of the British Isles have a Prime Minister, but there is only the one King. But many of the Prime Ministers are descended from ancient kings, such as Owain Glendwyr of Wales." Matyushin had read up on British government for this assignment. "I do not recall the name Oberon," he added. Unfortunately for the Secret Police they had never obtained such books as *A History of Wizardry*, or *The Selighe and Unselighe Courts* ,which were an important part of British history. And Matyushin did not care to admit that the one book on Wizards that he had had tried to read had been completely incomprehensible to him. He found the concept of magic so far fetched and unbelievable that he had given up his reading of *Famous Wizards and Witches* in disgust. He had been supplied with copies of Simon's books by Count Pozharsky, and those had suffered the same fate as *Famous Wizards and Witches*. He could not understand them, even though he read English very well indeed. Like almost everyone else in the Department he had taken a turn spying upon the Wizard and his dragon and he still could not believe that such a fabulous creature as the dragon existed, despite the evidence of his own eyes. Nor did he believe that someone could perform magic. It was all a trick, he was convinced, and he hoped to unmask the trickster.

He turned to Anatoly's Colonel, who participated in these interviews. "Colonel Danzas, will you allow this young man leave so that he may accompany the English Wizard into the countryside?"

The Colonel, a stern man with extreme military bearing, gave his consent with little or no thought about the matter. One did not deny a request of the Secret Police. Everyone in the briefing room knew that it was not a request, but an order.

"From this moment on consider yourself on extended leave," Zemstov told Anatoly. "Where exactly does the Wizard want to go?"

"He only specified a heavily forested area. He said it should have many old – very old – trees," said Anatoly.

Zemstov and Matyushin exchanged glances again. "It is probably something to do with our Navy – shipbuilding no doubt," Zemstov said.

"You must keep his every action under strict surveillance, Lieutenant! I shall tell you how you may file your reports during your journey. We shall not suggest places for you to take him, for if you appear to guide him too closely he might not reveal the true purpose of his mission."

Anatoly's heart sank. He did not think that Simon was in the least bit interested in the Navy or shipbuilding. And he would still have to write those damned reports! But what could he do but agree?

Mikhail told Simon everything he had seen that morning, describing the Ice dragon and how it had swooped from the sky, snatching Sacha.

There were no good maps in the Rostov household, so Simon provided Pavel with enough money to go to Smirdin's the bookseller on the Nevski Prospekt, to obtain the best map possible.

Simon had a confrontation with Ekaterina and Yuri. He was appalled by the fact that they would do nothing to rescue Sacha. When Count Pozharsky arrived, summoned by Simon, he was equally indifferent. To Simon's demand that the egg be returned to the Ice dragons, he said flatly "Nyet! We will never return the egg! All this furor over a serf!"

Yuri and Ekaterina were appalled and terrified when Simon shouted at Pozharsky "This boy is a member of your nobility – a Count like yourself – not that that should matter! This is a *child* who will die a horrible death unless we take action!"

"You said that dragons don't eat people," returned Pozharsky mildly.

"I also told you that I know next to nothing about Ice dragons!" Simon retorted. "For all I know people form an integral part of their diet!"

But Pozharsky could not be swayed. His government would not let their policy be dictated by the demands of an animal. The egg would stay where it was.

Simon left the Rostovs and the Count in disgust. How could they be so indifferent to Sacha's plight? He had never met with such care for nobodies!

Out in the courtyard Tatya waited with Lakota for Pavel's return. She had not been allowed to be present at the interview with her aunt and uncle and Count Pozharsky. One look at Simon's furious expression as he came towards them answered the question that she had been about to ask. She felt terror overwhelm her again.

"Your relatives and that idiot Pozharsky –! " Simon said angrily. "He refuses to release the egg and they don't caret that Sacha could be in mortal danger!"

Tatya sobbed audibly, hands clasped in front of her. The face she showed to Simon and Lakota was pitiful. 'What can I do?" she said in a whisper.

"We will do anything we can to help you," Simon promised her."I shan't let those idiots stop us from rescuing your brother!"

It was at this moment that Pavel arrived.

Mikhail had insisted on poling up the smallest *droshky* and taking Pavel to the Nevski Prospekt his own self. This was done without asking permission from Yuri. It would be faster than a hack, for was not he, old Mikhail, the best coachman in all of St Petersburg?

Pavel had asked the bookshop clerk to find him the best and the largest map available. This he had done. Simon was gratified to find it was a good-sized, very detailed topographical map of the entire country. He spread this on the ground so that Lakota could see it as well as the rest of them.

Luba came out of the kitchen with a tray of hot tea, and joined the others. "I am packing you a big basket of food to take on the journey!" she announced. "No matter what Ekaterina Feodorova says!"

"Did you find something of Sacha's?" Simon asked Tatya who handed him a neckerchief. "He wears that a great deal," she said, "But it was laundered today."

"Excellent !" said Simon. He took his wand out of his breast pocket and bent over a flat package that lay on the ground. This he tapped with the wand and it sprang up and out, revealing itself as a bulging satchel.

168

Everyone jumped backwards, eyes awed in their faces. The satchel opened itself and an interior pocket opened. A chain with a diamond shape weight flew up into the air and Simon caught it.

Mikhail, Pavel and Luba crossed themselves. Tatya watched anxiously.

Simon tied the scarf around the gold chain and then stood over the map. He swung the chin around in a wide circle, which grew faster and smaller as his anxious audience watched. The golden weight had come nearly to a stop when suddenly it began to pull in the direction of the bottom of the map.

"South and west," Simon said thoughtfully, carefully watching the direction of the golden weight.

Unnoticed by any of them, Anatoly had entered the courtyard and stood behind Mikhail.

Simon took his wand and tapped the map with it A small image of a flying dragon appeared on the paper, in perfect proportion to the map scale As they all watched it flapped its wings and flew a little ways across the paper. "That will stay on the map and show us exactly where they are going," he explained.

"I estimate him to be about two hundred and fifty miles ahead of us," said Lakota. "It won't be easy to catch him up, for his wingspan is greater than mine."

"I'm all packed," said Simon. "We can set out within the hour."

"I want to come with you!" said Tatya urgently.

"That isn't a good idea –" Simon began, but Luba interrupted him.

"She can't stay here, Wizard! Now that the master and mistress think she is your whore they will give her to Evgeny Yurovich and he will make of her life a misery, if he doesn't kill her with beatings and ill-usage!"

Simon acknowledged the truth of this even as he thought of the difficulties of taking her along on what might be a strenuous and futile trip.

He made up his mind quickly. "Very well, I'll take you. But you can't go wearing those clothes – you'll freeze to death. Could you possible wear trousers? You'll need a warm

169

jacket as well and boots and gloves." He knew that there would be no possibility of obtaining a ladies' flying suit here.

"I know just the thing!" said Luba. "Nothing is ever thrown away in this house! Evgeny Yurovich's old things are in trunks in the attics – some of them will probably fit you! There is everything from hats to boots up there!"

"But what of this egg the Ice dragon wants?" said Tatya as Luba tried to drag her towards the house.

"We'll take it with us – we have no room to negotiate without it and I would rather not try to fight an Ice dragon, even with magic," Simon said.

"But Pozharsky won't let us have it!" Tatya protested.

Simon grinned at her. "I don't intend to take no for an answer!"

"What is going on?" Anatoly interrupted loudly. From what he had heard, it sounded as if they were plotting something. And he was shocked to hear both Simon and the dragon speak fluent Russian – which they were doing for the benefit of the serfs.

Simon looked up from the map. "Sacha has been kidnapped by an Ice dragon. The dragon has threatened to kill him unless we return the egg that was stolen from him." He went on to explain about the egg that Pozharsky had in hiding.

"But if the Count won't release it, what can you do?" Anatoly pointed out.

"I'm going to steal it," Simon said calmly. "And if you do not promise me you will not interfere, I will use a memory charm on you that will make you forget the last year of your life." He leveled his wand at Anatoly.

The lieutenant at once declared that he had no desire to interfere "In fact, you'd best take you with me !" he suggested rather recklessly. "If you are heading south and west you are heading to where I come from! I know that area well – the entire region is covered in my relatives!"

"Can I trust you?" Simon asked, rather skeptically. "Lakota, what do you think?"

"On my honour as an officer and a gentleman, I will not betray you and will do my best to help you," said Anatoly quickly as the dragon bent his head to look into his eyes.

There was something completely mesmerizing about those great blue draconic eyes. Anatoly felt as if he were falling into a deep pool and that every one of his thoughts was being read and analyzed.

"He's telling the truth," Lakota announced, breaking eye contact.

Anatoly staggered back from Lakota's gaze and would have fallen had not old Mikhail caught him under the elbow and said "Steady, steady there, Lieutenant!"

"But how can you steal the egg?" Tatya was saying as Anatoly recovered himself. "Is it not closely guarded?"

Lakota laughed. "There is nothing that can be guarded from Simon, *Mam'selle* Tatya! Unless another Wizard put a very powerful spell on it – even then Simon could probably break it," he added proudly.

"But won't you have to wait until evening when it is dark? That's hours and hours away!" Tatya cried. "They could be even further ahead by then!"

"You get your things and have the Lieutenant help you pack Lakota's harness," Simon directed. "I'll be back with the egg in about five minutes." And so saying, he disappeared.

"Less than five minutes!" said Lakota at the gasps that followed this vanishing.

"Where did he go? And how did he leave?" stammered Anatoly.

"Why, to get the egg, as he told you," the dragon said. "He dematerialized. It's a fast way Wizards can travel. They can go hundreds of miles in minutes if they want. I wish dragons could do it.

In less than five minutes as Lakota had predicted, Simon was back , with a cloth wrapped bundle in his arms.

"Did you have any problems?" Lakota asked.

"Savva was on duty. He is having a nice long nap and when he wakes will not remember I was there," Simon returned. He looked at the rest of them, still standing where he had left them. "Come on!" he ordered. "We need to pack and get out of here. I arranged an illusion so that it will look as if the egg is still there, but it will only last for a few hours and then there is bound to be an outcry. We should be long gone by then."

It was another hour before Lakota was finally all packed up and ready to take flight. The egg was in magiced cloths and tucked against his chest where it could feel the heat from his body. He had chewed firestone and could feel his flight gases building up.

Tatya had found clothing to fit amongst Evgeny's outgrown garments. She had also packed both her and Sacha's belongs up in a bundle. It made a pathetically small package.

Mikhail gave her the wind-up toy to place in the bundle. "Tell Sacha Ivanovich I never meant to be cruel," he told Tatya with tears in his eyes.

"I will give him your love," Tatya promised the old man. "Mikhail – I have decided that we will not come back here. I will get a position scrubbing floors or working in a factory if I have to. Anything is better than this!"

"That is the right thing to do," said the old man. "God bless you, Tatiana Ivanova."

She kissed him and the others good-bye. For it really was good-bye. She was determined, that whatever happened, she would never return to live under the Rostov roof.

Anatoly returned briefly to his barracks, packed hurriedly and changed his uniform to civilian dress. He brought along a brace of pistols, ammunition and a rifle.

He arranged for the care and exercise of his horse while he was gone and spoke briefly to his Colonel, telling him that the Wizard wanted to begin looking for Elves immediately, now that he had permission.

And at the last minute Vron insisted on going. Janus said he could not bear to live here without Tatya and Sacha. Anatoly obligingly tucked the cat into the front of his jacket as Simon did Janus, since the jacket Tatya wore was too big and he would slide right out. Simon resolved that when they stopped for the night he would magic up a better traveling method for the cats.

Anatoly was exhilarated at the thought of another dragon flight. And this promised to be an adventure as well.

Under ordinary circumstances Tatya would have been apprehensive and afraid of flying on a dragon. She also would have been embarrassed to wear trousers that clung to her legs like a second skin. But she gave it scarcely a thought as they prepared to depart. All she could think about was what was happening to Sacha.

Simon strapped them both in, gave them each an Elfin cloak to keep away the effects of the high cold air, and showed them the straps built into each seat of the six person saddle on Lakota's harness that they could hold to steady themselves. Mikhail helped Simon, now clad in his flying suit, load the luggage into Lakota's breast harness.

"Can he carry all of this and three people as well?" Anatoly asked Tatya. He sat in back of her – Simon would sit in front of her, right behind Lakota's first spinal ridge. A ridge separated each saddle pad.

Lakota heard this and turned his long neck to say, "I can carry six adults and ten times this amount of luggage with ease. And I'm not even a truly big dragon."

Simon, climbing up to his seat, said "Is every one secure, even Vron?"

Anatoly checked the black Tom cat. Janus had told him to sink his claws, front and back, into Anatoly's jacket, and curl into a small ball. This he had done. He was terrified, but he trusted Janus and the thought of being separated from Tatya was insupportable.

Simon fastened down his straps, testing them as he always did. "All secure," he told Lakota, told everyone to stand well away and the blue dragon leaped into the air, leaving the serfs on the ground, calling good-byes and blessings. In no time at all the dragon and his passengers were a dwindling speck in the early afternoon sky.

17

A Wing and a Prayer

Under the strictest orders, Count Pozharsky reported at once to the Summer Palace when the egg was discovered missing.

The Summer Palace had been built by Peter the Great. It was a small building for a palace – only fourteen rooms. It sat where the Neva and the Fontanka canal met at the corner of the Summer Gardens; a solid, two story, sensible structure that seemed almost to be growing out of the water. It was shaded by large trees, its wide and latticed windows letting in much light and air.

Count Pozharsky, carrying a thick letter case, waited for his Imperial Majesty in the spacious but starkly simple Turnery on the lower floor. The walls were paneled in dark wood, with shining wooden floors devoid of rugs. On the immense stove were blue and white Dutch tiles, showing the sixty gun Russian sailing ship that had been built to Peter's own design. An instrument made for Peter by the famous Dinglinger of Dresden was in the room. This instrument showed the time of day and the speed, force and direction of the wind through the medium of lines connected to the weather vane on the roof.

The room was simply furnished –a sturdy table of Russian oak, a large carved Dutch cabinet, a few chairs, and Peter's own Admiralty chair, covered in golden velvet, its arms ending in carved human hands and its feet eagle's talons.

Pozharsky knew better than to even think about sitting in this chair. He did place one of the other chairs in the room opposite it, so that it would face the Admiralty chair across the breath of the oak table.

But he would not sit until the Czar invited him to do so.

Nicholas did not keep him waiting. What had begun with the theft of the egg was too important.

174

The Czar nearly always wore a uniform of some type. and today was no exception. It was particularly suited to one of his military bearing.

"Ah, Pozharsky," he said in his cold voice. "Your note of this morning indicated that you have important news regarding our most pressing problem?"

Pozharsky bowed low. "Indeed I do, your Imperial Majesty. Matters have turned out far better than we have hoped and what has happened, I hope you will agree, has been fortuitous for us and far better than our original plan."

The Czar invited him to be seated as he seated himself in the Admiralty chair.

Pozharsky, in succinct fashion, outlined what had happened at the Rostov home and the theft of the egg.

"But how did the English Wizard accomplish this?" the Czar demanded. "There were guards – he could not just walk out with it."

"We think he did something that the English call *dematerialization*, Majesty," said the Count. "We have learned that certain amongst the English Wizards can vanish in one place and turn up in quite another – sometimes many miles away, in a matter of minutes. This Wizard's father actually teaches this skill at Trinity University in Dublin."

"A very useful skill," commented the Czar dryly. He made a steeple of his fingers and looked over this at his Third Section operative. His arctic glance was deep and penetrating. "And have your spies in England completed their investigation into this Wizard's talents?"

"Yes, Majesty," said Pozharsky. He lifted the letter case he carried onto the table and opened it. Inside lay a thick sheaf of papers and a book. "As your Imperial Majesty no doubt remembers, this investigation was begin last summer. It is now complete. I received the final report only yesterday. We have thoroughly looked into his background, his education and his family, with a particular emphasis on his expertise in magic. All reports have been most satisfactory indeed. From what we can find out from bribing various individuals he is accounted a Master and an Adept – the highest level of proficiency." He pulled the book from the case. "This, Majesty is a magical book that lists all of the Wizards and the Witches in the British Isles and their rankings. According to this book

175

Stillfield passed all of his tests – and I understand that they are difficult indeed – with 'no higher honor'. In addition he is an expert on dragons and a Master Druid, which is yet another difficult magical discipline."

"Most satisfactory," said the Czar.

"And may I say, Majesty, that I think the outcome we desire will be inevitable," Pozharsky said, returning his papers to the case and passing it to the Czar, for Nicholas would want to read all of the reports his own self.

"I leave today to follow his trail. Tcherpnin went with him – another fortunate happenstance – ostensibly to search for *Elves*. So we will be receiving reports along the way. Zemstov coached the Lieutenant in how to file his reports."

"And the Lieutenant has no idea of the real purpose of this assignment?" the Czar inquired.

"None, Majesty. He is the perfect dupe – innocent, honest and honorable. The questioning has made him very uneasy and according to Matyushin he has no more idea than a puppy would what we want of him. But he is a useful tool."

"What is *Elves*, Pozharsky?" then queried the Czar.

Pozharsky spread his hands and shrugged. "I think they are mythological creatures, Majesty, like our Firebird." He was better read than his colleagues and had actually spent time in the British Isles. "I think we need not concern ourselves with creatures of whose very existence I am in doubt."

"Do not be too certain of that, Count! Before this business started we thought Wizards and Ice dragons only legends or something long vanished. But I will not keep you. Send your reports directly to me." He drew a heavy signet ring from one finger. It was deeply engraves with the double headed eagle. "Use this ring as your seal and any communication will be given top priority."

"Thank you, Majesty." Pozharsky rose and bowed and backed out of the room.

Tatya could never have imagined what it would be like to fly on the back of a dragon, high in the sky. It was rather frightening to be so high up. But the straps holding her in place were very secure and well maintained. She found it comforting to cling to the handle in front of her.

They were going so fast that tears filled her eyes. The Wizard had warned her to wear a knit cap that cam well down over her ears and she was glad that she had taken his advice, for elsewise her hair would be loose by now and streaming over her shoulders.

It was also cold. They were not very high – the Wizard had explained that they were only several thousand feet above the ground – but it was colder up here and the rush of wind made it even chillier. Tatya was grateful for Evgeny's old jacket and gloves. Her cheeks felt as cold as if she had walked to the market in the depths of winter. She was even more grateful for the Elfin cloak and the hood on it. It had molded itself to her body and came down over her legs. No amount of wind seemed able to dislodge it and it was incredibly warm, but light.

But in truth she scarcely noticed the discomforts. All she could think about was her brother and what might be happening to him. Where was the Ice dragon taking him? Could they catch up in time to prevent Sacha's death? What hadn't the Ice dragon given them a time and a place to exchange Sacha for the egg? What did the Ice dragon expect them to do? Her mind worried at this as they flew. They could not talk at the speed Lakota was making.

Anatoly was excited. Even the fastest horse could not make speed like this! It was exhilarating to see the scenery speed along beneath them, so far below that the towns and dwellings were doll-sized. Each sweep of the dragon's wings sent them further along – effortlessly. The dragon had not boasted – he easily carried the three passengers and the luggage with no sign of fatigue. To Anatoly's eyes the beautiful opal wings looked too frail to hold the bulk of the dragon aloft and he resolved to ask the Wizard what kept the dragon in the air. What stories he would have to tell his family! And now he was to see an Ice dragon as well – a creature of legend. Perhaps they could even stop at his home and his family could see him dragon-back!

Both Simon's and Lakota's thoughts were the same – to make as much time as possible to save Sacha's life. Such was their concentration – Lakota thinking only of speed and Simon making plans of how to contact the Ice dragon to make an exchange – that they failed to give proper heed to the weather.

It had been a cloudless summer day when they left St Petersburg, with perfect summer temperatures. The further south they flew, however, the heavier the air became. Simon failed to keep a weather eye behind them as he usually did and he did not see the clouds building up, although the anvil shape of the towering thunder-head was concealed by low level stratus clouds. The cold front causing the convection in the clouds was behind them and Lakota, usually weather sensitive as dragons were, failed to notice it at the speed he was making. In his defense, it was a rapidly forming, fast moving storm. But it was a nearly fatal error.

The first warning was a sudden brilliant flash, Lakota startled, back-winged, looking as if he was standing on his hand legs.

Tatya shrieked. She thought that they would slide right off the dragon's back. But the safety straps did their work. Anatoly grabbed the front of his jacket where Vron clung. The black Tom was shaking with terror. "I've got you!" Anatoly said in Russian, He wasn't sure how much the cat understood.

"DOWN!" Simon yelled. There was nothing more dangerous for a dragon than lightning. Only a fool would stay in the air during a thunderstorm. Cloud to cloud lightning was the most dangerous for a dragon and it was also the most common lightning.

Lakota dived. He did not dare try to spiral down, Diving was perilous, but not as risky as remaining in the air for a dragon filled with explosive flight gasses.

With great effort, due to the rush of wind. Simon turned and gestured to the others to bend low over Lakota's back. He wished he could tell them to cling hard with their legs as well. But both Anatoly and Tatya did this instinctively. To Anatoly, being a cavalryman, it was second nature. It had been years since Tatya had been on a horse, but she had learned to ride bareback as a girl and did not think twice about wrapping her legs around Lakota's sides.

Lightning flashed again and Lakota gave a shriek. "Simon!" he screamed. "I'm hit!"

178

One wing suddenly collapsed and hung loose and they began to fall rapidly towards the ground.

By late afternoon Volunvoshka reached Mount *Stredny Baseg*. He had flown at his maximum speed. His immense wing span – twice that of Lakota – had easily covered the many miles between St Petersburg and the Urals.

He had decided to give his hostage into the Wizard's keeping. He had no facilities to keep a boy, and he reasoned that the Wizard could put a spell on the boy to keep him from running off. Volunvoshka had no desire to hold the boy in his talons the entire time until the egg was returned.

He landed on his back legs with a thump and let out a roar to let the Wizard know he had arrived.

Sacha, securely held in the dragon's left front talon, was both frightened and relieved to be out of the sky. Once the dragon had gone aloft with him he had been afraid to move, terrified that he would slip from the grasp of this immense dragon and fall to his death. He could not imagine what the dragon wanted with him. When he saw how far they had come, his heart sank and he wondered how any one would ever find him – if he lived through whatever it was they wanted of him. The chances of rescue looked nonexistent.

Illya came out on the small porch. "What do you want? The Master says to tell you that he is busy."

"I've brought him a hostage to hold for me," said the Ice dragon. He held out the claw holding Sacha so that Illya could see him.

"Where did he come from?" Illya asked. "I thought that you had cleared out all of the people here!"

"St Petersburg," said the dragon. "Now fetch your Master, boy, before I turn you into an icicle!"

Illya turned on his heel and hurried back into the house.

Sacha desperately wanted to know what was going to happen to him. But this dragon terrified him. He was not friendly like Lakota. His voice was harsh; his tone impatient and disagreeable.

The Wizard came out next, scowling. "What have you done, dragon? Whose child is this?"

179

"You will not recover my egg so I took matters into my own talons!" Volunvoshka snarled. "This child belongs to a house where people regularly visit the place the egg is kept. Their young one for my young one! I left a note saying that the egg should be returned or the boy dies."

Karachev surveyed Sacha, noting the boy's shabby clothes and dirty hands. "This boy is a serf, dragon. No one will care if he disappears. You might as well eat him and be done with it."

Sacha seeing his death in front of him, yelled, "I am NOT a serf! I am Count Alexander Ivanovich Kustodiev!"

"And you dress like a peasant because –" Karachev said silkily.

"My sister, Countess Tatiana Ivanova Kustodieva, insists that I wear old clothes for gardening. It is my hobby," he said, praying that he would be believed. "She says that I have ruined too many of my good clothes by digging in the dirt."

Karachev looked closer. The clothes were not as bad as he first thought. They had been of good quality at one time. He could not know that Sacha wore Evgeny's cast–offs. And he had heard of stranger hobbies amongst the aristocracy.

"Very well," he said at last. "And you want me to do what with this infant Count?" he asked the dragon.

"Bespell him so that he cannot run off."

"Put him down," the magician directed. As Volun-voshka complied, Karachev waved his hand and a collar, such as Illya wore, appeared in his hand. He bent to Sacha and fastened this about his neck.

"Hear me, young Count," he said in a threatening voice. "This is the exact obedience collar as my slave wears. He has found out – quite painfully – that to try to run away whilst wearing it is impossible. So unless you wish to suffer horrible pain I suggest that you do not try to leave this clearing. For now I will put you in my slave's charge."

He motioned for Illya, who had remained on the porch, to come forward.

Karachev took Sacha by the shoulder and roughly shoved him towards Illya. "Here, boy, here is some company for you. Find out if he can sing or play or has any useful skills

180

at all. Being a damned aristocrat I doubt if he can do anything other than eat his silly head off."

The Wizard then turned to the dragon. "You and I have much to discuss," he said, sneering. "For I doubt you've thought this little scheme of yours through to its logical conclusion!"

18

Beneath the Dome

Even Anatoly screamed in terror as they hurtled towards the earth. The fall was faster than Lakota's flight and the force of the wind the dragon's fall created was enough to almost cause the riders to be torn from the saddle.

Simon, in the front nearest Lakota's neck, could not even try to get his wand. It would probably be ripped from his hand.

With a great effort he put out a hand and shouted "*Tarde!*" in Wizard's Latin, hoping that the lack of a focus stone would not impede the force of the spell. The fact that he spoke the spell aloud made it all the more powerful.

But it worked. Immediately the headlong fall slowed. Simon was then able to take out his wand, and pulling energy from the ley lines he felt beneath him, he commanded "*Regio mollis!*"

It was as if a giant hand reached up put of the earth and took Lakota in its palm. With lightning repeatedly flashing over their heads, they were deposited gently in a wide meadow.

"Dome!" Lakota gasped as soon as they landed.

With his wand Simon pointed at the earth and then drew it in an arc high above them. A violet curtain followed his wand , making a dome over their heads. The curtain followed the wand to make a complete circle, and left the dragon and his riders enclosed in what appeared to be a giant, upside-down violet bowl.

Simon was out of the saddle and on the ground as soon as this task was completed. He went at once to Lakota's side.

The dragon had drawn his wing up against his side as soon as they landed. He was moaning a little in pain, but spread his wing back out when Simon asked him to show it.

The very end of the wing had been struck – like a bird's wings, this part of the dragon wing was known as the fore edge and the first several sections of membrane and hollow bone were called the primaries. Lakota's first primary was blackened and shredded.

Simon drew in his breath sharply. It was a terrible injury.

"It hurts!" said Lakota, his voice full of tears.

"I can give you something for the pain," said Simon, and raised his wand. All Wizards were taught simple pain spells for use when a Wizard Healer was not immediately available. He pointed the wand at the injured wing and a violet light wrapped itself around the wound. This served to immediately deaden the pain.

"That's better!" said Lakota gratefully.

Anatoly had helped Tatya slide from the saddle. They both looked about them in wonder at the dome. Outside it rain had begun to fall heavily and yet they were as dry as if they were in a house. Thunder boomed and lightning flashed almost constantly. It was a very bad storm.

"What is this thing?" Anatoly whispered to Tatya, not wanting to interrupt Simon's examination of Lakota's injuries. He also reached inside his coat and took out Vron and placed the Tom on the ground. Janus had jumped from the front of Simon's flying suit as soon as he had touched the ground. She now came up to Vron and touched noses with him.

Simon overheard the question. "This is a dragon dome," he explained. "It protects the dragon from lightning."

"Too bad you didn't think of this when we were up there in danger of crashing to the earth!" said Anatoly.

"It can't be done in the air," Simon returned ruefully. "It has to be firmly attached to the earth because the energy to make it has to be drawn form the earth. No one has yet devised a protection for the air – it would have to be something like a giant soap bubble. We do have a deflector shield, but it doesn't cover every where it would need to."

"Is he badly hurt?" Tatya asked anxiously. The dragon was standing with his head down, nose touching the ground and his eyes closed. He held out the injured wing awkwardly.

"It's a bad injury. The nerves in the wings are extremely sensitive and any injury causes a great deal of pain," Simon answered. As he spoke he was removing various flat packages from the breast harness.

183

"Could I have my harness off, please?" asked Lakota faintly.

Simon did this quickly, with a simple spell, disregarding the tangles it fell into. "I've got Stuart's medical book here," he told the dragon."There's an entire section on dragon medicine."

Simon silently blessed his brother for supplying him with this book. As the book was magiced, it opened at one to the chapters that dealt with draconic injuries. And it showed Simon the section on "lightning strikes".

There were two spells and two potions – one for the dragon to drink and the other to make a salve to spread on the injury. And reading them, Simon was relieved to find that all the ingredients he would need were amongst the medical supplies and in the new traveling Wizards' kit with which his great uncle Lyonshall had gifted him.

"We might as well set up the tent," Simon told Anatoly and Tatya. "We won't be going any where for a while. I have to make some potions and quickly before he goes into shock." Already the blue dragon was a paler shade of blue – not a good sign.

"I'll set up the tent," Anatoly offered, and Tatya timidly offered to help Simon with the potions.

"I would rather you take care of the egg," said Simon and briefly told her how to set it in the cradle and check the wrappings. "And don't worry, *Mam'selle* Tatya," he added reassuringly, "as soon as Lakota is comfortable and the storm ends I will do what we call a finding message to the Ice dragon and let him know that we are on our way with the egg so that he will not harm Sacha."

Outside it was getting darker and darker as the storm intensified. The wind had risen and they could hear it shrieking around the dome. It appeared as if this was not just one storm but perhaps a band of them. At one point marble-sized hail came down, making a noise like pebbles falling on glass. But even this did not disturb the dome. Inside they were safe and dry.

As Anatoly put up the small tent Tatya carefully placed the egg in the cradle. It was still quite warm to the touch and the cloths protecting it were also warm.

She had never seem anything like it . It was really rather beautiful – a crystalline white streaked with brilliant silver. But it was a lot smaller than she had expected. Dragons must be quite little when they first hatched.

Anatoly finished with the tent and joined her. "Look at the size of that tent!" he said in amazement. "From the outside it looks scarcely large enough for two children! But on the inside it is bigger than many drawing rooms and is furnished! There is even a kitchen and a washroom! And it was all folded flat! Truly , magic is a wonderful thing!"

And they watched in amazement as Simon brewed the potions. Ingredients flew out of his bags. The bottles unstopped themselves and measured in silver measuring spoons to dumped into mortar and pestles or beakers which hung in the air. The pestle ground the ingredients by itself A mage fire burned beneath a beaker, heating the contents, while an animated spoon stirred it at just the right speed.

It seemed no time at all before two vessels were ready – one with a green liquid brew, and the other with a thick unguent that smelt rather enticingly of herbs. Simon stirred honey into the drink as the book directed, to make it more palatable to Lakota, and held the basin while the dragon drank.

In order to drink from a small basin Lakota folded his tongue and used it as if it were a straw. His colour, which had steadily worsened, began to come back all at once, for the drink, combined with a spell, was very efficacious.

Simon then very carefully and tenderly spread the ointment over the wound, all the while telling Lakota how brave he was and how this would help his pain and speed up the regeneration of the membrane. Lakota could not help but wince – even the gentlest touch hurt the raw, torn skin. But he *was* very brave and bore it as best he could. But both he and Simon were glad when the wound was well covered.

"I'm sorry, Simon," the dragon said as soon as he could speak. "I was not paying attention to the weather!"

"It's not your fault!" Simon insisted. "It's just as much my job to keep an eye out for thunderstorms! I'm the one who is supposed to keep rear watch!"

He put down the empty vessel and began to stroke the dragon's eye ridges. Lakota sighed and laid his head on

Simon's shoulder. Long used to this expression of draconic affection Simon braced himself and continued his soothing stroking.

"How long before he can fly again?" inquired Anatoly, coming up behind Simon. He had not understood what they had been saying to one another for both Simon and Lakota had spoken in English.

"About a fortnight, if the ointment does its job regenerating the membrane," Simon answered.

Anatoly stared at him. "*Regenerate!* Do you mean that the skin will grow back?" he said incredulously. He had seen the injury and thought that it would be a miracle if Lakota ever flew again.

"Oh, yes," Simon assured him. "If I was a trained veterinary Wizard Healer I could regenerate it right now. But that's specialized training and I don't have the right magical energies for healing. All I can do is brew the potions which will begin the process and help it along."

"I wish Stuart was here," said Lakota wistfully.

"He's only a first year medical student, Lakota," Simon reminded the dragon. "I doubt he's studied regeneration yet. Stuart is my younger brother – he's a student of Wizard Healing at Edinburgh University." he explained for Anatoly's benefit.

"Will we be able to continue?" Tatya, having made certain the egg was warm, now joined them.

"Lakota needs to rest for a day or two," said Simon. "His colour is still not good and the potion he drank will make him a little sleepy."As if on cue Lakota yawned, showing huge, very white and clean teeth. "I think I will lay down," he said sleepily.

He removed his head from Simon's shoulder and carefully lay on his right side – it was the left wing that had been struck by the lightning.

Within minutes of laying his head on the grass he was asleep.

"As soon as the storm passes I will perform the spell that will send a message to the Ice dragon," Simon promised again.

"But how ever will you find him?" Tatya asked despairingly. Each moment that passed increased her anxiety about her brother.

"The message he wrote us is not in ink, but in dragon ichor. My message will sniff out the owner of that blood," Simon was quite confident that he could reach the Ice dragon.

"Magic is a wonderful thing," Anatoly said, sounding as wistful as had Lakota longing for Stuart. "The way you brought us safely to the earth! And all these things flying about and opening and pouring them selves! It's just —!" Words failed him. "To be able to do that!"

"But until the dragon has recovered, how will we proceed?" Tatya wanted to know.

"I daresay we will have to walk," Simon answered.

"I tell you, he took her four times! And never have I heard a woman scream like that!" Yuri still started perspiring when he thought about what he had seen last night. He now took out his handkerchief and wiped his face and patted his lips.

Evgeny had been raked over the coals by his Colonel this morning. He and Sumarokov would more than likely be posted to the ends of the earth. His Colonel had not been amused by the attempted rape. He had turned a blind eye to many of Evgeny's peccadilloes as he termed them, but this time Rostov had gone too far. He had better learn to confine his attention to women that were paid to put up with him.

When his father had first come to the barracks to see him Evgeny had stared when the old man had asked him for the name of a brothel that catered to unusual tastes. Evgeny knew for a fact that the elder Rostov had frequented the same place for a number of years. In fact, his father had taken Evgeny there on his fourteenth birthday, telling him it was time he became a man. But that house of ill-repute had proven too tame for Evgeny's tastes and he sought out other dens of pleasure where one could be more creative and a blind eye was turned to rough play, as long as one paid up.

He had listened to his father tell of what he had seen though the peep hole with increasing disgust.

She should have been his to despoil! But it sounded as if the Wizard had hurt her. "Scream, did she?" he said in satisfaction. As long as someone had hurt her... "Did he injure her badly?"

"No, no! You misunderstand me!" Yuri said. "She screamed in pleasure! And I have been with enough whores to tell when pleasure is feigned! This was real, I tell you! And as what they did... I have never even imagined such things!" This was not so – he had often imagined them but had never thought to see them.

His father had always suffered from a lack of imagination, Evgeny thought sourly. A wave of intense hatred, for both the English Wizard and his cousin swept over him. How dare she reject him in favor of a foreigner – in favor of the man who had humiliated and cursed him!

For cursed Evgeny was. He had visited a whore last night and had been unable to perform. This had never before happened to him. He had taken out his feelings on the prostitute by beating her badly. The same thing happened with the next two trollops he tried to bed. The last bawdy house he visited was of a higher type and when the little trollop screamed as he began to hit her, the very large man employed to keep order had thrown him from the premises.

He listened with interest to the rest of his father's tale. He had little interest in Sacha or the egg. What interested him deeply was the fact that his cousin had run off with the Wizard and another man.

"After what I saw her do last night she's probably taking both of them at once!" Yuri said bitterly. "Had I known what she was like in bed I would have had her myself long ago! We could have shared her!" He licked his lips yet again. "I must go now." Evgeny had given him the name of a place to go for those with depraved tastes and he could barely wait. Evgeny had said the women there would do anything one desired for enough money and Yuri's *rubles* were burning a hole in his pocket. Three times with Ekaterina last night had barely whetted his appetite. And his first act of the morning had been to visit his favorite whore house. He still craved more. All he could think about was what he had seen. He had not even gone into the office that day, more intent on seeking his pleasure.

Evgeny hardly noticed him leaving. He though back to what his Colonel had said that morning. The Colonel thought

188

that perhaps Evgeny should go on a protracted leave – perhaps a long sojourn in the country. Evgeny had scorned the idea, not wishing to leave the fleshpots and gambling dens of the city.

But now the idea seemed attractive. He would go after the Wizard and his cousin. The Wizard had to have a weakness and he would find it out. That was the way to defeat one's enemies. And he would have his revenge upon his cousin as well. Screamed in pleasure had she? Pleasure was not what she would scream from when he had her! His thin lips twisted cruelly as he thought of the painful and humiliating things he would do to her. Perhaps he would keep her in his rooms, naked, for his friends to use. Oddly, he also wanted her to beg him to take her as Yuri said she had begged the Wizard. He would use her until he tired of her and then drop her in the lowest sort of whore house.

It would seem forever before he could take his revenge.

19

The Message

Karachev was more than a little annoyed with Volunvoshka. The Ice dragon had not only foisted a boy into him – another no doubt useless mouth to feed – but close questioning revealed that the dragon had not provided for any communication to arrange an exchange for the return of the egg.

Not for the first time the Wizard was sorry that he had involved the Ice dragons in his plans. It had seemed beautiful and simple at the time – use the fearsome creatures to clear out the mountains without the expenditure of magical energies. Karachev's magical energies were difficult to gather, for he was a blood mage and a necromancer. Much of his power came from blood sacrifice, forcing demons to his will, or raising the spirits of the dead. These last two rituals were not something lightly undertaken. Some rituals took weeks to prepare and were complicated indeed. Blood magic was the easier but in these modern times it was becoming more difficult to find victims that might be sacrificed with impunity. The Secret Police seemed to be everywhere and if too many people went missing, they began to push their long noses in where they were not wanted. Karachev had had to leave Taganrog for this very reason.

He could not believe the stupidity of the Ice dragon in not leaving instructions behind – just a threatening note.

"How do you expect then to know how to communicate with you?" he asked Volunvoshka, later the same day that Sacha had been brought to him. The Ice dragon had been angered when Karachev criticized his actions earlier and had flown off in a rage. It was not until he had had time to think about the Wizard's comments that the dragon returned and this time listened.

"You shall have to return to St Petersburg and leave another note," the Wizard told him. "The people holding the egg need a place to exchange the boy for the egg. Knowing how dear most people hold their children, this boy's family is

190

probably frantic and all eagerness to return your egg. If as he claims, he is indeed a Count, that argues some influence, perhaps, with the Court. Do you have any idea who holds your egg?"

"No," said Volunvoshka sullenly. He did not appreciate being told that he had made an error in judgment. It stung bitterly to realize that he had made such a mistake. "I only know that people from the boy's house visit where it is kept. I could not see my egg but I could sense it. I had to keep well up in the air so that I would not be seen until it was time to snatch the boy."

"And who wrote the note for you?" Karachev inquired.

Volunvoshka bristled. "I wrote it myself!" he hissed. "With my talon and my blood! Reading and writing are skills I acquired long ago – they are very useful if one has to deal with human beings." His tone implied that humans were far inferior to dragon-kind.

"Then you shall not find it difficult to write another," said the Wizard sarcastically. "I shall tell you what you must say."

But the second note was never written. For on a strong breeze, straight at Volunvoshka, came a very small dragon. It was not even as large as one of the Ice dragon's ears. It came to a stop in front of Volunvoshka's face and hung in the air. And surprisingly, it was not a real dragon at all but was made of paper.

"What -!" exclaimed Karachev. He snatched the paper dragon from the air. "This reeks of magic!"

In his hand the paper dragon unfolded to a flat sheet of parchment. In the Cyrillic alphabet, in a very fine hand, it read:

"We have the egg and wish to exchange it for the boy. Do not harm him. The egg is well tended. Please indicate a time and place for the exchange. The map on the other side of this letter shows our present location. Please return this letter with your terms."

Karachev quickly turned it over and saw a map appear underneath his disbelieving eyes.

"This is impossible!" he muttered. "This had to have been made by a Wizard – or at the very least a talented Witch! There is no one capable of doing something like this in all of Russia!" Except for himself, of course.

"What does it say?" Volunvoshka interrupted. He did not care who or what had made it.

Karachev turned it back over and read it aloud. "According to this map whoever he may be is halfway here," he added.

He turned the parchment over again and studied the map, frowning slightly. "I don't like this," he said at last. " I am one of the last Wizards in Russia. The power raised to fight Napoleon nearly twenty years ago killed most of them – for they were elderly to begin with. There are a few doddering old fools left in the Caucasus, in the Cheroskiy and the Verkhoyansk mountains... but Old Aleksandrov, who lived in the Ozhugezhurs, died last year," he went on as if talking to himself. "And the Witches left are pitiful creatures such as Baba Yaga – no match for me." Could they have gotten one of these pathetic old nonentities to help them? No, there wasn't enough time for that – unless... His eyes narrowed as he thought hard. "Unless Nicholas had already found himself a tame Wizard – perhaps my old rival – Tenisheva! Well, he's learned a trick or two since I knew him if this is his work!" he said, in reluctant admiration. "This is a neat little bit of magic!"

Volunvoshka had listened to this soliloquy with increasing impatience. "I will meet them tomorrow," he thundered. "I care not if there is a Wizard."

"You fool!" said Karachev in scorn. "This Wizard is your enemy! You could be flying into a trap! We don't know why they took your egg! It could be that they have need of a very dead adult Ice dragon or perhaps they think that removing you will put paid to my occupation of these mountains. No, this needs time for study." He folded the parchment and tapped it against his teeth thoughtfully. "We will meet them in a fortnight's time," he said at last. "We will meet them at –" He unfolded the map again and held it up the Ice dragon's snout. With one long finger he pointed at the map. "Here, near the Volga."

192

He would not listen to Volunvoshka's sputtering and increasingly hostile protests, but instead produced a quill and an ink bottle from the air and scribbled a reply. "I will accompany you," he said as they watched the paper fold itself into the shape of a dragon again. Karachev held it on the palm of his hand and watched as it raised its wings and launched itself into the air. "If it is Tenisheva he will need to be eliminated." He gave a hard laugh that held no mirth. "*Anyone* who thinks to thwart my plans will need to be eliminated."

Sacha had followed Illya into the house. He noticed at once that the older boy wore a sullen look and glared at Sacha as if he had arrived at the house just to make his, Illya's, life miserable.

Sacha was a naturally friendly soul and had no wish to be at odds with his fellow prisoner. Therefore he said "I can do my share of the work."

"What do you, an aristocrat, know about work?" said Illya scornfully. "I have enough to do around here without waiting on a Count!"

"I may be a Count, but my sister and I are quite poor since my father was sent to Siberia, and we live with horrible relatives who treat us like servants," Sacha said frankly. "My sister works as a maid and I work in the stables and in the yard. I only said gardening was my hobby so that man would not give me to the dragon to eat," he added.

Illya looked at him doubtfully.

"I am used to working hard," said Sacha. "Won't it be easier for you if I help you? I can chop wood and haul water and clean things. Many hands make light work!"

"That's true," said Illya grudgingly. "What did you say your name was – or do I have to address you as Count whatever your name is?"

"No, call me Sacha! Sacha Ivanovich. Nobody calls me Count Kustodiev," was the reply, with a friendly smile lighting Sacha's face.

"I'm Illya Timofeiovich," Illya returned, beginning to think it might not be such a bad thing to have this little aristocrat here. At least it would be some one to talk to. Karachev just barked orders at him.

When Sacha caught sight of the *balalaika* and expressed fervent admiration for anyone who could play and begged for a tune, Illya's disgruntlement turned to pleasure.

When the storm passed and Lakota slept Simon wrote a note on heavy parchment to the Ice dragon. This was written on an invisible desk, by an invisible hand holding a quill as Simon doubted his ability to write Cyrillic easily and legibly. He could not ask either of his companions to write it as it had to be done magically. Anatoly and Tatya watched in amazement as the letter then folded itself into the shape of a perfect little dragon and took off into the sky.

"There," said Simon. "I've instructed that note to find the dragon whose blood was on the kidnapper's note. There's a map on the reverse side to tell him where to find us. Hopefully we will hear very soon."

"But how will they know where to send it?" Tatya asked anxiously. They were in the tent, sipping a cup of tea from a pot brewed on the magical stove and eating sandwiches made from a huge ham and fresh bread that Luba had packed for them.

"If they follow my instructions and write their reply on the bottom of my letter it will return to me as would a homing pigeon."

"This is truly amazing!" said Anatoly in awe. "However did you learn all of these things? Can everyone in England do this?"

"No," said Simon, "there are many non-magical people. And as for where I learned it – the first year or so I was tutored by my father. And then I attended the Tara Druidry school until I was seventeen and then took my baccalaureate degree at Trinity in Wizardry. I spent a year and a half in America studying Dracophilology – "

"I wish," said Anatoly wistfully, "that I could do just *half* of what you can do! It must be wonderful to have such power!"

"We never think of it as power," said Simon, "for we consider that immoral and unethical. A lust for power is evil – what we would consider black magic. Magic is a tool. The three functions of magic are to produce, to protect or to

194

destroy. And White magicians such as myself take an oath NOT to destroy."

"But where does magic come from?" Anatoly persisted. "Can anyone become a Wizard?"

"Magic comes from five main sources," said Simon, seeing that they were really interested, for Tatya too was listening intently. "In the tradition I was taught, there are five sources – the energy inherent in every living thing, which through time has been gathered in to nodes, or centers; from the four elements and their creatures, and from mind magic – psychic energies."

"And the other two?" prompted Anatoly.

"Those are black sorcery – blood magic – gathered from the psychic forces of pain and death and the acts of raising demons or the spirits of the dead. Not only would an honourable Wizard never use black magic – it is punishable on pain of death to do so in the British Isles or in America." Simon continued. "And to answer your other question – no, not everyone can become a Wizard. You have to have a predilection for it – most people are born with it and when one's aura manifests itself –"

"What is that?" asked Anatoly eagerly. Tatya seemed content to just sit back and listen.

"Everyone has an aura – rather like a full body halo. And it usually becomes apparent when one is about six or so," Simon explained. "People who have the potential to become magicians have auras of blue, ranging to violet. The colour deepens from blue to violet sometimes with study and proficiency. Non-magicals have various colours of yellow. Healers, such as my brother Stuart, have green auras. Orange indicates a person who is very ill – either physically or mentally. A red aura means the use of blood magic while one never wants to see a black aura for it is the indication of the worst evil imaginable."

"Do we have auras?" Anatoly looked hopeful, rather like a very large puppy hoping for a treat. "Can you tell?"

Simon looked at them with his Othersight, expecting to find only yellow auras, but to his surprise they both glowed with steady blue lights.

"You both have the potential to learn magic!" he said in some surprise.

195

Anatoly looked as if Christmas and his name day celebration had all come at once. "Can you teach us?"

Tatya was not as sure that she wanted to learn magic and said so, doubtfully.

"It might be a good thing, *Mam'selle*, if you were to learn *defensive* magic," Simon suggested.

"To protect myself from such as my cousin?" she said eagerly. "Oh, yes! That I would like to do!" She remembered how the horrible Viktor had slammed into the wall and Evgeny had followed him. She would love to be able to do that! No one would ever be able to hurt her again and she could protect Sacha as well.

By the time that Lakota awoke, feeling hungry, Simon had, as a good teacher should, used the spell that awakened their dormant magic and taught them both to ground and shield and to make a mage light.

Evgeny had no trouble getting leave. His Colonel was glad that Rostov had taken his suggestion. Let someone else deal with him!

To Evgeny's delight Viktor was given leave as well. Viktor wanted his revenge as much as did Evgeny and they spent some time discussing just what they would do to both the Wizard and to Evgeny's cousin when they caught up with them.

Both of them had deluded themselves into thinking that it was only because the Wizard had caught them at an unguarded moment that he had been able to interrupt their attempted rape. If they stayed alert and found out his weaknesses, they could defeat him. Were not all of the Wizards and Witches in the old tales defeated by clever young heroes such as themselves?

And with many obscenities and ribald laughter they planned the vengeance they would take on Tatya. Evgeny recounted to his friend what his father had told him of the scenes through the peep hole.

"And we could have had that!" said Viktor in disgust,

"Don't worry, we will have that and more!" said Evgeny confidentially.

By the simple expedient of threatening Pavel with a drawn sword they found out in which direction the dragon had flown. People were have bound to have seen a dragon in the sky, Evgeny reasoned – it was not a sight one saw every day. They could follow their route that way.

Both his parents and his sisters were out when Evgeny visited the family home. As once again he was short of money he felt no compunction in breaking into his father's strong box and taking most of the piles of *rubles* that lay in it. His eyes gleamed as he saw the large amount of gold. Wherever had the old man come by so much money? And he had not offered to share it! That was selfish indeed.

By late afternoon they were in civilian dress, packed, mounted and ready to leave the capital. Both were well equipped with weapons, for as Viktor pointed out, if they saw the Wizard before he saw them they could disable him by shooting him.

"But only to disable," said Evgeny. "I don't want him to die quickly. In fact, I'd like to make him watch us have our fun with my dear cousin!"

Viktor agreed – it would be very amusing.

Count Pozharsky had left scarcely an hour after Lakota leaped into the sky. Since he had operatives watching the Rostov house he had no problem discerning the direction in which they were going – in point of fact he had a shrewd idea of where they would eventually end up.

The Count never mounted a horse unless he could help it. He traveled in a comfortable carriage that contained everything from a portable bar complete with several varieties of vodka to a seat that changed into a bed.

Since like most Russians he thought that the only way to travel was at top speed he made excellent time. The Imperial Seal allowed him the choice of the best horses at the various places he stopped for fresh teams. He ignored the bumps and ruts of the roads with equiamity – Russian roads were not very good. He watched the scenery flash by, with a complacent air, hands folded across his stomach.

He wanted to be there to see if all unfolded as he had hoped – and planned.

20

Magic Lessons

When the message from the kidnapper arrived Simon and Anatoly at once consulted their map. The rendezvous point was some distance from where they were now and since they had to walk it would take the better part of a week at the very least.

Tatya could not understand why the Ice dragon wanted to wait for two weeks before exchanging Sacha for the egg. She wanted her brother back as soon as possible and she thought that the Ice dragon must want the egg returned just as quickly. She fretted over the delay.

Simon had no comfort to offer her. He could not imagine why a delay had been suggested. But one thing was certain – the reply had not been written by the dragon. A human hand had penned it. The answer had been written with ink and quill, not talon and ichor. The Ice dragon had a human helper.

Simon did not spend mush time wondering about who might be helping the dragon and why. He was too concerned over Lakota, for the blue dragon, although he claimed to be hungry, only ate three of the roasted geese with cranberries that Luba had made for him. His eyes seemed glazed to Simon – a sign of fever in a dragon – and his scales were still not their normal shade. He also seemed lethargic and uninterested in what was happening around him. This was highly unlike him. Lakota was intensely curious and under ordinary circumstances would have been asking all manner of questions and been interested in the fact that both Tatya and Anatoly were having magic lessons. When told of this he only said "That's nice," and slipped back into a doze.

Of course, Simon realized that some of this was due to the potion he had taken. Sleep was necessary for the regeneration process and he would be in less pain if he were unconscious, but Simon could not help but worry. He wished that there was a draconic veterinarian available – many veterinarians at home specialized in dragon health – but the chance of finding one here was nonexistent. He would have to trust in the book.

The potion had to be repeated every twelve hours and the unguent reapplied every six hours until regeneration began. The book claimed that this would begin within twenty-four to forty-eight hours. After that the potion had to be administered daily, with frequent applications of the salve until regeneration was complete.

Not only did the book advise against moving the injured dragon for the space of at least a day after the initial treatment, but all of Simon's experience with dragons told him that his dragon friend was better off resting as much as possible and eating lightly.

Simon had restored the dragon dome once he had sent and received the message, for the sky was still threatening and thunder rumbled in the still, heavy air. They were glad of this after a simple supper of soup and bread from Luba's generously packed baskets, for the heavens split asunder once more, with brilliant jagged bolts of cloud to ground lightning. One huge blue charge split into three descending shafts that struck the dome. But it ran harmlessly into the earth.

Tatya shrieked – she had been afraid of lightning since she was a little girl and had seen a barn struck at Mikhailovskoe and the animals in it all killed by fire. Somehow she found herself clinging to Simon, burying her face in his shoulder as shudders shook her. She scarcely noticed as he stroked her hair as if she were Holly and whispered reassurances that the dome was entirely lightning proof and no harm could come to them as long as they stayed in it. She only noticed that suddenly she felt safe and protected.

As hail began to fall, she pulled away from him, feeling slightly ashamed of herself, and could not meet his eyes. Making light of her distress, Simon suggested he give them another magic lesson to take their minds off the violence of the storm.

With one last look at Lakota – who had slept through the lightning strike – they entered the tent and sat around the table. The cats had already retreated to the tent the moment the thunder began rolling.

199

In the old tradition in which Simon had learned his magic – and so it had been since the time of Merlin – beginning magicians first learned the rituals of the magic Circle, the pentagrams and the cardinal points. But in the last twenty years a new theory of teaching magic had been evolved – that of practical magic, in which the pupil learned to do things that were of practical use first and when a good groundwork in this had been laid, then the rituals were learned. Nowadays, with all of the new advances and discoveries in magical practice, only great workings required specific rituals. With adult pupils such as he had now, Simon though it best to use the newer teaching method. It would allow them a sense of accomplishment that memorizing rituals would not.

Accordingly, he taught them the simple charm of calling an object to them.

He used two cut crystals from his Wizard's kit. Since crystal easily absorbed energies they were the ideal medium to use for beginners. The charm was a simple *advenire* in Wizard's Latin, but the concentration needed and the feeling of the energies in the object that was the difficult part.

It was always interesting to any teacher to see how his pupils responded to his teachings and learned from them. Anatoly was an eager pupil – almost too eager. He wanted to rush in and *do* before he sufficiently understood what he heard. Tatya was more cautious. She wished a full, complete understanding of theory before she actually did anything.

Before the evening had ended they both could call a crystal to them from a distance of six inches. Tatya's crystal actually rose up an inch off the table, while Anatoly's stubbornly insisted on skidding along the table top. The two cats watched with interest. Neither one of them cared for the storm and found that watching the humans stopped them thinking about it.

Both pupil and teacher were exhausted. Simon had done quite a bit of magic that day, and as he pointed out to his pupils, magic had its price. Beginners always found it fatiguing. It was nowhere as easy as it looked.

Simon chose to sleep not in of the beds in the tent but out under the dome beside Lakota. He would have to make a fresh potion tonight for the dragon to drink – it had to be

200

made fresh each time, according to the book. But that would be several hours away and in the meantime he could get some much needed rest. In the morning they would make Lakota some strengthening broth. Anatoly had already offered to take out his gun and get a brace of birds for the broth

The egg was being watched by Tatya. Simon had resepelled the coverings to keep it at the proper temperature. However, he was concerned that it seemed suddenly to be growing harder. He did not want it to hatch under these circumstances. If Lakota felt well enough tomorrow, perhaps he could talk to the egg. A dragonet usually had a good idea of how long it would be before it was hatched.

A hatchling would be a rather large problem on their journey. The newly hatched dragonet, after it's first feeding of meats needed to eat it's shell for the calcium it contained, had a voracious appetite and ate almost every hour. A hatchling could double in size the first week. They would spend all of their time finding food for and feeding a ravenous dragonet, and have no time to travel. The dragonet would have to walk, for it would not be able to fly for almost a year. And that would increase its hunger.

To feed a growing hatchling as they traveled to the *rendezvous* with Sacha's abductor would be a task of Herculean proportions. Dragonets were not only fed vast quantities of cooked meat but were also given blends of milk, grain and honey or bread and milk four times daily. Greens and other vegetables were also fed as were fruits. A healthy dragon ate a varied diet.

When Simon gathered some blankets and a pillow and went to bed, Lakota looked at him sleepily and said "I'm glad you're here with me," and lifted his right wing for Simon to crawl under. With thoughts of Lakota's health, of the dragonet, of his new pupils and of their coming journey swirling in his mind, Simon at last fell into a fitful sleep.

Sacha had observed many things since he had been brought to this place. Illya had told him they were high in the *Uralsky Knrebet*. Sacha was not exactly sure where this might be as his geography lessons had been conducted under a blanket with an elderly book smuggled from the nursery, lit a single flickering candle. His sister had always been afraid that Ekaterina would see the light and demand to know what they were doing, wasting a candle.

Illya's notions of place and distance were not much better. All of his education had been of cloth and finance. He had the vague notion that they were at least one thousand miles from St Petersburg.

Such a distance to Sacha was nearly incomprehensible. And this place was entirely alien to anything he had ever known.

He knew that he had been born in the country and lived there until he was five but all of his real memories were of the city. Sometimes when Tatya spoke longingly of Mikhailovskoe a vague something stirred in his mind as if remembrance were struggling to come to the surface, but it never coalesced into any recognizable form.

To be so lonely, to see no other dwellings, to see no other people – it was all strange and new and a little frightening. The most frightening thing of all was the collar around his neck. Like Illya had, he tried to find a way to remove it. But unlike Illya, Sacha did not test the limits of his imprisonment. He was too used to being punished and had no desire to be beaten by someone else besides Uncle Yuri. Something in Karachev's voice and eyes had told Sacha that the Wizard meant what he said.

A little porch in the back of the house served Illya as a bedroom and it was here that he conducted Sacha when Karachev ordered then to bed. Illya had been pleased with Sacha – the younger boy had fetched wood for the stove, chopped more wood for the morning, scrubbed the dishes and swept the floor – all without being told and had done a good job as well, without complaint. After supper, when Karachev brusquely ordered Illya to play, Sacha had joined in the songs with a sweet soprano while Karachev watched them with hooded eyes. The Wizard, since that first night when he captured Illya, had never praised or criticized Illya's musical talents. But tonight he said "More," in an almost pleasant voice. Usually he said "Stop when I tell you to stop," rather nastily.

It was late before he let the boys go to their beds. "Enough !" he said abruptly, and waved them away. Sacha's last glimpse of him was his hawk like profile bending over a huge tome, a great shadow flickering against the opposite wall, cast by the firelight.

As they were preparing for bed – which consisted of each of them wrapping himself in a blanket and laying down upon the floor – Sacha asked Illya "Is he a good Wizard?"

Illya had blown out the single tallow candle that Karachev allowed him. He gave a short humorless laugh. "Good? He's the worst of the worst! I've seen him raise demons! He murders people and drinks their souls! I've had to bury dead bodies of the people he's killed!"

This was said in a whisper, for there was always the possibility that Karachev would punish them for talking. As the Wizard could do this without leaving his chair, Illya wanted to take as little chance he dared.

"The Wizard I know," Sacha inched closer to Illya and lowered his voice further, "is good. He does *White* magic," he added, remembering what Simon had told him.

"You know a Wizard? And he has not enslaved you?" said Illya in disbelief.

"I told you – he is a *good* Wizard," Sacha repeated. "He gives me presents and has let me ride on his dragon. I think that he will probably come and rescue me," he added hopefully, although he had no notion how this could be accomplished. He had a vague idea of the two Wizards fighting over him, with a very ill-informed idea of a Wizard's duel or perhaps the two dragons would fight high in the air.

Illya thought his new companion was somewhat naïve. In the last year in Karachev's service, he had come to believe that there was nothing and no one that could defeat or even upset the black Wizard.

"You may be rescued when they return the dragon's egg – I know that much. Someone took an egg from that great Ice dragon and he wants it back. That' why he took you – to exchange for the egg," he said on a large yawn.

Sacha was puzzled by this. He knew of no egg. He wanted to ask more questions but gentle snores told him that Illya had fallen into sleep. His questions must wait for the morning.

Count Pozharsky, in his well equipped *lineika,* made very good time. As he pretty well knew where he was going he left the tedium of planning the trip to his coachman. Accustomed to the road conditions, he ate an excellent lunch of cold chicken, caviar on *blini,* and a cherry vodka. In spite of the sway and lurching of the coach he took out a book of the poems of Alexander Pushkin – it was a copy of *Ruslan and Ludmilla.* He soon became immersed in this. His mind was tranquil and his soul satisfied. Once again his plans had come to fruition and he had been able to serve the Czar. He would be well rewarded.

Evgeny and Viktor had been fortunate as well. Many people had seen the dragon's shadow pass over head – it was not easy to see Lakota against the deep blue sky of summer. But his shadow was a different matter. If the weather remained fine the two Hussars would have a clear trail to follow. With Evgeny's stolen cash they had no problem getting the best horses at the various places they stopped when a change of mounts became necessary. It also proved necessary to have more than a little vodka at each stop and by the time they finally put up for the night they were quite well to live and took to their bed with a barmaid for company. They were delighted to find, that as drunk as they no doubt were, that the Wizard's impotency spell had worn off. The barmaid, a lusty young woman, was delighted, too. She was even more pleased when, slipping from bed after they had done with her, she found Evgeny's purse of pilfered loot carelessly deposited on the carved bureau. She helped herself to a good portion of the contents while Viktor and Evgeny lay in a drunken stupor, for they had consumed even more vodka both during and after their throes of passion.

As so often happens after a violent storm, the next day dawned bright and sunny. It was a perfect summer day; the temperature and humidity moderated by the tempest of the day before.

Simon awoke a little after dawn, the early light making it rather difficult to sleep. He was the only one awake – even Lakota still slept. Both the cats had slept in the tent.

Simon examined the dragon's wing as soon as he rose. It still looked bad, but already seemed less raw. Right after

204

breakfast would be time for another potion and the salve could be reapplied then as well.

The first thing he would do, though, was take down the dome. If they were to stay here today, they should move the tent from the middle of what Simon suspected was a hay field and perhaps move it nearer to the trees. If Lakota were still feverish he would probably prefer to be in the shade as well. Right now it was no doubt cool, but the advance of the day might bring heat. They needed to find a source of water as well.

Simon got out his wand and with a single sweeping motion, and a silent "*diffugere*" dispersed the dome.

And to his surprise, he was not alone.

For there, in a solid circle about him where the edges of the dome had stood, were white- clad bowmen, all with long bows of ivory, notched, with silver-tipped arrows pointing at him. They wore grim expressions.

And they were Elves.

21

Yasnaya Polyana

Simon straightened up slowly, allowing his wand hand to drop by his side. These Elves did not look friendly. On the contrary, they looked as if they would just as soon shoot him where he stood. Simon had enough experience with Elves to know that before he could raise his wand and silently speak an incantation, he would be full of arrows. Elfin arrows had a magic of their own and always found their mark. They flew truer and faster than other arrows and even the greatest of human Wizards had no defense against them. The best thing to do was to show the Elves that he was not hostile and meant no harm.

The Elf who appeared to be the leader now demanded, in Russian, "Who are you and why do you do magic so near to our home?" He was slightly taller and looked to be older than the others, with silver hair that flowed to his shoulders. It was tucked behind his pointed ears and a silver coronet with an amethyst in the center held his hair back from his forehead. Under the soaring brows his eyes were large and green and angry.

The other five Elves with him were younger, but, like him, they were garbed in a white silken version of Russian peasant dress of high-collared shirt, baggy trousers and impossibly shining knee high boots into which the trousers were tucked. The shirts and trousers both had bands of beautiful embroidery in coloured silks, metallic threads and small gemstones, about the neck, cuffs, along the front closure and down the outside leg of the trousers. They all wore embroidered belts as well. Each wore a dagger with intricate silver handles set with gems at the belt, and several wore embroidered bags slung over one of their shoulders. Even their quivers for the silver-tipped arrows were heavily embroidered.

Simon bowed low, and laid his wand upon the ground as he did so. "My compliments to you and yours," he said pleasantly, addressing his remarks to the elder Elf. He spoke

Russian, as they did. "I am indeed sorry if I worked my magic near your home. But I had little choice – my dragon was struck by lightning and injured. I had to tend him."

The sharp green eyes had not missed the bulk of Lakota sleeping in the background. "What sort of a dragon is that?" he demanded suspiciously. He had not lowered his bow, not loosened the bow string, with its arrow ready for flight. The other younger Elves copied him.

"He is an American dragon," answered Simon, wondering if these Elves even knew anything about America.

They did not, for the elder Elf growled, "Do not feed me your tales, Sorcerer! Tell me what I want to know or else you shall die – and the dragon with you."

It was at this moment that the sun rose above the trees and shone directly in Simon's face. The star that Oberon had placed upon his forehead, flared and a young, golden-haired Elf standing by the elder Elf gave a gasp. "Silverhair! He wears the mark of favor! See the star upon his brow!"

"What nonsense is this?" growled his elder. "Stories from our ancestors' time! You spend too much time amongst those dusty scrolls, Greenleaf. Little wonder your skills with the bow are not as good as they should be !"

The younger Elf flushed and looked shame-faced, but nonetheless insisted, "You may ask the Elders if you doubt me, but that is the mark of favor used in the Eld days when we had dealings with humans."

Silverhair looked somewhat disconcerted, as if surprised his junior would dare to speak so. Once again he turned to Simon. "Is this true, Sorcerer? Do you have Elfin favor? And if so, who has so honored you?", his tone implied that so honoring Simon had obviously been a mistake.

"I bear the mark of Oberon's favor," Simon answered.

"Oberon!" said Greenleaf excitedly, lowering his bow. "That is a name from our mythic history! Elf King of France and the Isles to the West!"

"Do not lower your bow!" said Silverhair sharply.

"I come from the Isles of the West," said Simon, "From Ireland. King Oberon asked me to seek out the Elves of Russia." He directed his remarks to the one called Silverhair. This Elf was the one he had to convince. The younger Elf, Greenleaf, was ready to accept his word, as were at least two of the others. Save for Silverhair, they were all very young – amongst humans they would probably all be counted as adolescents. Simon guessed that this might very well be a training mission where the older experienced Elf taught his juniors the skills they needed to know in hunting and scouting. The bags several of them wore were more than likely game bags.

It was at this moment that Lakota stirred and woke up. Since he was one of the fortunate few who instantly wake up he took the situation in at a glance and said "Why are you threatening us with those bows? We are Elf friends!" The start shone brightly on his forehead as well.

"See! See! The dragon bears the mark too!" said Greenleaf excitedly. This time he was careful to keep his bow high. "You see it too, do you not, Evenstar?" he asked of the Elf standing beside him.

This Elf was a dark haired young woman, tough and fit and looking far more warrior-like than did Greenleaf, who had a scholarly look about him.

"I see it too," she admitted, "And it is true that I have heard tales of this mark from my Grandsire. But that was long ago and far away. We have no reason to trust the word of a Sorcerer. Our experience with Sorcerers has been unfortunate."

"That was almost one thousand years ago!" Greenleaf said impatiently. He began to lower his bow once again, but a speaking glance from Silverhair changed his mind for him.

"What more might I do to prove my honorable intentions?" Simon asked. "I give you my word –"

"Your word means naught to us, Sorcerer!" Silverhair interrupted grimly. "My people trusted a sorcerer once and it led to the destruction of our homes and caused us to flee for our very lives! We will take you to the Lady – she will be able to judge your heart."

"I should tell you – there are more of us," said Simon carefully. "We have four companions – a man, a woman and two cats. They still sleep in the tent."

"Wake them then," Silver hair directed. "If this dragon matters to you there will be no treachery. Else he dies."

Simon went into the tent and a few moments later emerged with a yawning Anatoly and Tatya, looking frightened and clutching Vron to her breast. Janus trotted out and looked at the Elves in pleasure.

"Oberon will be pleased!" she said to no one in particular.

Silverhair would not allow then to pack up, but told two young male Elves, Redberry and Brightwing, to guard the tent and their other possessions. That left him, Greenleaf, Evenstar and another young female Elf called Goldflower to accompany their prisoners.

"We shall take you to our home, *Yasnaya Polyana*, to be judged by the Lady," Silverhair said. "But you must be blindfolded, for it would not do for outsiders to see the way in to our secret places."

At a brusque nod from him, Redberry and Brightwing laid aside their bows and stepped forward with bits of cloth they withdrew from the game bags. These would have ordinarily been used to wrap the game they caught, and like everything else of Elven manufacture were far too fine for the purpose intended.

Since when he woke them Simon had warned them to submit to everything the Elves asked, Anatoly and Tatya accepted the blindfolds with good grace. Even Lakota and Janus allowed it, but until Janus explained the necessity to him in Cat, Vron protested, hissing and slashing with his claws. He finally compiled, but only because Tatya carried him. Janus rode on Simon's shoulder.

Each of the humans was led by an Elf. Silverhair himself guided Lakota. The dragon, equipped by nature with a sense that kept him from stumbling into things, had an easier time of it than did his human friends, who tripped and blundered through what felt like very thick woods.

As Simon knew, *Yasnaya Polyana* meant 'Clear Glade'. It was an interesting name for an Elfin home, for it implied a home amongst the trees. Simon was used to the Elfin home being within the Hollow Hills – a vast underground kingdom that was invisible to those who were not invited in. Within the Hollow Hills it had been magiced to look as if the sun rose and set and the seasons passed. One had no feeling of being inside a mountain or underground.

Millennia ago, though, the Elves had lived amidst trees, for they had been the guardians of the forests. The dryads were the keepers of individual trees, while the gnomes cared for the animals. But when the Elves had fled the Continent and come to reside in the British Isles they had retreated to the Hollow Hills for safety's sake, and walked but little among the trees of the earth above. In olden times the way to the Elven groves and glades had been magiced — but the way had always been open to those who used magic and could read the signs. Simon could not fault Silverhair for his caution. He would have done the same.

It seemed an eternity until at last they came to a stop and Silverhair allowed them to remove the cloth about their eyes.

They stood in an immense glade circled by ancient trees. It was a bright place, full of sun and a pool sparkled in the midst of it, with a quick flowing stream filling the pool from a small waterfall on one side and flowing away from it on the other. A rustic bridge, covered in flowering vines, crossed the stream at the lower end.

The first overwhelming impression was of flowers and gardens. Everywhere one looked were flowers of all colours and types. Even under the trees in the deepest shade there were blooming plants.

The next thing one noticed was the silence. There seemed to be no people at all about. Wind chimes and several Aeolian harps sang in the warm breeze, but there was no hum of conversation.

Then Simon noticed that behind the screen of vegetation there were houses in the trees. Here and there were glimpses of stairs climbing the sides of the huge trees, a window or a porch showing between the curtains of vines and leaves. He could only assume that a sentry had warned of their coming and that the Elves had retreated to their homes until it was deemed safe for them to venture out. He could feel their eyes upon him.

Silverhair led them to the base of a raised platform formed from earth and grass. "Wait here," he ordered shortly. Then he turned to Simon, hand outstretched. "I will have your wand, Sorcerer."

210

With no demur, Simon handed it to him. Silverhair sought to disarm him. The Elf could not know that he did not need the wand for magic.

Before they had left their camp Simon had been allowed to pick up his wand and put it in his breast pocket. Silver hair had assumed, wrongly, that Simon, being blindfolded, would not be able to use his magic. That night have been true one thousand years ago, when only the strong and physically perfect could wield magic, but it had not been true for a very long time.

Simon could feel both Anatoly burning to ask questions and Tatya's fear. Lakota was a trifle indignant – he was not used to being treated like this by Elves, who usually nade much of him. Oberon's people considered his colour 'lucky' and welcomed his presence Underhill. Vron was still upset – his ears were flat against his skull and his tail lashed back and forth. Janus was her usual imperturbable self.

They did not have to wait long – within a few moments of their arrival at the foot of the grassy dais, there was a stir at the foot of the largest tree in the glade and a small procession came towards them.

In the front were two female Elves, clad in the lightweight but incredibly strong chain mail of Elven forging. They wore swords and had bows and quivers slung across their backs. They moved with grace and economy of movement, and looked as if it would be most unwise to make a threatening move near them. Behind them came three Elfin women in silken gowns of blue, rose and lavender. Directly behind then came a beautiful Elfin lady.

She was clad all in green , with a chaplet of silver set with moonstones on her long dark hair. Her eyes were green as her gown. They were expressionless as they looked at Simon and his companions, but widening a little as she saw Lakota.

A chair had been place on the grass as they had waited and she now sank into this. Her ladies adorned the grass at her feet and the guards stood at the sides of the chair, standing with feet slightly apart, each with a hand on the hilt of her sword, ready to defend the Lady should anyone offer her violence or insult.

211

She was a very beautiful lady, in the fashion of Elfinkind, with features almost too perfect to be real and a certain alien something that was more than just the pointed ears and soaring brows or the narrow face. Her hands and feet were narrow as well and her waist so slim that it seemed as if a mild breeze would snap her in twain. But Elfin looks were deceptive. She probably was stronger than Lakota.

"What have we here, Silverhair?" she asked in a low voice as she settled herself in the chair.

"My patrol came across the source of the magic we felt yesterday, Lady," said Silverhair with a graceful bow. "It is as you suspected – a Sorcerer." He indicated Simon. "He claims to have Elfin favor."

"I can see a mark upon his forehead – and I see it upon the dragon and the cat as well," the Lady stated.

"Greenleaf claims that this is a mark of the Elf Friend," said Silverhair dismissively. It was obvious that he set little store by Greenleaf's opinion.

The Lady stared at him for a moment. "Darksky is our eldest historian and he speaks highly of Greenleaf's scholarship," she said in neutral tones that nonetheless implied a rebuke. Silverhair flushed and opened his mouth as if to speak and then closed it again. Simon received the impression that Silverhair was not very often reproved and he did not like it.

The Lady then turned to Simon. "I am Moonbright, Lady of the Elves of Clear Glade. And you are?" It was a polite command.

With a low bow, Simon formally introduced himself and his companions. He spoke slowly and formally, and was gratified to see that the others followed his lead, bowing low and remaining quiet. With Elves it was best to speak when spoken to.

"Simon Stillfield," mused the Lady. "That is not a Russian name. Your two human companions are Russian, as is one of the cats."

"That is correct, my Lady," said Simon. "as I told the leader of your patrol, I, Lakota and Janus am from the western Isles – the British Isles – and the country of Ireland, where the Elfin High King Oberon reigns in the Hollow Hills. My family has long been Elf friends and when King Oberon

212

became aware that I was to come to Russia he bade me seek out the Elves he hoped would still be living here. He is saddened that the two great houses no longer know one another. "

"What you say may very well be true," said the Lady. "But we have reason to mistrust sorcerers." Her voice changed so that there was a hint of steel in it. "Will you submit to a test of your heart? It will show us if you mean us good or ill."

"And if I fail the test, Lady?" Simon asked in some trepidation

"Then you all will be put to death," she said calmly.

22

The Test

"No!" Lakota protested. His tail was lashing and his ruff stood up around his neck, a sure sign that he was agitated. "Simon is a White Wizard! You seem to think he is some sort of necromancer! We, none of us, mean you any harm!"

The looks the Elves gave him were astonished that a dragon spoke up to them. "Be silent, beast!" Silverhair commanded. "This is between your master and the Lady. I know not by what strange magics you speak -"

"There is no magic about it!" Lakota said angrily. "I can speak because I am an intelligent being!" Steam came from his nostrils.

In a few moments he would be breathing flames. Simon spoke soothingly to forestall this. Lakota, he could see, was again in pain, and it made him irritable. Carefully, with an eye to Silverhair, and with no gesture that could be interpreted by that hostile Elf as threatening, Simon went to the dragon and lay a calming hand on his shoulder.

"Lakota, we have nothing to fear from a test. They will see that we come in friendship," he told the dragon. "I will stand surety for the others," he told the Elven Lady. turning back to face her.

"Come to me, then, Sorcerer," she said.

Simon reflected that he was becoming very tired of all these people who seemed to forget that he had a name. Anatoly and Tatya both called him 'Wizard' as did most of the Russians he had met. Now the Elves were calling him 'Sorcerer'. At home, that term was only used for a black magician. The preferred term was Wizard or Mage, or more formally, Magus. It made him feel somehow set apart and different – a feeling he did not like.

But with no protest he went to the foot of the dais and waited expectantly. He had no idea what would happen. He could feel both Tatya's and Anatoly's eyes boring into his back and Janus and Vron crouched low on the ground, their tails

214

lashing back and forth on the grass, every once in a while giving voice to a low hiss. Lakota's anger could be felt, through the bond they shared

The Lady first asked for his wand. Silverhair, who had held it all this while, presented it to her with a bow – Simon noted that like their counterparts in the Hollow Hills, these Elves prized formality.

She studied his wand intently, touching it carefully with her fingers, as a blind person might. And her expression became surprised. "This was a gift, freely given, from a Great Tree!" she exclaimed.

"Yes, it was given to me by Father Oak, one of the Eld trees of England, when I first began to learn magic," Simon answered.

"And how did you convince the Tree to gift you?" asked Silverhair, sneering as if he suspected Simon to have coerced the tree.

"My father, who is a Druid of the *Île de la Sein*, asked Father Oak to give me a wand," Simon told him, knowing what the mention of a Druid would probably mean to the Elves.

And as he had thought it would, a murmur ran around the assembeld Elves. " A Druid! The people of the Trees!" Simon heard someone say excitedly.

"It is easy to claim these things," said the Lady . "I do not read in this wand that it belongs to another hand than yours, or that it has ever been used for evil – but these may be clouded with magic. Can you talk to the trees, then, Sorcerer?"

"I can," said Simon. René had taught him the language of the trees many years ago. "I am a Druid as well."

"Then you will speak to the oak tree that is our home and ask of him that he bow to us," the Lady directed.

"I doubt that he will bow to you, Lady," Simon said frankly, "for the oak is a proud tree, the tree of Jupiter, the tree of wisdom and authority. He is the Tree of Thursday, the tree of independence and stands against injustice. The oak is the king of the waning year, ruling from the winter to the summer Solstice." And then Simon drew a line in the air – a vertical line with two horizontal lines midway on its left side. "This is his symbol."

215

This symbol, traced in violet, hung in the air.

As Simon had hoped, this display of tree knowledge impressed his onlookers. All Elves were highly attuned to trees and a black magician would not have known the tree lore, for the trees would not have allowed him to the knowledge, nor would a black Sorcerer been able to have used violet, the colour of highest power in white magic.

Tatya, watching all of this, was afraid. She could not understand what these beings wanted or what all the talk of trees signified. All she could comprehend was the hostility these people seemed to have towards them- and how it might affect their rescue of Sacha. There had been one delay after another. Even today, knowing they must remain in one place so that Lakota might rest, had made her feel sick with fear. What if they could not reach the *rendezvous* in time? What would happen to Sacha if these people kept them here, or even killed them as they threatened? She would have failed Sacha. And she had pledged to herself that she would never forsake him.

Anatoly, on the other hand, felt confident that the Wizard would soon have these Elves wrapped around his thumb. The Lieutenant found everything endlessly fascinating – a prime adventure. Even the thought of the report he must soon write could not dampen his spirits. It was an effort to remain silent as the Wizard had directed them, when he was bursting with questions and comments. Having no experience of Elfin arrows he was not especially afraid of the bow-men. He could give a good account of himself in any set-to. And the vast majority of the Elfin warriors he had seen were women, he thought with the easy contempt of one raised in a patriarchal society.

"You do indeed seem to know the Trees' secrets," said the Lady, "And like you, Sorcerer, we doubt that that oak would bow to us, or to anyone. But we will still look into your heart."

With this she put out an imperious hand to the young Elf clad in lavender, who came to her feet at once and gave the Lady a short rod, rather like a wand. But it was not carved, nor did it have a tip of any sort. It was of Elder, the tree most associated with the seeing of other dimensions. It was the tree of second sight and so potent in magic that a whistle carved of it could make Faeries dance to its tune.

The Lady touched the rod to Simon's brow and to his heart.

Immediately he felt as if he was falling forward into a deep pool. And in order to swim back to the surface where light and air waited he had to lay bare every secret of his heart, his innermost thoughts and feelings. As he had often read (and thought it a cliché) his life passed before his eyes – not just past events but his strengths, his weaknesses, his ambitions, failures and accomplishments, even things of which he was ashamed. All the while he heard her low voice murmuring things such as "That was not well done of you," or "You were very right to do so." She examined every memory and became intimately acquainted with the people and the places he knew. Memories that he had pushed to the back of his mind came forth – memories of his horrible cousins, the neglect he felt at the hands of his grandparents, his early childhood loneliness, the happiness he felt at finally getting a real family to call his own – all passed before him again as if they had happened yesterday. Again he studied magic, attended the Druidry, sat for his examinations and journeyed to America. He lived once more that year and a half in America, experienced the joy and the loss that the trip had brought and watched Lakota's egg hatch. She saw his classroom, his family life and why he had come to Russia. And she saw his visits to the Hollow Hills, the high regard in which Oberon and Titania held him and his family.

Abruptly, it was as if he had resurfaced after a near drowning experience. The entire event was so like to being submerged that he was almost surprised to find he was not wet and sputtering.

To those watching to seemed as if he had just stood in front of the Lady – there had been no change in his posture or demeanor. Only Lakota, who had a mental bond with Simon, could even begin to guess what he had been through.

When the Lady was done with him, Simon sank to the ground, his legs no longer supporting him. It was if he had indeed swum for his life.

217

"There is no evil in your heart," the Lady announced. She lifted her head and looked up at the surrounding trees. "He is indeed an Elf friend!"

This seemed to be a signal, for within minutes the glade was full of Elves of all ages, eyes bright with curiosity.

Anatoly came forward and helped Simon to his feet as Lakota stretched out his long neck and touched Simon anxiously with the tip of his soft snout. Janus wound herself around his ankles, purring. Simon exchanged looks with Tatya, whose eyes were huge with anxiety. She tried to smile back at his look of reassurance, but failed. Vron, sensing her worry, copied Janus and offered her his sympathy,

The Lady rose and clapped her hands. "Prepare a feast for our guests!" she ordered. "They will wish to rest and refresh themselves." At her nod several Elves came forward to conduct the now honoured guests to a place of rest.

"Our tent and supplies –" Simon began.

"Will be brought to you here," the Lady finished smoothly. "Our healers will tend your dragon's injury as well. You would be well advised to lay down upon your bed, for a heart search is a taxing undertaking. When you awaken there will be a feast to share."

"And may we partake of your food with impunity, Lady?" Simon asked boldly, for there were cases of food eaten in Elfin halls that enchanted mortals who ate it.

"You have passed our test – you are an Elf friend. We do not wish you to carry tells of enchantments to our cousin across the sea," she answered. To Simon's relief, she did not seem insulted by his question.

He then bowed low and said, "I am your servant, Great Lady," in Elfish.

Another murmur of astonishment ran around the crowd. Simon felt everyone staring at him. They had obviously never heard a human speak their language. Simon was glad to find that it was still their language. Oberon had been worried that they might have forgotten it and therefore forgotten part of their heritage.

Simon and Anatoly were led towards one tree, while Tatya, accompanied by both cats, was taken to another. Janus could sense that Tatya was more than a little nervous about being led off in a crowd of young Elfin women, so the familiar

218

decide that she would stay with her. After all, Janus was quite familiar with Elves.

Tatya had an experience the like of which she had not had in years – she was waited on hand and foot.

Two of the young lady Elves – they introduced themselves as Ravenwing and Starbright – appropriately, Ravenwing was dark and her companion fair – took Tatya inside a tree – it was a huge beech. But it did not seem big enough on the outside for what was in the inside.

There was a beautiful sitting room, with the finest furniture of carved wood of work so exquisite that it made the new furniture Ekaterina had purchased at great cost seem the work of amateurs. There were actually windows in the tree – adorned with curtains of the lightest, finest gauze imaginable. There were works of art everywhere she looked – carved crystals, flowers made of jewels, paintings that upon examination proved to be of coloured grasses or chips of glass. And every where were embroideries of such skilled work that it took the breath away. Tatya was no mean needlewoman herself, but she could never have produced such work.

Ravenwing and Starbright gave her little time to look around her. They took her to a room where an enormous tub was sunk in the ground. The walls and floor were covered in gleaming glass tiles, each with a different flower trapped inside. High windows let in light and air. The tub of bright enamel was filled with steaming water that exuded a most delightful and intoxicating scent. Plants and vines decorated the room as well and Tatya thought she saw a bird flitting about. She definitely saw butterflies.

As swiftly and impersonally as a good French maid, the two Elves divested Tatya of Evgeny's old clothes and helped her into the tub.

She sank at once in water up to her chin. There was a seat, she found, that she could lean back in comfortably, and even a place to rest her arms. She had never before been in a tub this large – one that she could stretch out her legs and not be able to feel the opposite side of it with her toes. In Ekaterina's tin tub, she had to keep her knees up.

The water felt as if she was sitting in liquid silk. She had never felt anything like it. The two Elf maidens washed

219

her hair and poured over it a floral infusion that made it soft and sweet-scented. They complimented her on her hair, for all of the Elves had either very fair or very dark hair, and the honey gold colour of Tatya's tresses was new to them.

When she was done with the bath – and it did not last long enough for her – she was laid on a soft table and annointed with oils and silken powder. The long, skillful fingers of the Elves soothed and calmed her. Her eyes closed involuntarily. "Sleep," said Ravenwing's soft voice as Starbright threw a light but warm blanket over her.

And she did sleep, amazingly enough. Far better than last night when nightmares of Sacha's peril kept her waking every hour.

When she awoke, completely refreshed, they appeared again and gowned her in a silken dress, of yellow, embroidered its length and breadth with primroses and bound at the high waist with a cord of primrose. It had sleeves full to the elbow and then tight down to her wrists, fastened with innumerable amber beads, the sleeves ending in points over her hands. The neckline was heart-shaped and showed off an amber necklace and long amber earrings. On her feet were primrose slippers with stockings of the finest silk that somehow stayed up without garters. To Tatya's embarrassment, however, the Elves did not seem to embrace the concept of underwear. The dress went on over the bare skin.

Starbright looked at her puzzled when Tatya asked her about undergarments. "But why would you want to wear more than this?" the young Elf asked. She gave the ribbon tied at the neck of her own lavender gown a tug and it fell off in one smooth movement revealing a slim, nude body. "See! Now I am ready for the bath, or to worship – or for my lover!" She picked up her dress and put it back on. "Which one of the males is your lover?"

Tatya felt a blush rising. "Neither one of them!" she got out. "They are my traveling companions, that is all. I have never -"

"That is a shame," said Starbright. "They are both very attractive – for humans. Do you mean you have not had a lover at all?"

Tatya could only shake her head. "Do you have a lover?" she ventured shyly. Starbright looked as if she was barely fifteen or sixteen.

"Of course!" she exchanged a look of pure amusement with Ravenwing. "As soon as we are of age we take our first lover. We sample everyone that is offered."

"But what if you want to get married?" Tatya blurted out. "Wouldn't your husband mind that you are not – virginal?"

The two Elf maidens burst into laughter that sounded like the tinkling of bells. "What man would want an inexperienced girl to wife? That is why our first lover is usually a man of experience."

"And a young male goes to an older woman for his first lover," put in Ravenwing. "Only by tasting of many can we find the one who is our perfect mate for all our lifetime. I myself have had five lovers," she added. "Is it different then with humans?"

"Yes, " said Tatya, and briefly explained how it was with her kind.

"That is foolish," said Starbright. "How would you know if you are suited? You should sample each one of the males in your party and decided which one you like the best. Give the one you most favor a leaf from the oak tree and go into his tree with him tonight. You are very old not to have yet been loved," she added frankly.

"Perhaps one of our men will give her a leaf!" said Ravenwing, "I saw Greenleaf look at her –"

"He has no lover at the moment, for Evenstar now gives her leaf to Heron and goes to his tree," Starbright exclaimed.

"If he gives me a leaf, do I have to –" Tatya asked worriedly. Was this some custom that must be obeyed?

"Oh, no! If you do not fancy the one who offers you a leaf, you need only decline," Ravenwing assured her. "Now let us make your hair so beautiful that every man who is not yet mated will shower you with leaves!" she said enthusiastically.

Janus, who with Vron, who had watched all this without comment and had slept with Tatya, lifted a paw to her mouth. Tatya was quite certain that the cat was laughing.

221

Simon and Anatoly had had the same experience as Tatya. They bathed, were massaged and slept, separately, and then were dressed.

Simon was given a Wizard's robe of a blue that changed from dark to light as he moved, in shimmering folds covered in silver embroideries of the sun and the moon and the stars. Over this was a long vest of silver tissue edged with sapphires. A silver belt inscribed with runes was clasped about his waist and a amulet of the Elves' favorite moonstone was about his neck. There was even a pointed hat to match the under-robe. He recognized the spider silk that was spun by Elfin ladies, and having stayed beneath the Hollow Hills, was not overly concerned with the lack of underwear. Elves felt differently about these things and the ones he knew took no offense if their guests did not participate in their sky-clad rituals or in their easy morality. Once he was of age, which in Wizard law was eighteen, his parents left it to him as to how much or little he took part in their worship services and accepted the offers of Elfin maidens.

Shortly after he was dressed he was joined by Anatoly, who had a bemused look about him. They had been valeted by two young male Elves, and had provided Anatoly with a heavily embroidered version of their own dress.

"I have never felt anything like this!" he exclaimed, gingerly touching the sleeve of his shirt. "I am afraid my touch will ruin it."

"Very little can ruin it," Simon told him. "That material is strong and tough enough for you to run through a bramble bush and emerge unscathed. It is spider silk and is woven with magic. The Elves keep spiders as if they were silkworms and the ladies spin and weave the silk for these clothes."

Anatoly had taken in Simon's outfit. "You look like a Wizard in a picture book!" he said admiringly. "Would you know what this means?" He unfolded his other hand, which he had kept by his side. In it was an oak leaf. "The Elf who was my valet said it was from the Lady Birdsong."

Simon grinned. Some customs hadn't changed in one thousand years.

222

"Lady Birdsong would like you to return to her tree with her tonight and share her bed," he said. "She finds you attractive and bed-worthy. You can refuse her if you like –"

"One of those beautiful women wants to *sleep* with me?" Anatoly said in disbelief. "Why would any sane man refuse-!?" Then he added, "Wait! Will there be any repercussions?"

"An angry Papa Elf with a bow to your heart if you do not make an honest woman of his daughter, or a jealous husband or male friend?" Simon said, correctly surmising his worry. " No – the Elves have a different code of morals than do we. If she gave you a leaf, she is free to do so. She is an unmated maiden and she is free to sleep with all she desires. It is expected that she do so before she takes a permanent mate."

"And this is how they signify their interest – they give you a leaf? Anatoly asked. "Are you certain that she means to - "

"There is no doubt about it," Simon assured him. "You can ask her if you want – be direct. She will not be embarrassed. She will probably find it amusing," he added, remembering the very first time he had been given a leaf.

"What a wonderful place!" said Anatoly enthusiastically.

223

23

Elfin Wine

Anatoly's enthusiasm continued to mount. If he had thought the Elf maidens beautiful whilst in their everyday garments he was stunned by their loveliness when they dressed for a special occasion in silks that sensually caressed their lithe bodies as they sparkled with jewels and wafted strange, enticing floral perfumes. He was given many appraising glances from their slightly slanted eyes and had more than one leaf pressed surreptitiously into his hand.

Simon was presented with no leaves – but he was not surprised or disappointed at this omission. He had rather expected it. These Elves seemed to distrust Wizards and that they still thought of him first and foremost as a Wizard was very obvious, seeing what they had given him to wear for the feast. With all of their magics and their arrows that never missed they still feared being bespelled. And too, the Lady might have thought that Tatya was his partner after seeing into his mind. The Elves were very honorable about not disturbing pairing and bondings between humans. They even honoured what they thought of as foolish customs. As far as Simon knew, neither of his sisters had ever been offered a leaf – for the Elves knew that humans prized chastity in their young females. And Simon's parents had never been propositioned, for they had been married by the time that visits to the Hollow Hills had become a regular event in their lives. The Elves would not attempt to break that bond.

The feast was outside under the stars, for while they had slept the day had rapidly turned to night. A low horseshoe shaped table had been laid out and the participants sat upon cushions filled with the fluffy seedheads of dandelions. These were incredibly soft and comfortable, for of course, more Elfin magic had gone into their making.

In contrast to the Hollow Hills the place settings were rustic – Oberon's court favored fine china and crystal. The plates here were quite beautiful, though – highly polished wood carved about the edges with a pattern of vines while the table ware was silver, heavy and old fashioned – the forks had only three tines – and all the handles were of carved horn. They drank from horn cups and there was no table cloth – placemats of woven grass decorated with vines marked each place.

A place had even been made for Lakota at the table. The dragon had been seen by an Elven healer and several children had made him a floral garland to wear about his neck. He had made it known that he liked his food cooked.

Simon and Anatoly had arrived at the feast site before Tatya and were seated in places of honour, flanking the Lady and an empty place. Lakota was on one side of Simon, between them an empty seat (that Simon correctly surmised was for Tatya) and Anatoly on the other side. There were two bowls set on the table top for the cats. They too had received Elfin attention and had been brushed and adorned with silken ribbons. Janus took this all in good part – she was quite used to Elves and their liking for dressing everyone up to the nines, but Vron was unused to bows or collars of any kind and kept pawing at his ribbon adornment.

When Tatya finally appeared it was on the arm of Silverhair, who it turned out, was the Lady's consort. After delivering Tatya to Simon, he escorted Moonbright to the feast, seating himself by her side at the head of the table.

Simon scarcely aware of this, nor its significance. His eyes were all for Tatya.

Why had he never noticed before how beautiful she was? In that garish negligee, as much as it had exposed, she had never looked this enticing. The Elfin silk made the most of her figure and the amber jewelry complimented her sparkling eyes of the same colour. Her shining hair had been piled high upon her head in intricate loops and curls and woven with amber beads and fresh water pearls. She smelled of some Elfin perfume, made of the essence of summer flowers and subtly blended to ensnare the senses. Simon had always preferred the floral Elfin scents to the musky ones popular with society ladies.

He leaped to his feet and took her hand from her escort. With great care he seated her comfortably amongst the cushions. "You look beautiful!" he said softly as she sank into the cushions.

225

Tatya was still self conscious about wearing nothing but the spider silk Elfin gown. She was used to wearing a chemise, a corset, a corset cover, drawers and several petticoats beneath a dress of heavy material. She was more covered by just her underwear than she was in this dress. And she would not have wanted to be seen in public in just her underwear! She noticed how the fabric clung to the Elfin maidens and showed off their every curve. Somehow the fabric seemed to adjust itself to its wearer. That it was doing the same for her she had no doubt.

But she had seen admiration in the eyes of several young Elves and now the Wizard too looked at her that way and told her how beautiful she was. It had been a long time since she felt even barely attractive. All of the male attention she had received was from Evgeny – and she had come to realize that all it mattered to him and his friends was that she was female. Viktor had voiced this, but much more crudely, when he was laying on top of her in the linen room.

She looked away from the Wizard in some confusion, blushing, and not knowing that the shy colour in her face and the sweeping down of her long lashes were even more captivating. To cover her confusion, she reached for the horn cup and took a sip of the liquid inside.

She had never had anything so delicious. It was at once like nothing she had ever had and yet like everything she liked most. It was almost clear, just slightly red, and cold – it had to be magic, for there was no ice and the cup was not cold to her touch. "What is this?" she said in wonder. "I cannot begin to describe what it tastes like."

"Rose wine," said Simon. "It's an Elfin specialty – non-intoxicating, refreshing and delicious. I daresay you can-not describe the flavour, for it tastes differently to everyone. Just enjoy it."

Eagerly, Tatya took another sip. It was wonderful! Better than anything she had ever had before.

She suddenly envied the Wizard. He enjoyed things like this all of the time. He seemed perfectly at home among these strange beings and she suddenly wondered if anyone had offered him a leaf. She liked the way he looked in his Wizard's robes – a little strange and rather exciting.

The Lady made a short speech welcoming the honoured guests and then clapped her hands for the feast to begin.

Many non-magical people held that Elfin or Faerie food was but glamoured weeds. One could eat and eat in the Hollow Hills and never assuage one's hunger.

Perhaps this was true for those the Fair Folk held in contempt, but Simon had never had that experience. They ate well beneath the Hollow Hills and there was no worry about enchanted food that would numb humans to how much time had passed. And the Lady had assured him that they could enjoy this food with impunity.

This was indeed a feast. There was a roast pig, done to tender perfection, and several types of roasted game birds. There was venison, tender and moist, cooked on a spit. Vegetables of all kinds had been cooked in imaginative combinations and steamed, pan-fried and baked with sauces and glazes. Breads, sweet and savory, were piled high in rush baskets. Rice and potatoes had been done just right in at least a half dozen different manners There were cheeses, pastries and fruits to tempt the most exacting appetite. Fresh fish – steamed, poached, baked and fried excited the cats' interest ands Lakota was given a sheep, roasted in a pit and stuffed with chicken and vegetables.

Used to the excess of Elfin feasts, Simon took a little of each thing offered him and advised his companions to do the same. Elves could stuff themselves to excess and never know the pangs of indigestion or even put on weight. Unfortunately it was not the same for humans.

He was glad that they seemed to be serving rose wine. Some of the Elfin wines were so intoxicating that they took humans by surprise. One or two sips was all that it took to become drunk – and the reaction could be extremely unpredictable. Sometimes humans could not tolerate the wines. Some of them elevated or depressed the spirits. Some people became convinced they could do anything, as if they were a God. Others became suicidal. And on others the wine acted as an aphrodisiac. To the Elves this last was no bad thing as they much enjoyed congress with humans. For Anatoly, this might mean a very, very pleasant memory. But Simon was determined to keep a watch on Tatya . She had

227

shown him that she was a highly moral person, a lady born and bred. She would not easily forgive herself if she, under the influence of honey mead, ended up in bed with one of these male Elves, several of whom had given her provocative glances. For all he knew, she had gathered any number of leaves. But he doubted whether or not she would accept any of the offers. She was genuinely afraid, he thought rather regretfully, of intimacy. And who could blame her after what she had suffered at the hands of men? Luba had told Simon what Tatya's life had been like and he had wished to kill both Yuri and Evgeny.

She was certainly lovely enough to tempt any of these Elves, he thought, stealing a glance at her as she daintily ate a roasted squab. Like their human counterparts male Elves liked the strange and the new and to them nothing could be stranger than human females with their oddly coloured hair and round ears. Human females also had different forms than did the Elf maidens – they were generally more curvaceous, with wider hips and larger bosoms. Elf maidens were very slim hipped and had small breasts, with little variation. And Elves were either dark or fair. Red heads, copper-coloured hair, true brown and honey brown such as Tatya's were unknown and therefore prized by Elven males, as would be her amber eyes, which were unusual even by human standards.

In the course of the meal, however, Simon lost track of Tatya. She was borne off at one point by a group of chattering Elf maidens, among them Ravenwing and Starbright who wanted to show her a special gown that another young Elf was having made. Simon was being kept busy answering Anatoly's questions, conversing with the Lady and her consort and Greenleaf the young historian and helping Janus and Vron to various fish dishes.

Lakota was quite happy and content. He assured Simon that he was not in pain at all – the Elfin Healer had given him something and the wing had actually begun regeneration. He was having a fine time – the food was wonderful and he was looking forward to the singing and storytelling which would no doubt follow the feast. He had noticed harps and other instruments on the dais. There were Elfin children in

228

this glade and they were all making much of Lakota, bringing him tidbits and stroking him. He was in alt.

Ravenwing and Starbright took Tatya off in a laughing group of girls to an immense beech, where lived Windsong, another young Elf. She was to be married soon, they explained, and she wanted everyone to see her wedding gown, which had been finished that very day.

Windsong greeted the arrivals happily. Her tree home was again, far bigger than it looked from the outside and Tatya only received a fleeting impression of a comfortable room lit with golden light before the Elf maidens conducted her into a back room.

Hanging in the air as if it were on a seamstress's dummy, was a beautiful gown.

It was the green of summer leaves. Over the full skirt and fitted bodice was a network of tear shaped *diamente* on intricate lines of silver. It looked like an early morning spider web covered in dew, and that was, Tatya was to find out, exactly what it was. The boat shaped neck ended in huge, puffed, short sleeves. Windsong showed them her veil, which was a silver spider web. She would wear a crown of daisies, her favorite flower and had silver shoes to wear with it as well.

"Why is it green?" Tatya asked. Although it was a most beautiful gown she could not imagine wearing green for a wedding. Most people would consider that unlucky.

"What other colour would you be married in?" said Ravenwing, astonished.

"In society our wedding gowns are pure white, while the peasants wear red," said Tatya.

All of the Elfin maidens cried aloud at this. "But pure white is the colour of mourning!" said Starbright, horrified. "Pure white is the colour of snow, when the flowers are dead! Even our hunters do not wear pure white – it is faintly blue – and they only wear that because it will take on the colours around it if it is necessary to disappear. But pure white -! We only wear that for a death! How horrible to wear the colour of death on one's wedding day! Truly, the ways of humans are very odd! And red is the colour of blood!"

"Green is the colour of life and of the trees themselves," Starbright explained. "For us it is the most fortunate colour we could wear. The trees will bless those who wear their colour."

"With us, white signifies purity and virginity," Tatya explained.

The Elfin maidens dissolved in laughter. The concept of virginity and chastity, Tatya reflected, was as foreign to them as underwear.

But somehow she could not censure them for their beliefs. Would she not feel the same if she had been raised to think it permissible to take as many lovers as she liked? She had grown up in a house of liberal ideas and knew enough not to impose her standards on others. She had musc to think over as she walked around the dress, admiring it. The workmanship was exquisite – there were women in St Petersburg who would commit murder to own such a gown. Somewhere in the background she could hear music beginning.

She did not see Ravenwing and Starbright whispering to the others, looking at her at they did so. She did not see the speculative glances turn to mischief and glee. Simon could have warned her that Elves took great delight in manipulation, and thought nothing of rearranging the lives of their human friends. Elves always thought that they knew best and were far wiser than humans.

She was not at all suspicious when Ravenwing asked a few casual questions about Anatoly and Simon. Tatya admitted that she did not know Anatoly all that well – in fact, she had met him but a day before. She did not think either he or the Wizard had a sweetheart, but she did not know for certain.

"I gave the other one my leaf!" admitted a dark tressed Elf called Peachblossom.

"And so did four others – and he had Birdsong's first!" said Ravenwing dryly. "You will have a long wait for your turn, Peachblossom!"

This sent them into gales of laughter. Tatya could not imagine having a conversation like this with other young women of her age and class. Not only did one not speak of such things, but there would be such jealousy. These young

Elves seemed totally free of that emotion. Peachblossom took their teasing in good part, declaring that she could be patient, even waiting until tomorrow when he would be well-rested. "It is very pleasant to make love on the banks of the river when the sun dapples the water and our bodies," she said cheerfully.

They were all sitting now on piles of cushions. One of the young women brought around a tray of drinks in small fluted glasses. Hoping it was more rose wine, Tatya eagerly took a glass.

This was something different. It was a honey-coloured drink, thick and smooth. It warmed her as it went down and left her wanting more. "This is very good!" she said to her hostess.

"Have another glass – there is plenty. I make it myself," said Windsong.

"She's famous for it!" said a very fair Elf, Silverbird.

For some reason this caused more laughter, and they began to talk of places to make love other than the bedroom and what were their favorites.

Tatya should have been embarrassed by this topic but she was not. A warm glow was spreading throughout her body and she began to have thoughts about sunlight on water and the moonlight peering between swaying leaves. Windsong offered around a bowl of plump, ripe cherries and Tatya took a handful.

They were exquisite – sweet and dark. She ate all she had eagerly and when Windsong offered more, she took them without a second thought. She accepted another glass – her third – of that delicious drink as well and polished it off. The cherries and the drink were even better than the food at the feast. She was warm – almost too warm.

"I think it's time we found the Wizard!" said Ravenwing, with another laugh. She reached out a hand and pulled Tatya to her feet.

"Windsong, I don't know if I can wait for the human! You are cruel to feed us your delights when I have no chance of a partner until the morrow!" said Peachblossom plaintively.

"There is still time to cast your leaf," said Windsong carelessly. "Any male will be glad to have it from you, especially now!"

"My brother has always favored you, Peachblossom," said Silverbird. "And he has not received anyone's leaf this evening, for Goldflower gave Redberry her leaf yesterday. He is all alone. You can lay with the human tomorrow. "

"Oh, poor Wildleaf! I will go to him at once! I cannot bear the thought of him being alone!" A little unsteadily, with very bright eyes, she left at once, pulling an oak leaf from the bosom of her gown as she left.

Tatya was feeling very odd. She felt hot and cold and excited – almost as if she could jump out of her skin. When Ravenwing suggested that they find the Wizard, she thought this was a brilliant idea. She could not think of anyone she wanted to see more than she did the Wizard. Just thinking about him increased the excited feeling and added to the flushed warmth of her body.

All the young Elf maidens were leaving – they were all bright eyed and eager to be gone. A few of them each clutched a leaf. Others murmured names of those they had gifted with a leaf before or during the dinner.

When Ravenwing pulled Tatya along with her it seemed like the best idea in the world to stop as the Elf girl directed and pluck a leaf from the oak tree.

"Give that to the Wizard," Ravenwing directed. "He'll know what to do even if you don't!"

This struck Tatya as so exquisitely humorous that she began to giggle. Ravenwing began to snicker too and they ended in holding each other up, shrieking with laughter.

"After tonight you'll see why lovemaking makes us so happy," said Ravenwing at last. "And you'll thank us tomorrow! Perhaps while you're here with us you can have many hours of enjoyment with many, many men – or just one if you prefer! "

Why had she not realized earlier what a good idea this leaf giving was ? Tatya thought, amazed at her own stupidity. Her reluctance to go to bed with the Wizard now seemed foolish. Now she wanted nothing more – she could barely think about anything else. Every part of her throbbed with longing and she ached for his touch. Ravenwing was a wonderful friend to give her this opportunity, and she stammered her thanks.

"Go to him," Raven wing gave her a little push, adding with a ribald laugh, "He is probably the only one left at the feast table – everyone else is better occupied!"

The moon was bright – Tatya could see as well as if it were daylight in the brilliant moonlight. All about the glade were poles with torches lighting the way as well.

The way seemed long to her, so eager was she to see him and present the leaf that was crushed in her hot hand. The silken gown she wore that had seemed so immodest and inadequate suddenly felt as if it was too heavy to bear and she longed to feel the cool night air on bare skin. Why did she not suggest that they go into the woods, where she had heard several of the young women mention there was a pool that sparkled with moonlight and a mossy bank where two lovers could be comfortable. It sounded ideal.

Simon was growing anxious. Tatya had been gone a long time. Most of the young women she had left with had returned and eagerly carried their male friends away, leaving him alone at the table. Even Janus and Vron had disappeared. Lakota, stuffed with good food, was fast asleep a little ways off.

Simon knew all too well what the bright eyes and eager air of the Elf maidens meant. And he was afraid that Tatya might even now be with a male Elf and would be shamed and regretful in the morning. He had seen the looks some of them had given her. And what she offered – and she would offer, definitely, if what he suspected was true – any of them would take.

"Here you are," said a husky voice behind him.

Startled, he whirled around, the hem of the silken robe he wore flying out and the embroidered silver decorations flashing in the moonlight.

Tatya stood there, holding out a leaf to him. "Please, take my leaf and we shall go into the woods. They told me of a pool where we can swim and make love on the bank. Take the leaf," she repeated when he made no move to do so,

"They've given you an aphrodisiac," he tried to explain. "This is not your idea – you probably had honey-mead –"

233

"And cherries!" she interrupted. She came closer and picked up his hand and put the leaf into it.

"There!" she said happily. "You've taken my leaf. Now you have to make love to me – Ravenwing said so. And I want you so much!" she suddenly giggled. "Do you know that all I have to do is pull this ribbon and I'll be naked? Elves don't wear underwear! Isn't that shocking? But it 's very handy for swimming and for your lover, they told me. I want you to be my lover, Wizard!"

One part of Simon wanted very badly to take her up on her offer. He found her extremely attractive. But the gentlemanly part of him that had been trained into his nature ever since he was a small boy would not allow him to take advantage of a young woman who was not in her right mind and had been drugged with honey-mead.

"Not here!" he sprang forward and took Tatya's hand as she began to pull at the ribbon at her breast that held her gown on.

"Why not?" she said. "The cushions are nice and soft and the moonlight is lovely…"

It rather horrified him that she was ready to take off her clothes in such a public place and expect him to make love to her there. How much of that stuff had she had?

"Lakota's a light sleeper," he said, nodding at the dragon, who several feet away, was snoring softly. "I'll take you to my quarters."

"And we'll do it there?" asked Tatya happily. "Perhaps then we can go to the woods and do it again?"

"Definitely," said Simon, mentally going through his Wizard's kit to think of remedies for honey-mead infatuation. Elfin aphrodisiacs were difficult to combat, especially since he wasn't sure how much honey-mead – or cherries, another potent passion fruit imbued with Elfin philter that she had taken. And getting the information from her might be nearly impossible.

Tatya went with him quite happily. She still had an overwhelming urge to remove her gown but they would be at his assigned tree in a few moments and they could begin making love. Even a few minutes seemed too long to wait, for she was on fire.

However, it seemed an eternity to Simon before they reached the tree and his Wizard's bag. Anatoly, who had gone off happily with Lady Birdsong and had shown Simon several other leaves he had received, would probably tell him he was a fool to not take what was so eagerly offered. But he could not – he could all too well imagine her face when the effects of the honey-mead had worn off and she realized he had acted as badly as her cousin almost had – and after he had given her his promise to be her friend.

24

Happy the Bride

When they reached the guest quarters Simon had been assigned, he went at once to his Wizard's bag and opened it magically.

He left Tatya standing in the middle of the floor, looking about her with interest.

"How much honey-mead did you have?" he asked casually, as he began to take packets of herbs and several beakers from the satchel. She might not remember how much she had drunk.

She giggled. "Two or three glasses," she said after a moment's reflection. "Or maybe four? And a lot of those lovely cherries! I never had such delicious cherries!"

Three or four glasses of honey-mead? Simon thought in horror. One small glass was enough to shed the inhibitions of the most prudish person in existence! No wonder she was so free and easy! Three glasses would make an elephant overly amorous. And to add cherries to that mixture! He felt a surge of anger at the Elf maidens. They should have known better. And he should have known better, he admitted to himself, and warned her about honey-mead and the manipulative nature of Elves. Aphrodisiacs were always very much in evidence at any Elfin celebration or feast. These Elves obviously were not used to dealing with humans and perhaps even thought that they were doing Tatya a favor by introducing her to the delights of love.

At least she had come to him, and not to a male Elf. He could make certain that she retained her chastity.

"What is that you are doing?" said Tatya's voice from behind him.

"I'm making us a magical drink to – er – increase our pleasure," he answered. He knew of nothing that could counter that much honey-mead. But a sleeping potion could work... He mixed and stirred feverishly.

"Don't take very long – I am growing impatient! Oh, this bed is nice and soft!" she said with another giggle. "Aren't you going to take off your clothes?"

"As soon as this is ready," he said, turning to look at her and nearly dropped the beaker he held.

She had taken off her gown and was laying back against the pillows of his bed.

"Put your gown back on!" he yelped.

"Why? Don't you like me like this?" she said provocatively.

"Yes, but I want to undress you myself," he said, thinking fast and noting that his hands were shaking.

She pouted but stood up and pulled the gown back on.

But the third time she took it off he gave up.

The potion was finally ready. It had taken far longer to brew than he remembered – or perhaps it just seemed that way. It was a very potent sleep-inducing potion and worked almost instantaneously.

Simon poured the blue liquid into two glasses from his Wizard's satchel and sat down beside her on the bed. He was very conscious of her bare beauty and her over-bright eyes and the way her breasts rose and fell with each breath she took.

"I can't wait any longer!" she said, twining her arms around his neck, almost spilling the mixture.

"First drink this," he said and added, inspired, "This is your first time – this drink will guarantee that you feel only ecstasy, not pain."

"Really?" she took the drink in one hand, leaving the other around his neck and sniffed it. "It smells good – and it's a pretty colour." She raised it to her lips and downed it on one gulp.

"Now, Wizard, you can make love to me!" And she reached for his belt.

Before her fingers had done more than touch the belt she gave a sigh and toppled over sideways, sound asleep.

She was a limp as a rag doll. She would no doubt be embarrassed in the morning when she awoke in his bed, completely unclothed, but Simon was too tired to cope with

237

inserting her back into her gown, even with the aid of magic. He covered her with a soft thistledown-stuffed coverlet.

The day, and especially this evening, seemed to have lasted one hundred years.

Simon made himself a bed on the floor with some cushions. In spite of his exhaustion he could not fall asleep right away. He had too many things to think over. He kept thinking that one of the worst effects of honey-mead lust intoxication was that the drinker clearly remembered everything that happened the next day, unlike becoming drunk with a human drink such as wine or whiskey, which often caused forgetfulness. Tatya would remember every thing she had done and said. How were they to continue on this rescue mission with this between them? She was still somewhat diffident with him since he had seen her in that shocking *negligée*. She would be shamed and embarrassed beyond belief after this night.

If he were a Wizard Healer he could use a spell of Forgetting. These were used in occasions of shock, to give a person time to heal, when the shock could then better be dealt with. Simon had seen a Wizard Healer use a spell of Forgetfulness on his mother, when she had seen something that had sent her into psychic trauma. In spite of the fact that he had threatened Anatoly with a Memory Charm he could in actuality not do that.

But he was not a Healer and it was considered completely unethical for a non-Healer to use these spells. Even a Healer had to have permission from the patient or his family to use such a powerful spell.

What was to be done? He thought far into the night, falling into an unrestful, fitful sleep only just before dawn.

Tatya awoke to a chorus of birdsong and a soft warm breeze full of sweet scents.

She had never slept so deeply. She could remember no dreams and many times her sleeping hours were filled with nightmares. Why had she slept like that? And then she sat up, and discovered she was completely naked under a feather light coverlet.

238

And everything came back to her in a rush – the spider-silk gown, the feast, the wedding gown and that drink Windsong had served.

And the Wizard! She could have moaned aloud when she thought of how she had acted with the Wizard! What had come over her? How could she have been so wanton? She covered her face with her hands as she relived everything she had said and done last night. Had she really given him a leaf and insisted that he make love to her? Had she really taken off that gown and waited for him on his own bed, urging him to hurry up?

How was she ever to look him in the face again? He had seen her naked – more than once now. It was embarrassing – it was humiliating! What made her act so contrary to all she believed?

Had he done it? Had he made love to her? she thought feverishly. The very last thing she remembered was him giving her a drink and she was reaching for his belt – she blushed to remember that!

But after that it was a blank.

Quickly she flipped back the covers and examined the bed, remembering what Janus had said about the signs of lost virginity that Yuri would look for.

But the bed was spotless, and only the indentation of her body and her head was in the feather mattress and in the pillows.

There were signs that someone had slept on the floor – a pile of cushions and a blanket in disarray. The robes he had worn last night hung magically on the wall as was the gown she had worn. But of the Wizard there was no sign other than his satchel and other luggage.

Had he once again played the gentleman and left her untouched? It looked as if he had. He had done something to her to make her fall asleep and forget what she had wanted so badly last night.

At first Tatya was grateful to him, but the longer she lay in the silken bed the more she began to wonder if she had indeed been fortunate.

She would shortly be seven and twenty – almost past the age for love and romance. If she ended in scrubbing floors or doing factory work to support herself and Sacha she would probably never meet the type of man she could feel anything for. She would never know what being loved meant. She had realized some time ago that she would probably never hold a child of her own in her arms – which made her heart ache with yearning – but perhaps she was stupid, as the Elf maidens suggested – not to know what being loved was like.

And who better than to initiate her into the joys of love than the Wizard? As Luba had said, he was kind – and honourable too, for he could have easily taken advantage of her befuddled state last night.

And she found him very attractive – she was always conscious of him and found herself looking for him when he was not close by. He was patient – she recalled the magic lessons and how simply and gently he had explained everything. He would not be contemptuous of her inexperience.

The more she thought of it the more she desired it. It would be a beautiful memory for what she did not doubt would be long lonely days ahead. She would have been loved once, even if the two of them were not really 'in love'. She had to admit it – the Elf maidens' easy enthusiasm had made her curious and given her a certain longing...

Accordingly, instead of getting dressed in the primrose embroidered gown she stayed where she was, as she was, and waited for his return.

After less than two hours sleep Simon had crawled from his bed and gone for a walk. He had come to a decision the night before and decided to stand by it, but he still was conflicted with doubts. He suddenly wished that he could talk to his father.

But that was impossible. He could not even write a letter – they were far from where he could insert it in a diplomatic bag that would be in Ireland posthaste. He had tried scrying and as they had feared it did not work at this distance.

And there was no time. What needed to be done had better be done now. " 'If 'twere done, 'twere best done quickly'," he quoted to himself

As early as it was, he went to see the Lady (for Elves did not sleep even half as much as humans and usually awoke with the dawn no matter how late that had stayed up the night before) and shared a breakfast of bread and honey with her and her consort. She was delighted with his request and expressed herself all eagerness to help in any way possible.

The only thing left to do was to go back to his tree and wait for Tatya to wake up.

To his surprise she was sitting up in his bed, waiting for him. She had not dressed, but held the coverlet up to her chin.

"Hello," she said shyly. "I have been waiting for you."

"We have much to discuss," he said. She wore a most peculiar expression – he was unable to read it. Was she angry with him or just embarrassed?

"Tatya – about last night –" he began, feeling more than a little awkward.

"Don't apologize," she said quickly. " I know that you did not take advantage of me and the wanton way I was acting."

"They gave you honey-mead – it is drink that releases the inhibitions and makes one –"

"Lust maddened," she finished.

"Well, yes," he admitted. "Elves don't think about these things the way that we do – to them love making is a gift to be enjoyed with anyone that offers as long as they are heart-free. Once they marry they are as faithful as anyone would wish. But before that – they probably thought they were doing you a favor. They more than likely have not had much contact with humans in the last one thousand years –"

"They did do me a favor –" she interrupted. "They made me realize that I have been foolish. And I want you to make love to me – now – and that is not honey-mead talking!"

And closing her eyes and turning her head away, she let the coverlet drop.

He was silent for so long that she turned back to look at him. She let the coverlet remain where it had fallen, below her breasts.

"Why, Tatya?" he asked softly, making no move to come to her as she had thought he might. "Do you think you owe it to me? You owe me nothing –"

She shook her head. "No – but I will be seven and twenty on my next birthday. No one has ever wanted to marry me and never will. I have no dowry and my father is disgraced. I will never go back to my aunt and uncle and I will probably end in working in a factory to support myself and Sacha. I don't want to die without knowing what love between a man and woman means."

He looked at her for a long moment and then finally came to the bed and sat on the edge of it. He reached over and very gently pulled up the coverlet so that she was covered again.

She was conscious of a feeling of bitter disappointment. "Don't you want me?" she got out. Perhaps he found her repulsive!

He laughed rather uneasily. "I want you more than you can imagine! But I want you to marry me first."

"What!" Her eyes grew wide and she stared at him.

"I know that you do not love me," he began "but I want to make things right between us. It is my fault that you cannot return to your aunt and uncle – they think that I made you my mistress. I should never have cast that illusion so that your uncle saw his fantasies played out in our images. Your reputation is ruined. And now the Elves and probably Lieutenant Tcherpnin think we are lovers as well. If this gets out you will be fair game for anyone. And your idea of working in a factory makes me shudder."

"It would be no worse than living with my aunt and uncle has been," she said, her mind whirling. He wanted to *marry* her?

"If you marry me I can provide – handsomely – for you. If you find we do not suit my country allows for divorce. It takes an Act of Parliament, but I have relatives in very high places. If we were to divorce I should make a generous settlement on you and you would never have to worry again about providing for yourself," he said earnestly.

"But you don't love me –" she stammered.

"I like and respect you, far more than any female I have ever met. I enjoy your company. Many people marry with less in common than that."

Tatya had always imagined that if ever she married it would be for love. But then again she had never imagined that she would end as an unpaid drudge in her aunt's house.

"And Sacha?" she asked. "What of Sacha?"

"He would be more than welcome to make his home with us and I will pay for his education and see that he too has sufficient funds to make his way in his chosen profession," Simon promised. "And if you still want to have – " he hesitated briefly "relations with me I can assure you that there will be no issue unless you desire it. There are many fail-proof contraceptive spells –"

"Unless you desire it" – she *could* have a child! Everything inside her melted when she thought of cuddling a child of her own, of suckling it at her breast...

To be married, even without true love, to a man she liked and respected, to have Sacha provided for, to perhaps have a child – this was so much better then the future she had envisioned for herself. He was kind and honourable.

"I will marry you, Wizard," she said quickly.

"You have made me very happy," he said in relief, and picked up her hand to kiss it. "But I do think it is time you began calling me Simon and not Wizard. You will have to practice, for I have asked the Lady to marry us this afternoon."

"The Elf Lady?" she said in confusion. "But how can she –"

"It is a legal marriage in Ireland – to be married by an Elf. I doubt that it is here. But just to be certain, the Lady tells me that there is a Russian Orthodox church less than a day from here. We will be married there again. Any papers needed, since I am a foreigner here. can be provided magically."

He put down her hand and stood up. "There are no doubt any number of young Elfin maidens who want to help beautify you for the wedding, so I will leave you to them." And very softly he added, " But I doubt you could be any more beautiful than you are now. '*But beauty's own self she is when all her clothes are gone.*' "

Tatya felt a blush rising all the way from her toes.

243

There were indeed a laughing, happy troop of young Elves who descended upon Tatya even before she had a chance to get out of Simon's bed. They pulled her from the bed and took her to bathe in an enormous tub that was strewn with what they called 'wedding herbs".

Several of them shed their gowns and joined her in the tub, scrubbing her back and hair and telling her with much laughter that the bride did nothing for herself – they would bathe and dress her – she had to save all of her energy for the wedding night!

Nudity did not seem to bother the Elves at all – it seemed as natural to them as wearing an excess of clothing did in Tatya's world. She put her inhibitions aside and let herself enjoy the experience.

She was washed and brushed and massaged with fragrant oils. Her nails and toes were given attention too and painted with something that sparkled.

When her hair had dried they piled it in a crown on top of her head. "This is the marriage knot," Ravenwing explained. "When you are in the bridal bower your husband will want to see your hair – for among our people only a married woman lets a man see her hair down. All he has to do is pull this one hairpin and it will fall down around your shoulders."

"Even your lovers don't see your hair down?" Tatya asked in amazement.

"Of course not!" Ravenwing said, tossing her head. "There must be some mystery left for marriage!"

This seemed absurd to Tatya for the lover got to see everything else, but when in Rome –

To her surprise and confusion Windsong offered her the use of her wedding gown.

"But surely you want to keep it for yourself!" she protested.

"It would be a great honour for my House if you would consent to wear it!" said Windsong sincerely. "It will be something to tell my grandchildren – that A Wizard's lady wore my dress at her wedding!"

Windsong really meant what she was saying. Tatya remembered that the Elves did not seem to know the human traits of jealousy or possessiveness. She had already heard

Peachblossom being teased about an early morning encounter with Anatoly and realized with a shock that two of the other young women and been with him too. None of them were jealous of the others but had taken their turns. Tatya clearly remembered her cousins' fight over a young officer who had merely danced with them.

She accepted Windsong's offer and the young Elf was delighted.

"I only hope that it will fit me," Tatya said, looking at Windsong's extreme slenderness. Windsong had been one of the ones who had helped bathe Tatya and she had not bothered to resume her gown. She was as slim as a young birch. Tatya knew herself to be slender, but she was thick-set compared to Windsong. And the Elf was slightly taller.

The group exploded into laughter. "Try it on," said Windsong.

Since the young ladies preparing Tatya for her wedding had not offered her anything to wear when she came out of the bath she was ready to put on the Elfin gown, for of course there was nothing to go underneath. She stood up from the stool they had seated her on and two of the Elves lifted the gown and dropped it over her head.

She gasped in pleasure as the silken folds fell about her. The gown she wore last night had been a sensual delight – this one felt incredible. Suddenly it did not seem to matter that there was no underwear.

And it fit perfectly – as if she had gone to the finest *modiste* in St Petersburg and had many, many fittings. It was molded to her breast and waist and then stood out in a bell-shaped skirt as if there were five petticoats between it and her skin rather than just the thin fabric. It was exactly the right length. And when she tried on the silver shoes which looked impossibly tiny – the Elf maidens had very small feet – those fit as well.

"You cannot try the veil until we finish dressing your hair," Ravenwing said. "All brides need a floral wreath – what is your favorite flower, Tatiana?"

Tatya's very favorite flower was the daffodil. She loved the sight of those brave yellow banners blowing in the still chill wind of early spring, telling her that the long winter was over. But it was June and daffodils were no longer in season. When she voiced this, Ravenwing smiled and sent Peachblossom out to get flowers for a wreath. Tatya supposed they would find something else yellow.

It also struck her that she was no longer embarrassed by the nudity of her attendants – for those who had joined her in the huge tub had not bothered to dress again. Nor was she bothered by her own nakedness, she realized as Ravenwing helped her out of the dress, so that they might finish her hair.

"The Wizard will admire you very much when he sees you in this dress," said Starbright. "You have a very fine figure – you might almost be an Elf, your hips are so slim."

"But her bosom is bigger," Silver bird pointed out. "Human men like big bosoms."

"So do Elf males!" giggled another Elf called Evenstar. Tatya recognized her as one of their guards from yesterday. She had been one of those that had scrubbed Tatya's hair. She looked much less intimidating in her current costume of nothing at all. "Heron says my continual practice with bow and arrow has increased the size of my bosom. What do you think?"

She leaned backwards and presented her breasts to the others who very critically looked at her.

Tatya's mind boggled when she tried to imagine this scene with her two cousins or any of their young friends.

They had just decided that Evenstar's breasts were indeed bigger and most had decided that they too, would take up archery when Peachblossom returned with an armful of daffodils.

Daffodils! In June! Tatya's mind reeled. She did not feel up to inquiring where they came from.

Peachblossom had left to get the flowers without clothing herself. Now she giggled again. "I saw my human lover of this morning as I went to the meadow to gather the flowers, He nearly fainted when he saw me! Why do humans make such a fuss over the lack of clothing? Even when we made love he wanted to only lift my skirt because we were out of doors and there were others out along the river.! I hope you and the Wizard do not do that for your Wedding night, Tatiana!" she said.

"But we will be indoors –" Tatya said.

She was greeted with a chorus of "Oh, no!"

"The Wedding Bower for the first night is out of doors," Starbright informed her. "even in winter. But we prefer to marry in the summer."

"And the first night is actually the afternoon," added Ravenwing. "It is very important that you be outside if you wish to conceive a child. Once you become with child you should always sleep outdoors so that your child can be as close to the natural world as possible."

They did not consider living inside a tree close to the natural world? Tatya thought.

She was surely going to have one of the strangest weddings she had ever heard of.

Anatoly had had a wonderful evening – and morning. No less than four Elfin ladies had desired his company and he had done his best to please then all.

He had never imagined there could be any one like these Elf maidens. They were completely uninhibited and direct. This morning he had been with an Elf called Starbright who took him to a pool in the forest where they swam without bathing costumes and then made use of a soft mossy bank. An hour later Starbright had delivered him to Peachblossom, who took him to a river bank and there with several other Elves fishing further downstream, shed her gown and invited him to partake of her. It was incredible. Elves were amazing. And just now, he was telling the Wizard. he had seen Peachblossom running about the glade as bare as the day she was born and no one even looked at her!

Simon was getting dressed for the wedding. A robe had come for him – another Wizard's robe – this one of green – the traditional Elfin wedding colour – embroidered with runes of gold. The long vest was gold and the amulet was gold set with a huge emerald.

"Elves don't think anything of nudity the way we do – none of the Faerie creatures do," Simon explained. "Among the lesser Faeries – the flower Faeries for instance – many of them wear no clothes at all. One becomes accustomed to it."

"How do you ever get used to it?" Anatoly said. "I could not take my eyes from her! She laughed at me! And this morning on the riverbank –" he actually blushed. "There were others there – who saw!"

247

"They more than likely ignored you," Simon told him. "Elves don't care about watching anyone make love. To them it is a natural thing like eating or sleeping. It is just another pleasure meant to be enjoyed. If you had looked closely I daresay there would have been other couples enjoying each other. Elves prefer to be out of doors and think nothing of sharing an area with others."

"A wonderful place!" said Anatoly fervently.

He became aware that Simon was putting on an elaborate costume. "Is there another feast?" he asked.

"No, there's a wedding," answered Simon. "You had better get dressed yourself. You'll find clothing on your bed."

"Who's getting married?" Anatoly asked.

Simon smiled. "I am."

Lakota, who Simon had thought might protest this sudden marriage, for he had seemed so relieved that Simon would not after all marry Birgit, was thrilled about the wedding. It made him happy that Tatya and Sacha, his good friends, would be part of their family now.

Even Janus expressed her approval. "I like that girl," she said frankly. "But be tender with her, Simon – she has been much abused. Vron told me. It made me want to scratch several pairs of eyes right out of their owners' heads! I wish there was a way to give those Rostovs what they deserve!"

In the late afternoon when the lowering sun sent long shadows chasing across the glade, broken by stretches of green-gold light, the Elves gathered in the middle of the glade.

All of the Elves wore green decorated with embroidery as a blessing and a compliment to the bride and the groom. The women wore flowers in their hair and flowers were everywhere one looked

Upon the dais a consortium of harpists played one of the heartbreakingly lovely songs of the Elves.

At a rustic altar made of carved wood the Lady stood waiting. Unlike a human wedding where the groom waited for the bride, Simon would meet Tatya and take her on his arm and lead her down between the lines of Elves to where the Lady waited. As Queen of the clan, although they only used

248

the simple title of 'the Lady', she had the authority to marry her subjects.

Simon was bowled over when he saw Tatya being led to him by a bevy of green-clad girls. The dress she wore flattered her golden complexion and sunlight caught in the silver gauze of the gown's overlay and her veil, which was swept back by a crown of daffodils.

She offered Simon a shy smile as she took his arm and they proceeded towards the Lady.

It was a very simple ceremony. The Lady bound their wrists together with a silken cord of green and bade then be true to one another as they had chosen each other from all the others they might have had. They each consented to 'this person and no other as my one and true mate' and exchanged rings of gold, carved with runes. This was not a part of the Elven ritual, but Simon had asked that it be incorporated. The Lady then led them to the four cardinal points – North, South, East and West – around the altar. This was to remind them of the journey of life they were to take together.

A small fire with blue flames was then lit in front of the altar and, holding hands, they jumped over this together, signifying the old life they were leaving behind ending and a new life, purified by the fire of love, beginning.

Lastly the Lady called upon the Elfin pantheon of gods to bless their union – the Lord of the Tempests, the Ruler of the Spirits, the Lady of the Flames, the Lady of the Earth, the Lord of the Waters, the Lady of the Stars and the Lord of the Sun and the Elves' most potent deities – the Lord of the Trees and the Lady of the Moon – to bless their union.

Then they were led beneath garlands of flowers to the Bridal Bower. This was in a small dell deep in the woods. A vine-covered arbor arched over a bank of moss for their bridal bed.

Tatya could smell wild thyme and other heady scents as the Elves offered their congratulations and then slipped away. In no time at all they were alone.

Golden sunlight poured down through chinks in the vines, turning the bed of moss to gold. It made an inviting couch.

"Tatya," said Simon earnestly, "if you'd rather wait –"

""No," she said. "I want you to love me." And she untied the ribbon at the neck of her gown and it fell to the moss beneath her feet. This time she stood before him unashamed and in her right senses.

Simon caught his breath. She was exquisite. His golden girl.

"I'll use a contraceptive spell –" he began.

She came closer to him and put a finger on his lips. "No – I want to have a child – your child, Simon"

He took her in his arms and they sank down on the sweet scented moss, the most joyous of nuptial couches.

25

In the Forest

It was a magical night for Simon and Tatya. After making use of the Bower they went to the pool Tatya had heard of and swam in the silken waters made silver by the light of the moon. They loved one another again on the bank of the pool and then lay cuddled on the moss, their only covering the moonlight coming through the trees.

Tatya thought that she had never been so happy. For the first time since her father had been disgraced and banished she felt as if there was something to live for besides her brother. She herself actually had things to look forward to – a new home, hopefully a child and getting to know her new husband – and this wonderful new activity! The Elf maidens had been so right! She chuckled to herself, a small sound in the depths of the forest and snuggled closer to Simon.

His arm tightened about her as he heard her laugh. It was a happy laugh. Marrying her had been an excellent decision. Her eager response to his lovemaking had delighted him. It had been her idea that they go to the pool 'as the Elves did' and left their wedding finery in the Bower. To his surprise she swam like a fish and played in the water like an otter. Simon had learned his swimming skills from the Merpeople on the Irish coast and they chased each other and ducked and swam all over the surprisingly deep, clear pool.

In between lovemaking they had talked and talked – of everything – of their childhoods, of their families, of their educations and likes and dislikes. They had even more in common than Simon had thought. They quoted poetry to one another – both loved it and both had tried to write it – and neither was very good at it. They both loved music and dancing – but it had been years since Tatya had danced.

There was so much lacking in her life that he could make up to her, so much that she had missed, he thought as she fell asleep against him, breathing softly. She could dance to her heart's content in Dublin, in beautiful clothes he would buy for her. Never again would he see that look of hopelessness that she all too often wore. From now on her life would be happy – he would see to it. She had spoken longingly of a family – well, she would have a large and loving family now. And he hoped they would have children. He had seen the look on her face when she said she wanted a child. He wanted children himself.

Yes, this had been one of the best decisions he had ever made.

And perhaps one day they would fall in love.

Morning came all too soon. The sun was well up by the time they woke, for the nights were short in June as Midsummer's Day drew near.

Simon was awakened by a large splash and a sheet of water covering him. He sat up with a start, sputtering a little.

A silvery laugh greeted him. "Come in!" his new wife called gaily from the center of the pool. "When I lived at Mikhailovskoe in the summer I started every morning with a bathe in the river!"

Simon grinned. He had been afraid that she might be a little shy this morning. But she was treading water in the middle of the pool, making no attempt to hide herself from him.

He stood up and dived in a long, slow motion that sent him underwater straight towards her. He came up through the cool water thoroughly awake and grabbed her, pressing close to her. "You look beautiful all wet," he said, kissing her. "You don't mind that it is daylight and we are naked?"

"There is an old Russian proverb "A pretty girl is not afraid when men see her in the bath but an ugly girl is frightened to death". You make me feel beautiful!" she said putting her arms around his neck. "I liked what we did last night," she said a little shy suddenly, looking down, her long lashes making shadows on her cheeks. "I hope we do it often."

Simon could not help it – he laughed aloud in sheer joy and kissed her again. "They will be waiting for us – there will be a wedding breakfast –"

"Can't they wait a little longer?" she said. "Love me again, please."

They *could* wait a little longer, he thought. He could show her how the Merpeople made love underwater, with the aid of a little magic.

It was going to be another hot day Volunvoshka thought in disgust. The sun had come up in a blazing red-gold ball and already the early morning dew had melted away. Heat simmered on the fields below the mountains and a haze hung on the horizon.

The Ice dragon was in a thoroughly vile mood. Not only was he suffering terribly from the heat – even sleeping on the remains of the glacier had not helped much – but he was incensed about the time Karachev was taking to exchange the egg. Why did he want to take so long? When he had grumbled about this and threatened to go after the egg himself yesterday the Wizard had waved his hand and Volunvoshka had found that suddenly he could not leave the mountains. It was as if an invisible fence were in his way – no matter how high or far he flew he could not get over or around it.

How he hated that Wizard! As much as he hated the boy Illya and his *balalaika*! And now the other one was singing too – it was more than a dragon could bear. How he was to wait calmly until Karachev fetched the egg he did not know.

For he was very afraid that the egg would hatch before the exchange could be made. He and his mate had calculated just to a nicety when it would hatch. And that should be within the next two weeks. He writhed in real pain when he thought of the hatchling clawing its way from the shell with no one to tend it properly. It would want meat when it cam forth – red meat and how would those stupid humans know what to do for it? It would be so hungry that it would attack them and they would kill it – for it would be relatively small and helpless – flightless, with talons not yet developed and little, new teeth that could barely shred. It would not even be able to spit ice.

And no one had been talking to it! It would emerge from the shell with no language skills and no knowledge of its noble heritage! These were all things that a dragonet learned in the shell – dragon language and at least one human tongue and the proud history of the Ice dragons and its own lineage, repeated by its parents as they tended the egg. The dragonet – his dragonet – his son! – would be an outcast among his own kind without language or historical knowledge. The dragonet had to repeat his lineage when he was presented to the Council at one week of age. That was expected of every dragonet. It was a tradition engraved in stone. And his son would not be able to do that. He would be disgraced – his whole family would be disgraced.

How he was to face his mate ever again Volunvoshka did not know. She had uttered no word of reproach but he fancied he could see it in her eyes. This was her first egg. He had failed to keep it safe. What if she left him for another – one who could protect her eggs far better than he had? That sly Derzshavin was always finding some excuse to come to their tunnel and far too often he just happened on Khlebnikova when she was chilling herself on the ice. He had even tried to entwine his neck with hers once – which amongst dragons was the prelude to intercourse – but Khlebnikova had turned on his with a roar and repulsed him. She was a good and faithful mate. But she was also incredibly beautiful. Would she stay with him when he had failed so spectacularly to protect their very first egg? Too many males, not just Derzshavin, found her desirable.

He bellowed his anguish to the heavens.

Lakota was very eager to see Simon for he had something of great importance to tell his friend. Janus had prevented him from going to look for Simon. "It's their wedding night – leave them alone. They'll come when they are ready," the cat had said.

Lakota was not certain that he understood why Simon and Tatya needed to be left alone. At only five years of age it would be at least ten years before he came to sexual maturity and thought about finding a mate. He was aware that Elves did something together – male and female – that involved joining their bodies but he had never watched of course – for Simon had told him it was impolite. He really had very little curiosity about it. Simon had always made certain that his bond with Lakota was dampened when he had accepted a leaf from an Elf maid in the Hollow Hills. In America Simon had learned from those bonded to their dragon that the experience was quite overwhelming when the bond was open and one and one's dragon loved at the same time. But he had not even discussed this with Lakota, as the blue dragon was so young.

Janus seemed languid this morning, he thought as he waited impatiently at the edge of the woods. She had Vron had been spending a great deal of time licking each others' heads and batting playfully at one another. They had disappeared for a long time last night too – almost as long as Simon and Tatya had been gone.

Nevertheless he was impatient. There was more food being put out and another celebration in the offing. Why didn't they come?

Simon was enchanted when Tatya said they would walk back to the Bower as they were. He offered to call their clothes to them here at the pool, but she said "No we are among the Elves – would they call the clothes?"

"Well, no," he answered.

"We will do as the Elves would do," she insisted. In truth, it no longer bothered her. She felt somehow liberated and free. And she did not relish putting her constricting corset back on, nor her heavy undergarments. Simon had told her his family spent a fair amount of time in the Hollow Hills and Tatya had wondered for one wild moment if she was seriously depraved, because she looked forward to being in a place where clothing was optional and everyone made love out of doors.

They made their way back to the Bower and dressed again in the wedding finery. It was going to be a hot day and Tatya thought despairingly of Evgeny's heavy old clothes – and her corset. In two days time she had become completely spoiled by Elven silk and nudity.

She felt a bit self-conscious when they arrived back at the glade for everyone of course would know what they had been doing. But when Ravenwing and a few of the other girls came up to her and said with much merriment, "Wasn't it wonderful? Did you like it?" she nodded yes and was able to join in their laughter.

Simon was glad to see this. He was also glad that they had come among the Elves, for their easy acceptance of love-

255

making had no doubt helped banish the fears he had seen in her eyes after the aborted rape and that night in his room in the Rostov house.

After a delicious wedding breakfast the newlyweds separated. Simon wished to talk to Silverhair about the surrounding countryside and he could see that Lakota was burning to talk to him.

He was very glad that Lakota was so accepting of his marriage. The dragon had greeted them happily and had even touched Tatya briefly with the end of his snout – a draconic sign of affection.

Simon went to the guest tree and collected his map and brought it out into the sunlight. He smiled to see Anatoly going off with yet another young Elf maiden. The Lieutenant would not be eager to leave *Yasnaya Polyana*. But they had to leave today if they were to make the *rendezvous*, for having to walk rather than fly would slow them down considerably.

Silverhair, as Simon had found out, was the commander of all the patrols that went out every day to hunt and assure the safety and privacy of the community. As Simon had thought, the young Elves had been in training. The consort would know of the dangers in the countryside.

Simon asked Lakota to join them at the table where the map had been spread out, promising to talk to the dragon about what was on his mind as soon as they consulted Silverhair, for the Elf was about to leave on another patrol and would not return until the evening.

Tatya found herself with a bevy of Elfin young women again. This time they took her to a shady nook where violets still dotted the grass and a heady scent of flowers hung in the air.

"We have a gift for you!" announced Ravenwing. "But first you have to return Windsong's gown to her."

Tatya took it off – it was no hardship in the increasingly warm day to wear nothing. Again she thought with dread of her heavy clothes, suitable for flying, but a punishment to wear in today's heat.

She thanked Windsong for the use of her gown. "I shall never forget it – or any of you," she said sincerely, looking at the smiling faces around her.

256

"And we will never forget you and your wedding!" said Starbright. "But now for the gift." She clapped her hands and Tatya was surprised when all of the girls, who were clad in a wide variety of clothing, all slipped from their garments. One by one they lay their clothes at Tatya's feet.

"What is this?" she asked bewildered.

"Your wedding clothes! Don't humans get new clothes when they marry?" asked Peachblossom.

"Yes, but – " she protested.

"You didn't think we would let you wear those horrid things you were wearing when you came here, did you? What kind of hospitality would that be?" said Starbright scornfully. "Heavy and dull – one's body cannot breath in such things!" She walked over to a rock in deep shade beneath a tree and picked up something. "What is this thing?"

It was Tatya's corset.

"What is it used for?" Peachblossom asked.

When Tatya told them they all stared at her as if she was telling them lies. "But why would anyone want to do that to themselves? How can you breathe? The fabric of your clothes was bad enough!" Windsong exclaimed. "It must take all day to get undressed for love! What a stupid custom!"

Tatya felt an urge to laugh hysterically. Never in her wildest imagination could she have ever thought that one day she would be standing naked in a glen, explaining the use of corsets to about fifteen equally naked Elf maidens who had just given her, literally, the clothes off their backs.

"Let's dress her!" cried Starbright. "They're going into the woods so she must be dressed as if for patrol."

Treating her as if she were a life-sized doll, the Elf maidens dressed Tatya in a long Russian style tunic, loose trousers and knee high boots. They gave her a heavily embroidered belt as well, with a dagger attached. The clothes were cool and light – and there was no underwear – and no corset.

Ravenwing and Silverbird began to fold up the clothes they had given her. It was a wardrobe fit for a Queen with every type of gown and garment imaginable.

"But what will you wear?" she asked the Elf maidens.

They all dissolved in laughter. "It is too hot to wear clothes," said Ravenwing. "We will all be going down to the

257

river this afternoon and meeting our lovers, and why bother to be clothed when we are going to swim and love? Then tonight is our worship service for the Lady Moon. And we do not wear clothes when we worship for the gods must see us as we are."

"And everyone moon-bathes," put in Peachblossom. "There is nothing like moonlight for the skin!"

Tatya was then certain that she had become completely depraved for she wanted nothing more than to join these naked laughing girls at the river and there meet *her* lover and moon-bathe with him. She wished that they could stay here longer.

But Sacha had to be rescued. She felt suddenly guilty for she had given him scarcely a thought in the past night and day.

Every single one of the girls then hugged her and wished her well. Tears filled Tatya's eyes. In such a short time she thought of them all as her friends. They had taught her so much.

She watched them walk away, laughing and talking, down to the river. She then turned back to the glade, picking up her bundle of clothes which was surprisingly light.

And behind her, on the ground, forgotten completely, lay the corset.

"What is it, Lakota?" Simon asked when at last he was done talking to Silverhair and the Elf had left with his patrol. He had sensed the dragon's increasing impatience as they planned a route.

The blue dragon was bursting with his news. "I have been talking to the egg!" he announced. A dragon could talk mind to mind to a developed dragonet while it was still in the egg.

"Does it know when it will hatch?" Simon asked quickly, rather dreading the answer. He was very much afraid that it would be before they could make the exchange.

"Within a fortnight," Lakota answered. He knew as well as Simon did what this meant. "It's a male dragonet."

"I was afraid of that," Simon said, frowning. "What else did he tell you?"

258

"He was not very nice –" said Lakota. "His name is Zaandam, he says – imagine, he chose his own name before he was even hatched!"

Amongst the dragons that Lakota knew the choice of name was made when the dragonet was a hatchling, by careful consideration between a dragon and his human friend, or what was more common in the British Isles, by the dragonet's parents or guardians.

"Why do you say he is not very nice?" Simon inquired.

"Because all he talks about is killing and blood! He says I am stupid to be friends with a human and humans are the enemy. His ancestors told him so when he was still an embryo," Lakota explained indignantly. "I told him that he was the stupid one – that humans are good and kind and treat dragons wonderfully! He said I was your slave! And that I should eat you and then be free!" He quivered with indignation. "As if I would ever eat you!" He rubbed his chin on Simon's hair lovingly. "I told Zaandam that it was very wrong to eat people and he laughed at me. I don't like him at all, Simon."

A hostile, man-eating dragonet about to hatch! Wonderful! Simon thought as he returned Lakota's caress.

"Can you control him if he hatches before we can exchange him for Sacha?" he asked Lakota as he scratched behind the dragon's ears.

Lakota sighed in bliss. "I think so," he said "He won't have flame and can't fly and he will be little – but I hope we can get rid of him before he hatches. The funny thing is that he talks about *freezing* me! What does he mean by that?"

Within the hour they were packed and ready to go, Anatoly reluctantly leaving two naked Elf maidens who hung on each of his arms. He looked rather dazed, but helped Simon pack up Lakota's breast harness.

Simon was very pleased with the state of Lakota's wing. Regeneration had begun and was progressing rapidly. The Elfin Healer had given it his full attention and as Elfin healing magics were potent – they had brought back Simon's father from near death – Simon was glad to have the Healer's skills used on Lakota. Lakota declared the pain to be gone.

Still it would be a week at least before he could fly again and they had a long walk ahead of them.

Simon noted Tatya's new clothes with approval. He and Anatoly had been supplied as well with Elf-made clothing. With the Elfin cloaks from Oberon they were well prepared. It would be difficult indeed for these Elf-made clothes to rip nor tear nor get dirty.

The cats finally showed up, Janus looking rather sheepish, when it was time to leave. The Elves had made a comfortable and safe traveling basket for the cats on the last saddle of Lakota's six-seat saddle.

Farewells were brief but heartfelt. The Elves wished them Godspeed and told them that it was a good day to travel, for tonight was the worship of the Lady Moon in the splendor of her fullness. Anatoly rather wistfully wished he could stay for that – the Elf maidens had told him of it. Everyone went sky-clad – which he found out meant naked – and it sounded as if this moon-bathing turned into a regular orgy. He would never be able to forget this place and the nubile Elf maidens. His spirits lifted when they told him he was now an Elf friend and welcome back at any time. What a place to spend his annual leave!

When they had walked some distance beyond the glade Simon held up his hand for everyone to stop.

"I don't want to alarm anyone," he said, "but we had better be on our guard. Silverhair told me that tomorrow, if we make good time, we will be in a Witchwood."

"Can we not go around it?" Tatya asked, not liking the sound of this at all.

Simon shook his head. "It's a large wood and to go around would add a day or maybe two to our journey. We can't count on Lakota's being able to fly again soon, and will have to make time on the ground."

"Is a Witchwood what I think it is?" said Anatoly.

"Yes," said Simon shortly. "And this Witch is *not* a White Witch. In fact, from what Silverhair told me, she sounds singularly unpleasant – if not dangerous."

At one time, Tatya thought, she would have scoffed at the very idea of a Witch as peasant superstition. But so many wonderful things had happened – she had been saved by magic, flown on a dragon, and now was married to a Wizard and learning magic herself. "What is the Witch's name?" she inquired.

"Baba Yaga," Simon answered.

26

Baba Yaga

"Baba Yaga!" Anatoly said disbelievingly. "I thought she was only a Faerie tale told by nursemaids to make the children behave!"

"Legends very often contain a great deal of truth," said Simon. "What do you know about her?"

"She's an ugly old Witch with blue skin and a big hooked nose," said Anatoly, remembering the tales his *nyanya*, his nurse, told him and his sisters. "Her favorite food is humans – especially children – and her mouth opens wide enough to swallow anyone she wants to eat."

"She lives in the birch woods and has a house that is built on chicken legs –" Tatya began.

"And the house is made from the bones of the people she has eaten!" Anatoly finished.

"My old *nyanya* at Mikhailovskoe said that she had fangs of stone like knife blades and that her glance could petrify anyone who gazes into her eyes. And she flies through the woods in a mortar, using the pestle to steer it," Tatya continued.

"Sometimes she travels with Death, eating the souls of the people he claims," Anatoly said.

When this recital had started Lakota had looked at each of his friends as if he suspected that they were joking. Now he burst out "But Witches are good! They don't eat people any more than dragons do! Simon's mother is a Witch, and his sister Holly. And Ninon and Aisling are Witches too – they're all good! I thought we could not go through the Witchwood because it would be rude since she hadn't invited us!"

"Your mother is an ugly old hag?" Anatoly asked Simon in interest.

Lakota was insulted more than Simon was. "Lady Diana is one of the most beautiful women in Dublin!" said the dragon, his ruff beginning to flare.

Sometimes, Simon thought, he forgot just how young Lakota really was. He might be twenty-five feet long, but even in dragon years he was still a child and still saw everything as a child would.

"Russian Witches are different than our Witches in the British Isles, Lakota," he said soothingly. "And not all magical people are good – remember the stories you heard from Tuathail, Uncle Lyonshall's dragon, about the evil necromancer my parents had to fight?"

Lakota nodded slowly. As Simon spoke quietly his ruff began to flatten. He did not look happy however. "Will this Baba Yaga eat us? I don't think I want to go in this Witchwood if she might eat us!"

"She won't be able to eat us – I have spells that will protect all of us – the new Deflection Charm can even protect us from a basilisk or a Gorgon. And her petrifying gaze may not work on you and me. As far as I know a fully qualified Wizard or a dragon need only fear a basilisk or a Gorgon," Simon reassured him.

"I am glad to hear that." said Anatoly. "I've no wish to become a Witch's supper!"

"Tonight, when we camp," Simon promised, " I'll put a Deflection Charm on each of you and teach you how to cast your own protection. I think our lessons for a while will be all in defense."

Tatya was happy to hear that the magic lessons were to resume. She had enjoyed the two she had and still was rather in awe of the fact that she could not only make a light of any size or any brilliance whenever she needed it but could actually make things come to her. Simon told her of his female relatives and friends who belonged to something called a Coven and she had a new ambition – to know enough magic to be asked to join this group.

They traveled most of the day save for the hottest part of the afternoon when they found a shady place to sleep for a while. Lakota could not walk as far or as fast as he would have been able to ordinarily. In spite of his brave words about the pain being gone, Simon's bond with the dragon and his observation told him that Lakota was hurting by the time they halted.

263

Before they slept Simon gave him another potion and reapplied a fresh batch of unguent to the damaged wing primary. In order to travel through the forest Lakota had to keep his wings folded tightly against his sides but it felt better if his injured wing could be spread out.

They halted for the night as dusk began to fall. Simon did not like the way that clouds were stacking up in the west and decided to cast a dragon dome. It was well that he did so, for by full dark a thunderstorm growled and raged overhead.

Once the tent was set up and a fire burning merrily – a mage fire that would burn nothing but could heat a pot and warm those who sat about it – Simon checked the egg. It had traveled in Lakota's breast harness, wrapped in its bespelled cloths for warming, where the blue dragon could monitor it.

It was definitely becoming quite hard – a sure sign that it was bound to hatch. Dragon eggs became rock hard from the large end up as they matured and this one was like granite on that end. Even the semi-transparent smaller end had become opaque. The silver bands twisting through the surface shone brightly and the exterior of the egg itself had taken on a crystalline brilliance that was very striking.

Simon was torn – on one hand this was an unprecedented opportunity to study Ice dragons, and as a Dracophilologist he wanted to be there when the egg hatched and the little-known species of dragonet emerged. But given the difficulties of handling a normal hatchling and what Lakota said about the personality of this dragonet, it was far better that he be returned to his own people before he hatched. If only they had this egg in the controlled environment of an Egg Incubatory, like the large facility in Dublin! What a wonderful chance to add to the body of knowledge about dragon breeds!

Tatya, Anatoly the cats and Lakota watched as Simon checked the temperature of the egg, listened to it with his stethoscope and tapped it with a small silver hammer. To Tatya and Anatoly's shock, the egg tapped back.

"How can it do that?" Anatoly demanded. " We had many chickens and ducks on our *dacha* and they none of them ever did that!"

"Dragons are not chickens!" said Lakota a little indignantly. "We are fully conscious in the egg and can learn

264

and even talk to other dragons mind to mind! No chicken can do that!"

"Can other reptiles do that?" the Lieutenant asked next.

Simon intervened, for he could see that Lakota was becoming offended.

"Dragons are not reptiles," Simon told him. "They are a unique species – *Dracones dragonii* – unlike anything else on earth. We think that they are born inside an egg because of the necessary nutrition an egg provides. Dragon mothers can't nurse their young. As soon as the dragonet becomes a viable life form he or she begins to eat the interior of the egg – what you would call the white. This is eaten right up to the inside of the shell. This is one reason we think that the egg becomes hard – it protects the dragonet from premature hatching. Otherwise the shell would be paper thin and the dragonet might come out too soon, unprepared to face the world. Once he is hatched he will eat the shards of the shell for the calcium it contains. But his parents or Egg Tenders will need to have red meat – a lot of it – ready for him."

"We're starving when we come out! And it takes a full day to get out of the shell – it's hard work!" said Lakota, his temper recovered.

"Is this one going to hatch soon?" Tatya asked. The shell had changed in appearance just since she had first seen it.

"I hope not," said Simon with a sigh. "I don't know how we'd care for a dragonet under these circumstances. It is a full time job for the dragon parents to care for it – even the Incubatory where Lakota hatched has to have three shifts of Egg Tenders to care for a hatchling. We simply haven't the time or the equipment to properly care for a hatchling."

After a supper of soup and bread, which had been supplied by the Elves, Simon taught his pupils a simple defensive spell which consisted of picking up two rocks and slamming them together. "You can do this with two people that are attacking you or command a rock or log or other hard object to slam into your attacker," he explained. The command was *"Verberare simul"* in Wizard's Latin, which he made them repeat aloud until he was satisfied that they said it correctly. Without a wand a pointed finger would suffice. But without the correct inflection a spell might not work or it might do something else entirely. That was why beginners in magic were always made to speak their spells out loud.

As it had been the last two times Tatya was slower to pick up the spell than Anatoly but when she had it firmly in her mind she did it better than he did. Indeed she seemed to be deriving a great deal of pleasure m slamming the two rocks into one another.

"I was imagining them to be Evgeny and his horrible friend," she told Simon later as they prepared for bed. She had wondered what the sleeping arrangements would be but the tent seemed to know that she and Simon would be sharing a room and had provided a spacious bed on the opposite side of the tent from Anatoly's room.

She had felt a little shy – she dearly wanted to make love but she was afraid Anatoly might hear them. Simon assured her that the privacy spell he cast would prevent Anatoly from hearing an entire herd of water buffalo in their room.

With this assurance Tatya shed her clothes and sat on the side of the bed brushing her hair. She had noticed how much Simon enjoyed looking at her and decided to give him every opportunity. When he removed his garments as well she was interested to note that male Elves did not wear underwear either.

"You do not have to worry about those two any more," he told her, watching her brush out her waist length hair. "Even if for some reason I am not there to protect you, I shall teach you enough magic so that no one will ever hurt you or even frighten you again. And Lakota will protect you as well," he added. "You're part of his family now. In fact, tomorrow I'll give you a dragon whistle to wear, to call him if you need him."

Tatya felt her heart swell – to never have to be afraid again! To have the protection of a powerful Wizard and a dragon! And to be able to protect herself – if she had known how to slam rocks together those two could have never laid a hand on her! No one would ever handle her again unless she wanted it. It made her feel strong and independent.

But right now she wanted very much for *Simon* to handle her! The look she turned on him was so shining that he suddenly could barely breathe. She was so beautiful, with her wavy honey-brown hair streaming down over her breasts! Wordlessly, he patted the bed beside him and she dropped the brush to leap at him.

They awoke early to take advantage of the cool early morning air.

The thunderstorm of the night before had done little to change the weather pattern – today would be hot and sunny again.

Simon, Anatoly and Lakota perused the map. The little dragon figure spellcast on the map had come to rest high in the Urals. Simon wondered if this was the dragon's lair. Although he knew few real facts about Ice dragons, what little he did know indicated that Siberia was their home. This was certainly far from Siberia. It was a mystery why a native of that far northern region had strayed this far south.

Having made excellent time the day before it was decided amongst the six of them that they would stop again when the midday hours became too hot for comfort. Even Janus and Vron felt the heat.

The three humans were glad for their Elfin garments. The spider silk was cool and allowed the skin to breathe easily and wicked the sweat away from their bodies. When the sleeves were rolled up for coolness they stayed rolled and the collar opened itself as much as propriety allowed. Even the boots were as comfortable as going barefoot.

Tatya wondered if the Elf maidens were spending these hot days in a state of nature, swimming in the river and making languid love in the deep shade of the trees lining the river. It was a programme that appealed to her very much, and fleetingly she wished that they might have remained with the Elves.

But Sacha had to be rescued.

"I wish we could fly!" said Lakota wistfully as they started out after eating breakfast and breaking camp. "It's so nice and cool up in the air!" Since Lakota did not feel entirely well, he felt the heat much more than it would have normally.

It was also warmer than Ireland – in Russia, a country that they had thought would be chilly.

With the aid of the magiced map and a non-magical compass they plotted a route that would keep them beneath the trees of the forest. To travel directly beneath the hot sun was not only unbearable but foolish. Sun burn and sun poisoning were always a possibility.

As they journeyed the atmosphere of the woodland changed subtly. At first it had been open, with many sunny areas, full of birdsong and the scatterings of squirrels and other little animals. Flowers bloomed in the sunny spots and shade-loving plants could be seen beneath the trees.

The deeper the wood became the darker it grew – and more silent as well. By mid-morning all the noise of the birds had vanished. The trees, which had seemed friendly earlier in the day, had taken on a dark and sinister aspect. Even the slender white birches seemed to leer at them and the almost black needles of the fir trees kept the sun from shining.

In spite of the darkness it was very hot and still, without a breath of wind stirring to make the woods less oven-like.

Tatya found herself walking closer to Simon. Janus had climbed to Simon's shoulder while Vron rode on Anatoly. Even Lakota looked about him nervously and said in a whisper, for the wood seemed to call for whispering, "I don't like this place at all! Is this the Witchwood?"

"Yes," said Simon. "I don't like it either, Lakota. There is an atmosphere of pain and death here – and of evil." He felt Tatya's hand slide into his.

Anatoly had tucked his pistols into his Elfin belt and slung his rifle over his shoulder. He was also repeating his rock slamming spell over and over to himself. Last night Simon had put a Deflection Charm on everyone, but Anatoly wished that it had made him feel strong and invulnerable. He had never doubted his own bravery – since he had been in the Guards he had fought in various skirmishes here and there in the Empire, and had hunted wild boar, bear and wolf with what his father called the 'right amount of fear' – meaning that he was not over-confident of his hunting skills and respected what the animals could do to him. But there was

268

something about this wood that made him want to turn around and run back out into the sunlight.

He stole a glance at the Wizard, who did not seem perturbed by the foul atmosphere of the wood. Of course he was a very powerful magician and probably not afraid of anyone or anything since he could no doubt vanquish it with the vast store of magic at his fingertips. Anatoly fervently hoped that one day, he, too, would be a very powerful magician – if he lived that long.

The wood became thicker and darker. Lakota began to have trouble getting through the trees. He was a slim dragon, without great bulk, but the trees seemed to be deliberately blocking their way. "They're grabbing at me!" he complained.

Simon took out his wand and pointed it at a birch tree that looked as if it had bent over to confound their passage in just the last few minutes. In what sounded to Tatya and Anatoly as if he was mimicking the wind in the branches, he commanded the trees to let them pass.

At once, the trees obeyed. The crooked birch straightened and the firs drew back their branches,

But this necessity had an unfortunate consequence. A great shriek came from deep within the forest and a sound of something rushing through the trees was heard.

"Who dares command the trees in my forest?" came a loud, grating voice.

From the trees directly in front of them burst a strange and terrifying sight. Standing in a gigantic pewter mortar was Baba Yaga. She steered the mortar with a matching pewter pestle and glared at them with baleful black eyes set deep in her blue-skinned face.

She was twice as tall as an ordinary man. Her face was twisted with malice, her mouth but an ugly slash from which protruded two fangs of stone. Her nose was an immense hook and nearly met her pointed chin. The wild tangle of her hair was confined only by a red kerchief. She wore a dark blue dress, with a red apron tied around her waist. All were well-worn. Her hands were huge and big knuckled. Anatoly nervously estimated that each hand was at least as big as his head.

She lifted the mortar menacingly at them. "How dare you?" she hissed. "How dare you tell my trees what to do?

This is *my* wood! Such as you – *humans* –" she made of it a dirty word –" are only fit for my supper!"

"We only pass through your wood," said Simon. "And if your trees had allowed us to do so I would have not had to command them."

Baba Yaga laughed – a hideous cackle that made the hair rise on Anatoly's head and Tatya clutch at Simon's arm.

"My trees are very good servants – they look out tasty tidbits for me," she said, grinning maliciously at them and proving that her teeth were indeed made of stone. "I prefer children – they are far more tender, but I've no objection to eating such as you when I'm truly hungry! And I see you've cats with you – nice for snacks!"

Both Janus and Vron crouched low on the chosen shoulders – hissing and spitting, their fur on end and their ears laid back.

Lakota had hung well back in the dusk of the trees but now came forward when his friends hissed. "You leave us alone!" he shouted. He did not like her at all.

The Witch stared at him. "What are you, creature?" she demanded.

"I'm a dragon!" said Lakota. thinking fleetingly that people in this country were very stupid about dragons.

The Witch laughed in derision. "Don't give me that! I know a *real* dragon – Chudo-Yudo! He's my son! He has many heads and is monstrous! You have only one head and are tiny!"

Lakota opened his mouth but at a sign from Simon he subsided.

"All we wish is to pass through your wood quietly and peacefully. We will soon be gone," Simon said in pleasant, even tones to the Witch. It was always better to try diplomacy rather than fling magic about indiscriminately.

The Witch was sniffing the air, her long nose quivering. "You smell of magic!" she declared. A sly smile crossed her ugly features. "But I have eaten those before who fancy themselves magicians! Know my power and be afraid!" she shrieked.

The woods parted and through the parting ran a house on chicken legs. It ran straight towards the Witch and halted in front of her. As Anatoly had said, its walls were made of human bones while the roof was of straw – thatch, as it was called in Ireland.

"My oven is always hot!" she said. "Who will be first? I can swallow you whole, but I much prefer my meat cooked and done to a turn!" She cackled again, sounding much like fingernails on a chalk board.

Her eyes began to glow with an eerie blue light which suddenly shot out towards them.

Instantly a violet shield sprang up before them and deflected her malign and petrifying glance.

She screamed in rage and leveled her pestle at them. She jumped from the mortar and ran forward, opening her mouth, which turned into a huge cavern with stone teeth like stalactites and stalagmites.

"*Glaciere!*" Simon shouted, leveling his wand at her

She halted in mid-stride, frozen as if a deadly arctic wind had blown upon her. Only her eyes moved and they glared with hate at Simon.

"Will she stay like that?" Anatoly asked quickly.

"Until I release her," Simon said.

Tatya became conscious of the faint sound of some-thing crying ever since the house had arrived in the clearing. Now that the Witch was silenced she could hear it clearly. With horror she realized what it was.

"Simon!" she exclaimed, turning to her husband, "There are children in that house! They are crying!"

"Can we get them out of there?" Lakota cried.

"There seems to be no door," said Anatoly worriedly.

"My *nyanya* always said that Baba Yaga went in and out the chimney so that she needed no door. The victims she kept in her pantry could never escape because the was no door or windows!" Tatya wrung her hands. "Oh, we can't leave then there! But how can we get them out?"

"Vron and I can go down the chimney and see if we can find a way out," Janus offered.

"No need," Simon pointed his wand at the chicken leg house and commanded "*Liberare!*"

The bones split apart and out tumbled six serf children ranging in age from about eleven down to five. There were four boys and two girls, the eldest a sturdy looking boy that reminded Tatya of Sacha.

271

The littlest ones still had tears on their cheeks. Tatya ran to them and knelt on the ground. spreading her arms out towards them "You are safe, dear ones! The Witch is banished!"

The children seemed to know immediately that she meant them no harm and rushed to her, eager to be hugged and reassured.

The eldest boy went bravely up to the frozen Witch and aimed a kick at her knee. Then he spat on her. "She was going to eat us – she was fattening us up!"

He turned to look at Simon and Anatoly. His eyes grew big as he saw Lakota.

"He is a friendly dragon – he won't eat you!" said Simon reassuringly.

"How did you do this?" the boy asked, obviously ready to trust anyone who had had the best of Baba Yaga,

"This gentleman is a very great Wizard," said Anatoly. "His magic was far stronger than hers."

"Simon!" Tatya screamed. Children's terrified screams joined hers

The chicken-legged house had been enchanted by its evil mistress to hold onto the things she deposited in it. While Tatya had been comforting the children it had repaired itself and now long bony arms were grabbing at the children.

As fast as Simon moved, Lakota moved faster. A long tongue of flame shot from his mouth and ignited the straw roof of the chicken legged house.

The house screamed and began to run in circles as the straw went up in a whoosh! of flame.

"Oburere! " Simon leveled his wand at the house. It was immediately engulfed in flames in every part. Quicker than an ordinary fire it burnt to the ground, leaving a heap of bone ash and scorched chicken legs. The smell was terrible.

As they began to gag at the stench Simon commanded *"Irritum odoratus,"* and the clearing was filled with the scent of a summer meadow. The children were round-eyed with awe.

When he recovered his composure the oldest boy introduced himself as Terenshichka. All of the children he said, were from the same village of Treblinkova which lay to the south near the edge of Baba Yaga's domain. Some of them

272

had been her captives since early spring and had given up hope that they would not be eaten. She delighted in teasing and tormenting them, said Terenshichka. Except for gobbling them down, nothing made her happier than tears and fright. She had eaten three other children when she deemed then plump and toothsome enough. She stuffed them full of honey cakes and other sweets, the boy explained. He had talked the others in this group into eating just enough to keep from getting hungry so they would not get fat enough to tempt the Witch. The three who had died had been greedy and had taken all that she offered. They were from another village and paid no heed to Terenshichka's good advice.

"She couldn't understand why we weren't getting fat!" said Terenshichka. "But there were rats in the house and they were glad to make off with the food we didn't eat. She kept the rats so they would run over our faces and nibble our fingers and toes."

One of the little girls still clinging to Tatya gave a convulsive shudder, remembering the rats.

Simon's face had grown steadily grimmer as he listened to Ternshichka's recital. When the boy told them that the Witch had steadily been eating all of the children in the area, he made up his mind and pointed his wand at the frozen witch. "*Mutato lithum!*" he said loudly.

With a loud *crack!* the Witch began to change. First her boots turned to stone and then the change ran up her legs as if she were changing colour. Quickly her body and arms changed into grey rock, and then her neck, face and head. The last thing left alive were her eyes, blazing hatred. Then they, too, glazed over and became blank.

Simon was not yet finished. "*Friere, pulvie,*" he ordered and the statue crumbled to dust.

The children went wild, clapping and screaming in delight. "No more Witch! No more Witch!" they chanted.

"You killed her!" said Anatoly in surprise. "I thought you told us that White Wizards don't destroy!"

"There is one exception to that rule," Simon said. lowering his wand. "As a practicing White Wizard I am obliged by the oaths I swore to impede or destroy any black magician, necromancer or sorcerer I encounter. Of course, we can try to reform them, but in such a case as this I really

273

doubt that there could have been any change for the better. Torturing and eating children is pure evil."

"Shall we take these children back to their parents?" Tatya asked.

"Oh, yes, lady!" said one of the littlest girls. "We would not be afraid if you were to take us home!"

"From what Terenshichka tells us their village lies to the south of here – right on our way," Anatoly put in. The idea of little ones finding their way home through this scary wood did not sit well with him.

"Simon!" Lakota said eagerly. "They could ride me – I wouldn't feel their weight at all! I'd *like* to carry them!" he added as he could see that Simon was about to protest the dragon's invalid status.

"Of course we'll take them home!" Simon said, giving into Lakota's wishes. "It wouldn't be right not to see them safe home."

The children had been startled when Lakota spoke. He looked at them in his usual friendly fashion. "Would you like a ride on my back?" he asked in the Russian they had all been speaking. "It would be much less tiring for you."

Some of the children were afraid of him, but Simon took out a bag of dragon treats and encouraged the two oldest boys, Terenshichka and Alexei, to feed Lakota. When the rest of them saw how gentle he was they soon overcame their fear. The other two boys, Mstislav and Levky, were only about eight, while Trinka and Anna, the girls, were very little – Anna barely five and Trinka six.

Tatya could not bear to think of how frightened they must have been and how much their mothers must have suffered, knowing they had probably been stolen and eaten by the Witch. She ended up in mounting Lakota too, for the two littlest ones had already come to think of her as a temporary mother and would not be parted from her.

"I shall send a message to the Elves tonight," Simon said to Anatoly as they started off again. Janus and Vron had joined the group on Lakota's back, and were being hugged and kissed by the children. To hug a purring cat was a great comfort.

"To the Elves?" Anatoly looked at him puzzled.

274

"They are the Guardians of the Forests. They will be able to purify this wood and make it healthy and friendly again," Simon explained.

"Good thing!" remarked Anatoly. "I don't think I have ever been in a less appealing place!" He was a little disappointed that he had not had the opportunity to use the defensive spell he had learned.

Behind them, the first breeze to penetrate the dark wood in many a year lifted a bit of the fine powder that was all that remained of Baba Yaga. Soon there would be nothing left of her evil. She would be but a nursery tale in truth.

27

The Cherry Orchard

Treblinkova was a village in mourning. In the wooden *ibzas* there was no singing or laughing, only the sound of mothers and fathers praying before the icons of their own special saints in the 'beautiful corner' of their humble homes, begging that somehow their children might be returned safe and sound. Six children were missing from six different families. Their 'little father', César Stepanovich Doboujinsky, owner of the great estate of Ostanchino which encompassed the village, was a kindly master and had mounted an expedition into the birch forest to look for the children.

Nothing had been found – the men who had gone into the wood came back with tales of eerie and horrible laughter and strange noises that terrified even the stoutest of hearts.

The Holy Father, Grigory Alexieovich Zheverzheyev, had at first prayed almost ceaselessly that the children would be returned. It would take a miracle, he knew. They all were well aware of what had happened. The children had strayed too far into the forest or been tempted in by HER wiles. She had taken children from all of the villages in the area.

Years ago, when the current parents were but babes themselves, the Witch had stayed in the northern part of her woods, where a road ran towards the west. Her depredations were all of the travelers there.

Over the last fifty years the road had gained an evil reputation. It was now avoided and had fallen into disrepair. Indeed, it was no longer on the newer maps. The Imperial cartographers, of course, did not believe in Witches. They thought the road, and the wood it went through, heavily infested with bandits who robbed and killed their victims – including the men sent to mend the road. They recommended that the Czar send troops to clear out the wood but nothing was done. The area was not a priority. There were other roads, more convenient and in better repair that could be used.

The people who lived near the wood knew better. Even the priest, for he was a native of the region, knew that the Witch was very real and very evil. He knew that she had a voracious appetite and after it began to seem hopeless, counseled the serfs to accept that their children were gone.

But the mothers refused to give up. They continued to pray and hope, beseeching images of Saint Andrei, Saint Basil, Saint Isaac, Saints Peter and Paul, Saint Vladimir, the 'Bright Sun", Saints Boris and Gleb and most of all they begged the intercession of the Virgin Mother, she who was always portrayed in the icons with her Holy Child, to return the missing children to their empty arms.

For Treblinkova, this day had dawned like any other. There was always work to be done in spite of the grief that filled nearly every breast – the first cherries had ripened already, for the spring had been early and warm and cherries blossomed even before the apples. The fields were full of grains that needed tending, as did the cows, pigs, sheep, horses and chickens and vegetables grown on the estate.

To add to their troubles, there had been someone stealing cherries from the many orchards every night. No one had seen any sign of a thief and somehow the men set to guard the orchards always fell asleep. The little Father did not whip them for their carelessness, as was his right. He had lost a child himself, not to the Witch, but to a putrid fever. He could understand all too well the sorrow that shrouded every household – for all of the serfs were related to one another and each child was a son, daughter, niece or nephew or cousin to all. And great grief dulled the senses. Their bereavement was even worse then his, for he and his wife had been there with their small daughter when she died, able to hold her in their arms as she left them. But his poor people did not know for certain what had happened to their children. So he only scolded the men who slept on guard duty.

It was another hot day – the type of heat that made men irritable and small quarrels could easily turn into large ones. Usually there was a festival when the first sweet cherries were picked from the tall trees. Vast vats of sweet and sour cherry soup were made, with steaming *varenki* – cherry stuffed dumplings – and served, as well as many other

277

delectable treats. There was singing and dancing late into the long summer evening.

But no one had any heart for the Cherry Festival this year.

Pavel Nikolaiovich Vrubel was seventeen years old and had been put in charge of the beet patch that was nearest the road that lead away from the estate. Where it lead to Pavel did not know, for he had never been off the estate. Being a serf and the property of his master, he would probably never leave it. His master was not extremely wealthy and did not travel, as many of the great nobles did, with entourages of musicians, valets and maids and even their own apothecaries. But he was a kind master – food was plentiful, there were many festivals and celebratory occasions. When a child was born or a young couple married, the little Father was generous. Widows and orphans were taken care of with the same generosity. The whip was little used. It was not a bad life – Pavel liked working on the land and he hoped to soon marry Minka, the most beautiful girl in the entire village.

But his mother, Tasha, had not stopped crying since his little brother, Terenshichka, had disappeared. When she wasn't doing what was absolutely necessary in their home she was on her knees at the church, in front of the Iconostasis, with her gaze fixed on the icon of the Holy Mother and Child, praying ceaselessly that her son be returned. In spite of the priests' counsel of acceptance, Tasha Antonova could not accept that her small son was most likely dead.

It gave Pavel a sick feeling to think about his brother. Eaten by a Witch! Could there be a worse fate? Although a small brother could be a pest Pavel had been fond of Tishka, as they called him. For the sake of their family he wished that they could find out what had happened to Tishka. Even his father, Nikolai Vasilovich, had changed since Tishka's disappearance. Once a hearty, laughing man who had enjoyed a pipe, a glass of *kvas* and a joke, he had become morose and silent. Even Minka had grown sad, for her small sister Anna had been stolen away as well.

But there was nothing that could be done. Even the Holy Father could do nothing. When Nikolai had returned from the expedition to the woods he had only said that it was hopeless and then had not spoken for two days while Tasha cried.

Sweat running down his back, Pavel yielded his hoe in the beet field. Beets were an important crop – they made the good *borscht* that sustained many a family through the long winter. Pavel was proud to have been put in charge of the beet field and the small group of youngsters that worked it with him. They were all fourteen or older– less tempting to the Witch, it was thought. But all the same Pavel had them stand watch in rotations, for the slightest suspicious looking thing.

They had had their luncheon beneath the shade of a canvas awning provided by their master. There was deeper shade on the edge of the forest that bordered the road but no one wanted to go near it. Their master allowed them time to rest during the heat of the day until the sun declined somewhat.

They had just returned to their work when Sofia, who was perched on the fence watching, gave a shriek of excitement.

"It's them! It's them!" she screamed incoherently. "And they're riding a blue – a blue – *beast!*"

Pavel dropped his hoe and looked down the road where Sofia was pointing as she bounced up and down on the fence.

There coming down the road, was a strange procession.

A great blue beast with horns and folded wings walked down the road. Two men in brightly embroidered clothes walled beside it. And on its back were the missing children, waving and shouting happily, in company with another stranger and two cats.

Pavel and the other five in the beet field cleared the fence with a bound, shouting the names of the children as they ran fearlessly towards the beast.

Lakota, seeing the happy, excited people running towards them, stopped in the middle of the road and let Simon and Anatoly pull the children from his back.

The rescued children ran to their friends and relatives, to be swept up into their arms and kissed and hugged and

279

exclaimed over. There were many tears, but they were tears of joy.

Pavel knelt on the ground and hugged his brother to him. "Tishka! Tishka! We thought we'd never see you again!" he sobbed.

Tishka was crying too. "And my mother – "

"She has prayed every day and night for your return!" said Pavel. "It is a miracle!"

"No" said Tishka grinning through his tears, "It was a Wizard!" he pointed at Simon. "Pavel, he *killed* Baba Yaga! We need never be afraid again!"

Pavel stared at him. This could scarcely be true! Without taking his eyes off his brother, as if afraid Tishka would disappear if he did so, Pavel shouted "Dmitri! Run to the village and tell them!" Dmitri, a small wiry boy of fourteen, took off at a gallop.

Pavel stood up then, holding tight to Tishka's hand and bowed to the three strangers and their blue beast. "We welcome you to Treblinkova," he said. "You have given us a great gift!" As the oldest present it was his responsibility to treat these saviors properly. "How can we ever thank you? Please partake of our hospitality." The Russian word he used for hospitality was *Khlebosolstvo* – bread /salt.

There was no time for introductions, for within but a few moments, with shouts of joy and screams of happiness, what looked like the entire population of the village thundered towards them – Dmitri had run like the wind and the people of the village had barely waited to hear him out before they ran towards the road. And the main street of the village was not far away – just around a bend in the road.

César Doboujinsky, attracted by the noise, followed, on horseback, on the side of the road. He could scarcely believe what he was hearing – the missing children restored! How was it possible?

Doboujinsky's high-bred Rostopshchin saddle horse (a mixture of the finest Arab and English Thoroughbred stock) suddenly shied, almost unseating her rider. Doboujinsky patted his horse's shining black neck soothingly. "Be calm, Zäide," he advised the mare.

But when he saw what stood in the road he could not blame Zäide for shying. He only wondered way she had not turned tail and run.

Unlike the serfs Doboujinsky knew exactly what Lakota was. His fortune was only comfortable but his one great extravagance was books. He purchased books from all over the world, including many picture books for his children, Mily and Anastasia, when they were still in the schoolroom.

One of those books had been English – *"The Big Picture Book of Dragons"*. The children's English governess had used it as a lesson book. All of the Doboujinskys had been much taken with this book – it was Mily's favorite for years and he begged to look at it at each bedtime.

César had never thought to see a real dragon – much less on his own property. This one was a different colour that the ones in the book, though. But it was a handsome creature. How glad he was that Mily was home on leave from his regiment, having suffered a badly broken arm in a fall from a horse in a difficult jumping competition. The whole family was at home to see their favorite fabulous creature come to life!

He became conscious that the serfs were saying that Baba Yaga was dead – a Wizard had killed her! And the Wizard was standing there beside the dragon.

Another creature out of legend! César swung down from Zäide's back. At once one of the serfs sprang forward to take the reins from the little Father.

The chattering happy crowd grew silent and respectfully bowed as he advanced through their ranks. He halted in front of the strangers and bowed low, "I am César Stepanovich Doboujinsky. Welcome to Ostanchino!" he announced, "Whom have I the pleasure of addressing?"

Anatoly performed the introductions, making much of Simon's status as a Wizard. Bows and compliments were exchanged.

When Lakota spoke, returning his greeting with a bow of his head, a complete hush fell over the crowd and more than one person crossed himself or herself.

Doboujinsky looked pleased. His book had said that dragons could talk. Mily and Anastasia had both wanted to talk to a dragon. Now they would have that chance.

281

He found the Holy father at his elbow. "Is it true?" Father Zheverzheyev demanded. "The Witch is dead?"

The priest was still a young man – not yet thirty-five – but he had already the full black beard of the patriarch. The current crisis had put several streaks of gray into his beard and hair, however.

Anatoly overheard him and said "The Witch is indeed dead, Father! She will never eat a child again!"

"It is a miracle!" said the priest reverently, making the sign of the cross. He turned to look at the parents hugging children, everyone crying unashamedly. Tears stood in his own eyes as he said again, "It is a miracle!"

It was quite obvious that the journey would have to be curtailed for the day. All of the inhabitants of the estate insisted that the children's rescuers stay for a celebration. Simon grew embarrassed, for so many women knelt before him and kissed his hand. He agreed that they would stay for a feast only if the ladies would stop expressing their gratitude in such an overwhelming fashion.

César sent one of the men ahead to warn Marie Milovna, his wife, that they would be shortly having guests, among them a Wizard and a dragon.

There was no more thought of any work that day, save for the work necessary to have a celebration. The women set forth with a will to cook and bake. The men set up tables and seats out of doors to take advantage of the long evening hours.

Marie and Anastasia and several of the female servants ransacked the attics and found dozens of Chinese lanterns that had been last used on the occasion of Mily's birth. These were hung in every tree above the long tables as the air began to fill with savory smells.

Lakota's eyes gleamed as he sniffed the air. It seemed a long time since the Elf feast. He and Simon were the heroes of the hour – Anatoly had told the villagers how Lakota had set fire to the chicken-legged house. Lakota was not uncomfortable with the villagers' gratitude as was Simon – he did not mind the caresses of the children (the adults were too nervous to come very close to him) and since their gratitude had so far manifested itself as bowls of cream, he was quite content to be thanked. He could hardly wait for the pigs he smelled roasting to be done.

The Doboujinskys were an old provincial family of the best type – warm, caring, tied to their land. They had no airs about them and were as happy for their serfs as they would have been had it been one of their own children returned to them. It had been an arranged marriage for Cesar and Marie, but they had come over the years to genuinely love one another.

Anastasia was their eldest – a tall, rather plain girl with a very kind heart. Her brother Mily was a handsome, quicksilver youth – the pride of their family. He was an junior officer in a cavalry regiment – he was horse mad – but as excited as a boy at seeing a real dragon.

The celebration lasted far into the lengthy summer twilight. There was singing and dancing, story telling, and the recitation of *byliny,* the unrhymed narratives of great heroic deeds. There was much laughter – the relief and joy were almost overwhelming to the people. Before the feast there was a special thanksgiving at the village church.

Before too long there was an almost carnival atmosphere – Lakota gave rids to the children and the entire five pound bag of dragon treats was finished off. *Kvas* flowed freely.

It was quite late when everyone at last staggered to their beds. Simon, Tatya and Anatoly were quartered in the modest country manor with the Doboujinsky family.

Anatoly lay awake for a while – he found that his mind was quite restless and the many events of the day went round and round in his brain so that he could not rest.

He had been very impressed by the magic that he had seen that day. Could he learn to do that? He was intelligent enough to realize that it looked easy but was far from it. The few lessons he'd had proved that – he didn't think that he had ever worked so hard in his life as when he tried to make that crystal come to him or make the rocks fly up in the air. He wished he could have learned magic as a small boy as Simon had done.

He was lost in a blissful daydream of himself as a full-fledged Wizard when he became conscious of noise from out of doors.

His window faced one of the cherry orchards where the trees stood, many still heavy with fruit. Mily, with whom he had struck up an instant friendship, both being in the cavalry and both willing to spend hours discussing the finer points of horseflesh, had told him of the cherry thief.

The light of a bright moon filled the room. Anatoly slipped from bed, thinking to himself that the thief was rather stupid to steal cherries in moonlight – he could be seen and identified. It was probably one of the adolescent boys, doing it on a dare.

The casement of the window stood open to the still and warm night air. Cautiously, Anatoly went to the window, not needing a mage light for the room was quite light. Using the curtain as a shield he looked out towards the cherry orchard.

A branch creaked. There was definitely something in one of the trees.

As he watched a sudden bright light shone through the leaves, a brilliant golden light that illuminated the entire orchard.

Anatoly caught his breath. It couldn't be!

But all the old tales told him by his *nyanya* came back to him.

Her favorite foods were cherries and golden apples. She shone with a bright golden light, gleaming from her red and gold body.

It was the *Zharpesta*, the Firebird.

Before he had met Simon and Lakota Anatoly would have scoffed at the idea of the Firebird being real. Now he knew a Wizard and a dragon, had seen a legendary Witch come to life and was learning magic himself. He had no trouble believing in the Firebird.

There was a stout trellis climbing the side of the house. Anatoly quickly shed his night clothes and pulled on his Elfin garments.

A sturdy rose had entwined itself about the trellis – Anatoly was glad of the protection of the Elfin fabric for there were many thorns. The trellis was heavy and strong enough to use as a ladder. He jumped down the last few feet where the climbing rose became thick and impenetrable.

A strange stillness lay over the orchard as Anatoly headed for the trees as quickly and quietly as he could.

The Firebird did not seem to notice him. She was intent on her feast.

Anatoly passed a serf, sound asleep at the base of a tree. No doubt she had bespelled him. But why was he himself immune to the spell, Anatoly wondered.

If only he could get a tail feather! To possess such was lucky – good fortune came to the possessor of a Firebird feather. His sisters could have a better chance at making good marriages. His mother and grandmother could have new gowns and would never have to scrub floors again. Good fortune would lift the look of care and sorrow on his father's face. Anatoly was not sure what form the good fortune would take, but he wanted it for his family. They had sacrificed so much so that he could have an excellent education and join a good regiment. A Firebird feather would go a long way to paying them back.

Without making a plan at all, he ran lightly to the foot of the tree she was in and began to climb.

He had climbed many a tree in his youth and had no trouble in ascending the cherry tree. It was an older, large tree, as high as Lakota was long.

She was greedily eating cherries, fixated on the sweet, ripe goodness of the fruit. She was also beautiful beyond belief.

The Firebird shone with an unearthly light. She was as large as a ring necked pheasant with a sweeping, drooping tail of many curved feathers. The feathers were scarlet, trimmed with gold and her head was golden, too, with a little crown of scarlet. Her taloned feet and legs were golden as well.

Anatoly had never wanted anything so badly as he wanted that feather. He reached out and touched and –.

She turned and looked at him. He pulled his hand back, suddenly feeling as if he had desecrated a shrine.

Her eyes were huge and dark, not like a bird's at all, but like a girl's and, like a girl's, her lashes were long. Her golden beak was curved like a raptor's.

"You must be a magician," she said in a soft, sweet voice. "Else you would have fallen beneath my sleep spell."

285

"I am a very poor sort of magician as yet, lady," he replied, not certain how to address her. "I have only begun to study magic."

"And you want my feather to help you become a great magician?"

"Can it do that?" he asked in confusion.

She gave a low laugh. "My feathers are very powerful, magician. That is why men have always sought them. Why did you, if not to enhance your magic?"

Anatoly explained about his family and how poor they were in spite of a noble name and how he was expected to marry well to recoup their fortunes.

"And why did you not make a good marriage as yet?" she queried, cocking her golden head to one side.

It should have seemed fantastic, sitting in a cherry tree in the early hours of the morning, having a conversation with a bird, but somehow it did not.

"I want to marry for love," he said shortly. "I don't want a marriage based on her money and my noble family name."

"Some would say that was a good bargain,' the Firebird pointed out.

"Not without love," he said.

The Firebird looked at him for a moment and then said very abruptly, "You may take a feather."

"I couldn't – not any more!" he stammered.

"You don't want it for yourself and the fact that you no longer want it tells me that you deserve a feather," she said. "Here." She raised her wing and a long flight feather fell out and, as if on a breeze, went to Anatoly's hand. His fingers closed about it. The feather was warm to the touch.

"How can I ever thank you?" he cried.

"There is no need," she said calmly. "I am free to bestow my feathers where I wish. You could have had it had you stolen it but it is much more powerful when it is freely given."

"Will I ever see you again?" he blurted out. She was so beautiful – like nothing he had ever seen.

"Do you want to see me again, Anatoly Aloyshovich?" she asked, so low that he could barely hear her.

286

He did not pause to wonder how she knew his name. "More than anything else in the world," he said sincerely.

"Then we shall see each other again. My name is Marushka."

Before he could say anything further she spread her wings and took to the sky in a blaze of crimson and gold sparks. He sat in the tree watching her long after she had disappeared, holding the still warm feather tightly in his fist.

28

Closing In

Ekaterina awoke in a bad mood – Yuri had demanded her martial duty again the night before – and the day progressed steadily downhill from there.

Less than a week ago that little slut had run away with the Wizard, leaving no one to do her work. Ekaterina had had to endure the endless complaining of her daughters that there was no one to do their hair properly or to iron their petticoats without scorching them. Since the boy was gone too, there was no one to clean the boots, help in the stables or weed the garden. Ekaterina was finding out, as so many other miserly people did ,that one can simply not fill a void by increasing the work of the other servants. There were only so many hours in the day and only so many tasks one person could do, since the Rostov household was understaffed to begin with.

Ekaterina's character was not such that the absence of her niece and nephew made her appreciate all that they had done. Instead she became furious at them and resentful about what she thought of as their ingratitude. She conveniently forgot that she had treated them badly, both physically and mentally, and saw only that she had given them a home when she had not had any obligation to do so. And this was how they repaid her!

And if that were not bad enough, they had seen a considerable drop off in the amount of invitations they received, since the news of the Wizard's departure had gone around St Petersburg. No one cared too much for the Rostovs, but they had been willing to put up with them in order to have the company of their charming and unusual guest. Without him, the Rostovs were *persona non grata*.

And this morning had arrived the most unwelcome event of all.

Ekaterina, head aching from her daughters' shrill complaints, had been still in her wrapper, at her breakfast when, quite unexpectedly, Yuri returned home. He would have scarcely had time to get to his office.

"Are you unwell?" she demanded, putting down her glass of tea with a bang on the crumb-covered table cloth.

He did look rather green, she thought without compassion. "If you're going to be sick, don't do it in here!"

Yuri slumped into a chair opposite her. "They sent me home," he said, passing a hand through his thinning brown hair. "They said to come home and wait for a caller."

"A caller!" she echoed. "But who – ?"

"I don't know!" he said angrily. "They didn't tell me! But the way they said it – it's nothing good, I can tell you that!" He was very much afraid that his superiors had found out how many hours he had been at the whorehouse when he should have been at the office. He could still not stop thinking about what he had seen in the Wizard's room and bothering Ekaterina twice a night had done little to assuage his lust.

Ekaterina did not need to ask who 'they' were – 'they' could be any one of Yuri's superiors in the Foreign Office – and every single person, it seemed, was his superior.

"You had best go above stairs and get yourself dressed," Yuri said, looking at her for the first time. "You can't greet callers in your curl-papers and wrapper."

But she had no time even to rise from the table. Boris came into the room and presented a card on a silver slaver. "The gentleman's just come, *Madame*," he said

Yuri grabbed the pasteboard card before Ekaterina could retrieve it.

"Prince Andrei Arcadiovich Ovsyannikov," he read aloud. The name meant nothing to him. There was nothing on the card besides the name.

"I never heard of him," said Ekaterina, sniffing dismissively.

"Most people have not heard of me, *Madame*," came a cold voice "and after I am through with them, most people wish they had never met me."

Startled, Ekaterina jerked her head around to meet the coolly appraising gaze of an elegantly attired man who stood in the doorway of the dining room.

He was quite tall and very slender, clad in the most beautifully cut clothing Ekaterina had ever seen. He looked as if he had stepped from a bandbox or just that minute come from the hands of his extremely skilled valet. He was as beautiful as an angel, with handsome, refined, aristocratic features – the sort of good looks normally only found on stage actors.

But he was a dark angel – dark of hair and eyes and as cold and as proud as Lucifer. There was no human warmth in his face, and the glance that slid over the Rostovs was completely impersonal.

"Who are you to invade our –" Yuri began to bluster, coming to his feet. But one look from those dark eyes set him silently back in his seat.

In spite of the summer weather the Prince wore a cloak with an astrakhan collar slung over his shoulders. He raised a long slender hand and snapped his fingers.

From behind him a small figure, carrying a huge satchel, scuttled crablike into the room.

In a gesture that should have seemed theatrical but was not, Prince Andrei swept the cloak from his shoulders and tossed it to the little man, who deftly caught it.

The little man, a small, wizened figure in brown, then carefully placed the satchel on a chair, and folded the cloak over the back of the chair. With a brush drawn from a breast pocket, he whisked the crumbs away from the table top. He then put the satchel on the cleaned area, and whisked the chair seat clean as well. This he then offered with a bow to Prince Andrei.

"Thank you, Vakhtangov," said the Prince. "Vakhtangov is my assistant," he said to Ekaterina and Yuri. "He is invaluable to me. You will be seeing a great deal of him during the investigation."

"Investigation?" Yuri faltered, exchanging horrified glances with Ekaterina. "What investigation?"

"What is your business with us?" Ekaterina demanded shrilly.

The Prince looked at her as if she was something unpleasant one might find beneath a rock. "You may think of me as a Financial Comptroller," he said at last. "I report directly to his Imperial Majesty, the Czar."

"Financial Comptroller?" Yuri repeated weakly, his stomach making a sudden crunch.

"You have been advanced a considerable amount of Imperial monies," said the Prince, confirming Yuri's worst fears. "The Czar naturally wishes to know that it was spent wisely and for the reason for which it was disbursed."

"And now," he added in his passionless voice as Vakhtangov begin to pull papers from the satchel and arrange them neatly in front of his master, "I shall want to see all of your household records, current receipts and expenditures, from the very moment of the English Wizard's arrival."

Ekaterina swooned – landing face down in the butter dish.

It was not until the third night on the road that Evgeny discovered that quite half of the plump purse he had taken from his father's strongbox had in turn been stolen from him.

Of course, by this time he could not name or even guess at the identity of the thief. There had been too many inns, too much vodka, too many barmaids and too many villages that all looked the same to bleary eyes and aching heads.

It seemed all of a piece with everything that had been going wrong. They had been unfortunate in the horses they had hired – the landlord had sworn they had the blood of the Dons – the same horses on which the Cossacks had harassed Napoleon's troops. The endurance of the Don horses was legendary. But the two screws allotted himself and Victor had proven broken in wind and lame.

Both he and Viktor had suffered a repeat of the damned Wizard's curse. Neither one of them could see that the copious amounts of vodka and every other liquor available they had been constantly swilling might have to do with their lack of ability between the sheets. And one tavern trull had had thé gall to laugh! Their attempt to punish her insolence had failed when she proved to have a very large brother. Viktor still sported a black eye.

And yesterday they had lost the dragon's trail. No one had seen it in the sky. At Victor's suggestion they had steadily gone southwesterly, the original direction in which the dragon had flown. Evgeny had been certain that some one

291

would have seen it. How could even a stupid peasant fail to see something that big?

But no one had.

Count Pozharsky reached his goal quite comfortably in his swaying *lineika*.

His goal was a small town, near Perm, in the foothills of the Urals. This, the Count had decided, was a good vantage point for the events about to unfold. Here he could swiftly send messages to St Petersburg, for there was an outlet of the Imperial courier Service and his ring, gifted him by the Czar, guaranteed his messages top priority. He had the power to call in troops or police as was necessary. But hopefully it would not come to that.

He wrote daily to the Czar to keep his Imperial master apprised of the situation. Nicholas would expect no less. The Count sent another message – an important one – deep into the mountains with the aid of a heavily bribed, surly trapper.

The Count was well known here, for he had stayed at this very small hotel when the current situation had first developed. The innkeeper was glad to have his custom and the Count was treated as a very honoured guest. The food was excellent as was the vodka and *kvas*. The landlord offered his guest the use of his daughter as well, to which the Count was not adverse, as he had pleasant memories of the girl, a buxom beauty of eighteen, from his previous stay. He had brought with him a collection of his favorite poetry and between the food, the beverage, the girl and his books, the Count was quite content to wait for what would come.

Sacha had quickly realized that Illya had not exaggerated when he said that Karachev was "the worst of the worst".

Although he resembled closely the picture book that Sacha had found in the old nursery, Sacha soon discovered that an evil Wizard in a book was a far cry from one in real life.

Sacha hated the feeling of 'wrongness' that permeated the house on the mountainside. It mad him feel someone defiled. He could not exactly say why he felt that way – but it made his flesh creep. He soon learned to avoid the arcane symbols chalked on the floor – stepping inside one of them made him feel sick and dizzy.

There were rows and rows of glass bottles lining the walls and Sacha could swear that there were THINGS leering at him from inside those bottles. The bottles, of all shapes and sizes, held different coloured fluids. When Sacha looked directly into any one of them he could see naught but a swirling mass of colour. But over his shoulder he could catch glimpses of glittering eyes that disappeared as fast as he could turn around.

When he spoke of this to Illya the older boy assured him that he did not imagine it – there *were* things in the bottles – evil things that were best left alone. Some of them were demons and if they escaped from the bottles they were hungry and ate everything in sight – including humans. Karachev called them up from the depths of Hell and then tricked them into the bottles to await his bidding. Naturally enough, they resented being trapped in the bottles and were eager for revenge – and they didn't care who they took their revenge upon.

And some of the bottles held different eyes – these eyes were human. Sacha could not bear to look at these, for they made his heart ache. These eyes were full of sadness. Illya told him that these were the remnants of the souls that Karachev had 'eaten' during his blood magic rites. They looked that way because they had no hope of Heaven and had died unshriven by the priest.

As were most Russians, Sacha was deeply religious and found this even more horrifying than the demons. He began to think more and more about these poor souls and to wonder if there were not some way that they could be helped. Surely Simon, whom he thought of as *his* Wizard, could release these people, most of whom, Illya told him, were serfs. Sacha imagined what it would be like if this had happened to Mikhail or Luba.

Sacha wished that there were some way he could know if his friends would come for him. As carefully as did Illya he eavesdropped on Karachev and the dragon. And what he heard confirmed what Illya had told him. There was an egg and the dragon wanted it back.

293

Sacha knew that his sister would do anything for him. Would she be able to convince Simon that the egg should be returned? Sacha knew that the egg might belong to someone important – he doubted that they would release it to free him – an unimportant nobody, as his aunt all too frequently reminded him.

When he heard that someone was coming with the egg his hopes rose. He prayed to Saint Andrei and Saint Basil – his two favorite saints – that Simon and Lakota would come and rescue him – and Illya, who he had come to like – and free the souls trapped in those horrible jars.

And perhaps put an end to that evil sorcerer as well.

29

Another Wedding

To Tatya's chagrin, she and Simon slept in separate rooms. She realized the necessity of this, for they had asked the priest to marry them again. Anatoly, thinking quickly had informed the priest that his friends had been married in a Gypsy ceremony (for of course they had promised the Elves to keep their presence a secret) and the Holy Father saw at once the necessity of them being reunited under the aegis of Holy Mother Church.

It did not suit the Doboujinskys' notions of propriety that a couple married only by the Gypsies share a room. There would be time enough for that after the proper ceremony. César Doboujinsky did not anticipate any trouble in obtaining the papers necessary for a foreigner to marry a Russian national – the person in charge of such things in the largest town near to the estate was a friend of his and once Vyazemsky heard of the singular service performed by the Wizard in ridding the area of the Witch, he would be happy to expedite matters.

So Simon was conducted to one guest room, while Tatya was put in another. She was amazed by how much she missed him – not only the lovemaking, but the comfort of someone to cuddle against, the warmth of another body and the feeling of security it gave her not to be alone. Since their marriage and the magic lessons had begin the fear that was always with her had somewhat abated. She now had a protector and was learning to protect herself. True to his word, Simon had given her a dragon whistle and she wore this around her neck. It was a beautiful thing – silver, on chain of the same metal and etched in a floral design. One note from that whistle and Lakota would instantly fly to her aid. It was especially attuned to him.

All the same, it took her a long while to fall asleep that night.

The next morning Simon, on a borrowed horse and once again in European clothing, set off with César Doboujinsky to the nearby town of Gatchina to get the necessary papers. Mily bore Anatoly off to look at his cavalry mount, a Strelets from the Ukraine who much resembled a large Arab. This left the three ladies to discuss the wedding over the breakfast tea glasses.

Since it was a fine summers' day they were seated outdoors, at a table placed beneath a stand of trees. A pristine white cloth covered the table's surface and the table was laid with the finest French china and Tula made flatware, that seemed to be of gold but was of silver gilt made with an arabesque floral design. The *samovar*, too, was of silver gilt and resembled a dragon. To Lakota's disappointment it was a Chinese dragon, but nonetheless, he was charmed with it. He lay by the table gazing at in appreciation.

Anastasia could not stop looking at him. To actually see a dragon, a real dragon, here, at her own home, and to find him so good-natured and obliging – it was beyond anything she could have imagined.

Anastasia had attended the Smolny Institute, the school for girls, in St Petersburg and still kept up a voluminous correspondence with half a dozen former classmates. The letters she wrote seemed so dull compared to those of the other young women, most of whom had married and were out in the world. But now she would have the most exciting letter of all to write and with the added fillip of the wedding of a Wizard and his lady.

Marie's concern was over what Tatya would wear for a wedding gown. "My own dress," she explained, "would never fit. You are taller than I and I was plumper by far. Anastasia has nothing fine enough."

At this moment they were interrupted by a delegation of three of the serf women, who bobbed curtseys as their elected spokeswoman said, "Pardon us, great lady, but the Holy Father tells us that there is to be a wedding. Since the young lady is to marry the Wizard who freed our children, we would like to offer her the use of our wedding garments."

The speaker was Tasha Antonova, Tishka's mother. She held a large basket covered with an embroidered cloth.

The other two women were mothers of other children rescued from Baba Yaga.

"That is the very thing!" cried Marie. Turning to Tatya she said, "The women in this village are needlewomen beyond compare! Their wedding garments are exquisite!"

"It would do us much honour," put in little Anna's mother shyly, " if the lord and lady were to be wed as Russians." By this she meant that the union be performed with the traditional peasant celebrations. This was at once agreed upon and the three serf women spread out the contents of the basket on a clean section of the tablecloth, while more glasses were sent for so that all could have tea.

The garments were astonishingly beautiful – especially the *kokoshniki*, the headdresses. These were of great importance, because by tradition a married woman had to hide her hair from the gaze of the stranger. Tatya knew that the shape and size of the *Kokoshniki* varied from region to region. Each town had its own style, and by her *kokoshnik* one could tell where a maiden came from.

The three in the basket were high like crowns and heavily embroidered with pearls and thread of gold over silk and velvet. One in particular took her fancy – shaped like a tall diadem, it was covered in red velvet, fashioned in a design of gold feathers and river pearls. A fine gauze veil hung down from behind, all edged with the finest handmade lace. Large pearls adorned the edge of the *kokoshniki*.

The gown which matched it, had unfortunately been ruined by a careless spill of *kvas*.

Tatya remembered that one of the gowns given her by the Elf maidens was red, embroidered with a feather design. She had wondered at the time how the Elf girl could give up such a beautiful garment.

But now it seemed that it was meant, the other women exclaimed when she fetched the gown from her room. It matched the headdress as if they were made for one another. In the basket was a jacket of cloth of gold, bordered with pearl embroidery, with gold needlework on the very full sleeves of fine cambric. These were tied up with a brilliant blue ribbon and finished with falls of lace. Tatya would wear the gown, the jacket the dress, and boots, heavily tooled and bright red, that belonged to the third woman. The other three mothers of the returned children would supply the embroidered petticoats, the ribbons to braid in her plait and the stockings and garters.

The arrangement was highly satisfactory to all concerned and by the time that César and Simon returned with the good news that matters were well in hand and the wedding could go forward. The ladies had decided on all the particulars of the wedding, down to the foodstuffs to be served at the feast.

Lakota had wandered away while the females all talked of wedding clothes. He found it boring. He also found it difficult to understand why Simon and Tatya had to be married again. He was glad that Simon had wed Tatya – he liked her and Sacha and was happy that they were to be part of his family – but one wedding was enough.

He walked around the estate, watching the serfs at work in the field and touching noses with the horses that were bold enough to approach him. The cows and sheep ran away, but Lakota had always considered them animals of very little sense. The bolder horses included a young stallion, a Karabakh, gold with black points and a distinctly Persian look about him. Lakota could almost understand horse talk, for it was close to dragon in the many gestures of head and body language. But most of the horses, particularly the mares that had foals to protect, were afraid of him. This made the blue dragon sad, for at home he often played with foals. There was a large Thoroughbred breeding farm near Amberwell and the owners were glad to have a dragon interact with the foals.

Home! Lakota realized that he was homesick. He missed the rest of the family, Cerridwen, and all the familiar sights and sounds of Dublin. He missed Irish voices and the way that it was for dragons at home. He missed playing dragon-ball and talking to other dragons.

He also missed flying.

At home, there was a large draconic hospital attached to the Dublin Incubatory where he had hatched. If he had suffered a lightning strike at home his wing would have been regenerated in a day, two at the most and he would have been right back in the air. There were veterinarians at home that did nothing but treat dragons.

He sighed and lay down near the stallion paddock, where the young Karabakh ran and leaped, full of himself that he had touched noses with the creature the others were so afraid of.

Lakota lay his chin on his forelegs, feeling more than a little sorry for himself and rather depressed as well. He wanted to go home. And he wanted to fly! Dragons were meant to fly – not to walk!

Simon found him there a short while later.

He could see at once that something was wrong. Lakota's ruff drooped miserably and the dragon's expressive face looked sad. His posture was dejected as well.

Lakota did not even raise his head as Simon approached and Simon became alarmed. "Lakota!" he exclaimed. "Are you feeling well?"

Lakota looked up, raising his head only slightly. "I want to go home, Simon," he said a little tearfully. "I miss home dreadfully."

Simon came closer and began to stroke the dragon's sensitive eye ridges. "I know," he said softly. "I miss home too. But we have to save Sacha first, so he can come home with us."

On a long sigh Lakota said, "I know – but everything would go so much faster if I could only fly!"

"Have you looked at your wing today?" asked Simon. He himself had not checked it since the early hours of the morning when he had applied the unguent and made up the daily potion for Lakota to drink.

Lakota shook his head. He stretched out the injured wing and bent his long neck around to look at it.

Simon went to this side and checked the injured primary.

"It is almost healed!" he said jubilantly. The regeneration had speeded up remarkably. It was no doubt due to the Elfin Healer's skills. And Simon had been assiduous in applying the cream and having Lakota drink every bit of the decoction.

"Might I fly soon?" Lakota brightened visibly.

299

"Perhaps in another two days we'll try it." Simon promised him. "First of all we have this wedding –"

"But you're already married!" said Lakota 'Why do you have to do it again?"

"Because here in Russia an Elfin marriage is not a legal marriage," Simon explained.. "It is legal at home in Ireland –"

"We do these things much better at home," Lakota grumbled. "And if I can try flying the day after tomorrow, you'll go up with me – just you?"

"Yes," Simon promised.

Lakota rubbed his nose affectionately on Simon's hair. "I like everyone else," he explained "but it's special with just you and me."

Simon felt the same. He, too, could hardly wait to get back in the air again. He could not comprehend how earthbound people could stand it. The closeness of his bond with Lakota was such that it was almost as if he was flying himself when they opened their minds to one another.

The wedding was a joyous occasion for the entire village. Unlike most, this marriage had not been arranged by the marriage broker, the *svakhi*, who was a venerable old woman of the village.

The evening before the wedding the Simon was conducted to the generously sized bath house for his first Russian style bath, and then he spent the evening with all of the men of the village and Anatoly, César and Mily as well. They passed the time in singing, story-telling and drinking *kvas*. The singing was breathtakingly beautiful – the men's voices naturally harmonizing in the old songs.

Traditionally, a Russian bride sat weeping in the corner of her *izba*, surrounded by maidens who sang sad songs. She was now to become a slave – she who had been free. Tatya at first found it difficult to weep, for she was quite certain that being married to Simon would be in no way any form of slavery – but she managed to produce enough tears to satisfy the women of the village, when she found that all she had to do was think of returning to Ekaterina and Yuri and the tears came freely.

She sat in a corner of the Doboujinsky parlor, as she had no *izba*. César and Marie were to stand in place of her parents. Too, the parlor was large enough for all that wished to attend. Like Simon she was moved by the beautiful singing of the girls of the village.

The next morning Simon was brought to the house in a ribbon and bell-bedecked carriage. pulled by two golden Karabakh mares. Red handkerchiefs had been tied to the carriage as well and they fluttered in the warm wind. It was another hot, beautifully clear day.

Simon had been provided with clothes by the young men who brought him their best to try on until things were found that fit him properly. He wore a long blue coat, called a caftan, buttoned to the throat over a finely embroidered shirt and his own Elfin trousers and boots. He also wore a flat blue cap.

He had been carefully coached the evening before as to what he must do. Now he dismounted from the carriage and went to the front door of the house and knocked on the door. It was answered by César playing the role of the father of the bride. Simon gave him a few symbolic *kopeks* – the bride price. Then while everyone celebrated and feasted – there were tables laden with food of all kinds – the pair to be wed sat side by side in a corner, not even speaking. Simon longed to ask Tatya questions – for she had attended serf weddings before at her father's *dacha* – but he had been told that it was traditional to remain silent at this point and he was well aware that this wedding meant a great deal to the people of this village. It was a way for them to express their gratitude.

Since neither Simon nor Tatya had family present, the villagers took it upon themselves to be their families and, in a moving ceremony, they, one at a time, filed before the couple, blessing them. Simon and Tatya bowed low to each one. Each person received an icon and some black bread sprinkled with salt...

Then the entire party went to the church.

Simon had never been inside a Russian church until the Thanksgiving service on the day of their arrival. He was interested to see that there were no pews – the congregation stood throughout the services.

The exterior of the wooden church was crowned with four onion domes of differing heights, each surmounted by a tall cross. The carving was done with extreme skill – although the shingling of the sides and the roof reminded Simon of the gingerbread houses the Delamar cook made each Christmas.

Inside the church was a vaulted ceiling and columns on each interior wall, all carved in the floral motifs the Russians loved so well. There were individual shrines everywhere one looked, complete with brilliantly coloured icons.

But the glory of the church was the iconostasis, the icon screen, the symbolic border between heaven and earth. It was completely decorated with icons and concealed the sanctuary. This both connected and separated the priest and his congregation. The central door was called 'the Royal door' and its opening and closing during the service had many meanings – the creation of the world, and the resurrection among others. Only the priest and the Czar (during his coronation), was allowed behind the Royal Door. No woman, not even the Czarina, was permitted to go behind that door.

The richly painted icons were of tempera paint on wooden panels. The iconostasis rose three tiers against the wall, each picture of a saint or a religious scene, bright with primary colours and gilding. All were framed with ornately carved frames, some adorned with gold leaf and river pearls. All of the icons were in a special order, but movable, revealing the special events that were taking place in the kingdom of Heaven behind the screen. Simon could not help thinking that Tatya would find the Anglican church rather drab after this glory of art.

Holy Matrimony was one of the mysteries of the Holy Orthodox church. A man and a woman were united by the Holy Trinity. Each of the acts of the mystery had special meaning and significance.

Beautiful gilded crowns were held over the heads of the bride and groom during the ceremony. Father Grigory blessed the rings by taking them in his hand and making the sign of the cross over them. "The servant of God," he intoned "is betrothed to the maid of God in the name of the Father, the Son and the Holy Spirit."

Simon and Tatya then exchanged rings. It had been explained to Simon that the rings are the symbol of betrothal and their exchange signified that by themselves the betrothed couple was incomplete – together they are made perfect.

The wedding service began immediately after the betrothal service. Simon and Tatya were given lighted candles which they were to hold all through the service. The candles symbolized the willingness of the couple to receive Christ into their lives.

Their right hands were joined when the Holy Father read the prayer that beseeched God to "join these thy servants, unite them in one mind and one flesh." Their hands would remain joined throughout the service to symbolize their 'oneness'.

Then came the Crowning, the climax of the service.The crowns were the sign of the glory and honour of God which crowned them during the ceremony. They were now the Queen and King of their own kingdom – their home – with God's help and guidance. Father Grigory, taking the crowns, held then over the bridal couple's heads. "The servants of God, Simon Renovich and Tatiana Ivanova," he said "are crowned in the name of the Father and of the Son and of the Holy Spirit. Amen." The crowning was followed by the reading of the Epistle and of the Gospel – of the marriage at Cana of Galilee where Christ performed his first miracle – turning wine into water. In remembrance of this blessing wine was given the couple – the 'common cup' of better life, symbolizing the sharing of joy and sorrow and the representation of a life of harmony.

Father Grigory then led them around a table on which reposed the Gospel and a Cross, the former containing the Word of God and the latter the symbol of the redemption of Christ. This was their first walk as a married couple. The Church as symbolized by Father Grigory, was leading them in the way they should walk. This way was represented by the circle they made – the center of which was the Gospel and the Cross. A beautiful hymn was sung as they walked, that told them of th sacrificial love they must have for one another – a love that must and should be willing to sacrifice all for the other person.

Simon and Tatya were returned to their original places. Father Grigory, looking very solemn, blessed them, saying "Be thou magnified, O bridegroom, as Abraham and as blessed as Isaac and as increased as Jacob, walking in peace and working in righteousness the commandments of God. And thou, O bride, be thou magnified as Sarah, and as glad as Rebecca, and do thou increase like unto Rachael, rejoicing in thine own husband, fulfilling the condition of the law, for so it is well pleasing unto God."

After the ceremony there was more food, dancing and singing. Every so often during the feast the villagers would cry " *Gorko!*" (bitter). At each cry Simon and Tatya had to kiss to 'sweeten' the meal.

Simon found it rather odd that the men and women did not dance together, but in separate groups.

The feast and celebrating went on far into the night. Even Lakota and the two cats celebrated.

It seemed a long time to Simon before they were allowed to slip away to a room prepared for them by Marie and Anastasia. The party, César assured them, would go on very well without them.

Simon told Tatya how beautiful she looked din her Russian bridal dress. Her hair had been braided with ribbons in the maiden's single plait down her back. As a married woman she could now wear her two plaits wound around her head in a coronet again.

"Are there any more traditions I must know of before we seek our bed?" he asked her in a teasing tone.

"I can't think of any," she said, suddenly, absurdly, feeling shy again.

"There is one line in the Anglican marriage service that I have always liked and somehow it seems particularly apt here, tonight." he said.

"And what is that?" she asked.

"*With my body I thee worship,*" he said and took her in his arms.

304

30

Rusalka

Simon woke very early, his internal clock working efficiently. Lakota wanted to test his newly healed wing before anyone else was awake, in case he found himself unable to fly. He was quite self-conscious about being confined to the ground.

Tatya lay curled on her side, facing him, still sleeping soundly. This second wedding night had been quite as joyous as the first.

She seemed to be happy, but yesterday Simon had been assailed by doubts. Had he done the right thing by marrying her? Was he perhaps doing her a disservice by taking her into what would be a completely alien world? The Church service yesterday had only served to underscore the vast differences between them. In Dublin, and probably in all of Ireland, there was no Russian Orthodox Church – she would not be able to worship as she was accustomed. And that was only the beginning of it. The entire culture was different from what she was used to – even food would be strange to her. He suddenly realized that he did not even know if she spoke a word of English. English – and Gaelic – would be necessary for her new life.

He gave a long sigh and pulled the counterpane up over her before he slipped out of bed, quietly, so as not to disturb her. The problems he envisioned would have to be dealt with later. Before they could return to Ireland Sacha had to be rescued and the egg returned.

He dressed quickly, not bothering to shave, as eager as was Lakota to see if the wing was healed enough for flight. Since they would be going neither high nor far, he pulled on his Elfin clothes rather than the flying suit.

He scribbled a note for Tatya, in French, leaving it on his pillow so that she would be certain to see it when she woke up.

305

The early morning was misty and damp, thick with fog, which did not augur well for the coming day. Simon could smell rain on the slight breeze. If Lakota could fly, perhaps they could get above the clouds. Otherwise it would be a poor day for traveling.

Lakota was waiting anxiously in the big meadow near the house. He had been awake since first light.

"Look, Simon!" he said eagerly as Simon approached. "Look at my primaries!" He presented his wing for Simon to view.

The healing was complete – the damaged skin had completely regenerated. It was still somewhat paler than the surrounding skin, but it would darken in time.

"How does it feel?" he asked Lakota after a minute inspection.

"As good as new! There is no pain left at all!" Lakota furled and unfurled his wing rapidly. "I am certain that I can fly!" he announced, his eyes shining. "Please, Simon, get my harness!"

Simon went to the stable tack room, where they had made room for the large dragon harness. The only persons about this early was a pair of sleepy serfs, measuring out sweet feed to the horses.

From long practice Simon was able to harness Lakota without aid – the dragon helped with the process by putting his head well down and wiggling to get the harness to slide into place. Since they were both impatient it seemed a long time for the harness to be properly adjusted and fastened and for the safety inspection. Neither of them would have dreamed of taking off into the air without this careful scrutiny. Only the most dire emergency would be an excuse for not checking the harness.

At long last all was ready and Simon climbed up Lakota's foreleg and strapped himself into the first saddle seat, which was almost on Lakota's neck. The Elfin cloaks had been with the harness – Simon grabbed one of these since the air was so damp.

When Simon gave the word, Lakota launched himself into the air spiraling up, flying easily.

Lakota gave a great bugle of excitement, and Simon, feeling the cool air rushing past, gave a shout of joy that echoed Lakota's. It was wonderful to be up in the air once more! The blue dragon's wings beat easily, showing no signs of strain. lifting them up in to the clouds.

The clouds were low lying nimbostratus, gray and ragged, probably created by the fog that had been warmed by the early mid-summer sun. Some fifteen hundred feet up they burst through the cloud cover into a sunlit sky.

The deck of the clouds was thick and spelled a nasty drizzle for the day on the ground. The horizontal spread of the cloud was as far as the eye could see and might cover hundreds of square miles completely obscuring the scene below. But this presented no problem to the day's flight – Simon had a compass that could be attached to the saddle and like all dragons, Lakota had an innate sense of direction

Lakota made a huge circle and then, at Simon's prompting, descended again, spiraling downwards to make a nice landing almost exactly where he had taken off.

Lakota hopped from one foot to another impatiently as he waited for Simon to dismount and examine his wing.

"No sign of stress or strain!" Simon announced, after a thorough perusal of the primaries from all sides.

"Then we can fly today instead of walking?" Lakota demanded.

"I don't see why not," Simon replied. The wing had healed much faster that he had even dared to hope. He gave a great deal of credit to the Elfin healer. "But we will stop early this afternoon. You must tell me at once if it gives you any pain or distress." He resolved to keep a close eye on his dragon friend – Lakota, so overjoyed to be in the air again, might do too much and do the newly healed wing a mischief.

Lakota agreed happily. In less than two hours, after packing up, a filling breakfast and many fond farewells, they were in the air again, all three of the riders in the warm Elfin cloaks, and the cat's flight basket lined with an Elfin cloak as well.

At two o'clock that afternoon Simon called a halt to their journeying for that day. Lakota, to his critical eye, was tiring a little. They could spare the time, for with the blue dragon airborne once again, they had made excellent progress towards their goal.

Once camp was set up for the night in a forest clearing, they consulted the map. Two or three days flying at the most, Lakota said, would see them at the *rendezvous* point, where mother Volga met the Kama river, before the Volga poured into the *Kuybyshev Ras*, a great stretch of water.

The closest town to the meeting place of any size was Vyatskiye Polyany, where, as it happened, Anatoly had relatives – an aunt, uncle and several cousins. They lived outside the town on a modest *dacha*. Very few persons in Anatoly's family were flush with the world's goods.

If, as was feared, the egg would hatch before they could exchange it for Sacha, Anatoly's family could help with tending it. If Anatoly knew his young cousins, Arcady and Feodor, they'd leap at the chance to feed a dragonet.

For the egg was definitely harder. Zaandam, Lakota reported, was becoming impatient to come out. But the shell was not quite brittle enough for him to crack it and emerge, for which Simon was thankful. He hoped they could manage to get to the estate of Anatoly's relatives before the fierce Zaandam was with them.

Their camp was in a pleasant forest glade, rather like that of the Russian Elves. But there was no water close by. Lakota insisted he could smell it within the close-set trees of the birch and fir forest. The trees were too dense for him to make his way through – Simon could have asked the trees to part for the dragon, but he wanted Lakota to rest. Janus and Vron, who could have sniffed out the water, had unaccountably disappeared as soon as their paws had touched the ground.

Simon therefore decided to use his wand as a dowsing stick and find the water. Tatya went with him while Anatoly took out his gun, eager to find some game for the pot. Lakota, who was actually feeling quite tired, offered to guard the camp and tend the egg. He did not like taking care of Zaandam, for the dragonet in the egg always wanted to talk to him and Lakota disliked the topics of conversation – which seemed to be mostly those of violence and boasting. But he thought egg-tending his duty – he was after all the only one who could talk to Zaandam and he was well aware that it was very important that they knew when the egg would hatch.

But he did complain to anyone who would listen just how horrible he found the dragonet's personality.

The wood they traversed was indeed very thick It was typical of the forests of the great Russian central plain – mostly coniferous, with a mixture of deciduous trees – birch, larch and beech, amongst others. The footing was thick with fir needles and dead leaves.

Unlike Baba Yaga's wood, this was an inviting forest, with no feeling of menace. Simon wondered if the trees, like those in the British Isles, had guardians or dryads. When he asked Tatya she told him of the *leshii,* the forest spirit, who laughed boisterously in the woods and tried to lead people to become lost. He was invisible, but did show himself before misfortune struck. He stole children who were abused by their parents. Tatya also told Simon of the *polevoi*, who haunted meadows.

At the very least, Simon reflected as the wand pulled him along towards water, Tatya was accustomed to hearing about these spirits, even if she was not used to seeing them. Perhaps it would make the visits of leprechauns, brownies, flower Faeries and other creatures of the Selighe Court a bit less disconcerting for her at home in Ireland.

Home! He could only hope that she would come to regard Ireland as home. He was not certain if she had even thought about how different her life was to become or the difficulties that lay ahead. He was reluctant to speak of it to her before the current difficulties were resolved.

They were quite deep into the forest now. The wand steadily pulled at Simon, Tatya marveled that water could be found so easily. She wanted to learn to dowse and he promised that he would teach her.

Far away they heard the report of a gun – Anatoly had obviously found something worth hunting.

As if reacting to the gunshot the wand gave a convulsive leap in Simon's grasp and pointed straight out, pointing at a grove of slender white birches.

They pushed their way through the trees and came upon a beautiful, still pool, fed by a narrow stream.

It was a great deal like the pool where they had spent the latter part of their first wedding night. The trees that ringed it were not as ancient as those in the Elf wood, but the banks were as mossy. Dappled sunlight was reflected in its depths, not moonlight, but the dark water was just as inviting.

Tatya had brought two covered pails with her and bent over the pool to dip these into the water "Perhaps," she suggested to Simon over her ,shoulder, "we could return here to bathe as we –"

She never finished her sentence for with a blinding speed something shot up out of the pool and took her by the neck, and dragged her beneath the surface of the water before Simon had time to react or she could even scream.

But Simon wasted no more time. "*Spire infra aqua!*" he shouted and made a clean dive into the pool, following the trail of agitated water and bubbles left by Tatya and whatever had grabbed her.

The spell allowed him to breathe underwater as easily as he did on land. A mage light at the tip of his wand illuminated the murky waters.

The pond was filled with aquatic life – fish. frogs, turtles and many weeds. And to Simon's horror, among the weeds were a vast amount of human skeletons. Some were clearly old and covered in weed, but others, still bare, showed signs of having been stripped of flesh and gnawed. But none of the bones were very new or very recent.

It had to be some sort of water creature, like a water–leaper or a nixie – both of which lured victims into their pool or river and devoured them. Simon could only conclude that whatever had seized Tatya was too hungry to wait to entice her into the water. With desperate anxiety he swam faster, using all the tricks he had learned for propelling himself through the water from the Merfolk. He would never be as fast as they were – he had seen Merfolk out-swim dolphins – but practice had made him a much more streamlined and therefore speedier swimmer than most humans. He hoped and prayed that he could reach them before Tatya drowned.

The pond was not deep or large – less than fifteen feet in depth. At the very center Simon found them.

Tatya was in distress – her eyes wide and bulging. She looked as if she was holding her breath admirably but

310

was running out of time. Silently, swiftly, Simon pointed his wand at her and repeated the underwater breathing spell.

She turned as much as she could towards him whilst in the creature's grasp, shocked and grateful that she could suddenly breath.

And the thing holding her arm in long, clawed fingers turned towards him as well.

It was roughly humanized, and clad in what Simon thought at first to be a cloud of green pond weed. As it turned rapidly in a burst of bubbles, Simon saw that the green weed was hair. And it was very clearly female – voluptuously so. She was naked and green of skin. If she had been on land and her hair was dry, it would have reached her ankles. Her face was now twisted with rage and she hissed, letting go of Tatya when she saw Simon, exposing sharp teeth.

Simon now knew what it was. It was a *Rusalka*, a Russian water spirit – like the nixies of his native land. He had been told of them in St Petersburg. They used their lush bodies and seductive charms to lure young men to their deaths beneath the waters of lakes and pools such as this. Tatya, wearing male dress, had probably been mistaken by the hungry *Rusalka* for a young man. The water creature was angry because she had discovered Tatya was not a male. They only fed on the opposite sex. But now the *Rusalka* had legitimate prey – Simon.

Tatya, Simon saw, was rapidly heading for the surface of the pool. Good! Her lungs were probably full of water. She was sensible – perhaps she realized that he could not fight this creature and protect her at the same time.

Ssssoooo, came a long sibilating voice in his mind. *You would rescue the female? I let her go when I discovered her sex! I do not eat those of her gender! But I can and will –* she bared her teeth in a horrible leer – *eat you!* she lunged at Simon at incredible speed, webbed hands outstretched and mouth opened to bite. Webbed feet propelled her through the water.

A pulse of violet energy shot out of Simon's wand and knocked her backwards in the water, tumbling her over and over, A shriek of pain sounded in his mind. But she recovered quickly, rolling hard forward and came at him again.

311

He continued to shock her with surges of violet light, throwing her backwards each time. Shrill screams of pain and rage filled his mind, but she was tenacious and kept coming at him, determined to kill him. As he kept stunning her he swam back and up, hoping to reach the surface before she became immune to the rays of light. He could not use enough energy to kill her, for there was a danger to himself – a killing stroke could end his life as well as hers, for the water was a conductive medium for the power of his wand.The level which would put an end to her menace would kill every bit of life in the pond.

Tatya crawled out of the pond, lungs heaving and limbs trembling, to collapse on the bank beside the abandoned pails. She could barely breath, even though Simon had done something to help her. Without his help she would have drowned.

All at once she was violently sick and up came a vast quantity of pond water that she had swallowed. She began to cough and more water came up from her lungs. Through the spasms of coughing she scanned the surface of the pond. Where was Simon? Did that thing have her talons in him?

The dragon whistle still hung about her neck and she raised it to her lips. It was a terrible effort to summon enough breathe to blow it.

Within minutes there was a thunderclap of wings and Lakota, doing great damage to the trees about the pond, landed with difficulty.

"What is it?" the dragon cried.

"Simon!" Tatya managed to gasp through another bad spell of coughing. "In pond – water spirit!"

Lakota plunged into the pool without a thought of any danger to himself. At his size, to him the pool was only a puddle. With his huge lung capacity he could dive beneath the water for quite a long time and dragon sight enabled him to see easily in the murky depths.

He saw them at once – Simon, tiring, trying to swim backwards to keep sending energies from his wand and the green female creature gaining on him.

Lakota could move and strike quickly. And now he did so, drawing his long neck back and striking like a cobra. He did not miss, but grabbed her in his mouth. Closing his large teeth on her flesh. He immediately lifted out of the water, the *Rusalka* struggling and screaming. But she was no match for dragon strength.

He was not certain what to do with her at first – he could not eat her, for she was too like a human being. The metallic taste of her blood was horrible. But she was evil – and he remembered what Simon had done to Baba Yaga. Like Simon, he had seen the skeletons on the floor of the pond.

He flew upwards in a spiral, going higher and higher, while his mind was filled with her curses and threats. When he was a full mile above the ground he opened his mouth and let her fall.

He had done the right thing he consoled himself – she was evil and would only keep eating people, but all the same he shuddered and felt sick. He had never killed anyone before and it left him feeling as if he needed comfort rather desperately and someone to tell him that he had made the right choice. He turned in the air and began to swiftly fly back to where he had left his human friends. He did not need to ascertain whether or not the *Rusalka* had survived the fall. Nothing could fall from that height and live.

Simon crawled out of the pond shaking with fatigue. He could barely walk. He staggered to where he saw Tatya laying on the mossy bank. She lay so still, so pale. There was ample evidence that she had been sick. But now she was flat on her back – her long hair a tangled mess about her. She looked as if she was not breathing.

Simon fell to his knees beside her, so frightened that he himself was scarcely breathing. "Tatya," he whispered, picking up a limp hand, "Tatya, *acushla*."

Acushla – the Irish endearment meant literally 'pulse of my heart' and it came easily and naturally to his lips.

It was then that Simon realized that he loved her – that he wanted to spend the rest of his life with her and if she was dead, a large part of him would die with her.

His heart lifted when he saw her long lashes flutter and she looked up at him, with first confusion and then relief in her eyes. "What happened ?" she asked hoarsely, trying to sit up.

313

Simon put an arm behind her shoulders and helped her sit up to lean against him. "It was a *Rusalka*. Lakota grabbed her and flew off with her in his jaws."

"I hope he eats her!" said Tatya viciously and began to cough again.

Simon held her until the spasm passed, stroking her wet hair. His heart, which had been in his throat when he thought she night be dead, settled down again. He suddenly felt extraordinarily happy.

There was a loud crashing in the trees and a heavy thump and they looked up to see Lakota regarding them anxiously.

"I dropped her!" he blurted out, with a guilty look.

"Did she struggle? It was more than likely an accident –" Simon began, seeing the distress on Lakota's face and the way his ruff drooped.

"No, I dropped her deliberately!" Lakota confessed and he hung his head, now contrite and sickened anew by what he had done.

"Good!" said Tatya clearly and coughed again.

Lakota looked surprised and then said "I thought she was evil, Simon – it looked as if she eats people! Did you see all those bones? I tried to think what *you* would do!"

"You did exactly as you ought, Lakota," Simon said, in a bracing tone. "She was very evil and evil should be destroyed."

Lakota felt marginally better – it would take some time before he could think of killing her without shuddering and feeling twinges of guilt.

"She tried to kill me," Tatya said. To Simon's distress she began to cough again.

"We need to get you into a warm bed," he said in concern.

"I can take you both back to camp," said Lakota eagerly. "My harness is still on – it will be safe and faster, even though it's wet."

Before he joined Tatya dragon-back Simon filled the two pails with water – the gathering of which – a simple, everyday act – that had nearly cost them their lives.

314

31

An Ill Wind

Anatoly returned to their camp shortly after Lakota had deposited his friends in the sunny clearing.

The Lieutenant had shot a brace of pheasants and, anticipating only the pleasure of eating the plump birds, was shocked to hear of the *Rusalka*.

"I wish I had been there!" he said rather wistfully.

Simon, busy brewing a medicinal tea for Tatya, retorted, "I'm glad you were not, else I should have to had to rescue two of you!"

"I could have shot it!" Anatoly returned, a little hurt.

"One look at her and you would not had time to raise your gun," Simon said. "Her enchantments are very powerful. Fortunately she has little sway over a fully trained Wizard."

"I can't wait to be fully trained!" Anatoly said. His tone seemed to imply that he believed it was something that could be accomplished in very little time.

Simon did not dissuade him – instead he occupied himself in carrying a large mug of tea to where Lakota sheltered Tatya beneath his wing.

It had been the dragon's suggestion that she be wrapped in blankets then be put in under his wing and be laid against his side where his flight cavities were still warm. This had been done and the blankets were warmed by magic. Lakota dried her hair with his heated breath.

Lakota lifted his wing as Simon and Anatoly drew near. "She's been coughing a great deal," he said anxiously.

"She swallowed a great deal of water," said Simon. "But it needs to come up."

Tatya was more than half asleep due to the warmth. She roused at Simon's touch and looked up at him. "So nice and warm …" she said drowsily.

She was so nearly asleep that in the end Simon propped her up while Anatoly held the cup so that she might sip it. She could only manage half of it before she was sleeping in earnest.

Lakota insisted that she remain in his charge and chewed more firestone so that his cavities would retain their heat.

"Did I smell pheasant?" he asked with interest of Anatoly as Simon tenderly folded the blankets around his wife.

"I shot five of them – I was very lucky," Anatoly said modestly. In truth, he was a very fine shot. "I'll make some for our dinner."

"You can cook?" the dragon asked in some surprise.

Anatoly grinned. "My father insisted that whatever I shot or fished out of a stream I should be able to prepare it to eat. We were poor – we had but one old manservant to accompany us when we hunted and my father felt it was too much to ask him to do all of the work."

"I'll roast four of the birds and use one to make some broth for the Countess," he continued. "My mother always said that there was nothing like poultry soup for sickness or shock. I'll use some of the herbs and dried vegetables in the supplies if I might."

Simon nodded. He thought that he would add some of Oberon's journey bread to the meal. It had restorative properties that they needed at the moment.

In the morning Tatya was much improved. She had passed a somewhat painful night, coughing up the last of the water she had breathed in. Simon used the stethoscope from his egg kit and checked her lungs – they sounded clear. She insisted that she was able to go on – Simon worried about the effect of the cold air on her breathing, but Lakota said he would fly as low to the ground as he could. Since he was a small dragon this was easier for him than it would be for one of the larger breeds.

Lakota studied the sky anxiously before they left. "There are a lot of *Cirrus Uncinus*," he said to Simon as they were packing up his breast harness. "That could mean bad weather coming! Perhaps even another thunderstorm!"

"*Cirrus Uncinus?*" queried Anatoly. "What do you mean?" He looked up at the sky as if there was an explanation there.

Simon pointed up at the thin, hook-like clouds in the otherwise blue sky. "We commonly call them mare's tails for

316

they look like the tail of a horse – but the scientific name is *Cirrus* – wisp of hair – *Uncinus* – hook. They often mean deteriorating weather conditions to come."

"In 1803 an Englishman named Luke Howard named all of the clouds, with the help of his dragon Kelvin," added Lakota.

"Dragons are born with weather knowledge," Simon said , "and they study weather as well. It's always a very good idea to listen to a dragon when he talks about the weather!"

"At home I go to the Tara Druidry which has a Draconic Collegium and I study weather, draconic and human history, mathematics and languages – and a lot of other things." Lakota said proudly. This had been his first year at the Collegium – he was five – the age which a dragon was considered ready for school – and he was an excellent student.

"Will there be another thunderstorm?" asked Tatya, shivering. Simon quickly put an arm about her and held her close.

She did not want to be up in the air in another thunderstorm. She had grown very fond of Lakota and did not want him hurt again and in spite of the fact that Simon had saved them from falling to the earth to certain death, it was not an experience she wished to repeat.

"I think that we can make our destination before it becomes a thunderstorm," said Lakota confidently. No more that Tatya did he wish to be in another thunder-burst.

"Vron and I will watch the clouds too," Janus offered. She and Vron had finally come out of the woods on the previous evening, offering no explanation as where they had been. From the satisfied smile on their faces Simon had a fair idea of what they had been doing. *Another litter of kittens*? he wondered.

It was agreed amongst them that at the first sign of the weather worsening they would leave the air and take shelter under a dragon dome. None wanted to repeat the earlier near tragedy. They might not be so fortunate a second time.

The weather indeed continued to grow more threatening as the hours passed. The *Cirrus Uncinus* clouds were associated with high level winds which, if he went high enough, could cause problems for a dragon. Simon and the cats as well as Lakota kept a weather eye out for developing thunderheads. The heat that had been apparent every day was ideal for helping to develop these huge anvil-shaped clouds – or *cumulonimbus incus*, *incus* being the Latin for anvil.

They went up again after a brief luncheon, against Simon's better judgment. They were so near to their goal that Lakota insisted he could out fly any bad weather and by the evening they could be where the exchange was to be made. He had been talking with Zaandam and he was afraid the egg would hatch within the next two days. Dealing with a ravenous dragonet would be easier when they were on the ground.

Simon gave in when he was informed of the egg's imminent hatching. The last thing he wanted to suffer was the unpleasant dragonet as a passenger while they still had to travel in the air.

Volunvoshka had calculated to a nicety just when he thought the egg would hatch. It would be within the next two days, he was certain. And what would happen to the dragonet? If Volunvoshka had been able to cry he would have done so. But his father had soon taught him, with beatings form his heavy spiked tail, that an Ice dragon, particularly a powerful and strong male, did not indulge in the luxury of tears. That was for the weak and for females.

This morning his mate had arrived. The Wizard had lifted the barrier briefly so that she could enter. And that meeting had not gone as he had thought it would.

Khlebnikova was the most beautiful dragoness that Volunvoshka had ever seen. Even after having her as his mate for two years he still had trouble believing that she had chosen him. She was a princess of Ice dragons – her father the equivalent of the human Czar in their society. She had huge eyes that glittered like ice, a sinuous body and a long, regal neck. Other males looked at her with undisguised desire, and as was usual in their community, offered to fight her mate to prove their worth to her.

But it was up to the female to decide whether or not her mate would be challenged. So far she had refused every male that had offered. Would that change? Volunvoshka had often wondered miserably – for he had failed her.

When she joined him on the glacier he could not meet her eyes. A quick glance reveal her long face to be almost expressionless as was her voice when she asked for news of the egg.

"We will exchange a hostage for him very shortly," he said. "I sent you news of this – why did you come? Did you feel that I would make a mull of this too?" he added bitterly.

She did not speak for a moment. "I did not think that," she said at last. "It is only that I could not bear the waiting any longer. I had to be here for myself – to see. I have prayed every night to the Dragon Lord and it seemed to me that he wanted me to come here. I had such a feeling of urgency that it felt like a sending."

The Ice dragons believed that a strong feeling came from their Dragon Lord and that such a feeling was meant to be acted on, for in their religion it was seen as a commandment from the Dragon Lord. Such a feeling was known as a sending.

"I do not blame you, my mate, for the theft of our egg," she added, seeing his depressed stance. She understood why he would feel the way he did. A male was supposed to be the guardian of the family. "We did not ever think that men would come and take our egg! They have never bothered us in the past – they were too afraid. As much as I want our young one back do I want to understand *why* they have taken it. This must not happen again. If we know why we can stop them."

She moved closer to him. "I do not wish to allow another male to challenge you. I chose you from all the other males in our community. I have never regretted my choice. We will have our young one returned to us, I am certain,for I have dreamed of it." Dragons were great believers in the truth of dreams.

Moving still closer to him she began to wind her neck about his. "Come," she said in a low, sensuous voice, "let us make another egg! There can be no better place to couple than here on this ice. I have been too long without your attentions and I yearn for you."

319

Filled with elation. Volunvoshka returned her caresses eagerly. She did not blame him! She would not cast him off! He let out a bellow of triumph that shook the mountains as they rose into the sky. He would chase her, feeling the need to mate grow until it was almost unbearable. Once he caught her, (and she would not try very hard to evade him) he would entwine his body with hers and glide to the ice below where the act of mating would be completed.

But in the back of his mind he still wondered what would happen to the dragonet. Who would care for him? Another egg, although it would be welcome, could not replace the one that had been taken.

In spite of her reassurances and her conviction that all would be well he still worried. Her faith in him made him more determined that ever to recover the egg and redeem himself in his own eyes, even if he did not have to do so to her. Khlebnikova's trust at once shamed him and filled him with pride. He did not deserve her – he was determined to prove his worth to her so that she would never regret her choice.

Later that afternoon she was confident that they had made another egg – for she had intertwined her neck with his at least three times. This had enflamed him to heights of passion he had not felt since they first began to share a cave. He hoped she was right on all counts.

Prince Andrei took three interminable days to go through the Rostov accounts.

Each minute scrap of paper or receipt was scrutinized with a magnifying monocle that the Prince wore on a velvet ribbon around his neck. The Rostovs were questioned as to each expenditure. He wished to see each item that money had been spent upon. Their word was not enough for him. His crab-like assistant was everywhere, poking his nose in the closets, chests and even the privacy of bedrooms.

Quite the worst part was that they could not read on the Prince's features any indication of approval or disapproval. He was emotionless. He arrived early and stayed late. He would accept nothing from them – he even brought his own *samovar*. He would not wish to be accused of taking bribes, he said coolly when Ekaterina demanded if her tea was not good enough for him. And then he added, "And I doubt your tea *is* good enough for me, my good woman."

At the end of the three days, by which Ekaterina and Yuri were almost prostrate with nerves, the Prince called them into their own parlour and said without preamble, " I am done here. I shall now present my case to the Czar."

"And – ?" Yuri said daringly.

"My dear Rostov, it is in the hands of his Imperial Majesty! Once I have made my report it is no longer my affair! But if I were you," he added coldly "I should make certain that I had a good warm coat. It can be quite frigid in Siberia."

"Siberia!" Ekaterina shrieked and once more fainted dead away.

The weather seemed to stabilize for a bit and Simon was hopeful that they could reach the destination between the Volga and the Kama before flying became dangerous or impossible. The clouds were indeed developing into *cumulus*, which could become thunderheads, given the right conditions. But at the rate Lakota was flying he hoped they would be safe on the ground before the thunderstorm broke.

They were now flying below thick cloud cover. The cloud base was some 2000 feet, and higher in places. There were some pockets of wind – Lakota had expected this for the *Cirrus Uncinus* usually meant wind – in the higher elevations. He had hoped to avoid the turbulence by flying low. He was a skillful flyer and managed to avoid too much discomfort for his passengers.

The cats were the first to notice that the sky to their rear had suddenly become a curious copper colour. Janus called out to Simon, "Look behind!"

He turned his head sharply and saw the strange colour. Anatoly and Tatya turned to look as well. She gasped aloud and Anatoly muttered a curse. This could not be good! Leaning forward Simon said urgently to Lakota, "Down!"

The dragon looked behind, and saw the sky,"Oh, my–" He was unable to finish the sentence, for a violent downdraft seemed to shoot up from the earth with the force of a heavy artillery gun. It slammed into them and with Lakota's wings spread out wide and acting as if they were sails, spun them in a dizzying circle at high speed.

With the wind came heavy, blinding rain. It too, appeared to be spinning in a circle, but was actually hitting the ground with such force that it spun outward and upwards, forming a curl – a curl in which the blue dragon and his passengers were caught. Lakota could do nothing – his wings and all the flying tricks he knew were as naught against the force of the wind. Simon could not raise a hand or make himself heard against the roaring wind. The one spell he could think of that might be of use in this situation and tried to utter, was lost in fury of the weather. Helpless, they spun away into the clouds.

32

Zaandam

The blast of wind seemed to last forever, turning them over and over in its violence. Lakota struggled to pull in his wings as much as he could, for the thin skin could be torn by a strong gale such as this. Grimly, each rider held onto the straps as the cats, claws rammed into the sides of their traveling basket, howled in terror.

And then, as quickly as it had begun, it was over. Lakota snapped his wings open and glided to the earth.

Both Anatoly and Tatya were nauseated, their stomachs heaving from the turbulence, and, quickly dismounting, staggered away from Lakota to fall to their knees and be sick. Simon was in little better case, but his first concern was for Lakota and any damage to his wings.

"I'm all right!" Lakota gasped, his sides heaving like bellows, and his head hanging. "I don't think I tore anything! But I'm so sore – and dizzy."

Simon, feeling rather dizzy himself, examined each wing Lakota kept them stretched out so that he could do this easily. "I don't see any damage," he said relieved.

"Let us out!" came a plea from the basket and Simon scrambled back up onto Lakota's back and undid the fastening of the cats' traveling compartment. The Elfin made basket had survived the rough treatment it had received from the wind and had probably saved the cats' lives. The way they had spun and turned over in the air – the cats, if they had been traveling as was usual, in the front of a jacket, would have probably slipped out and fallen to their deaths.

Janus, fur all on end, was the first to emerge, on wobbly legs. "We were sick," she said in a faint voice. Simon lifted her down onto Lakota's front leg and then turned to help Vron, equally disheveled and dazed. Lakota carefully lowered them to the ground where they slid off and teetered away to sink on the grass.

Simon went to where Tatya sat on the ground, head hanging. "Are you all right?" he said anxiously.

She could barely raise her head. "Everything is spinning!" she said and would have fallen over if he had not sat down and pulled her against him.

Anatoly, close by, was laying on his back, face up to the sky. He gave a groan and said "What in the name of all that is Holy *was* that? I never saw anything like that in my life! And I never felt this bad before – oh!" he turned over quickly and was sick again.

"Oh, this is terrible!" said Lakota, much distressed by seeing his human friends so ill.

"Are you not sick?" Tatya asked him, her eyes closed as she leaned against Simon. It was very comforting to be held in spite of the fact that they were laying in a muddy field in the rain.

"Dragons don't get nauseous – they're rather like horses – if they vomit it means something is very wrong." said Simon.

"You're not sick either," she said.

"I've felt a lot better," he admit, with a wry smile, "But I've flown a great deal more than you have and been in some rough weather –"

"But nothing like that!" interrupted Lakota. He was still shaken. "And I don't know where we are!" he added, sounding worried. "Simon, I got all turned around – and my head isn't right yet!"

"Don't worry about it right now,"said Simon soothingly. "We need to get dry and out of the rain and have some tea. I'll put up a dome and if you would dry the field with your breath, Lakota..."

Glad to have something to do, Lakota did this as soon as the dome was erected and the heavy rain blocked.

Simon felt very much as if he would like to go to sleep for a long, long time after this operation, but the tent had to be put up and the tea made and he seemed to be the only one in any fit case to do these tasks.

Even the cats lapped at some restorative tea and Lakota eagerly drank a basin of it. He was not nauseous, but he was dizzy and disoriented. Lakota dried everyone's hair; the cats fur as well They staggered into the tent, allowing wet garments to fall to the floor, and fell into bed, sick and

324

exhausted. Lakota, too, went easily into a deep sleep, for such were the properties of the tea.

Both cold and hot air was blowing on Simon and he stirred uneasily. A wind was calling his name and he murmured "Go away," for he was warm and comfortable with Tatya cuddled under his arm.

"Simon! Wake up!" came a low urgent voice. "Wake up! The egg is hatching!"

As Simon woke he realized that it was Lakota speaking and he opened his eyes. The sensation of both hot and cold was explained for Lakota had put his head under the tent's side and lifted the canvas, allowing the cooler air to enter. His breath, close to Simon's face, was hot. His eyes were anxious.

"I thought he told you that it would be two more days!" Simon protested, carefully sitting up.

"He says the egg was shaken up by our flight and he can break it easily," said Lakota, shivering. "Oh, Simon, I don't like this at all!" he whispered, not wishing to wake Tatya who still slept.

Simon doubted that a shaking could make the egg readier for hatching – but he had seen cases when a determined dragonet could emerge from the egg before the shell was completely ripened. And such obstinacy seemed part of Zaandam's personality, which, according to Lakota, was characterized by impatience and arrogance.

"We've still a haunch of beef left," Lakota continued to whisper,"for his first feeding."

Simon grimaced as he began to get dressed. A haunch of beef would scarcely suffice. He hoped that Anatoly was feeling better today and up to hunting, for they would need several deer at the very least for the first few days alone – unless there was a *dacha* or a village near where they could purchase cows or sheep. It was a fortunate thing that he had a money belt full of gold, Simon thought as he hastily finished dressing – they were going to need it. A hatchling was an expensive proposition.

If an Ice dragon egg were the same as those of other dragons the hatching would take anywhere from twenty to twenty four hours. That was an average. Simon had seen hatchings go much more quickly and some much slower. It depended on the size and strength of the dragonet – and how eagerly he or she wanted to be out in the world.

Sometimes a dragonet needed help – either from its parents or the Egg Tenders at the Incubatory. Claws were still relatively soft at this stage and the dragonet still had its first small teeth and only a bubble of gas that came out as a thin stream of flame. It was better to help the emerging dragonet than see it exhaust itself and perhaps be unable to eat – which was so important to its health. Simon had read of dragonets dying of the effort of hatching, in the old days, before well attended hatchings had become commonplace.

With Lakota's help he rolled the now heavy, very hard egg out of the egg cradle and onto its side. A long crack had already appeared near the top and ran down the side. This was in order – the dragonet usually came out of one side of the eggshell. At about 10 to 13 hours after hatching began the dragonet would stick his long tongue out of a good-sized hole and test the air, panting a little after its exertions. Then with renewed vigor it would attack the shell.

Simon was indeed worried about the hatching – they had to have meat and plenty of it – the moment that Zaandam joined them. He would be ravenous and ready to eat anything that looked good to him. Western dragons would never eat a person – this taboo was deep in their blood. But he did not know about Ice dragons – they could be human eaters. And he could see by the worried look on Lakota's face that his dragon friend had had the same thought.

"He says he'll be out in an hour or less, Simon!" said Lakota. "I don't see how he can be! How long did it take me to hatch when my egg was that far along?" He nosed at the cracked egg.

"Another sixteen hours," Simon answered. "To judge by your egg and the other eggs I've seen hatch, he's been working at it about five hours."

"I think it was shorter than that – he just woke me up!" Lakota complained.

"We don't now anything about Ice dragons, Lakota – I daresay that they could hatch faster –"

Lakota sniffed a little contemptuously. He did not want to admit that the little Ice dragon, whom he cordially disliked, could be his superior in anything.

As they watched, the egg gave a great shudder and the crack spread across the egg's face. An energetic clawing could be heard.

"We'd better get that beef ready!" said Lakota, eyes widening.

Four hours later it seemed as if Zaandam would soon be with them. A thick stew of beef and broth simmered gently in a kettle. Anatoly had gone hunting and had brought back two deer, with Lakota's help as game transport.

Simon was a trifle worried about getting the dragonet to eat his eggshell after his first meal of meat. Some dragonets refused to eat it – when the parents were with the hatchling, it obeyed their command to ingest the shell and get the advantage of the calcium and other nutrients. But dragonets, sometimes satiated with red meat, refused to chew the shell. Incubatories had pulverizers that the shell could be crushed in and added to the next feeding – which was usually an hour or less after the first.

Tatya and Anatoly, looking far better than they had earlier, were doing all that they could to help. The deer, gutted and cleaned, were now roasting on spits in fire pits, and Tatya had made mugs of soup for everyone.

Both Tatya and Anatoly were fascinated by the hatching. It was far different for Simon too – the Ice dragonet was coming from the egg far quicker than any hatchling he had ever seen – and he had lost track of just how many hatchings he had been at. He pulled out his notebook and quickly sketched and made notes.

And Zaandam had began talking as soon as there was a hole big enough for him to stick first his tongue and then his snout through. Most dragonets chattered – eager sentences about how pretty the world was that they could see through the shell, talking to their parents, words of gratitude to their helping attendants – but Zaandam offered little save threats and curses. He threatened to kill everyone if they did not have meat ready for him and cursed the slowness of his progress in clawing the shell to pieces.

327

"Where did he learn those words?" said Lakota, embarrassed. "Not from me!" With the help of Oberon's spell they understood the Russian curse words and many of the swears were in Dragon as well.

"You're too well-bred to use language like that," Simon said dryly as a particularly colourful phrase came from the egg. He was totally disinclined to help the Ice dragonet get out of the shell any faster. Lakota was right – Zaandam was most unpleasant. It would be a pleasure and a relief to hand him over to the adult Ice dragon.

With a final crack the egg broke and a head emerged from a large hole. He gave a lunge outwards and the shards fell away around him.

"Meat!" he demanded, licking his lips, and looking at everyone belligerently.

Lakota put his snout underneath the handle of the steaming cauldron and swung it towards the dragonet.

Without a word of thanks Zaandam plunged his head into the cauldron and began to noisily gulp down the meat.

"No manners at all!" thought Lakota in disgust. When he himself had emerged from the egg, he had said "Please, may I have something to eat? I'm so hungry!" And Simon had been there waiting for him – Simon, who had been talking to him and reading to him since his egg had arrived in Dublin. He had had his first mouthful of meat from Simon's hand, which had helped to create their bond. And he had expressed his gratitude properly, not like this rude lout.

Zaandam looked up, globules of meat hanging from his jaws, and said threateningly "There had better be more where this came from!"

"I think I had better go and get some more deer!" said Anatoly, looking at the amount the dragonet was putting away in horrified fascination.

"He's rather pretty, though," Tatya stood a little closer to Simon. The dragonet ate so fiercely – completely unlike Lakota, who had better table manners than her Uncle Yuri.

Indeed, he was a handsome dragon. He was dazzlingly white, with silver edges to his scales. Since he was so young, his body, snout and neck were short and almost stubby – only his tail was a bit longer, for balance when he walked. His legs, too, were short and his spinal spikes and those of his tail were mere bumps. In the weeks to come these would grow and form rapidly His wings were very small and still furled – he would need to dry off – in ordinary circumstances the dragonet's mother would lick him off or the Egg Tenders would dry a dragonet with toweling. Lakota flat out refused to lick him and he did not want Simon to go too near to Zaandam. The blue dragon grew so agitated that Simon had to promise to keep his distance.

"He's dangerous!" Lakota insisted. "I'll feed him myself!" With this he dragged one of the two roasting deer off the spit and gave it too Zaandam, who, with a muted roar, dug into it as if he had not just devoured an entire haunch of beef. Again there was no word of thanks or appreciation.

Simon's fears proved groundless, for after eating the deer – bones and all, much to Lakota's disgust – the dragonet gave a large belch and then gobbled down the egg shell. He then lay down on the grass and began to pick his teeth with a claw. Meat juices ran down his chin and chest but he made no effort as Lakota would have, to clean himself. Soon he was snoring – loudly.

" Can't we get rid of him now?" Lakota said to Simon. "I could take him up and drop him far from here!" he added eagerly.

Simon sighed. No more than Lakota did he like the rude and demanding Zaandam

"We have to exchange him for Sacha," he reminded the dragon. "I don't like him either but I am not going to take the chance of something happening to Sacha because we don't have the dragonet."

Tatya, who had drawn closer to Simon when she saw with what ferocity Zaandam attacked his food, slipped her hand into her husband's and squeezed it gratefully. She was so thankful that he still thought first and last of her brother's welfare. She had been so lucky to marry him!

Simon faced the fact hat he might have to bespell the aggressive dragonet. He hated to even think of it – a bespelled dragon was a sad thing, In America he had seen dragons that had been bespelled to work the gold mines in New Spain – a process which only served to point out the hypocrisy of the Inquisition, for an institution that decried magic and those who practiced it had no hesitation in using it to further their own ends. There were many brave souls and their dragons who risked their lives to rescue both bespelled dragons and slaves from their cruel masters.

But if Zaandam was to be a threat to their lives he would have no choice. He hoped that Lakota would be able to control the dragonet. There was a little less than a week until the exchange was to be made and they had yet another problem – even Lakota had no idea where they were at the moment. They had been completely blown off their course.

33

The Cham of Tatary

Zaandam ate two more deer before nightfall. The third deer was not cooked – he scorned the niceties of civilized behavior and wanted raw, bloody food.

Lakota was completely repulsed by his behavior – the dragonet ate savagely, did not mind the bits of meat that hung from his jaws and made no effort to clean himself after he ate. And worst of all, in Lakota's book, he had no gratitude for all the effort that everyone was going through to meet his incessant demands. He laughed at Lakota's protests in a sneering, superior way that was very hard for the blue dragon to bear.

"I don't like him at all!" Lakota, his ruff fully extended, said to Simon after Zaandam finally fell asleep, his stomach bulging. "He is rude and mannerless and dirty! If all of the Ice dragons are like him I never want to meet another one!"

"And he's damned greedy!" remarked Anatoly, coming up to them where they stood watching the dragonet sleep. "I bagged four deer today – and at this rate the game will be eliminated in this area in but a few days' time."

"At first light we need to find out where we are and if it is at all possible to purchase some cattle and sheep from somewhere near by," said Simon thoughtfully. "Someone has to stay here who can control the dragonet – which I can if needs be. But if you would be so good, Lakota, to take Anatoly aloft and scout out the area?"

At the thought of a solo dragon ride Anatoly brightened, but Lakota protested. "I don't want to leave you and Tatya and the cats alone with *him*! What if he tries to eat you when all the deer are gone?" All the loathing that he felt for Zaandam was in his voice.

"I can protect all of us from him – he has no flame and is still relatively small. He has no defenses against magic that I can sense," Simon assured him. Zaandam was about the size of a good-sized setter. But that would change rapidly. He could double in size in a week.

Lakota still looked uneasy. "You must promise me that you won't go near to him, nor even lay your wand down until I am returned! Perhaps we could give him a sleeping potion from Stuart's medical kit!" he added hopefully.

It would take far more sleeping potion than they had available to stun even a dragonet the size of Zaandam. "There are control spells that I can use – I don't like to do so, but I will if our lives are endangered – don't worry so!" Simon reached up and stroked Lakota's forehead.

The blue dragon nuzzled him affectionately. "Well, I do worry! He's so horrible! And he doesn't like people! I don't understand him!" He could not imagine life without people – especially Simon.

Reluctantly, Lakota finally agreed to flying over the countryside with Anatoly, both to look for cattle and sheep, and to take their bearings. They had to find out how badly they had been blown off course and resume their travels. Transporting the dragonet would be difficult as of course he could not fly – it would be almost a year before he could begin even short flights, for the wings were the last thing to strengthen and grow.

But Simon decided to worry about transporting the dragonet later – first of all they had to feed his voracious appetite – and orient themselves.

Before they all retired that evening Zaandam awoke and demanded another deer. Anatoly decided to hunt again at first light – for that left nothing but a small ham for the dragonet's breakfast – and since it was not bloody, but cured, he would no doubt make a fuss.

Lakota had been determined to remain awake and guard his human friends from Zaandam. He almost wished that the horrible dragonet would wander away in the night and they would be rid of him. But dragonets had a type of bond with those who fed them and therefore Zaandam would not leave a good source of food unless driven away. Since it was a fine night and it would be better not to expend unnecessary energy, they did not sleep beneath a dragon dome.

Lakota was worried about Janus and Vron as well – Zaandam eyed the cats as if they were some sort of dragon snack. Lakota begged Janus to stay well away from the dragonet. She was his good friend and he did not want to see her vanish in one gulp into Zaandam's maw.

She agreed readily, for she liked him as little as did Lakota. She had always been around dragons – since she was a kitten, both in the British Isles and in America when she had accompanied Simon abroad. But she had never seen one like this one. Zaandam was outside everyone's experience.

After supper Lakota requested that Tatya make him a cup of coffee – he had heard that it would keep him awake – but he spat it out in disgust, it was so bitter! "How can you drink that stuff?" he asked his human friends, who were all enjoying an after dinner cup.

"This is exceptionally fine coffee!" said Anatoly in surprise. He had learned to like coffee when stationed in Turkistan, for normally Russians preferred tea.

"Ugh!" Lakota reiterated and went to the stream for a long draught of water. They had been fortunate to land in an area that had a small stream and a natural pool deep enough for dragons to drink from. The pond life seemed to be confined to frogs and minnows. The blue dragon thought that he could not have borne Zaandam *and* another *Rusalka*.

Lakota was glad when the cats went into the tent to sleep with Simon and Tatya. He was gladder still when Simon put a spell on the tent that would alert them to Zaandam coming near it – attuned to the dragonet, so that he, Lakota, could still approach it without setting off the alarm.

In spite of his best intentions Lakota fell asleep before midnight. He slept deeply and dreamlessly and did not awaken until terrified squealing and bellowing awoke him just after dawn.

Abruptly Lakota awoke and found that they were surrounded by horses and cattle. Zaandam was bellowing "Meat! Meat!" and moving as fast as his stubby legs could carry him, which was not as fast as a horse or even a cow could run.

"Simon!" Lakota shrieked as Zaandam lunged towards a slow moving cow. As Simon and the others tore from the tent Lakota briefly flew above the melee and grabbed Zaandam by the scruff of his neck and took him aloft.

The dragonet screamed in rage, demanding to be put down at once. "I will eat it! I will!" he yelled, thrashing about.

Keep quiet or I'll take you up higher and drop you! Lakota threatened in dragon mind speech. *You cannot eat those cows – they're not yours! Nor do we EVER eat horses!*

"I don't care for your stupid rules!" Zaandam yelled out loud. "I am hungry – I am going to eat! And those horse things smell good!"

Lakota shook him like a rag doll. *Listen to me! All dragons must obey the law! You can only eat what is paid for, what is yours! To do otherwise is thievery!*

Below him he could see men on sturdy horses arriving, and bringing the herds together. They were all dressed alike in round fur hats with flat tops, long flowing caftans and knee-high boots. Rifles hung over each shoulder and belts of ammunition crossed over their chests. Several of the men had pulled their guns from their shoulders and were aiming them up in the air – at himself and Zaandam, Lakota realized. He winged higher, out of range. He saw Simon gesturing angrily at the men but could not hear what was being said over the noise of the herd animals and Zaandam's continued threats and imprecations.

But the rifles were lowered, and Tatya, who had run back to the tent , came back with Simon's purse. Lakota saw the glint of gold as coins changed hands and two of the mounted men began to cut several cows from the herd.

There! Simon has paid for some cows for you! Lakota told Zaandam. He hovered in the air as two men took the cows behind their tent, away from the rest of the herd and quickly dispatched them.

As the smell of blood rose in the air Zaandam struggled in Lakota's hold. Disgusted, Lakota, spiraled down and let go of Zaandam while he was still a foot or so above the ground.

Clumsily, the dragonet landed and lumbered eagerly towards the dead cows, salivating and snapping his jaws. He fastened on one at once and began to tear at it, growling at Lakota as the older dragon landed.

"It's mine!" Zaandam threatened. "You stay away! I'll kill you!"

"As if you could!" said Lakota, his voice full of scorn. "And I don't want your cow! Why, it isn't even cooked!" He was revolted by the way Zaandam wolfed his food and crunched the bones. He even ate the hooves!

He was growing hungry, though. He knew that Simon would not fail to consider his needs. He could wait for his meal to be cooked – *he* was not a barbarian!

He turned his back on the sickening spectacle of the gorging dragonet and walked over to where Simon and Anatoly were talking with a herdsman. The balance of the riders were trying to bring the herd to order – Zaandam, unlike Lakota, smelled like a predator to them. But Lakota's appearance and size were not what they were used to and they showed every sign of wanting to flee. Finally, the herders were given a signal and they began to move the herd away.

"Ho!" said the short-legged, rather swarthy man who appeared to be their leader. He spoke Russian with a distinct accent, speaking loudly as if his throat were hollow. His utterances were sudden and abrupt. "We never expected to find dragons here in our grazing land!"

He had a rather Oriental look to him – his eyes were slanted in his broad, flat face, his hair dark and he wore a thin mustache that drooped down on each side of his mouth and a tuft of dark hair on his chin.

"We are not trespassing, I hope?" said Simon "We were blown here by the storm –"

The man waved a hand as if to dismiss Simon's concern. He grinned, showing a gold tooth. "Not at all! It's added a little excitement to our day and put gold in our pockets! If you need any more cows –"

"We'll need quite a few," Lakota put in gloomily. He can eat more than I thought possible!"

"A talking dragon!" the head herdsman interrupted, looking admiringly at Lakota. "That's something out of the old tales!"

"Are your people Tatars?" Anatoly, who had been studying the herdsmen, asked suddenly. "I've heard of you –"

335

"Who hasn't heard of us? But we are the last of the Golden Horde that came here with the great Temuchin, the great Cham, Temuchin's grandson, Batu took Kiev and his empire lay as far as the Adriatic. We are the last of that Golden Horde, the last of the true blood. We have held ourselves apart from the other peoples of this land and kept our blood pure. But now, we are not warriors, we are herdsmen, but we are still people of the horse!" he added proudly. "And I am the leader – the Cham – of Tatary. I am Tarquin and I am the last Cham in the direct line, for I have neither son nor daughter." He paused, looking sad for a moment.

Simon performed the introductions and invited Tarquin to have coffee with them. "My wife is preparing it at the moment, as well as fried ham, eggs and bread."

Tarquin accepted at once, saying it was a long time since he had broken his fast. "And we can discuss how many cows you will need as well!" he added jovially, jingling the purse that hung at his waist

"I would like a cow too, please!" Lakota put in.

"I purchased for you a side of beef that was roasted yesterday," Simon told him

"One of my men is fetching it –" said Tarquin "It's cooked in a pit and smoked with spices – you'll like it!"

"Oh, thank you!" said Lakota gratefully. He was growing hungrier by the moment. He would have waited patiently for it to cook but this was better. And unlike the boorish dragonet, he would properly express his gratitude.

The humans were very pleased to discover that the storm had not blown them that far off their course. Tarquin declared them to be less than a day away from their goal, as he showed them on their map. "But I'd be very careful thereabouts if I were you!" he said after polishing off two large slabs of ham, a platter of eggs and three cups of coffee. "We've heard rumors that there is a great sorcerer in that region. Word is that he has cleaned the Urals of every human being that made his living thereabouts. He's got a huge dragon at his beck and call – one that makes your dragons seem tiny. They also say he's a black magician."

"My husband is a White Wizard," Tatya put in, pouring Tarquin another cup of coffee. "He defeated Baba Yaga."

"Is that so?" Tarquin looked at Simon in interest. "That should be a good tale! I could eat another slice or two of that fine ham while I hear it!"

Anatoly told the tale while Tatya cooked more ham.

Tarquin was an excellent audience. He was properly awed at the right places and slapped his knee in glee when Anatoly told of the Witch fading away into dust. "Ho!" he said. "I guess *you* won't have to worry about a black sorcerer!"

Simon was quiet – he did not like the sound of this. Perhaps this black sorcerer *was* in league with the Ice dragon who had kidnapped Sacha. It began to seem as if there would be more than a simple exchange involved.

Tarquin informed then that his people were traveling in the very direction that they wished to go – and that they were more than welcome to go with the herds.

Given Zaandam's needs, this would be a fitting solution. They gratefully agreed. Tarquin had quantities cattle, sheep and goats – all of which he was willing to sell.

Outside the tent, Lakota's cow had been delivered. As Tarquin had said. it was smoked, with some Oriental spice that Lakota found very much to his liking. After thanking the men who delivered it, Lakota lay down to enjoy his meal. He did not know nor really care where Zaandam was – after two whole cows that dragonet ought to be sleeping.

"I want that!" came a loud voice.

Lakota looked up sharply . A few feet away Zaandam was staring at him greedily.

"You've had two cows!" Lakota said indignantly. "Others besides you are hungry! "

"I'm still hungry!" said the dragonet belligerently.

At this moment Simon came around the corner of the tent and seeing something move, Zaandam lunged at him.

"NO!" Lakota screamed and lunged himself. He grabbed the dragonet and threw him across the field where he hit a large tree and fell to the ground. He looked up, shaking his head and then hauled himself to his feet. "I'll freeze you!" he said, his voice growing shrill.

Eyes narrowed, Lakota said "If you ever make a move towards Simon – or any human or anyone I hold dear, I will incinerate you! I don't like you in the least and I would not mind turning you to ash!"

"What's incinerate?" Zaandam demanded, his tail lashing. Even the thick-skinned dragonet could tell by the tone of Lakota's voice that the older dragon was extremely angry and meant every word he said.

"This!" Lakota let loose a long jet of hot flame and the tree behind Zaandam burst into fire, consumed in mere minutes. It fell into ash as they watched.

Simon had thrown up a protective shield the minute he saw Zaandam's charge. Now he stayed behind this, wisely not interfering. This was between the two dragons. Lakota needed to assert his authority over the headstrong dragonet.

Zaandam looked astonished. "But dragons spit ice!" he said, almost pleadingly. He knew himself to be largely immune to the freezing of ice – it might slow him down but it would not stop him.

"Not where I come from," said Lakota.

"That couldn't hurt me!" the dragonet said, some of his bravado returning.

"My flame can melt mountains and rock. You are only flesh and blood," said Lakota grimly. "You will do as I say or I *will* flame you! And Simon is a Wizard – he can turn you into rock – he just turned a Witch into rock and then turned her to dust so that she blew away on the wind!"

Zaandam looked from one to the other of them. In no good humor he said "Oh, all right. I will obey your stupid rules."

"You will only eat what we give you – you will not eat humans, or cats or horses or anything else that I tell you is forbidden," ordered Lakota.

Zaandam agreed grudgingly. "But I want another cow – right now!" he stated pugnaciously.

338

34

Waiting

It proved a good decision to join forces with the Tatar tribe. Simon couldn't see how they could have feed Zaandam without the Tatars. The ice dragonet ate more than any dragonet that Simon had ever known. He ate at least four cows a day, and several sheep and goats as well. But the Tatar herds were vast – they met several more groups of herders when they reached the confluence of the Volga and the Kama.

With the Cham's permission Simon cast a wide calming spell on the herd beasts so that they would not be terrified at Zaandam's feral scent nor at Lakota's appearance.

The Tatar people proved to be friendly and curious about their new acquaintance – they were also eager to take Simon's gold for the cows that Zaandam gulped down. He reflected that it was a very good thing that he had filled his money belt before leaving St Petersburg. At this rate, he would have to use Chenevix's letter of credit when they reached a large metropolitan area. As a Dracophilologist, Simon did not begrudge the dragonet his food – this was an invaluable opportunity to study the breed – but he did wish that the dragonet was a more pleasant companion. He was continually distressing Lakota.

Tarquin indicated that his people would be staying about a fortnight in the area of the two rivers – until the grazing was done and they attended a large market fair in the area where they would sell and trade their stocks and the handcrafts made by the womenfolk. As the exchange was due in less than a week now, this suited the party down to the ground. In that time the voracious dragonet would become someone else's problem.

They were all sitting about a fire one evening with cups of tea when Lakota said suddenly, "What if they don't want him back when they see what he is like? I can't imagine that even his parents would be happy to have him returned to them!" He looked significantly towards where Zaandam lay sleeping off another gigantic meal.

Anatoly and Simon exchanged uneasy glances. They had not thought of this possibility.

But Tatya sais soothingly, "Do not worry. Lakota. Mothers always want their children, no matter how horrible they are. My aunt Ekaterina loves Evgeny – and he is far worse than Zaandam! She just does not want to give him any money."

"That reminds me," said Simon and rose from his seat to give Tatya a little embroidered bag. "I saw you looking at those beautiful embroidered shawls this morning – you should be able to buy one if you wish."

The bag was full of *rubles* and *kopeks*.

"I can't take this!" she protested.

"Why not?" he returned. "I am your husband – it is my responsibility to give you pin money – and a dress allowance among other things. If we were in Ireland there would have been a legal contract before we wed, to spell out exactly how much you would get."

"But I brought nothing to the marriage!" she said, thinking of her lack of dowry. Most men would not have taken her without a portion.

"You brought yourself – that's enough for me," said Simon firmly and pressed the purse into her hand.

Later, when she was by herself, she counted it and was stunned at how generous he had been – it was four times what Yuri gave Ekaterina.

"I'm going to need some *rubles*, Simon," Lakota announced. "I want to have one of the women make an embroidered collar as a gift for Cerridwen and I have only English pounds."

"You have money?" Anatoly asked, rather astonished.

"I earned it!" said Lakota. "I'm a teaching assistant at Trinity University!"

Anatoly shook his head in wonder. "Why," he then asked, "is this Ice dragon so different than you are?"

"Because I am nice and he is not!" said Lakota, his tail twitching

"No, it's more than that," Simon said, smiling affectionately at the blue dragon. "You must remember – Ice

340

dragons are feral. They have no history of working and cooperating with man as British and American dragons do. It's been almost one thousand years since Merlin changed the dragons and of course, when America was settled, dragons went with the settlers –"

"And they discovered native breeds there!" Lakota interrupted eagerly "Like mine!"

"And those dragons were accustomed to existing with the Native peoples," Simon continued. "With Zaandam it is a question of survival – if he is mot selfish about his food he might starve. British and American dragons are accustomed to having their food provided – by their parents, by the Incubatory and then later by their employers or they can purchase their own food with their earnings. And there are pensions and homes for old, sick dragons as well. Western dragons never have to hunt –"

"I don't even know HOW to hunt! I don't want to kill anything! " Lakota put in. "HE doesn't know either – he wants me to teach him!"

"What did you tell him?" Tatya asked.

"I told him his manners would have to improve a great deal before I taught him anything! I hope he is off our hands before I have to teach him!" said Lakota.

"There seems to be little danger of his manners improving!" Anatoly declared. He had watched, in horrified fascination from a safe distance, as the dragonet had de-voured two cows that evening, growling and shooting threatening glances at any one who even looked his way. In two days' time Zaandam had become visibly larger and more intimidating.

"I want to be well rid of him!" Lakota sais rather wistfully. "He's not even civilized! No dragon I know would even want to acknowledge his acquaintance!"

"We won't be responsible for him much longer," said Simon. In spite of the sheaf of notes had had made, and the many sketches as well that would make the basis for a monograph that he could present at the next Dracophilology symposium that was to be held in Boston, at Harvard University, in the autumn, he would be glad to see the last of Zaandam as well. He suddenly wondered if Tatya would like Boston. He still had many friends there that he would like her

341

to meet and fond memories of that city as well. Perhaps Sacha could go with them...

After losing the trail rather abruptly Evgeny and Viktor had had a stroke of luck. They had kept going steadily south west, thinking that they might as well stay on the original direction given them by Pavel the footman. For them, this was a profound intellectual effort.

They stumbled across the town of Gatchina – they were actually lost – where the Wizard who had defeated Baba Yaga was still a nine days' wonder. They did not hear of the wedding, for César Doboujinsky's friend who had helped Simon obtain the proper papers was a close-mouthed man who saw no need to regale his neighbors with what happened in his office.

After that it was easier to track them. In the fair weather people had seen the shadow of the dragon passing over and were eager to talk about it.

Evgeny and Viktor earned much enmity on their way, for they did not even thank their informants properly, much less give them the small amount of coins expected. Evgeny resented giving even a *kopek* to a peasant, no matter how valuable his information.

As they drew steadily closer to their goal, even the length of time they had been traveling had not diminished their eagerness to revenge themselves on the English Wizard and they spent many an hour at night going on in sickening detail what they would do to Tatya when they had her naked and whimpering.

Count Pozharsky was quite snug in the Inn at Perm. With a bottle, a book and a girl he was more than content. The landlord's daughter proved a willing and talented partner.

When news of the noble visitor to the area became common knowledge he began to receive invitations as well and dined out and attended card parties.

And because of the proximity to the Urals, he began to hear more of the black sorcerer that had come to live there as well. He was even introduced to some of the refugees that had

342

fled the depredations of the Ice dragon. What he learned interested him.

He called in his spy and learned some more very interesting things. It seemed as if there would soon be a confrontation. And he wanted to be there to see it. Unfortunately, this was one affair in which the meddling of the Secret Police could not assure the outcome. For they had no way of influencing magicians.

Sacha and Illya had become great friends. It was a relief to Illya to at last have someone to talk to and Sacha heard all about Illya's family and village and how he had not wanted to become a cloth merchant. Sacha proved a sympathetic auditor as well as a great help about the house.

The boys overheard Karachev discussing the time of the exchange with Volunvoshka and his mate. The female Ice dragon was eager for the exchange to take place for she was worried that the dragonet had hatched and there would be no one to tend to its needs. In a way, Sacha wished he could assure her that Simon studied dragons and would know how to care for it, as would Lakota. Sacha was not even certain that the Ice dragons knew about Lakota, for they never mentioned him . But Volunvoshka had to have seen him – he had told the necromancer that he had been watching the Rostov home for days before Sacha was snatched. Of course, Lakota was not as big or as fierce as the Ice dragons – perhaps they thought him not worth mentioning.

In truth, Volunvoshka was completely contemptuous of Lakota.

"Barely twenty feet long," he said dismissively to his mate. "And blue! What sort of dragon is *blue*?" he added in disgust. "It's my belief that he is not a dragon at all but a lizard, magiced to dragon size by a Wizard! You know Wizards – they can not resist tampering with nature!"

His mate agreed with his assessment. They had no knowledge of any other dragons in the world. The Ice dragons were proud, insular and xenophobic. No one could be better than they were, so there *was* no one else.

Karachev was actually looking forward to a possible confrontation with another Wizard. He had settled it in his mind that the Wizard was his old rival, Tenisheva. He would positively enjoy flexing his magical muscles against a competitor. Such was his arrogance that he gave no thought to another Wizard other than Tenisheva. Who else could there be? He laughed to think that that fool of a Czar thought to challenge him with such a poor stick of a Wizard. The outcome was forgone.

And Karachev was worried next to naught about the dragonet. It mattered little to him. What was coming to matter the most were the energies that he would gather from Tenisheva when he killed him. He would make certain that his rival died in pain and agony so that the blood energies he could harvest would be all the stronger. Torturing and killing and ordinary human beings added to his power but to kill another Wizard and to drain his life energies –! That would make him powerful indeed.

As the time grew near for the exchange Tatya grew fearful. What if something went wrong? What if Sacha was already dead? What if that Ice dragon had eaten him or otherwise harmed him of Sacha had not cooperated? She wished desperately that they had some assurance that he was alive.

Simon, waking sometimes at night, would find her laying rigid in the bed beside him, trying not to cry but succeeding very ill.

He sought to reassure her as best he could. With the aid of the map he showed her that Sacha was still alive – for the scarf tied on the pendulum still swung to the same spot in the Urals – which it would not do, he explained, if Sacha were no longer among the living. He also tried scrying for Sacha, but there seemed to be some sort of etheric barrier in front of the mountains. If the sorcerer was indeed aiding the Ice dragon he was no doubt magically protecting then from scrying. It was what he, Simon, would do in the circumstances.

He was not certain that Tatya believed his reassurances. She almost desperately clung to him at night, seeking lovemaking as a relaxant – for after making love she could sleep for a while until bad dreams and anxiety woke her again. Simon only hoped that one day Tatya would love him as much as she loved her young brother.

Everyone would be glad when the waiting was over. Not for the first time Simon wondered why the long wait had been proposed.

Karachev could have told him. The necromancer wanted his rival to have time to learn to be afraid.

35

Rendezvous

The last few days before the exchange of Sacha for the Ice dragonet passed with excruciating slowness, enlivened only by the constant struggle to keep Zaandam fed and out of trouble. The dragonet was growing rapidly – in a week he was twice that size he had been when first hatched, and his appetite grew accordingly.

Neither Lakota nor Simon had ever seen a dragonet eat as much as did Zaandam. Lakota voiced the opinion that Zaandam was eating more than he actually needed – he was just greedy and ate so much because it was available.

The two dragons cordially hated one another. Zaandam barely obeyed Lakota, in spite of his fear of being incinerated. He was constantly testing his limits – threatening people and animals and laughing at their fear or anger. He tried to steal Lakota's food as well, until Simon put a magical impenetrable barrier around the blue dragon so that he could eat in peace.

Lakota longed to flame the dragonet or take him someplace far off and leave him there. He dreamed about dropping the dragonet from a very great height as he had the *Rusalka*. He would feel no guilt over doing that to Zaandam!

Only the knowledge that they needed Zaandam alive to exchange for his friend Sacha kept the dragonet from serious harm or even death. Lakota, normally of the most equable temper, had nearly reached the end of his patience. He had hoped that intimidation and his own good example would improve the dragonet but it had not worked out that way. Zaandam, if possible, grew worse each day – more demanding, more of a bully, more greedy, rude and graceless. Lakota had never hated anyone before, but he was getting to the point that the mere mention of the dragonet's name was enough to make him simmer with anger – literally. Steam trickled from his nostrils constantly – a certain sign of agitation.

Everyone was glad when the day marked for the exchange dawned. But it started badly. Zaandam demanded three cows for his breakfast and a sheep as well and ordered deer for his luncheon.

Anatoly, who was responsible for hunting down the deer, was as disgusted as Lakota. "It is as if I was feeding an eating machine!" he grumbled. He would have preferred at least a show of gratitude for the hours he had to spend tramping about in all kinds of weather, trying to find game for the churlish dragonet. But nonetheless he left early, before the others had even breakfasted, on his hunting expedition, hoping that this would be the last – for today should see the departure of the obnoxious dragonet.

A morning mist hung heavy the valleys and depressions and over the surface of the river. It showed every sign of burning off, however and the day promised fair and hot.

Tatya had slept very ill indeed the night before – until, at about midnight, Simon made her a cup of tea with a small sleep charm surreptitiously added. Perhaps he should have not done this without her knowledge, but she was too tautly strung and too worried over what might go wrong. And she was keeping both of them awake.

Over a breakfast of which she ate next to nothing she voiced her fears. What if the Ice dragon did not show up? What if Sacha were injured in some way? What if the adult Ice dragon did not like the way they had cared for Zaandam?

Lakota snorted with derision when he heard this, lifting his snout from the basin of grain, honey and cream he had been ingesting. "Not like the way we have cared for him? We've bent over backwards to please him! He has had the finest food – and the most expensive – and it is not our fault that he will eat naught but meat!"

For Zaandam had turned down all offers of cream and honey, or the grain Lakota enjoyed so much. The dragonet scorned fruits and vegetables as well, He wanted nothing but raw meat and mocked Lakota for eating those things – no *real* dragon, he said, sneering contemptuously, would eat such pap.

Simon sighed. He wanted this to be over and done with. The time set for the exchange was noon – and it would be a long morning, he was afraid. Between Tatya's fears and Lakota's anger and the fact that two days earlier he had had to confine Zaandam in an etheric barrier – for he would not stop chasing horses and snapping at them – it would be a blessed relief to end this entire affair.

The only thing he wanted to do once Sacha was safely with them again, was take his wife and brother-in-law and head home. It would not be that easy – Sacha and Tatya would need passports, and who knew what else – for that they must return to St Petersburg in all probability.

But Simon was dreaming more and more of home – of the pleasures of being with his family, of working in his Tower again. He would introduce Tatya to Dublin – buy her the wardrobe she deserved, take her dancing and continue her magic lessons. His mother and sisters would be kind to Tatya for his sake and would soon grow to love her for her own. If Sacha proved to have magic he could be enrolled at the Tara Druidry, or if not, go to Saint Pádraig's, an excellent school in Dublin.

So lost in this reverie that he quite lost track of the conversation and was startled when Lakota said his name loudly.

"Excuse me, I was woolgathering!" he said. He smiled at the blue dragon and at his wife. "I was thinking about home – I hope that we will soon be heading there."

Lakota looked wistful. "Oh, I do too!" he said. "I will be glad to leave here!"

With a jolt to her stomach Tatya suddenly realized what had never occurred to her before – she had been so focused on rescuing Sacha that she had though of very little else. Simon's words had brought home a rather frightening prospect.

She had to go and live on a foreign country amongst strangers. She did not speak the language – she knew only a few words of English and none at all of Gaelic. Simon's parents had no idea that he had married – and what if they did not like her? Perhaps there was someone else that they had wanted him to marry! And as much as she might wish it, they could not stay in Russia – Simon's family and work were in Ireland – and a wife always went where her husband led. That was the way that things were. She began to wonder if she had done the right thing in marrying him. What would Sacha think when she informed him that they were to go live in Ireland, so far from all that was familiar? What if they were miserable and unhappy in Ireland?

They were less than an hour from the *rendezvous* point.

Karachev, on a great black Orlov saddle stallion, rode out ahead of the two boys who were mounted on Steppe horses. These small , rather ugly animals were barely horse-sized, but were very hardy and could carry a tremendous amount of weight. This was fortunate, for in addition to the boys, each horse carried all the accoutrements the necromancer considered indispensable for his comfort. Karachev's horse, of course, carried only the Wizard.

High overhead the two Ice dragons flew. Karachev had done some sort of spell that prevented them from flying too far ahead. When Volunvoshka had protested this treatment, the Wizard had asked him, sarcastically, if he would rather walk, for that could be very easily arranged. Karachev did not want any one arriving at the *rendezvous* before he himself did so.

Khlebnikova managed to placate her mate, and they remained in the air together during much of the journey. Sacha was glad that she had come to be with them – he did not like the look in Volunvoshka's eyes and often thought that perhaps the Wizard did not have the control over the Ice dragon that he thought he had. Sacha also was fearful of the glares that the Ice dragon gave him and Illya, particularly when they had been making music. The female dragon seemed to enjoy the music but her mate did nothing but growl and lash his tail every time Illya took out his instrument.

Sacha couldn't help but wonder what had happened to the egg. Had it hatched? Were Simon and Lakota taking care of it? And too, he wondered if his sister would be there to meet him.

He kept his mouth shut when he heard Karachev talking about killing Tenisheva and stealing his powers – the necromancer had boasted of this to the dragons. Karachev knew nothing about Simon and Sacha was not about to enlighten him.

Illya, of course, knew all about the English Wizard, for his new friend had informed him of every particular. He had no intention of telling Karachev and did not need to be sworn to secrecy. To himself, Illya gleefully thought of Karachev's shock and surprise when he faced, not a doddering old wreck of a Wizard, but a young magician in his prime. It would serve the black-hearted scoundrel right!

They had been traveling for well over a week. Karachev did not even think of riding the dragon to the meeting place – it did not seem to occur to either the Wizard or the dragons that such a thing was possible.

Sacha much preferred a dragon like Lakota and the relationship he had with Simon. He dreamed that he might somehow be able to fly with his own dragon one day.

But Karachev's voice interrupted a pleasant day dream. "We shall set up here." He pointed his riding whip – a cruel, snake-like black leather lash which he had used on Illya – at a small meadow. "We are within a short distance of where we are to meet. Set up the tent," he ordered, swinging off the Orlov stallion.

The dragons, circling overhead, saw them stopping and plunged down from the clear sky as rapidly as eagles, landing with thuds almost on top of them.

"Is it time?" demanded Volunvoshka harshly, folding his wings so rapidly that the resulting wind nearly knocked Sacha off his feet. The Steppe horses shied and whickered anxiously.

"It wants but half an hour," said Karachev. "I am going to have a cold drink first – I am parched with all of this heat." In his gem-encrusted robes he did not look as if he even felt the heat. As usual he wore a close fitting hood and high boots. He wore his favorite red, today heavily embroidered with gold and rubies.

Volunvoshka seethed with impatience. When the egg was returned to them he would take his family and leave this benighted area of heat and scorching sun! Even up in the air it was far hotter than he liked. He was all anxiety as to what had been the fate of the egg. It must have hatched by now. If any harm had come to the dragonet he would eat the young Count without a second thought.

To take Tatya's mind from the horrors of waiting Simon gave another magic lesson. Anatoly had returned with two deer – he had had good luck – and Simon taught both of them to tap into the ley lines for defensive power.

He had been surprised at the raw, untapped feel of the Russian ley lines. A skilled Wizard could actually 'read' the signature of the last user of a ley line and these appeared to be unused for many, many years. Their power level was quite high and his two pupils easily accessed the potent force at once.

He gave each of then a focus stone to use in lieu of a wand – to Anatoly a sapphire ring that made the Lieutenant's eyes grow wide. "Is that real?" he stammered, looking at the great glowing stone Simon harded him so nonchalantly,

"Of course it's real!" Said Simon, amused. "Pray, what good would it do if it were paste?"

"And you're just giving it to me?" Anatoly asked.

"It's traditional for a Master to give his apprentices their first focus stone," Simon explained. "Later on, you'll want something better, of course..."

"Something better than this?" Anatoly repeated incredulously.

Leaving him staring at the sapphire in bemused wonder, Simon gave Tatya a diamond on a chain. It was a large, flawless stone of three carats, set in silver on a long chain that when he put it over her head lay between her breasts, hanging a little lower than the dragon whistle she still wore.

"But this must be so expensive!" she said, staring at it.

"Focus stones have to be fairly large and free from flaw," he said. At the stunned look on her face he said, "Tatya, we Wizards don't think of jewels as items of adornment or even expensive commodities. Jewels are tools, just as our wands and potions and grimoires. A good focus stone is a necessity. If necessary, a Wizard will save for years to buy a good one. The tradition of a Master giving the first stone to his pupil arose because very often the pupil is poor and cannot afford a decent stone. Fortunately I am quite well off and can afford high quality stones. And we always carry extra in case our favorite stones are cracked or lost. These are two of my extras. Please, both of you, accept these stones in the spirit they were given!"

They thanked him and spent the rest of the lesson marveling at the gleam of their stones and also feeling with awe how easily the power flowed through the medium of the stones, enhancing what spells they already knew. Their mage lights burned brighter, the objects they called came quicker and the defensive stones flew higher and faster and struck harder.

When it lacked only a half an hour to the exchange time, the Cham cane to see Simon.

One of the herdsmen, scouting around, had seen a Wizard, two boys ands two dragons in a field not far from where they were encamped. He had reported his sighting to his leader and the Cham felt he had ought to warn Simon.

"Ho!" he exclaimed. "Arvid said that he was a dangerous looking fellow – red robes with jewels as big as pigeon's eggs, and a black bearded face – cruel, Arvid called it. Two huge dragons – all white and silver. And two boys on horses. One of them sounds like the young fellow you're looking for!" They had confided to their new friend the reason for their presence in the area and he was all sympathy.

Sudden joy flared in Tatya's face. "Did Arvid say that he was well – in good health?" she demanded, clutching at Simon's arm.

"Bustling about raising a tent with the other boy," Tarquin assured her.

Trembling with relief, Tatya hid her face against Simon and almost sobbed. Sacha was safe and it sounded as if he was well! She felt Simon's arm slid protectively around her shoulders. She had never felt more grateful for his support.

Evgeny and Viktor, by dint of riding two hired horses almost into the ground, were nearly at the confluence of the Volga and the Kama. Their quarry had been easy to track – Simon and his party had made no attempt to hide and furthermore, they had been in this area for some little while and the gossips in the various villages along the route were more than eager to tell increasingly tall tales about the blue dragon, who grew bigger and more ferocious with each telling.

"Whatever are they doing here?" grumbled Evgeny rhetorically. He could not imagine what his cousin and her paramours were doing. The footman thought they had gone to rescue the brat – why hadn't they done it? Not that he really cared, though.

They finally had to stop and rest the horse and had taken the time to sport with a serf girl they had come across picking blackberries. She had not been willing but a handkerchief tied around her mouth and her arms and legs tied and spread-eagled with spare cravats had taken care of that.

They were eating bread and sausage while they rested themselves before taking her again. Mindless as to her comfort, they left her tied up while they ate. She lay in numb misery, far past the screaming and fighting she had done at first. Evgeny was disappointed – he truly enjoyed a fight with an unwilling woman, but Viktor was not as particular. He loved intercourse, no matter who with or what condition she was in. It was a standing joke in their regiment that Viktor would have lain with a toothless, fat, ugly, stench – ridden, ninety year old woman if her female parts all worked properly. And it was true – he was not fussy.

Now Viktor gave a satisfied belch and took a deep drink of a bottle of *kvas*. Crudely, he wiped the back of his hand across his lips. "We're too close to the road here," he said, thoughtfully, "Let's take her into the woods before we take her again."

He eyed the girl's naked body, for of course they had stripped her. Her shame and horror excited them both But there was something about a woman tied up and helpless that Viktor really enjoyed. And if her mouth was prevented from talking and screaming, even better.

"We could try what we've talked about doing to your cousin on her," he now suggested. He licked his lips in anticipation. What they could to to Evgeny's cousin had been a constant topic of conversation. No less than Evgeny did he want to finish what they had started in the linen room.

Evgeny had thought of very little else since that day. The thought that she had escaped him and that she had been the cause of his humiliation tortured him. He *would* have her – repeatedly! And this time Viktor would have to wait. This

353

girl was a poor substitute for cousin Tatya but she would do. Soon, very soon, he would have the supreme pleasure of having his cousin where she belonged – underneath him.

And on the road from Perm a carriage bowled along at a high rate of speed. Inside was Count Pozharsky, dozing. On the box, beside the coachman, sat the Count's spy, who had brought interesting and significant news that very morning.

36

The Challenge

No one had informed Zaandam that he was to be exchanged for Sacha and was to be given into the care of adult Ice dragons. Both Lakota and Simon hoped that the adults *were* the horrid dragonet's parents and would actually want him back.

Even the Tatars, although their coffers had been much enriched by Simon's gold for the purchase of cows, sheep and goats, would be glad to see the last of the repellent Zaandam. He was loud, rude, had dirty personal habits and had suddenly developed a routine of hiding behind a tent or a tree and leaping out at people with a loud roar and gnashing of teeth. Simon's magical barrier kept him from doing actual harm, but it was still frightening to have him leap out at one.

He laughed inordinately at anyone's fear and eventual anger – he thought it a great joke, although no one else viewed it as such. This was yet another reason Simon had put a barrier around him to keep from both pouncing on people and chasing horses. Lakota had scorched his tail several times but Zaandam's skin was thickening and he little felt this censure. That too, was unusual. Western dragons had thinner skins and dragon parents often used flame as a disciplinary tool.

A bare half hour befcre the exchange was to take place Lakota informed the dragonet that he was going to be leaving them. Lakota could not quite keep the elation from his voice – in all the etiquette the blue dragon had learned it was grossly impolite to let a guest know that you would be glad to be shut of him, but he could not help his joy.

"Why do I have to leave?" Zaandam asked suspiciously."I like the cows here!"

"You will be going into the care of another Ice dragon," Lakota explained.

"Suppose I don't want to go? Will this other dragon have good food?" Zaandam demanded.

"Of course he will!" lied Lakota, for he had no idea. "And probably things that you will like even better. After all, he is an Ice dragon as you are and will know what you like. And he will probably take you back to your own home and to your parents! Think how happy that will be!"

Zaandam considered this for a moment and said "As long as the food is plentiful and good – I *would* like to be with *real* dragons!"

Lakota winced and his tail lashed.This was a very sore point with him, for Zaandam, like Baba Yaga, has cast aspersions upon Lakota's identity as a dragon. Lakota was unused to this attitude – even though he was a different colour than most of the dragons in Ireland, not one of them had ever accused him of not being a 'real' dragon. But as Simon had told him, he had to remember the source of this insult – Zaandam was ignorant and not very intelligent. And ill-bred – Lakota had added.

The dragonet agreed to go with them to the rendezvous point. It was not far away – a short walk. But before they left Zaandam ate another sheep.

Simon tried to insist that Tatya remain behind in the safety of the tent surrounded by the Tatars. He had heard more and more of the black sorcerer that seemed to be working with the Ice dragon and none of it had been reassuring. Simon of course realized that most stories and rumors were exaggerated – he had heard stories about himself and Lakota that were so highly embroidered that they were scarcely recognizable, but the tales of the necromancer made him out to be very bad indeed. If the Ice dragon and his partner were not disposed to be conciliatory, the exchange could go very wrong – and he did not want Tatya in danger.

She could not see why she could not be present – it was her brother after all. Anatoly was to go! Why could she not?

Simon took her hands in his. "Anatoly is a soldier – he is well used to danger. If things go badly amiss – although I see no reason that they should – I shall have all I have to do to protect Sacha – I shall not be able to protect you as well."

"But I have learned to protect myself –" she protested.

Simon shook his head. "You've done very well," he said, "but what you have learned would be useless against a necromancer. It sounds as if this man practices blood magic. My father, who is a very powerful Wizard indeed, nearly lost his life in a duel with a blood magician. Please, Tatya, give me one less thing to worry about! I promise you that I shall ask Tarquin if he will deliver Sacha back here to you the moment the exchange is completed. The necromancer could very well use you against me."

Something in his tone gave her pause. Searchingly, she looked at him. "Do you anticipate trouble with him?"

"No, not at all. But forewarned is forearmed as the saying goes," he said lightly, seeing a worried look start to form on her features.

She looked deeply at his face for a moment more, as if somehow she could read his mind. Then at last she said, "Very well – I will wait here. But you promise that Tarquin will deliver Sacha to me as soon as you have him?"

"I give you my word of honour," he returned.

She squeezed his hands lightly. "Don't get yourself killed," she said in as light a tone as his.

How he wished that she would throw her arms about him and beg him not to go, declaring her love and saying she could not live without him! Then he chided himself – he sounded like a lovesick youth in one of the romantic novels Noelle so enjoyed. Even if she behaved so extravagantly he would still have to go to this meeting. He had to remember that they had made a marriage to save her reputation without a word of love between them. That he had come to love her was his own tragedy. So he only kissed her on the brow and left the tent to join Anatoly and Tarquin, who sat on a pair of the honey-gold Akhal-Teke horses favored by the Tatars.

Anatoly held the reins of a spare animal and Simon took these from his friend and swung onto the horse's back.

Lakota and Zaandam were walking along side the trio of horsemen, Zaandam complaining loudly that they had to walk so far. He was peevish that he could not as yet fly and looked at Lakota, first in dismay when told it would be a year before he could fly, and then accusingly, saying that Lakota was lying because the older dragon did not want the competition of someone who could no doubt fly rings around him.

This made Lakota so angry that steam came from his nostrils in a great billow.

"Ho!" said Tarquin. "You'd best mend your manners, young dragon, if you don't want to be smoked meat!"

Simon judged it best to intervene at this point and told Zaandam to mind his tongue if he did not want to be turned into a vegetarian.

"You can't do that!" Zaandam protested hotly and then looked at Lakota and said doubtfully. "He can't do that, can he?"

"Simon can do anything!" said Lakota, with a fond look at his friend.

Ahead of them, where the meeting was to take place on a flat, treeless area, Lakota could see two Ice dragons heading down from the air above. His long dragon sight enabled him to see clearly, from more than a mile away, three riders, among them Sacha, looking well and fit. He sighed in relief and said softly to Simon. "Sacha is well – I see him. But I don't care for the looks of the necromancer – cruel and proud!"

Simon hoped that this first impression was erroneous and the other magician would be amiable and the exchange could be conducted with no fuss and furor.

"Look, my mate!" said Khlebnikova excitedly as they circled above Karachev and the two boys. "That youngling is surely our egg, hatched!"

Volunvoshka looked and saw a well-grown hatchling walking alongside the enchanted blue lizard. "It can be no other!" he agreed, pride filling his voice. "See how well-grown and handsome he is!"

"He looks as if he has been well fed – for if he were not, he would scarcely be this large. He is strong and fit! We owe them the debt of gratitude – " she said.

Volunvoshka snarled. "We owe then NOTHING! They stole him away from us for reasons I still do not understand! They owe US a debt – and taking proper care of him does NOT cancel it out!"

358

They were heading downwards as he spoke.

Khlebnikova did not comment on his statement but said "Is that the blue dragon you spoke of? He does not look like a lizard to me. The blue is a pretty colour. But he is but a child!" She was honestly surprised at how young Lakota was.

"He is not a real dragon!" stated Volunvoshka as they landed. His son would have agreed with him.

Karachev, without dragon sight, had taken the precaution of bringing a very fine spyglass that had once belonged to a surveyor he had killed, after torture, who had the misfortune to work too near to the necromancer's dwelling at Taganrog.

He now raised this to his eye to study the little party heading towards him. A small blue dragon and an Ice dragon hatchling – two men in Russian dress and a Tatar, all mounted on the superb Persian type Akhal-Tekes.

But where was Tenisheva? None of the party wore Wizard's robes – had Nicholas dared to send non-magicians? Karachev's lip curled. Nicholas was even stupider than he had thought possible if he thought that non-magicians had even the slimmest of chances against *his* potent magics! As he continued to gaze at the party his eyes narrowed. The one in the middle – one with very fair hair – had a glow about him that spoke of magic.

And Karachev put down his spyglass and laughed to himself. This *child* was Nicholas's answer to his demands? A youth, scarcely out of boyhood? The Tatar he dismissed out of hand – and the other sat his horse like a cavalry officer – he had a faint, a very faint glow of magic about him – obviously an apprentice – not worth worrying about. The necromancer could not read the one real magician's strength – it stood to reason that if it could not be read, he hadn't much. In Karachev's tradition, one wore one's competence like a banner. He could not know that shielding was one of the first lessons a Celtic magician learned – they did not believe in flaunting their powers for all to see.

As they drew closer to the waiting party Zaandam began to show signs of wishing to run ahead and join the adult Ice dragons they could see ahead. In the first endearing emotion they had seen in the dragonet, he exclaimed in the exhilaration he had only shown for food "That's my mother and father ! I know it!" He lunged forward eagerly.

Simon was determined that they would have Sacha in their possession before Zaandam went to his parents and he quickly threw a restraining spell at the dragonet, who suddenly found himself compelled to stay by Lakota's side.

"I will go! I will!" he shrieked.

"Be quiet!" said Lakota in a sibilant whisper. "You'll go as soon as we have Sacha! There are rules to be observed here —and Simon can easily make you dumb as well!"

"You and your stupid rules!" said Zaandam savagely, his heavy lashing tail cutting wide swathes through the grass. His obvious anger caused the three horses to snort and sidle, tossing there heads uneasily. "My parents will not make me obey any stupid rules! They'll let me do as I please!"

Lakota doubted it. Although he had never known his own mother he had seen many other dragon mothers who were sticklers for discipline and manners – and there had been Matron at the Incubatory – an older female dragon who made the youngsters tow the mark. Surely even Ice dragons would not be that different? But Zaandam could find this out for himself – after today he would no longer be Lakota's problem, for which the blue dragon was extremely thankful.

Khlebnikova, too, showed signs of wishing to rush towards her hatchling, but Karachev allowed this no more than did Simon. She subsided with better grace than had Zaandam. As the dragonet drew nearer she noted with disapproval that her son bore the remnants of his latest meal in his teeth and on his chest. She knew well how a young male could barely be brought to clean himself, so intent was he on gorging, but he would find that his mother would not put up with such behavior – he would soon learn to be civilized or he would suffer her discipline.

At last they stood face to face – Khlebnikova stretched her long neck towards her son and they touched noses. "I am your mother," she said huskily.

"I knew it! I knew it!" exclaimed the dragonet, throwing a triumphant glance at Lakota. "And is this my father?" he asked, looking eagerly at Volunvoshka.

The older Ice dragon inclined his head, looking at Zaandam in pride. His son was well-grown and healthy – already he was a large as many a month-old hatchling. On the flight back to Siberia he would drill the dragonet in his lineage so that he could be presented to the elders as was proper. All was not lost. Perhaps the family would not be disgraced after all.

Karachev signaled to Sacha to dismount and motioned him forward. Sacha obeyed with alacrity, throwing a glance back at Illya, who looked miserable. The young Count stopped at Simon's stirrup and earnestly spoke to him for a moment, in a low voice, looking back at Illya.

Simon had released Zaandam and the dragonet had lumbered forward to be untied with his parents. "Did they feed you well?" his mother demanded, in between licking him clean with her long forked tongue.

"The cows were good," he said complacently, accepting her affection easily and basking in it. "But they would not let me eat the horses and *he*," he added, nodding at Lakota, "eats his food cooked and eats grain, milk and vegetables!"

Volunvoshka looked at Lakota in disgust, even less impressed by him close up. "Not a real dragon – I told you so!" he said haughtily.

More steam billowed from Lakota's snout.

"See, his ice is melting!" Volunvoshka stated.

Lakota tired his best to ignore this but his extended ruff and his twitching tail revealed his agitation. How he disliked these Ice dragons!

Unexpectedly, Khlebnikova stepped in. "This young dragon has helped care for our child!" she said sharply, her tone rebuking her mate. "We owe him courtesy, not derision! We are obviously not the only dragons in the world as we have always thought! And we should not mock this dragon just because he is different than we are."

Lakota looked at her gratefully. She seemed to be better mannered than the males in her family.

"You will say your thank-yous to your host, " she ordered her son "and express your gratitude properly as becomes one of our race. We would not wish other dragons to think us lacking in civility."

361

Zaandam obeyed with ill-grace, for something in her look told him that she would not brook his refusal. He was already realizing that he would not be allowed his own way as he had thought.

While the dragons were occupied, Simon, on prompting from Sacha, had offered to buy Karachev's slave from him, proposing a handsome sum in gold and the spare jewels he had in his luggage. Anatoly's eyes bulged when he heard the sum that Simon was willing to spend upon a stranger.

Karachev was not a wealthy man – the sum named – and the jewels – would be more than welcome. He could find another boy that played the *balalaika* as well as did Illya. He agreed to the purchase but then said abruptly "And does Nicholas meet my demands? What direction did he give you?"

Simon looked blank and then looked at Anatoly, who shrugged helplessly. He had no idea of what the necromancer was speaking.

"I'm sorry-" Simon began, "I don't seem to know what you mean. Are you speaking of the Czar?"

Karachev's looks grew thunderous. "Do not call him so! Do not play the innocent with me!' he threatened. "I know full well that Nicholas sent you here! He has been playing at cat and mouse with me for above a year! I fully expected him to have resurrected that old fraud Tenisheva! Does he seek to make me even more impatient? Does he think to intimidate me with *you?*" he sneered, sounding very like Volunvoshka.

Simon had no idea what was going on. But he did not like the look on the necromancer's face nor the tone of his voice.

Illya, overjoyed at the thought of freedom, had gone as far as he dared from his master without arousing the pain that his slave collar provided. Once Karachev agreed to his purchase, the collar fell from his neck, as had Sacha's and the two boys ran to Tarquin, who took them up behind him.

The Cham did not like the way that things were going. He had promised to protect the young Count and thought he should protect the other boy as well, for whom his new friend had just paid such a long price. He wheeled his horse and galloped off with the boys in the direction of the yurts that housed his people, removing them from danger.

The increasingly acrimonious tone of the conversation had attracted the attention of the dragons and Lakota went to stand by Simon, anxiously listening.

Volunvoshka threw the dragonet up on his back and then stretched out his huge wings, prepared to take flight for his home with his mate and hatchling.

"Stay!" Karachev commanded. "I may have need of you."

And Volunvoshka roared when he found that he could not leave the ground. His mate was similarly encumbered.

"Wizard!" said the Ice dragon angrily. "I do not fight your battles for you!"

"If you do not want your mate and your child destroyed before your eyes you will do as I tell you!" Karachev said menacingly, not taking his burning dark gaze from Simon.

There was something here that Simon could not understand in the least. What was all this talk of Nicholas? Why was this necromancer so angry?

"I have no fight with you, sir," he said diplomatically. "We came here but to exchange the dragonet for my wife's brother. I know nothing of the Czar or any connection he might have with you. I am not even Russian – I am from Ireland –"

It was obvious that Karachev did not believe him. "He cannot ignore me like this!" Karachev muttered and lightning flickered at his fingertips.

Once again. Simon and Anatoly exchanged glances. This could turn ugly. "Shields up," Simon said, *sotto voce*, glad that he had taught his pupils to shield using the power of the ley lines. He threw a shield about Lakota as well.

Karachev felt the power snap into place and reacted with a ball of blood red lightning that he threw at his opponents.

The horses, both Simon and Anatoly's Akhal-Tekes and Karachev's Orlov, squealed in terror as the magical energies broke around them. They bucked and plunged, doing their best to escape. All three riders slid to the ground and the horses ran off.

The red lightning ran over the shields and was absorbed by the ground.

363

"I will finish you!" Karachev thundered, "And anyone else Nicholas sends to thwart me!"

On a hill not far away, in the shelter of a grove of trees, Count Pozharsky lowered his spyglass. It had begun. He hoped that his gamble had paid off – that the English Wizard was all that was said of him. Elsewise, he did not know what they would do.

"How goes it, Pozharsky?" came a cold voice from behind him.

The Count was not easily startled but he jumped and whirled about and found the Czar standing behind him.

"Your Imperial Majesty!" he said, recovering from his fit of surprise and bowing low. "I did not look to see you here!"

"When I received your last *communiqué* I decided that this was something I must see for myself," said Nicholas in his autocratic fashion.

This was not unusual – Nicholas had a habit of suddenly descending upon various parts of his empire for inspections and to study various operations. He never gave advance notice and would think nothing of traveling all night at a very high rate of speed. Indeed, he had been in several accidents due to his predilection for haste.

"How goes it?" he now repeated.

"It has only but begun, Majesty," said Pozharsky, handing the spyglass to his Imperial master. "As we thought, the black sorcerer is of a volatile temperament and has leveled the first volley."

"And the English Wizard?" Nicholas took up the glass and put it to his right eye.

"Has only defended himself so far, Majesty," Pozharsky admitted. "Perhaps we had ought to have told him..."

Nicholas stiffened and lowered the glass to look at Pozharsky as indignantly as could a man with frozen facial features. "Do you question my wisdom, Count? These English are stubborn – he would have not cooperated with us for he would not have felt this to be his fight. No, my course was the best one. Only see how well it has all worked out!" His voice was smug. He was right – he was always right.

364

37

Vindication

Since Simon had indicated a desire to return to St Petersburg and from there to Ireland as soon as they had Sacha in safety, Tatya occupied herself in packing up their belongings for bestowal in Lakota's breast harness. She could not stop thinking about what might be happening during the exchange, No less than any of the others did she wish to rid herself of the awful dragonet and, even more, she wanted Sacha returned to her – and Simon to come back safe and unharmed.

It seemed an age since she had seen Sacha. So much had happened in that time! She would have a lot to explain to him.

She soon had everything ready to go, and, feeling warm, sat down on the grass behind their tent, where the canvas wall made some shade. In her hand she held the peony box Simon had given her that day, after their visit to the tea shop. She had never dreamed then that she would be married to him and about to start a brand new life in Ireland.

Since it was such a hot day she had chosen to wear one of the Elfin gowns – it was white, with a pattern of green leaves and vines that appeared to be all shades of green, as if they were shifting in the breeze and in the sun. The Elves were about twenty years behind the fashion, for it had an old style high waist and tiny puff sleeves. A deep décolletage exposed the tops of her breasts. She had not worn it before – she was eager to see if Simon liked it on her. Of course, it was held on by but a ribbon tied at the high waist and could easily be discarded, for there was naught underneath. She had ceased to worry about the lack of undergarments. for everything in her rebelled against wearing those hot and stiff items of torture – particularly in this heat. When they finally returned to civilization she would try to find and wear the most minimal of undergarments. She could not contemplate wearing ever again the heavy things she had worn before. She suddenly wondered what the Elves wore in the winter.

There was a pool nearby in a copse– perhaps they could swim there before they left – it was so hot that it would be very pleasant indeed. And if she and Simon were alone, perhaps they could make love as well.... it was amazing how much she liked that activity and how she had come to crave it.

She was idly opening and shutting her gift box, enjoying the blossoming flower and thinking of love on the edge of a cool green pool. She had no warning of danger; no sound told her of peril. The first thing she knew was that she was hauled to her feet and her arms were pinned behind her. Panicked, she twisted away and someone grabbed at her, catching the ribbon of the Elfin gown. It fell off.

"Hold her!" came a voice she knew all too well and as she was grabbed again, she looked up to see her cousin's cruel face peering at her. All the old familiar feelings of terror and paralysis flooded her being. This time there would be no escape from whatever depraved things he wanted to do to her.

"Well, well, cousin!" he said mockingly. "You really *have* become a whore! Even in the finest brothels in St Petersburg they don't undress that quickly! You must really pant for it! And what's this?" He came closer and grasped at the diamond – her focus stone – that hung between her breasts entwined with the dragon whistle. He gave a low whistle. "Take a look at this, Viktor! She's a very well-paid whore as well!"

That was Sumarakov's hot breath in her ear and his strong hands pinioning her arms. "Do you think she takes both of them at once?" he laughed and nuzzled the back of her neck and thrust himself against her buttocks.

"I wish I had started screwing you when you first came to us ," said Evgeny " if you like it this much!" He then said to Viktor "Remember when we paid a whore once to take on most of the regiment? We could have saved our *rubles* and used my dear cousin! She'd have done it for the enjoyment of taking all of us one after the other!"! He grabbed both of her breasts, one in each hand and squeezed them, rolling the nipples between thumb and forefinger. "You've got nice, full boobs," he said approvingly. "They're bigger then I recall, by God!"

"Regular sex will do that – makes the tits bigger," Viktor put in. Her bare body, held tightly against his, was exciting him.

"By the time we're done with her she'll have the biggest boobs in Russia if that's true! We'll take her back to St Petersburg with using her every chance we get along the way, and keep her in my rooms once we're back home. She can cook and clean as well as pleasure us. But I don't think I 'll let her ever wear any clothes!" said Evgeny with an obscene laugh. He stooped suddenly and thrust a hand between her legs, "Definitely not a virgin any more!" he said after his examination.

Suddenly Tatya's mind seemed very clear and almost cold. She remembered with perfect clarity a conversation with Anatoly and Simon when they had been talking about attack and defense. "Surprise is the essence of attack," Anatoly had said. "If you are out numbered, let them think you are not dangerous." Simon had agreed with this and told her she had an advantage now that she had learned to protect herself magically. "You don't look dangerous," he had said. "But remember – you ARE dangerous – now."

So she was not defenseless! She could use the magic that Simon had taught her! Oh, why had she panicked?

She let them handle her and make their crude comments, most of which, thankfully, she did not understand. She was waiting – waiting for them to let their guard slip, waiting for the moment that she could attack She said nothing to them, nor did she make a sound, now almost contemptuous of what they were doing.

"See how she wants it!" said Viktor gloatingly. "If you'll but let me have her half the time I'll make her serve at my card parties – and drinks and food won't be all I'll make her serve! Who'll notice the way the cards fall when there is a naked wench there to ogle?" To him, any woman that didn't fight wanted his attentions. And Evgeny's cousin was offering no resistance to anything they did, which so far had just been handling her, although in an intimate fashion.

"We can take her right here," said Evgeny. "There's no one around – they've all gone off to look at something – there's just the herd beasts about to hear her scream. And you'll scream, I can guarantee it!" he leered at Tatya and laughed, putting immense pressure on her breasts, and bending down to bite at her nipple. He wanted her to respond, to be frightened or beg to for it, as his father said she had done with the Wizard.

Why did it feel so good when Simon touched her breasts and so repulsive and vile when Evgeny did it? she wondered dispassionately. It was almost as if she was watching this entire byplay from a distance. She was waiting, waiting...

"Throw her down!" said Evgeny, beginning to pull off his clothing hastily. His eyes glittered strangely and she noticed that he was both panting and drooling a little. This she was certain, was not due to the heat.

And Viktor loosened his hold upon her arms...

NOW! Just as Simon had taught her she pulled the power from the ley lines and silently said the spell in her mind.

Victor went backwards so violently that he struck a pile of firewood that had been stacked in back of the tent. As he bounced off the wood several pieces of it struck him with the force of a cannon firing. With one screaming groan he subsided into unconsciousness.

She then, without skipping a beat, slammed Evgeny into the ground so hard that he could scarcely breathe. Rocks began to fly up from the earth pelting him mercilessly. He had had his breeches and drawers half off – this were down around his ankles and impeded his getting away from her attack.

"No! No!" he howled. Managing to stumble to his feet, he tried to run away, the half discarded breeches acting as hobbles. He fell to the ground again and tried to crawl away, attempting to protect his head with a crooked arm. Finally he collapsed on the ground, sobbing as rocks still showered him, bare bottom sticking up in the air. Then he, too, slipped into unconsciousness.

For several moments Tatya stood over them, breathing hard and clenching and unclenching her fists, unmindful of her nudity. Her breasts were going to be sore where he had manhandled her and her female parts hurt as well from his rough hand. Even her arms would be black and blue where Viktor had held her so tightly.

But she felt wonderful! Strong! In control! And vindicated! This time she had fought back! She had been frightened but had still been able to take charge! This time she had won! And she had done it her own self – she had not needed to be rescued! She had not even used the dragon whistle!

She could not help it – out there in the sun, as bare as the day she was born, in front of the bodies of her enemies, she did a dance of triumph, her hair falling down around her shoulders. Then she picked up her dress and calmly resumed it, looking around for her peony box. It had fallen some distance away when they grabbed her – fortunately it had not been damaged. Without a backwards glance at her would-be rapists she walked to the front of the tent, just as Tarquin and the two boys arrived.

"Sacha!" she cried in delight, as her brother slid off the horse and ran to her and they fell into each other's arms.

When they had greeted one another Sacha introduced her to Illya. "He's my friend," he explained simply. "He was Karachev's slave and the Wizard bought his freedom."

"And I do not know how I will ever repay him," said Illya miserably. He had had time to start worrying about the debt he now owed Sacha's Wizard. "Will he let me be his slave, do you think?" he asked hopefully.

"I am certain that my husband does not believe in keeping slaves," said Tatya without thinking.

"Your husband!" said Sacha in amazement. "You have married the Wizard, Tatya?"

"I hope you do not mind, Sacha, but he wants us to come and live in Ireland with him –" she said quickly, wishing that she had not blurted out her news in such a hurly-burly fashion.

"Mind?" Sacha interrupted an expression of sheer bliss spreading itself over his features. "Oh, sister, Ireland has always sounded to ne exactly as if it were heaven!"

"Ho! What is this?" came Tarquin's voice. They looked around to see him dragging Evgeny by the neck of his shirt as if he was a bulky parcel. "There's another one back there too!"

"Cousin Evgeny! What is he doing here?" Sacha said in amazement.

"He and his disgusting friend Sumarokov tried to rape me." said Tatya calmly. "And I taught them a lesson. I have been learning magic, Sacha!"

"Ho!" said Tarquin again and shook Evgeny until he awoke.

Dazed, Evgeny came awake and twisted in Tarquin's grip. The Cham was quite strong and easily held the Hussar, even though Evgeny was the taller by a head.

The boys began to snicker, for Evgeny was still half-clothed, his breeches and drawers still down around his ankles and his shirt pulled up around his throat by Tarquin's fist.

"Ho, rapist!" said Tarquin, "Do you know what we do to those who attempt to rape one of our women, or a woman of our friends?" He put his face close to Evgeny's and grimed in a very evil fashion, showing hjs gold tooth. "We castrate them!" he said in glee. Evgeny recoiled.

"Where is Simon?" Tatya asked Sacha quickly.

"Karachev is angry with him for some reason –" Sacha began but Illya interrupted him. "Karachev said that any Wizard who came to deal with him would be murdered and he would steal all of their magical energies!"

Tatya at once remembered Simon telling her, only that morning. *My father, who is a very powerful Wizard indeed, nearly lost his life in a duel with a blood magician.* What if he were killed?

And then she realized, when she knew she might lose him, that she was in love with Simon and that going to live in Ireland would not be difficult at all because he would be there with her. She would go to the ends of the earth to be with him. Nothing else mattered.

"I have to go and see what is happening!" she said to Sacha, her voice filled with urgency, "I could not bear it if he were hurt and I were not there!"

Sacha and Illya looked at each other – Sacha knew that his new brother–in–law would probably want him to keep her away and safe. He opened his mouth to voice this thought when Illya forestalled him.

"As we rode back here I saw a little hill, with some trees on it – we could watch from there," Illya suggested, and without waiting for approval of his plan, headed for the horse.

370

Tarquin watched without protest – his wife would do the selfsame thing – only calling "Ho! Lady Wizard! What should I do with this filth?" He shook Evgeny as a terrier shakes a rat.

"Oh, go ahead and castrate them!" she called back over her shoulder, as the three of them piled onto the horse and galloped off.

Evgeny began screaming as Tarquin shook him again. "Don't worry, rapist! My knife is very sharp – I've gelded many a horse!" the Tatar assured him. "It won't hurt that much!"

Simon had not sought to do else than defend himself, so far. He wanted to see what this sorcerer was made of. And with the untapped power of the many ley lines beneath him, he could keep up shields all afternoon with very little effort on his part, even with extending the shields to Anatoly and Lakota.

The necromancer was completely ignoring the power beneath his feet. All of his magic came from blood and death and pain he had inflicted on untold others and had collected and more than likely had stored in the jewels that adorned his person.

He saw Anatoly stir restlessly beside him, tired of remaining behind a protective barrier. He was a soldier, trained to attack.

Then Simon felt a surge in the ley lines – someone else had tapped into them, close. Another surge quickly followed and the necromancer began to be pelted with rocks.

"No!" Simon shouted at Anatoly. To do so could crack the defenses.

But the Lieutenant wore a look of grim determination on his face and ignored Simon.

"Kill him!" Karachev shrieked at Volunvoshka and pointed to Anatoly.

The big Ice dragon hesitated – and Karachev sent a red whip of energy to lash Khlebnikova, who cried aloud in agony and fell to the ground, writhing.

"Go or she dies!" Karachev commanded.

With a look of utter hatred Volunvoshka rose into the air and gathered his breath for a fountain of sub-zero ice that would kill Anatoly instantly if it reached him. Already cracks had appeared in the shield over him as he continued to throw rocks.

The Ice dragon shot out a powerful arc of ice that should have dropped down on Anatoly, a sure and horrible death, But the ice melted in mid air, turned to water by a powerful flame.

Volunvoshka, startled, looked up and saw that blue lizard hovering – *hovering*? Dragons could not hover! – in front of him.

"What did you do?" Volunvoshka bellowed.

"I won't let you hurt my friends!" Lakota stated. "I can melt any ice you can spit out! In fact, I could probably burn *you* to a crisp!" He was not so certain of that, for he could see that Volunvoshka's hide was very thick. But the Ice dragon could not know what his flame could do.

"Kill him, Father, kill him!" Zaandam was screaming from the ground, hopping up and down as if could somehow get himself into the air.

Khlebnikova lay on the ground where she had fallen, her long neck stretched straight out and her eyes closed, tail crumpled beneath her. She looked as if she were dead.

Enraged, Volunvoshka lunged at Lakota.

Lakota back winged and rolled away. Why, this was just like dragon-ball! Volunvoshka was much bigger than he was and had a far greater wing span, but Lakota realized that the bigger dragon was slow, and could not hover, nor back-wing.

He easily evaded the ice that Volunvoshka spit at him – and melted that which came too close with just a thin stream of flame. He had eaten a great deal of firestone that morning – just in case – and he could feel the high build-up of fire gasses in his stomach and flight cavities.

"Dragons don't spit fire!" Volunvoshka screamed. He had never seen anything like this damned lizard – flying backwards! hovering in one place, twisting and turning back on himself!

"Stay still!" he roared. "Stay still and fight like a dragon – so I can kill you!"

"I have no desire to be killed!" Lakota retorted, "And I AM fighting like a dragon!" He sent a long tongue of flame that reached Volunvoshka's tender stomach.

As the Ice dragon yelled in pain and tried to avoid the stinging flame he spat out a cloud of freezing vapor that Lakota met with a wide band of flame.

Busy with evading the Ice dragon, Lakota had no time to spare even a glance for Simon and Anatoly, The blue dragon was very confident that his human friend could handle anything that necromancer had to offer.

Hidden amongst the trees on a slight hill some ways away Tatya watched with her hands over her mouth and her heart in her throat. She had never seen anything so frightening. Red and blue energies filled the air as the two magicians dodged and feinted back and forth meeting with sounds like ten simultaneous thunderbolts. Simon was using Elfin levin bolts to try and crack the necromancer's shields and the necromancer was trying to destroy Simon's shields. Up in the air the two dragons were fighting, flames and ice vapors filling the air.

The two boys were round-eyed, watching. When Sacha had imagined a Wizards' duel he had dreamed of nothing like this – he had thought it would be like a duel between two gentlemen – shooting at one another in a civilized manner. He had never thought to see so much dangerous power coming so fast and furiously. Anatoly was still throwing rocks, which were doing little real damage but were still beginning to irritate the necromancer. The constant rain of stones interfered with his concentration and dented his shield.

Simon kept up a steady barrage of levin bolts. They used little of his real power and could quite effectively damage a shield. There was such a high power available from the untapped ley lines! The distant surge he had felt earlier had gone – now only Anatoly was drawing from it as well.

What was this all about? he wondered in a detached part of his mind. The necromancer had been hostile from the beginning – with no real reason. Now Simon was fighting for his life – and he would really like to know *why*.

38

Thwarted Desires

From another hill, Czar Nicholas and Count Pozharsky watched the battle below and above them.

"*Blagdos Christos!*" Pozharsky murmured, crossing
himself at the sight of the dragons in the air and the Wizards
dueling on the ground.

"The English Wizard is holding his own," said
Nicholas in satisfaction. The Czar seemed unperturbed by the
fire and ice in the sky and the power crackling and blazing
between the two Wizards.

Pozharsky heard murmuring and prayers behind
them as the members of the Czar's escort, a troop of Chevalier
Guards, drew nearer to see what was happening.

Pozharsky's coachman and his spy, a man called
Stefan Khristofvich Golovin, watched as well. A quick glance
showed that the coachman was terrified, but Golovin, whom
Pozharsky had never seen in the least bit impressed by
anything, was his usual unflappable self. He lounged at his
ease on a nearby fallen tree, his features unreadable. He was
a good-looking, dark haired man with strange eyes that
seemed a different colour every time one looked ay him. He
had a talent for blending in anywhere and could mimic a
nobleman as well as a serf. He was extremely useful to
Pozharsky, although the Count knew really very little about
him.

The horses were extremely restive, for both Volunvoshka and Zaandam were bellowing loudly – Zaandam
yelling encouragement to his father and Volunvoshka raging
at Lakota. In addition, the noise made by the energies of the
Wizards' battle was appalling as the powerful bolts boomed
and cracked against one another. The coachmen – for the
Czar had arrived in a coach – were having trouble controlling
their teams. The troopers' horses, more used to the noise of
battle, were not as frightened, but the noises they heard were
not those that they were used to.

Pozharsky could not imagine how the Czar could remain so calm. So much hung on this combat! If the English Wizard was to be defeated – it didn't bear thinking about it! Too much time had passed since the entire affair began and too much planning.

"Majesty," he said worriedly "have you given any thought to what the English Wizard will do if he finds out what we planned? When I look at the power that he has – I am quite frankly frightened as to what revenge he might take upon us!"

"Nonsense!" said the Czar without removing the spyglass from his eye. "We shall reward him handsomely. And he shall have the satisfaction of having done his duty."

Pozharsky could not point out to his Imperial master without reprimand that Stillfield owed no duty to Russia.

"I speak of course, Count, of the oath that these Wizards swear to, that they must rid the world of evil. And their can be little more evil that an usurper, a man so lost to the knowledge of what is the best for his motherland."

Golovin was the only one listening to the conversation between the Czar and his employer. The other men were too occupied in watching the conflict below, or soothing terrified horses. Golovin's hearing was keen and he carefully leaned towards the Czar and his companion. This was quite interesting and one never tired of gathering information. One never knew when the tiniest snippet might prove useful.

Pozharsky was still, even after nearly seven years of serving Nicholas, amazed at what the Czar knew. That piece of information had been an obscure item in the report he had delivered to his Imperial Majesty. But the Czar had obviously read and remembered every item in that report. His attention to detail and his interest in every aspect of government was astonishing.

"The English Wizard had changed tactics," the Czar announced. "Look, Pozharsky, he is now using a violet light. Did not that book on English Wizards call that the most powerful of energies?"

"I believe so, Majesty," replied Pozharsky, bringing up his own glass and focusing it on the fray.

Simon had indeed changed tactics. He was growing tired of this whole business, a tiredness not untinged by worry. This necromancer was indeed powerful. And he seemed determined to kill Simon – for still unknown reasons.

Simon was well aware that if he were killed the necromancer would be able to drain all of his powers and add them to his, and the necromancer would steal his soul as well – forever to be a servant of his evil. Blood magic was very powerful, and stealing the power of a White Wizard would only add to it. The necromancer would be a fool if he did not attempt to take Simon's power. He would assume that Simon wanted the same of him. He would never believe that that was quite the last thing on Simon's mind.

It was beginning to look to Simon as if he was going to have to kill this man whether he really wanted to or not.

Accordingly, he began using the energies of the ley lines to attack the necromancer's shield from all sides. It would now weakening –, for the more the necromancer attacked, the weaker the shield became. Attacking and defending at the same time was difficult, if mot impossible – it took a great deal of power to hold a shield.

Great bands of violet power began to assault all sides of the necromancer's shields. Simon hoped that this would awaken his opponent to the fact that he faced a most potent foe, as violet was the ultimate colour of power and Simon's magic was deep violet tinged with gold. He really did not wish to kill this man without reason. There were spells, new spells, that could strip a blood mage of his magics – they had been developed in the early part of the century, with the help of the Elves. But the blood mage had to be subdued, not actively engaged in attacking with all of his power at his fingertips.

Simon knew that he had done the right thing when he had killed Baba Yaga, but he had not been easy with doing it. Like Lakota, he had lain awake nights, once Tatya had fallen asleep, wondering if there could have been anything else he could have done. He really did not want to have to end someone's life again, even that of a blood mage.

The intense force of the violet energies, coming from all sides at once, began to work their magics upon Karachev's shield. His protection was visible only as a certain thickening of the air – not an actual violet coloured screen as was Simon's – but as the vigor of the ley line enhanced bolts struck the shield it cracked audibly. Anatoly's rock throwing had dented it deeply in places.

Simon dared not look up to ascertain Lakota's success in dealing with the Ice dragon. Like the blue dragon he had noticed how slow the bigger dragon was and he doubted that Volunvoshka could out fly Lakota. Nevertheless he was worried, for Lakota had never before fought another dragon, much less one bigger and more experienced. It was a fortunate thing that Karachev had rendered the female Ice dragon unconscious or the odds would not have been in Lakota's favor. Fortunately, the war-like Zaandam was kept on the ground by his inability to fly.

Behind Karachev Khlebnikova stirred feebly, trying to lift her head and at first failing miserably. She hurt so much! She had never felt such pain! Even her first mating and bringing forth her first egg – both of which were extremely painful – had not hurt this badly.

She moved again, carefully, and this time was able to straighten out her tail which had been caught beneath her body. It hurt to do that, but it felt better once her tail was in its proper position. She then opened her eyes.

Up above in the air her mate was fighting with the blue dragon. "Oh, no!" Khlebnikova moaned when she saw this, blinking her huge eyes to clear them. When she saw an enormous jet of flame from Lakota's snout take Volunvoshka full in the chest she moaned again in anguish. She saw Volunvoshka's ice fall away to earth as water, melted in the hot flame of his opponent's maw. Volunvoshka had a thick hide but how long could he stand up assaults such as that one?

She finally managed to raise her head and looked with loathing on Karachev. He was the cause of her mate's being in peril of his life! The black Wizard stood with his back to Khlebnikova, giving her not the faintest bit of attention, intent on breaking Simon's shield.

How she hated him! She drew in a deep breath and hissed, an icy vapor coming from her nostrils.

377

As she watched, his shields cracked and failed, as did Simon's. A violet bolt nearly caught the necromancer but he managed to push it away with a red surge that streaked towards Simon. Simon, throwing himself sideways, countered it, scattering the red energies into the ground.

Giving very little thought to what she was doing, Khlebnikova raised her head as much as she could and let out a stream of ice.

It struck Karachev unawares and he screamed, the red power he had been about to send at Simon flung into the air, where it narrowly missed Volunvoshka.

Karachev dropped to his knees, still screaming and began to claw at himself even as smoke began to rise from his clothes and from his flesh.

For female Ice dragons had another weapon – one that the males did not. Within their ice lay a deadly acid – extra protection provided by nature for the mothers who guarded their eggs. Nothing could be done for anyone, magician or dragon, who was sprayed with this acid. It was fatal. It was considered dishonorable to use it – the acid was an anachronism, a relic of another time when dragon battles were fierce and frequent and when one flight of dragons would try to destroy another flights' eggs in conflicts over territory and food.

But Khlebnikova felt no dishonour in using it against this necromancer. From the very first she had thought him an evil man and more than likely the author of all their misery. She might never know who had actually taken their egg – for all she knew it had been Karachev, wanting to secure her mate's services – but now Karachev was putting her mate and her child in jeopardy as well. It was too much to be borne.

Simon watched in amazement as Karachev fell to the ground, screeching out his agony. A terrible smell arose as his body began burning and he clawed helplessly at himself. His face contorted with fear and pain, the necromancer rolled over and over on the ground, seeking to put out the fire eating his flesh and bones.

"Did you do that?" Anatoly demanded, running up to stand beside Simon.

378

"No!" Simon put down his wand arm and ran forward, unable to watch someone in such torment without trying to do something to help.

"Stand back, Wizard!" came a great voice form the sky and Volunvoshka let forth a mighty blast of ice which completely covered Karachev, smothering him. Underneath the mound of ice the corpse kept dissolving – but the necromancer's suffering was at an end.

Then the big Ice dragon landed on the ground near to Khlebnikova and at once began to nuzzle her anxiously.

Lakota spiraled down as near to Simon as he could and he too, touched his friend with his snout. "Are you all right?" he queried worriedly.

"I'm fine," Simon assured him. "And you?"

"Oh, never better!" Lakota said cheerfully. "Simon, that was just like dragon-ball – dodging and feinting! In fact, it made me think of some new moves we shall be able to show the team once we are at home again!"

"A game! You thought that was a game?" Volunvoshka growled, turning to look at Lakota, his eyes narrowed. "But what else can one expect from a dragon who wears a saddle and allows himself to be used as a ferry for humans?", he added contemptuously, eyeing Lakota's harness. Zaandam, who had come to stand with his parents, growled too, in imitation of his father.

"That is quite enough!" said Khlebnikova, as sharply as she was able. "We have no quarrel with this dragon or these humans. You only fought because that evil Wizard threatened us. We have our child – let us go home! I long for my home and the summer ice fields of the Arctic! My heart is sick within me for the cold and the comfort of family and friends. Let us go, my mate – please!"

Tears stood in her eyes as she looked at Volunvoshka.

"Very well," he said at last, rather gruffly, for he had nearly lost her. He grabbed Zaandam and threw the dragonet up onto his back. "Place your claws under my scales and hang on tightly," he told his son. With one last malevolent look at Lakota he launched himself in to the sky, followed more slowly by Khlebnikova, who had the courtesy to say goodbye.

As Volunvoshka gained altitude Lakota exclaimed in disgust, "Well, of all the things-! That Zaandam is sticking his tongue out at me!"

"What a horrible way to die!" Anatoly said, looking at the quickly disappearing remains of the necromancer. Even the heavy coating of ice was beginning to melt, such was the potency of the acid.

"I am only glad that I did not have to kill him," said Simon gratefully. "But I would like to know *why* he wanted to kill me! And what was all that about the Czar?' He gave a long sigh. "Now we will never know." Then, turning to the his dragon friend, he said. "Lakota, have you enough flame left to clean this up?"

"Oh, yes," the blue dragon replied, and blew hot flame upon the mound of ice and flesh until nothing was left but a puddle of water and bone ash.

"I'm very glad that neither Sacha or Tatya was here to see this," Simon said to Anatoly.

"Since the horses ran off," said Lakota, "I can take you back to our camp. After all of that I'm hungry!"

From the ridge above the Czar watched as they climbed onto Lakota's back after the safety check, and flew off. "An excellent outcome, Pozharsky" he said.

"The English Wizard did not destroy hin," the Count pointed out.

"I care little for such distinctions," said the Czar coolly. "The black Wizard is dead and the threat he represented is completely finished. That is all that matters." He clicked shut his spyglass and said "I shall expect you in St Petersburg shortly, Count, with a full report of this incident."

"*Incident!*" thought Pozharsky incredulously as he bowed deeply to the Czar and then watched him enter the coach and order the driver to drive away at a gallop. Would he ever see the day in which the Czar ever lost his cold reserve?

Behind Pozharsky, no longer lounging on a log, Golovin had produced a small but powerful spyglass he often used in his spying. He had watched the Ice dragons kill the necromancer and watched the dragons land. He now took a good look at the two men who stood with the dragons and let out a startled exclamation, hastily suppressed.

He clicked the glass closed and put it in his breast pocket. This was an unexpected turn of events! And a matter he would have to take care of – after he collected his pay from Pozharsky.

39

Oci dushi

The moment she saw the necromancer fall, Tatya urged the two boys to get back on the horse and return to the tent. She had promised Simon that she would remain there, but with her new knowledge of her own heart, she had had no choice but to go and see what was happening to him.

They arrived back at the camp to find a scene of frenzied activity. There was a crowd of people, most of whom she did not know. None of them seemed to be Tatars – there were a group of grim-faced men on horseback and a *droshky* carrying a battered looking girl, wrapped in a blanket, with an older woman's arms about her. There was a large traveling carriage and a troop of Chevalier Guards. A golden double headed eagle was upon the door of the large *lineika* style carriage.

As Tatya and the boys rode up, a man turned to look at them. Although she had never seen him in person, she recognized at once the coldly perfect features of Czar Nicholas, familiar to every reader of the daily news-sheets.

"Ho! Here's the Wizard's lady herself!" announced the Cham, He seemed unimpressed that he had an Imperial visitor in his humble camp. "She'll tell you the truth of the matter!"

Tatya slid from the horse, closely followed by the boys and curtsied deeply before the Czar. "Your Imperial Majesty," she murmured. As the Czar politely returned her bow, she gasped at what she saw behind him.

Her cousin Evgeny and Viktor Sumarokov had been stripped and spread-eagled, tied to frames made of thick branches. Evgeny was trying to scream and curse – but the gag in his mouth prevented little more than a muffled noise. He had made his wrists and ankles bleed by pulling ineffectively against his restraints. Sumarokov hung limply in his bonds, sobbing and whimpering. Before them on the ground lay an oil cloth filled with sharp knives and a thing that country-bred Tatya recognized as a gelding tool.

"This is the lady I was telling you of, Czar," said the Cham, treating Nicholas as an equal – which did not set too well with his Imperial Majesty. "Tatiana Ivanova – she's married to the Wizard! And I caught these rapists after she had taught them a lesson with her magic!" continued the Cham.

"Surely you are Russian?" the Czar inquired of Tatya.

"Yes, Majesty. Before my recent marriage I was Countess Tatiana Ivanova Kustodieva," she answered.

He recognized the name; she could tell by a flicker in his eyes.

"And these men tried to rape you?" the Czar inquired, waving his hand at Evgeny and Viktor.

"They did, Majesty, but my husband has been teaching me magic and I was able to defend myself," She noticed Evgeny's eyes grow wide as she identified herself as Simon's wife.

"Would that my Sophie had had the same defense!" said a new voice bitterly.

A tall, distinguished-looking man with dark hair that had white wings at the temples, in European dress, had joined them. "As I told your Imperial Majesty earlier," he went on "those two –" he pointed a riding crop at Evgeny and Viktor – "came upon my daughter while she was out picking fruit in one of our fields. They brutally violated her again and again and then left her, naked, to stumble towards our *dacha* in shock. One of my serfs found her, cared for her and sent for me. I demand justice for my child, Majesty! She is only fourteen years old! No one in the family of Prince Aleksky Iraklovich Shchegolev will be treated like that! If needs be I will kill them myself!" His voice shook with rage.

The woman in the carriage who still had her arms about the girl said angrily, her voice full of tears, "What if a child should come of this? She will be forever shamed! Who will marry her now, particularly if she whelps a rapist's bastard?" She began crying holding the girl tighter against her. The child was still in shock and stared ahead vacantly, seeming to notice little.

"Does any one know the identity of these two men?" the Czar asked in his usual cold fashion.

"I do, Majesty, "Tatya said. "That one is my cousin, Evgeny Yurovich Rostov and the other is his companion in vice, Viktor Zukhaarinovich Sumarokov."

"Rostov," the Czar said thoughtfully. "is this miscreant any relation to Yuri Pavlovich and Ekaterina Feodorova?"

"His parents – and he is my cousin," Tatya admitted. "They are also Hussars –in Colonel Danzas's regiment." She was surprised that the Czar knew of her aunt and uncle.

The Czar's expression darkened. "These vile excuses for men are officers in one of MY regiments? And Rostov tried to violate his own cousin?" He turned and looked at the two with utter loathing. "I have just exiled the parents to Siberia for stealing from me –" he began.

Tatya gasped. Exiled to Siberia! In spite of Simon's many reassurances she had been more than half afraid that her relatives could somehow annul her marriage and drag her back to the old life, or at least keep Sacha from her. But if they were in Siberia…!

But at this moment Lakota landed near them, with Simon and Anatoly aboard.

Simon took in the situation at a glance and slid quickly from Lakota's back. He hurried to Tatya and took her in his arms, unmindful of the Czar or anyone else. "Did he hurt you?" he demanded.

"No! I used the magic you showed me and routed him utterly!" she said, so happy to feel his arms around her once more.

"Thank God!" Simon held her close, shooting a look of hatred at Evgeny and Viktor that did not bode well for their continued good health.

"What is going on here?" he asked of the Cham, as he reluctantly released Tatya, but keeping her hand in his.

"Ho, Wizard! We were just about to castrate these rapists!" the Cham said cheerfully, as if there were going to be a picnic or some other sort of fest.

Might I help?" Simon said savagely. He had felt Tatya wince slightly when he hugged her and he had no doubt that that filth had manhandled her.

"They must be court-martialed!" announced Nicholas. "We have enough officers here to perform a drumhead court martial."

"AFTER they are castrated!" said Tarquin firmly.

"I care little for what you do to them," said Nicholas. "They are a disgrace to their uniforms. I will not brook my officers behaving in such fashion, lacking all restraint and discipline!"

Tatya shivered and leaned a little closer to Simon. She had little doubt that her cousin and his companion would be found guilty. The court-martial would be but a formality – and Nicholas was well known to be a stickler for rules. She had never seen such a cold look of complete contempt on anyone's features as was on the Czar's face when he looked at Evgeny and Viktor.

"The court-martial will take place tomorrow," Nicholas announced. He beckoned to the captain of his troop. "I will leave you to appoint an officer to represent these men. Prince Aleksky, I shall stay with you at your *dacha* until this affair is finished."

The prince bowed low. "An honour, your Imperial Majesty."

Without a backwards glance at anyone the Czar returned to his carriage, leaving his troop, save the captain and one other, the Prince's *droshky* and his party to follow.

"We'll take these rapists away and geld then down by the river so the Lady Wizard won't hear the screaming," said the Cham.

"Are you really going to –?" Tatya said, a little sickened.

The Cham scowled. "You are a guest in our lands and your honour was nearly lost at the hands of these! We are dishonoured by their acts – we did not guard you properly and they must be punished. To prevent further rapes is the best way to punish such as these!"

"But they will probably be court-martialed tomorrow!" Tatya said.

The Cham grinned at her. "Then they'll go to Hell as eunuchs!"

Tatya continued to look troubled, but Simon held her close and said "They deserve everything that happens to them! Who knows how many innocents they have debauched?"

She shuddered. "Oh, Simon, that poor little girl! She was only fourteen! What if she has a child!"

"She will not – there is an herbal drink I can make up for her that will prevent conception. It can work up to forty-eight hours after the fact," he said soothingly, stroking her hair.

Anatoly, who had watched the entire proceedings with an air of astonishment, came up to them, his face puzzled. "Whatever is the Czar doing here?" he inquired.

"What?" Simon, intent on Tatya, had not given the Czar's presence a thought. Now he stared at Anatoly. "I can't imagine why he is here! Do you know, Tatya?"

She shook her head.

The two boys now joined then as well. In the background the Tatars carried off the two Hussars in the direction of the river.

"Are they really going to cut cousin Evgeny?" said Sacha with the ghoulishness of small boys.

"If what I hear is true, he deserves it!" said Anatoly firmly. "Your cousin and his vile friend are a byword in Petersburg! My Colonel always felt that they should have been severely disciplined years ago! I am glad you were not harmed, Countess," he said a little awkwardly, turning to Tatya.

"Right now," said Simon firmly, "my wife is going to go and lay down! She's had a dreadful experience and she used a great deal of magic. She's more than likely tired."

Lakota too joined the party. He reached out his snout to Tatya and she stroked it. "I wish I had been here to protect you!" he said. "I would have flamed them before I let them hurt you!" He had been talking to one of the Tatars and had heard the whole story.

"Why didn't Janus and Vron warn someone that those two had come?" the blue dragon added.

Tatya realized that she had seen neither cat all day. "I hope they have not got into mischief!"

"The only mischief those two have been up to," said Simon with a laugh, "will probably result in a litter of kittens!"

"Oh, good!" said Lakota, brightening. "I love kittens! And Tatya will need a familiar if she is to become a Witch!"

Simon took Tatya into the tent, leaving the others outside. He would let Anatoly tell the boys of the necromancer's death. He had more important things to attend to at the moment.

"Did he hurt you?" he asked Tatya once they were private. "Let me see!"

She untied the ribbon at her breast and let her gown fall to the floor of the tent. Ugly bruises had formed on her arms and her breasts.

Simon swore under his breath when he saw the discolouration of her skin. He went at once to the medical kit and returned with a pot of ointment. "This will heal those marks very quickly."

But then before opening the jar, he said 'Tatya, will this make any difference between us? Did he manage to make you feel –"

"As if I am afraid or disgusted by being naked before you, or find your touch repellent?" she finished for him. "No – when *you* see me like this I am proud and feel beautiful. And I ache for you to touch me. Oh, Simon! I was so proud of myself! No one like Evgeny can ever hurt me again!"

"I won't let them!" he said roughly.

"But I can take care of myself! I was so afraid for so long! I was afraid of my uncle's beatings, I was afraid of my aunt's tongue and afraid of Evgeny! But now I will never be afraid of people like them again! And you did that for me!" she said, her eyes shining.

"You did it for yourself," he said gently, and opened the little jar and began to stroke the ointment on her everywhere their brutal hands had injured her. From the extent of the bruising Simon had a fair idea of how they had molested her. He was very thankful that she did not seem to have been mentally damaged as well. She had stopped them before they had completed the rape.

Tatya closed her eyes as he anointed her. His fingers felt so good – calming and soothing and the ointment let a trail of warmth behind, penetrating deep and removing all of

387

the pain and discomfort. "That's a magical ointment, isn't it?" she said.

"Yes and in about an hour it will be as if you were never injured," he assured her.

"I love magic!" she said.

"Now get into bed," he commanded, pulling back the blanket. "You've used up a lot of energy – I felt you tapping the ley lines!"

"Only if you join me," she said, looking up into his face. In truth, she felt suddenly exhausted and was beginning to shake with reaction. But she wanted to lie in his arms. His touch could banish the last of the ugliness left by Evgeny and Viktor.

"Are you certain –?" he said, but what she saw in his face reassured him. "I must mix the potion for the little girl," he said, "for the sooner she gets it the better. But I will have Anatoly take it to her."

Tatya lay back on the bed and Simon tenderly covered her with the sheet – no more cover was needed for again it was a hot day. He kissed her on the brow and went about his task.

Tatya lay on the pillows watching him. How different he was from most of the men she had known! Tender, gentle and kind, but strong and sure too – the kind of man she had never thought to meet. He reminded her of her beloved father – with one difference. She could not ever imagine Simon allowing himself to be manipulated as her father had.

As she watched him work she said "Simon, the Czar said that he banished my aunt and uncle for stealing from him! He sent them to Siberia!"

"Quite frankly, I think Siberia is too good for them – I'd rather see them in Hell and your cousin and his rotter of a friend with them!" said Simon, rapidly stirring herbs into a beaker. He tapped the beaker with his wand and the contents turned a lovely rose colour. An enticing scent of cinnamon, cloves and allspice filled the room. He poured this into a jar and corked it.

"It is a good thing that they were banished, for they might have had me taken up for thievery!" she confessed.

"What?" Simon turned to look at her.

388

"Just before we left St Petersburg I sneaked into my aunt's room and took an amber necklace and earrings from her jewelry chest, and an icon from the wall as well. They were my mother's and she took them from me when we went to live with them," Tatya said in a rush.

"That was not stealing – you were merely recovering your lost property," Simon said. "She had no right to do that to you!" His blood literally boiled when he thought of the way those people had treated Tatya and Sacha. "Just give me one moment to give this to Anatoly and we shall talk more of this."

"And you will come to bed?" she asked eagerly.

"And I will come to bed," he promised and left the tent, jar in hand. In truth, he was fatigued as well, after expending all that magical energy.

When he had gone she slid the dragon whistle over her head and undid the clasp. She had added something to the chain several days ago. Now she slid it off the chain and then restored the chain to around her neck. The object she held tightly in one palm.

She heard Lakota take to the sky outside and within moments, Simon returned. "There," he said in satisfaction as he shed his clothes. "That is taken care of and that potion is full of magic that will help heal her mind as well as her body. I shall have to tell Stuart how very useful his book has been!" He lifted up the coverlet and slid in beside her.

He was more than half afraid that, in spite of her brave words, she might flinch away from him. But no, she melted into his embrace as sweetly and as eagerly as ever while he mentally uttered a deeply felt prayer of thanks.

"I have something for you," she said shyly.

"Better than this?" he said teasingly.

She blushed and laughed. "I want you to have this." She brought up he hand and uncurled it. On her palm lay a man's ring. "It was my father's – the only thing I have of him. I managed to hide it from my aunt for many years. It was sewn into my stays!"

"Oh, Tatya, you want to keep that –" he began, but she interrupted him, "No, no! I want you to have it – it is engraved in Cyrillic script. Are you able to you read it?"

Her head lay on his right arm, so he reached over her with his left and took the ring, holding it up to his face, *"Oti dushi,"* he read aloud. "From my soul."

"My mother had it made for my father when they were married," she explained. "Now I want you to wear it – it explains what is in my heart, too." She turned her head so that she could see his face. "I know that you don't love me yet – but I love you so much! And I will not be afraid to go to Ireland nor any place else as long as you are with me. And I shall even try to learn English!"

"Tatya, *douchenka*, I have known that I loved you since the *Rusalka* tried to drown you!" he said. "I hoped and prayed that you would come to love me too !" He gave the ring back to her. "Put it on my right hand – like my wedding ring, it will never leave my finger. And when we get to Ireland I shall give you a *Cloddagh* ring – a ring of eternal love and fidelity." When she had put the ring on jis finger – it fit perfectly – he said reassuringly. "And don't worry about learning English – I've a little plan for that."

As much as she pleaded he would not tell her what his plan might be. "It might not work out," was all that he would say.

"Do the Elves in Ireland behave as they do here in Russia? Do they moon-bathe and go without clothing?" she asked abruptly.

"And give each other leaves?" he asked. "Yes, they do. Did you enjoy living like that?"

"Oh, I did! I must be completely depraved! Or, maybe," she added, suddenly worried, "I *am* a whore as my cousin said! To enjoy being naked and making love so much–!"

"Listen to me, Tatya," Simon said, his voice growing stern. "There is nothing, absolutely nothing, wrong with enjoying those things! Why, my parents go to the Hollow Hills for much the same reason. And you are *not* a whore, no matter what your idiot cousin said!"

"How do you know your parents do that?" she said.

"I overheard my mother's maid telling the upstairs maid that 'Lady Diana is tanned all over – every inch of her!' " he said with a laugh. "And where else could that happen except beneath the Hollow Hills? You are going to love Ireland, Tatya. And I am going to spend the rest of my life making certain that you are never unhappy again! I want you to forget anything your vile cousin ever said or did and forget all of your disgusting relatives!"

"I know something that would make me forget them very quickly." she said placing her hand on his chest. "Love me, Simon," she whispered.

Anatoly, flown there by Lakota, had delivered the potion to the Shchegolev *dacha*. The Prince and Princess had been dubious of its value at first, but the Czar told them that he believed in the efficacy of these magical potions and as this was tantamount to a command they gave little Sophie the contents of the bottle as Simon had directed. Within minutes the colour had returned to her face and she emerged from her stupor. Of course, all of the terrible memories came rushing back and Sophie cast herself into Princess Anna's arms with a wail.

Anatoly explained, as Simon had done to him, that her memories would fade very quickly, especially after a good night's sleep and her injuries would be healed by morning as well.

"Truly, this is a miracle!" said the Prince in a voice that showed he was trying , with great difficulty, not to break down in tears in front of the Czar. "Will this wonderful potion restore her virginity as well?" he added hopefully.

"Alas, Prince, the Wizard said that it will not," Anatoly had to tell him. "He said that no one can do that – not even an English Wizard Healer."

Anatoly felt the Czar's cold eye upon him. "Lieutenant, you are of good family and are not married, I believe?" Nicholas said thoughtfully.

"Yes, your Imperial Majesty," said Anatoly with a sinking feeling.

"We shall speak of this more on the morrow, after the court-martial." the Czar gave Anatoly a measuring look.

Anatoly refused graciously the Shchegolev's invitation to dine, saying that he had something he had to do – the Wizard would wish to know how the potion had effected the girl.

When he rejoined Lakota outside he said to the dragon, "I want to find out what his Imperial Majesty is doing here, so far from the court! He has a reputation for showing up where you least expect him, but it seems strange that he has shown up here, just at this time. Will you help me find out?"

"I will ask Janus to speak to the horses!" Lakota offered. "They listen to all of the coachmen's gossip and in Ireland we say that if you really want to know what is going on, ask a servant!"

But in the end this proved unnecessary, for no sooner had Lakota made a landing and Anatoly slid from his back than, "Hallo, Anatoly Aloyshovich," came a quiet voice from the lengthening shadows beneath the trees.

Both Anatoly and Lakota looked up sharply. They had neither heard nor seen any one close by.

The man who emerged from the shadows was dressed like a hunter, with leather breeches and boots, and a gun slung over the shoulder of a rough frieze coat.

"Stefan Kriztofvich!" Anatoly exclaimed. If he had made a list of all the people he had never expected to see here, his Cousin Golovin's name would have topped the list.

"I saw your little display down there," Golovin nodded in the direction of the fight with the necromancer. "Very impressive! When did you learn to do magic?"

"Very recently," Anatoly admitted. "Lakota, this is my cousin, Stefan Khristofvich Golovin."

Golovin swept off his battered hat and bowed low. "Charmed. I have never met a dragon before," he said. "And I dareswear you've never met a black sheep! "

"Well, I've never been introduced to one, but I have eaten –" Lakota began and then stopped as he realized what he had said.

Golovin burst into laughter. "I can see that I have missed much – not being acquainted with a dragon! And cousin, I congratulate you on your family's good fortune. We all thought Great Aunt Sarafan Pavlova to be long dead! Who'd have thought she would cock up her toes now and leave all of her very handsome fortune to your father! And two of your sisters betrothed, even before the news of your father's windfall leaked out! Your fortunes are certainly improving!"

This was all news to Anatoly as he had not heard from his family since the beginning of this trip. He put his hand into his pocket, where the Firebird feather always rested. It was still warm to the touch and he had drawn comfort from it many times. Was this the good fortune that having this feather was supposed to bring? It certainly sounded as if it was! How much he wanted to see her again. Those eyes of hers, so human and deep, haunted his dreams.

"There's something else," said Golovin. "I think you ought to know why the Czar is here. I don't trust Nicholas and I think I need to warn you and tell you what he has done."

Anatoly and Lakota exchanged glances. "That is just what we were going to try and find out," said the dragon.

"And I can answer all of your questions – and possibly even those you didn't think of!" said Golovin.

And not very far away, on the riverbank, the Tatars were finishing up a gruesome task.

40

The Return of Marushka

Anatoly waited with extreme impatience for Simon to emerge from the tent. He was not about to interrupt them, but he was bursting to impart the intelligence he had learned. And he was burning with indignation as well at what his cousin had told him of the Czar and the Secret Police.

His cousin Golovin was a strange character. Bored with provincial life he had left home at fifteen to seek adventure. He turned up every once in a while, full of knowledge that no one knew how he had come by. He always knew all the latest family news even though he was seldom in their company. None knew how he made his living, for his father, who was married to Anatoly's mother's sister, had cut him off years earlier when he refused to come home and act out his proper role in the family. He had not looked particularly prosperous when Anatoly saw him that afternoon but, looking closer, the Lieutenant had noticed that his cousin wore very fine English-made boots and his rifle was a magnificent piece of workmanship.

Anatoly had met his cousin in some very strange places in recent years – on the steppes, once, where Stefan Khristofvich had been doing a duty as a caravan guard, looking very much like a Pathan, and in Turkistan, dressed and sounding like a Turk himself, among other places.

But the information he gave was always helpful and always accurate. Anatoly had no doubts that what he had been told today was true.

Eventually he became so tired of waiting for Simon that he took his gun out and got a brace of pheasants. These he cleaned and put them on a spit, with creamy butter he got from the Tatars mixed with herbs, spread under the skin. He set his roasting pit up close to the tent and, as he had hoped, the savory odor soon enticed Simon and Tatya from the tent, sniffing in appreciation.

"Just what we need!" said Simon, his arm around Tatya's waist. "We've had nothing since breakfast! How soon will they be ready?"

"I hope you will have an appetite left after what I have to tell you," said Anatoly grimly.

Simon noticed that only the Lieutenant and Lakota were present. "Where are the boys?" he asked, suddenly worried.

"They're fine," answered Anatoly. "I sent them off to bargain for vegetables and buy some cream –"

"For me –" Lakota put in.

"But I thought what I had to tell you ought to remain private," Anatoly continued, ignoring Lakota.

"This sounds serious," Simon said, exchanging looks with Tatya. He had never seen Anatoly look so bleak. His nature was generally sunny and all their adventures had not dampened his spirits.

"I have been informed why the Czar has honoured us with his illustrious presence!" Anatoly said, sounding almost bitter "And both of us have been duped and used as puppets by his Imperial Majesty! Let me explain –" he raised a hand as Simon began to speak. "I have some *kvas* here. Let us sit and drink and I will tell you what I learned and how I learned it," He produced three glasses and a bucket and poured then each a draft, including a small amount for Lakota in the bucket.

There was nowhere to sit but on the grass. Anatoly let them each take a sip before he told them how he and Lakota had met his cousin Golovin.

"My cousin is somewhat of a shady character but I have no reason to doubt his word – he has always been trustworthy," Anatoly said, swirling his *kvas* around in the ceramic cup. "He overheard much of this from the Czar and Count Pozharsky and some of it he pieced together from other information he heard that at the time did not make sense to him."

"A little over a year ago an expedition went to Siberia – a well equipped expedition with the Imperial Seal of approval. There were men in this expedition who were famous explorers, and mountaineers and a certain Dr. Quong Lee –"

"The Chinese Dracophilologist!" Simon interrupted, his interest stirred considerably.

"Yes. Their object was to steal an Ice dragon egg, which they accomplished. My cousin did not know the details of that – it must have been quite an adventure. Instead of returning overland to St Petersburg with their prize they came by tropical routes, hugging the shoreline of India and Africa."

"Which was more than likely too hot for an Ice dragon to follow them," Lakota put in. "I never saw a dragon that liked ice before! They couldn't seem to stand the heat!"

"Their object in stealing this egg was to lure you here, Simon Renovich!" Anatoly burst out, "And use you!"

"But why me?" Simon inquired "For a postal service?"

"There was never any idea of a dragon postal service! They were well aware that it would be impossible!" said Anatoly fiercely. "They needed a Wizard to challenge Karachev – that was his name – Vladimir Konstantinovich Karachev. The few Wizards we have left in Russia are superannuated and not up to facing down someone like Karachev. His old rival, Tenisheva, is practically senile. The Czar wanted you – because you are not only a Wizard, but a professor of dragon studies as well. His Imperial Majesty thought that tempting you with the little-known Ice dragons would be irresistible to a scholar such as yourself."

"That is despicable!" Tatya cried, her eyes flashing. "Why did he not just offer to pay Simon instead of tricks and lies?"

"The Czar felt that Simon would not care to be involved in what was not his quarrel – at least that is what my cousin Stefan Khristofvich thinks," Anatoly informed them. "Everything was planned as if it were an intricate chess game. The Czar used the stolen egg to insure that the Ice dragons would ask a Wizard for help and then used the Ice dragons to lure you here. Pozharsky even showed you the egg when he thought you were starting to think of returning to England."

"Would you have come?" Tatya queried anxiously of her husband. If he had never come to Russia–! It was a horrible thought.

"I don't know," he said slowly. In the mood he had been in after he broke off with Birgit, he might well have come, just to get away.

"But wait until you hear WHY the Czar wanted a Wizard!" said Lakota, feeling that this telling was taking far too long.

"Karachev was demanding that Nicholas turn over his throne to him – it was his by right," said Anatoly.

"Was he mad?" Tatya said incredulously "The Romanovs have ruled for centuries!"

"He claimed to be a direct descendant of Feodor, Ivan *Grozny's* son, by Feodor's lawful wife, Boris Godunov's sister."

"But Feodor was feeble-minded!" Tatya cried. "There were no children of that union!"

"Karachev claimed that a child was born, but was smuggled away, in fear for his life. The secret was kept all of these years until there would come an heir powerful enough to unseat the usurper. And that heir was Karachev."

"The Czar and Count Pozharsky gambled on the fact that the Ice dragons would want the egg back and would have to turn to a Wizard for help. There are historical instances of Wizards and Ice dragons working together. And it worked – too well. Karachev used the Ice dragon to terrify the people in the Urals, cutting off an important source of the Czar's income. And from what my cousin overheard they were overjoyed when Sacha was stolen because it made you take action immediately. They had some other scheme in mind to bend you to their will but my cousin did not find out what it was. And they used me to spy on you!" Anatoly burst out.

"I knew that all along," said Simon gently. "And I never held it against you. I daresay you were under orders. And it is what the FO warned me of, after all. It actually amused us –"

Lakota nodded vigorously. "Simon cast all sorts of illusions when we wanted privacy!"

"I had nothing to hide at any rate," Simon finished.

"Even the Secret Police, except Pozharsky of course, knew nothing of the real reason you were here. They persisted in thinking that you were sent hear to spy upon our military fortifications and capabilities! They even thought that the search for Elves had something o do with the Navy because you wished to go to a place with large trees."

Simon laughed so hard he almost fell over backwards. "Me! A military spy!" he said , wiping tears of mirth from his eyes.

Anatoly looked at him, puzzled. "I must say that you are taking this very well – I thought you'd be angry!"

"But I gained so much from this trip!" Simon said "New friends –" he nodded at Anatoly "enough material on Ice dragons for a monograph, enough experiences of Russia to address the Royal Society and, best of all – ", he turned to Tatya and smiled at her, "– I found the love of my life and she is going home with me! So I cannot be angry – I gained too much."

"I wish I could feel so generous!" Anatoly sighed. "I feel as if I were the stupidest fool in the world, not to see what they were doing!"

"Ho!" a voice interrupted and they all looked up to see the Cham, looking rather hangdog. "That rapist – the one who looked like a weasel – he's dead," he said abruptly, sinking down beside Anatoly and taking the bottle of *kvas* from him. He took a long swig and then wiped his mouth on the back of his hand.

He died of being–er – *gelded*?" said Anatoly delicately.

"No, no – he died of screaming! Burst a blood vessel in his throat and choked on his own blood! Stupid fool! We never meant to really cut them – just tease them with the knives until they repented of it! Threats work as well as deeds sometimes!" The Cham shook his head in disgust.

Tatya gave a gasp and turned to bury her face in Simon's shoulder. She had hated Sumarokov, but that was a horrible way for anyone to die. She found that she had not hated him enough to wish that fate on him.

"And my wife's cousin?" Simon asked, holding Tatya close. He hated for her to be distressed like this.

"Ho, that one's too busy cursing us – what a vile tongue he has! My men learned a lot of new curses today!" He shook the now empty jug of *kvas*. "Is his all you've got? And those birds smell good!" He licked his lips appreciatively.

"Of course, you must join us," Simon invited cordially. In truth he wished the Cham at the devil. Tatya was shaking against him – she was probably crying, but he knew she would not wish him to bring attention to the fact.

He was grateful when the boys arrived with vegetables and the Cham began telling them the Tatar way of preparing potatoes and carrots.

Anatoly, who could take a hint, went to fetch more *kvas* and a few more cups.

Lakota walked quietly over to Simon and Tatya and put his snout on her hair, breathing his soft, warm breath into her crown of braids. "Don't cry," he said softly. "I know how you feel – as if you killed him. But he did it to himself by being evil – just like the *Rusalka*."

Without removing her face from Simon's neck she reached up and stroked his snout. "I'm so glad we have you, Lakota," she said, sounding as if she needed a handkerchief.

"And I'm glad you and Sacha are in our family now. How happy we all shall be when we get home to Ireland!" Lakota said on a sigh, for his homesickness had returned full force.

"And we shall be heading home as soon as we return Illya to his home and tie up a few loose ends." Simon took a handkerchief from his pocket and gave it to Tatya.

She blew her nose vigorously and then said "I need to wash my face before they see –"

"I'll take you to the pool," Lakota offered. "You'll be safe with me."

Tatya accepted his offer and allowed Simon to help her up.

Simon watched them walk off with a full heart. Her hand was resting on Lakota's side and the blue dragon's head was bent down close to her, talking softly. How fortunate, how wonderful that those two had taken to each other so well! He would never have imagined it when they first met – she had been so frightened and Lakota had been so distressed about frightening her. Now they were part of the same family.

The birds were delicious and everyone ate in silence for a while, all of them hungry after the day they had experienced, enjoying the good food, until Sacha, who had been very quiet throughout the meal, said," What about all those souls Karachev had in the bottles? Can they be freed?"

399

Everyone turned to look at him.

"What is this all about, Sacha?" Simon asked. The boy looked very intent and rather sad.

"The people whose souls he stole are in bottles in his workshop in the mountains," Illya explained for his friend.

"Might you help them?" pleaded Sacha of Simon. "Their eyes look so sad!"

"If they are in bottles and their eyes are visible that means that he did not absorb the souls – he stored them for future use," said Simon thoughtfully "And I daresay that I could help – but I would need a priest to help."

"What about the priest back at Treblinkova?" Anatoly put in. "He seemed a decent sort and not at all in awe of magicians."

Lakota, who had been daintily ingesting an entire pheasant, said. "I would be glad to fetch him – if he gets here quickly we can go home quickly!" He realized as did Simon that they could not leave those poor souls trapped without hope of Heaven. They deserved to be released and go to their final home.

"He has demons trapped in bottles, too," offered Illya.

"Demons!" Simon looked startled and then said gravely "They must be destroyed. If Karachev is no longer there to constantly renew the keeping spells they can escape from the bottles and do terrible things to the world above. Once they are loose it is nearly impossible to capture them."

"What do you mean by the world above?" Anatoly asked.

"This, our world, is the world above to a demon, for they come from the world below – Hell," Simon answered.

"Do you know how to destroy a demon?" Tatya asked, her eyes wide in wonder.

"Oh, yes. Every *Magus Magistra* must destroy a demon as a part of his qualifying examinations," said Simon confidently. "Father Grigory will be helpful there as well."

The Cham looked at him, eyebrows up to his hairline. "Ho!" he said in awe.

It was decided that after the court-martial the next day the party would fly to Karachev's lair and then Anatoly would return to Treblinkova and beg Father Grigory's help while Simon prepared for the two ceremonies.

400

It was at this moment that Janus and Vron, after a full day's absence, strolled up.

"Oh, that bird smells good! I hope that you left enough for us!" she said. The two cats each wore the self – same satisfied smirk.

"Did we miss anything?" she asked and looked indignant when everyone laughed a little hysterically.

The next day a soft summer rain was falling when they awoke. The day was grey and misty and they were not surprised when a galloper from the Czar arrived, telling them that the court martial would be held indoors, at the *dacha* of Prince Aleksky.

Tatya had slept very ill the night before, in spite of the fact that she fell asleep with Simon's arms about her. This court-martial would be an ordeal – she did not know if she would be required to give testimony as to what they had done to her and how she had defended herself. She had scarcely been able to tell Simon what they had did and said, but she had done so the previous evening when they were in bed and it was dark. It had been easier to tell him in the dark. He had been angry that she had been subject to such indignities and crude language, but he had thought that they had been deliberately nasty in order to frighten her. He was probably right, but she knew that her dreams would be haunted by what they had done and said, even though her waking hours would be free of it. Making love with Simon yesterday had proved that.

But dreams were different and impossible to control. She did not know that Simon had already resolved to take her to a Wizard Healer when they reached Dublin and have those memories amended. so that she could sleep undisturbed.

Tatya wanted Sacha to remain behind with the Tatars but he insisted upon coming – he wanted to see his horrid cousin get what he deserved. And of course, Illya went wherever Sacha went.

Simon was thankful for the Elfin cloaks (but how had Oberon known how many they would need?) for by the time the party left for the neighboring *dacha*, rain was falling heavily. It might make their travel later in the day towards the mountains rather miserable...

401

The court-martial was short and over with quickly. Nicholas was much disgusted with the conduct of Evgeny and his only remarks when he learned that Viktor was dead, was regret that Sumarokov had so easily escaped his punishment.

The Czar waived many of the formal rules – surprising in one of his pedantic temperament and allowed a small panel of officers to listen to the evidence. He himself acted as Judge.

There was not much of a defense. Evgeny could offer no good reason as to why he had attempted to rape his own cousin and his excuse that he and Viktor had thought little Sophie Shchegoleva a serf was met with the contempt it deserved. "A serf is property," said Nicholas coldly, "and it is to the owner of that property as to its disposition. You should have ascertained if the girl' services were available and a suitable compensation offered. To use a serf in such fashion is theft of another's property."

Simon was nauseated by this cold–blooded description of a serf – a human being – as property. Members of his family had been in the fight to end slavery in all British colonies and it was revolting to hear a child described something to be deposed of as the wishes of as master, sold to a depraved individual such as Evgeny. He could never understand a mind that thought this way – yet another reason to be glad to be going home.

To Tatya's relief her evidence, like Sophie's was confined to identification of her attacker. She did not have to recount details, for Nicholas had a look of distaste on his face and waved away such considerations.

The Czar took no time to deliberate, but made his pronouncements quickly.

"There can be little doubt," he said, steepling his fingers and sitting very tall and stiff in his chair, "that the prisoner who stands before us is guilty of both crimes against these two females of noble birth and of disgracing his profession with such lewd and perverted behavior. Normally I would order him shot for his crimes. I will not tolerate such debauchery in one of my officers. But I think that execution is hardly justice for his actions. Therefore I exile him to Siberia for life, there to be put to hard labor for no less than thirty years. I shall personally write a note to the governor of the penal colony, ordering him to put this Rostov to the worst labor imaginable. He will also be stripped of his rank and disgraced in the eyes of his regiment. Let it be done!" He gestured to the members of the Chevalier Guard who had stood on each side of Evgeny's chair. He had been tied to the chair and was considerably disheveled and bruised, for he would not keep his mouth shut, shouting and muttering threats and curses on every one from Simon and Tatya to the Czar. The two officers, horrified that he would curse the Czar, had subdued him with the butts of their rifles. But even as he was dragged away he glared at his cousin over the blood-stained gag in his mouth.

Simon felt Tatya shivering as she stood beside him and he put a comforting arm about her. "Don't worry," he said softly so that only she could hear. We will never see him again."

"I know," she said. leaning gratefully against him, "No one ever returns from Siberia," she added, thinking of her father. "But why does he have to be so horrible?"

Simon reflected that to her such behavior was in-explicable. Perhaps she did not yet understand that some people were born warped, with twisted evil personalities and that no one as yet had an explanation for why this was so. Evgeny had lacked moral guidance all of his life, yet this alone could not explain why he was what he was.

Impassively, Nicholas watched Evgeny taken off. His expression indicated that he thought this a job well done.

Then abruptly he turned to Simon."You will be returning to St Petersburg before going to your home?" he asked, although his tone indicated this was more of a command than a question.

"Yes, Majesty," Simon answered, as if it really had been a question. "My wife and my brother-in-law will need to obtain passports."

"Then you will come and see me at the Catherine Palace – Pozharsky will arrange it," the Czar ordered

He then turned his attention to Anatoly. "Lieutenant Tcherepin," he said, "Prince Aleksky is much worried that his daughter will never make a suitable alliance. You are young, personable and unwed. I also understand that you are in search of a well-dowered bride. Sophie, though young, will have a magnificent dowry, for in light of what has happened here, an act of brutality committed by one of my former officers, I will contribute to her dowry substantially. I will present you to the Prince and Princess as their daughter's suitor. That is a direct order, Lieutenant. I will also make you a Captain in my personal guard."

Majesty –" Anatoly stammered, looking perfectly miserable but trying to conceal it. "I–" There was so much he wanted to say! But how did one defy a direct command of the Czar? This was not the way he wished to be wed! Both Prince and Princess Shchegolev looked quite pleased with this turn of events.

"No!" a clear voice rang from out the air. "No, he is mine!"

A golden shower filled the middle of the room, removing all of the day's gloom that many branches of candles had not. It was if a shaft of sunlight had suddenly burst from the heavy clouds. Dust motes seemed to dance in this radiance, but on closer examination they proved to be sparks of gold and red.

With no fanfare the Firebird appeared in the golden glow, hanging in the air, her bright feathers alight with colour. As they watched in surprise she lengthened and grew and changed to a beautiful maiden in a red gown, shining with exquisite gold embroidery. On her golden hair sat a *kokoshniki* headdress, pointed and with a floating veil of gold attached to it. She sparkled so that it made the eyes ache to look at her.

"Who are, *what* are you, *Madame*?" demanded the Czar in his cold voice. "And what business of this is yours? This man is one of my officers –"

She interrupted him with no regard for his rank. "I am the Firebird, the *Zharpesta*," she answered. "I am the very soul and spirit of Russia. And this man is mine. He carries my favour, a feather of mine, freely given."

When she had manifested herself, Anatoly's hand had gone at once to his pocket where the feather always reposed. Now he drew it out and uncurled his hand to reveal the brilliant gold and scarlet feather.

404

"And what do you intend to do with him?" the Czar demanded.

"Why, marry him, of course!" she said, with the sweetest smile in the world – one that pierced Anatoly's heart.

41

Going Home

The Firebird's words created a sensation.

"No, no!" cried Princess Anna. "My daughter must have a husband! Wild-eyed, she looked towards the Czar. He had promised that this young man of good family would wed her disgraced child.

"Be silent, woman," said the Firebird sternly. "Your daughter will make a magnificent match – a love match – but not with Anatoly Aloyshovich! I shall send her a husband, with one of my feathers, for good fortune for your entire family." This was a munificent offer – and Prince Aleksky realized it even if his wife did not. The Prince had a deep belief in the legends and traditions of his homeland.

"Hush, Anna Petrovna!" he said. "One does not question the gifts of the Firebird! One merely accepts – with gratitude." He bowed to the *Zharpesta* and said, "We thank you, great lady."

She looked pleased at his deference and inclined her golden head graciously.

Simon and Tatya were astonished at this turn of events, for Anatoly had told no one of his encounter with the Firebird. It had seemed too rare and precious to speak of it, even to people who had become dear friends.

But Nicholas was not pleased – his nature was autocratic and he much disliked having his plans counter-manded – even by the very soul and spirit of Russia.

Simon could tell by the clouds gathering on the Czar's brow that he was about to say something that might be dangerous. Simon had learned that one did not argue with creatures out of legend. He shuddered to think how Oberon would deal with someone who defied the Elf king as he very much feared Nicholas was about to do with the Firebird. One could, with great tact, disagree with Oberon, but it had to be done carefully. And Nicholas, an autocrat to his fingertips, had no tact whatsoever when it came to dealing with anyone.

Simon left Tatya's side and approached Nicholas. "A word to the wise, Majesty," he said in a conciliatory tone, low enough so that only the Czar could hear him. "When one deals with magical creatures it is far better to humor them, especially when they might have the capability to make one vanish from the face of the earth without a trace."

Nicholas looked at him, startled. "She can do that?" he demanded.

"I know little of the Firebird," Simon replied, "But I have wide experience of her kindred – and they can do that and more, quite easily."

"And I shall not hesitate to rid myself of you should you prove an impediment!" said the Firebird, proving her hearing was as supernatural as the rest of her. She then turned to Anatoly, and suddenly became a young maiden in love again. "Do you find fault with my desire for our union?" she asked him, almost shy.

"I have thought of little besides you since that night in the cherry orchard," he replied, looking at her with his heart in his eyes. It was if they were alone in the room, no one else existed – neither Simon nor Tatya, not the Czar, nor the Shchegolevs, nor the remaining Chevalier Guards.

She glided towards him, seeming to float rather than walk, leaving a train of iridescent red and gold sparks behind her.

Marushka took Anatoly's hands in hers. Her skin was soft but as warm as her feathers. "I will stay with you from now on," she promised. "Till we may be wed. You have important tasks to do yet, to help your friends. Those demons must be destroyed."

"How did you know –?" Anatoly stammered.

She smiled at him. "I know everything about you," she said.

"But why me?" he asked in sudden confusion.

"I am an immortal creature," she explained, "and the only one of my kind. But even we immortals need love and companionship. And what better companion and lover for an immortal than a Wizard? And one with a good and true heart," she added.

"I'm not much of a Wizard," he admitted, "I can only make a mage light and throw rocks!"

407

"But once you have completed your training you will be very good indeed, and you shall train others. I think that we all have seen that Russia needs her Wizards!" She turned to look at Nicholas. "Would you not agree?"

The Czar could do nothing but acquiesce. Nicholas might be an autocrat but he was not stupid. He was becoming aware that his country was not full of myths of magical beings, but was in reality, full of them and it would be good to have a magician, a trained magician, that he could call on in time of other-worldly threats.

Anatoly had only one demur. "How am I to complete my training?" he inquired. "Simon Renovich is to return to Ireland – "

"You must resign your commission and go to England, of course," said the Firebird matter of factly. "I am certain that your friend could help you with that." Her expressive eyes slid towards Simon. "But come, we must go – the demons become restive – already they have had several days to grow strong and try to escape their prisons of glass. I shall fly with you, beside the dragon." She released Anatoly's hands and shimmered yet again, reappearing in her bird form.

Lakota's saddle was full. All six seats were taken. The boys rode in the rear, just in front of the cat carrier, for the rear of the saddle ended just above the wings and there was not as much leg room there.

Illya was both frightened and elated to be riding a dragon. His friend Sacha acted as if riding the giant blue beast was an everyday occurrence (although in truth Sacha had only been aloft three times. That was three times more than Illya, though). The Wizard had promised that after his task in the mountains was completed they would fly to Topek and return him to his family. Illya could only imagine the sensation it would create in the village – a dragon landing!

And he could not help but wonder if his family thought him dead. It had been over a year since he had so stupidly decided to run away. He still did not relish the idea of becoming a cloth merchant, but there were worse things – such as being a slave. He had been very grateful that Karachev's death had cancelled the debt he would have owed Simon, for it would have taken a lifetime to pay off such a sum. From now on, he would do his best to be a good and dutiful son.

A stiff wind carried them quickly to the Urals and they found Karachev's house with little difficulty. Lakota, smaller than Volunvoshka, had little trouble landing in front of the building.

Already, people were returning to the mountains and to their work. In mysterious fashion the word and spread that the Wizard was no more and that the threatening Ice dragon was gone also. The dreadful silence of the mountains in Karachev's time was replaced by singing, the sounds of work and by children laughing.

No one had been brave enough to go near the Wizard's lair. It stood on the mountainside, already looking deserted.

Simon felt the vibration of black magic even before Lakota landed in the clearing before the house. He would not allow Tatya to step inside until he had ascertained the danger. Wand at the ready, he went inside, closely followed by Illya and Sacha, who knew the interior well.

Even the inside of the house had a deserted, neglected air. In only a few days time dust lay think everywhere and they heard a scurrying that spoke of a mouse invasion. At least Simon hoped it was a mouse.

With distaste, Simon saw the evil pentagrams on the floor, edged with not the names of angels in the celestial script, but of the great demons, Some of the symbols that he was familiar with had been drawn backwards and he noticed that neither one of the boys wanted to step in or near the red diagrams on the floor.

These were easily excised. A simple cleansing spell burned them away with a violet light, leaving an unmarked floor behind. There seemed to be a huge node of magic somewhere near this house and Simon was again amazed that Karachev had never learned how to tap into it.

Illya showed him the cupboards where the demons and souls were kept. Karachev seemed to have no sense of order, for the jars were indiscriminately shoved into the cabinets, souls cheek and jowl by demons. With his wand, Simon tapped each bottle and the flash of colour at the end of the opal that served as his focus stone, either red or blue ,

409

separated the demons from the souls. With the boys' help he placed them into two groups on tables that Illya and Sacha cleared for this purpose.

When this was done Simon did a general cleansing spell. Only then did he let Tatya come in.

Lakota and Anatoly had been dispatched to fetch Father Grigory. The Firebird had flown with them. Lakota would not be gone long – carrying only one rider, he could fly very fast indeed. But there were still preparations to make before Anatoly brought the Holy Father back.

Tatya and the boys watched as Simon drew a containment pentagram around the table that held the demons. When the time came to dispatch them this would protect them from the demons, for only he and Father Grigory would be inside the circle. This pentagram was drawn with his wand, the violet light rounding a circle and then crossing beneath the table to form the five pointed star. Around the circle at the four cardinal points were inscribed in celestial script – the names of the four great angels who were guardians of each point – Michael, Raphael, Gabriel and Uriel. When he said the spell that brought the circle to life the people in the room would feel the presence of thee great ones and might hear the rustle of their huge wings. Even now, their names glowed with heavenly fire, cleansing and purifying. As each name was drawn, the demons wailed in agony. The bottles rocked as they attempted to scratch their way from their earthly prisons. But Simon had replaced Karachev's dark spells with a pure white binding that kept them contained.

He drew another pentagram under the bottles that held the souls. But these cried in joy when the angelic names were written beneath them. For the first time since Sacha had first seen those eyes they held hope.

Father Grigory arrived shortly after all was in readiness. He had brought his most elaborate vestments, for Anatoly and the Firebird had impressed on him the urgency and solemnity of this undertaking. The Holy Father looked somewhat bemused – his first dragon ride in company of a Firebird. And now this!

Simon had hastily but accurately transcribed the priest's part in the rituals into Cyrillic, for the Holy Father's benefit. He also asked the priest to bless each ritual.

Tatya, Illya, Sacha and Anatoly stood inside a protective circle that Simon drew for them. He warned them that they must NOT step outside the circle no matter what they saw or what happened. The cats ands Lakota waited outside, while the Firebird sat high on a rafter. She was in no danger from demons.

The demons would be the first to go. The bottles were rocking on the table – there were over a dozen of them. Simon marveled at Karachev's being able to contain and control so many at once.

Father Grigory blessed the ritual before Simon began. The priest was wearing a pentagram that Simon had given him that would repulse the demons if one escaped – for they would instantly go to the nearest human and attempt to either subvert him or devour him if he could not be corrupted. "Will you cast them back into Hell?" he queried, nervously fingering the pentagram he wore.

"No," said Simon, "for if they are returned to Hell they can be used again by some other blood magician. Some friends of mine have given us use of a void in their domain. In this void the demons will sicken and die, for there are no people to corrupt, no Dark evil to feed from and no Light to try and pervert. They fade away to nothing and are gone forever. And no necromancer can possibly free then from Oberon's void."

Simon wore the green robes made for him by the Elves. Green was the colour of healing and was altogether proper for the ceremonies he undertook here today.

"First," he explained to the five watching him so intently , after the Holy Father had blessed the undertaking, "I shall open the door to the void." Simon raised his wand and pointed it to the air above the demon filled bottles. "Open to me, a friend of Oberon, void!" he said in Elfish.

Above the table the sky seemed to rip itself in twain and there came a roaring sound as if all of the winds in the world were within. The demons screamed. Their shrieks rose to a higher pitch as Simon awoke each cardinal point and the great angel whose name he spoke made his presence felt.

411

Like a great whip, power spilled from the end of Simon's wand, the fire opal on the tip glowing like flame. The tail of the whip gathered up the jars and threw them into the roaring mouth of the void. They all heard glass shatter and then more shrieks as the demons tried to turn back and race out the open maw of the void.

But they were too late. With a final roar like that of an oncoming cyclone the void slammed shut, then dwindled into nothingness. In less than a minute it was as if and the demons it now contained had never existed.

Anatoly, watching from the protection of the magic circle, thought to himself "I have a lot to learn!"

Simon closed the pentagram beneath the no longer demon laden table. The violet circle and its inscriptions faded away as it had never been.

Simon then asked Father Grigory to bless the next table as he invoked the help of the angels again.

There was a thunder like drumming and the room seemed full of mighty wings. The watchers could almost see , almost but not quite see, dozens of angels, cherubim, seraphim, archangels – all manner of heavenly beings. And they were singing – so beautifully. Father Grigory fell to his knees, tears rolling down his cheeks, but he still managed to say the prayers for the dead as Simon had requested. The other Russians knelt in their circle.

From the tip of Simon's wand a great white light broke and joined a light that seemed to be coming through the ceiling. The bottles full of souls began to dissolve and ghostly outlines of people – men, women and children, most of them serfs, began to stream upwards in the light, each escorted by an angel, all singing songs of welcome and calling "hosanna!" On each face was an expression of ecstasy. At long last they were going home.

The amount of souls seemed endless but as the last one disappeared, the light abruptly faded, the thunder of wings and the sweet singing fading too with the dying light.

And Simon staggered and would have fallen if Father Grigory had not leaped forward and caught him.

Tatya was by his side at once. "Are you well?" she cried anxiously, helping the Holy Father in holding Simon upright.

Simon shook his head. "Powerful spells such as those takes are rather stunning. And I used a great deal of magic yesterday. I just need a little rest, that is all." He gently kissed her cheek. "Let us go home, *acushla.*"

42

Loose Ends

Simon had hoped for only a few more days in Russia but it ended in being another fortnight.

Since it was closer, they first took Anatoly to his home, accompanied by the Firebird. His family was stunned to see him arrive on a dragon and even further surprised when they heard his news.

Resigning his commission! – very few officers in the service of the Czar ever did such a thing. But in the case, he had Nicholas's blessing, The Czar would even finance his Wizardly studies and an appointment as Imperial Wizard would be waiting upon successful completion of his education. The Czar also had given Anatoly a commission to recruit professors for the new Academy of Wizardry that was to be established in St Petersburg.

Nicholas offered the post of head of this new establishment to Simon, who turned it down without regret. He was a Dracophilologist and there was little scope for his profession in Russia. Sacha, who when tested, turned out to have magic as did his sister, wished to make Dragons his life's work as well – and his education in that subject could not be learned in Russia.

They remained with Anatoly's family nearly a se'enight, for there was the wedding to prepare for and both Anatoly and his bride-to-be, the Firebird, would have been disappointed if their friends had not remained to share in their joy. Anatoly and his new wife would come to Ireland in the autumn when Anatoly, although a few years older than most first years, would begin his studies. His bride promised that he would be completely fluent in English by that time.

The next task was to take Illya to his home. Another sensation was caused in the tiny village of Topek when Illya arrived dragon-back. And of course there was another celebration there that had to be attended.

His family had indeed thought Illya dead, and he was greeted as the prodigal son. To Illya's surprise and joy his father had realized that not everyone was cut out to be a cloth merchant, and had arranged, hopeful that his son would return one day, for Illya to attend an Academy of Music in Moscow, a famous school from which the graduates went all over the world to symphonies, and other orchestras.

Illya and Sacha, parting with regret, promised faithfully to write to one another.

Only then were they free to return to St Petersburg for the audience with the Czar, and to obtain passports for Tatya and Sacha.

To Simon's amazement the Czar showed his gratitude munificently. The monetary reward Simon almost refused, but thought better of it and determined to settle it on Tatya and Sacha. It would give them independence, and properly invested by the Duke of Chenevix's man of business, Mariposa, it could eventually yield handsome fortunes.

Nicholas also showered Simon with honors – the cross of St Andrei and a title as well. He made Simon a *Kynez*, a Prince of Russia, with all of the benefits and privileges thereof. Nicholas would become famous for his creation of Princes, no less than seventeen, including Simon. Although Simon did not feel that he deserved this – for the female Ice dragon had destroyed the necromancer. But Nicholas would not hear of his refusal. In his view, Simon had brought magic back to Russia.

When he asked what else he could do for Simon, the newly created Prince asked boldly for news of Count Ivan Kustodiev. Once he had learned of what had happened to Sacha and Tatya's father, Simon had decided that Count Ivan could just as well be exiled in Ireland, in comfort, with his children and resolved to do everything he could do to make this happen.

But they were informed, with regret, that Count Ivan had perished of a fever three years earlier. And notice had been sent to Yuri and Ekaterina. They had chosen to keep their niece and nephew in the dark.

Simon arranged for a proper headstone for his late father–in– law and for masses to be said for his soul. Tatya was much saddened by this and for a while, spent mush time in tears.

415

When they at last reached the Six Nations, Simon had Lakota take them first to the Hollow Hills, where he waited upon Oberon. He bore scrolls and letters from the Russian Elves.

Oberon was delighted with the success of his commission, and told Simon that he could ask a boon of the Elfin kingdom as a reward for a service well done.

Simon asked only that the Elf King grant his wife and brother-in-law complete fluency in both English and Gaelic. This had been his hope and plan all along.

This Oberon was happy to do and furthermore, marked then as Elf friends with the same gold star on their brows that Simon wore.

And thus, when they met their new family, Tatya and Sacha were able to speak to them in fluent English.

Epilogue

Dublin Ireland, April, 1833

"Perhaps this was a bad idea!" muttered Simon, pacing in agitated fashion about the tastefully decorated drawing room of his and Tatya's home in Dublin.

Several pairs of eyes watched him in sympathy. Sacha, Holly and René shared his vigil. Stuart and Noelle were still at their schools and bad weather over the Irish Sea had prevented Lyon and Ninon from joining them.

René regarded his son with sympathy. He well remembered the anxiety he had suffered when Diana had delivered their children. And with the twins it had been touch and go – they had nearly lost her.

"Courage, *mon fils*," he said as Simon once again ran his hands through his hair. "*M'sieur le docteur* has said that Tatya has been made to bear the children – but this always takes time, no?"

Holly, whose parents had chosen not to rear her on the new principles of ignorance of life and birth that were becoming popular, said, "Indeed, Simon, I have never seen a female *glow* as Tatya did while she was expecting! Why, she was scarcely ever ill! The Healer expected an easy delivery – he told us so!"

Sacha was miserable. huddled on a tufted velvet sofa. "Her mother *died*," he muttered, knuckling his eyes. He had come to love his new family, but Tatya was truly his and he feared losing her.

René rose and went to sit beside Sacha, placing a comforting arm about the boy's shoulders. "We have the best Wizard Healer in all of the British Isles, *non*? Everything will be of the best, Sacha. You will see! Very soon you shall be an uncle!"

The boy looked up, braced by the conviction in René's voice. He managed to smile.

A great roar suddenly shook the house as two dragons, Cerridwen and Lakota, bellowed outside.

"There!" cried Holly. "The baby is here!"

"How do the dragons know before we do?" asked Sacha.

"Dragons know many things that we do not," answered René. "You should ask that of Lakota, *n'est-ce pas?*"

Quick footsteps were heard coming down the stairs and crossing the hall. Dramatically, the sliding doors to the drawing room were thrown open.

"It's a beautiful boy!" Lady Diana cried. "And Tatya is fine – she had a very easy delivery and wants to see you, Simon!"

Simon took one wild look at her and headed at a run for the stairs.

"Our first grandchild!" Diana said happily, smiling at René.

Holly held up a tiny garment she had been knitting. "I finished the slippers just in time!" she announced.

"If I am an uncle, what are you?" Sacha said to Holly.

"I'm an aunt – as is Noelle. And Stuart is an uncle too," she replied, tying off the yarn of the tiny slipper and snipping it with a scissors from the embroidered chatelaine she wore about her neck.

"This baby will certainly have a lot of relatives!" Sacha remarked, thinking of the people in the Cotswold, and in Dorsetshire who were eagerly awaiting news of the safe birth. It was wonderful to be part of such a large family. René would be scrying the news to them and Sacha would go and watch, for the process fascinated him.

Upstairs, Simon quietly entered the sitting room of their spacious bedchamber. The curtains had been drawn, for the early spring afternoon was drawing to a close. A fire crackled in the hearth.

Nanny Sarah Pender, who had been nurse to Stuart and the twins, was in charge of the nursery and with the help of a newly hired nursery maid, Bridget, was preparing the cradle.

"You go right on in, Mr. Simon!" she said, beaming at the sight of the new father. "They're all ready for you. He's a little darling, he is!"

Dr. Ó Cennetig, who was cleaning and packing up his instruments in front of the fire, looked up as Simon approached. "Ah, Professor!" he said jovially, "Ye've a fine lad there and your lady is a brave lass. Would that all my lady patients gave me that wee bit of trouble – I'd be a less harassed man!"

Simon remembered the courtesy due to the physician. "My father will be uncorking a fine old Malaga to celebrate, Doctor, and would be glad if you could join him."

"Ah!" the doctor rubbed his hands together briskly. "Tis a cool night and that would be most welcome," he said.

The doctor looked as if he wished to go on talking but Simon paid him no heed. He wanted to see Tatya – and the child – his son.

The bedchamber was lit by soft mage lights and another fire burned in the Russian style tiled stove that Tatya had insisted upon. In the big bed, Tatya sat up amid a pile of cushions. Her maid, Aine, was fussing gently over her mistress. She had helped Tatya clean up, and put her into a lovely white lace receiving robe which had been a gift of her mother – in-law.

Tatya's head was bent over the tiny bundle in her arms, her attention on him. Simon though he had never seen anything lovelier.

"Here's himself!" cried Aine, catching sight of Simon. 'Tis a fine, darling boy, Mr. Simon!" she enthused.

Simon crossed the room to the bed and sat down by Tatya's pillow on the edge of the bed.

Without a word, Tatya pulled the swaddling blanket away from the baby's face and showed him to his father.

The baby was nearly bald, wrinkled and red – not particularly attractive, but to his parents he was perfect. He was asleep at the moment. Simon very carefully reached out and touched the downy little head. He felt a thrill run through his veins – together he and Tatya had made this little person.

"Have you finally decided what his name will be?" Simon asked in a whisper. They had made list after list of names, but Tatya had insisted that she would know what his name was when she saw him.

"Yes," she returned. "Alan René for your father. The next boy while be named for my father." Alan was the English translation of Alain, René's second name.

"The next one?" Simon stared at her. "Tatya, this one is scarcely an hour old and you are thinking about having another one?"

"Oh, yes," she said. "I am so much older than Sacha – I always wanted siblings – playmates. It will be nice for Alan to have a brother or sister close in age."

Women were amazing, Simon thought. He'd want to rest up for six or seven years before even considering another baby!

He looked back at her and was horrified to see a huge tear slipping down her cheek. "Tatya, *mo mhúirnín*, what is it?" he exclaimed.

"I'm so happy!" she sobbed. "When I lived with my aunt and uncle I never thought I would be so happy! With you, and my new family who love me as much as I love them, and my Witchcraft, this beautiful home – and now this!" She looked down at little Alan.

Simon picked up her free hand and kissed it. It was the right hand and on it she wore the *Cloddagh* ring he had promised her – two hands holding a heart with a crown above it. Like her wedding band, she never removed it.

"Now and forever," he said in Gaelic, for it was the language of poets, "you shall be my heart and pulse of my soul – I will give the rest of my life over to making you happy."

"Papa" thought Tatya "I hope that you can see me and your grandson. See how happy we are!"

And at that moment she felt as if a presence indeed was there, blessing them. And holding the baby closer, she leaned against Simon, content at last,

In far off China Dr. Quong Lee waited patiently while his grandson Hai fetched his writing tray.

April was still chill this year in the Sichuan province and the elderly Dracophilologist pulled a shawl more closely about his shoulders as he waited.

At last Hai, a solemn little boy, appeared, walking carefully so as to not drop the writing tray.

420

Dr. Quong thanked Hai gravely and told him that he might go and play.

He then bent to his task, with deliberation taking the pens that he used when writing to someone not Chinese, instead of the brushes more suited to his exquisite Chinese calligraphy. He had learned his English and his English style writing at a British school many years earlier in Macao
These skills had clung while the English religion he had learned there had not.

He was glad of these skills for he had a letter to write to an Englishman.

He took rice paper from the storage compartment in the tray and unstopped the ink bottle. Carefully, he dipped the pen in and shook off the excess.

He began to write:

My dear Doctor Stillfield,
As you are among the most eminent in our profession I write to you with a dilemma that this humble practitioner of the ancient study of the honorable and noble dragon cannot......

The End

www.ingramcontent.com/pod-product-compliance
Lightning Source LLC
Chambersburg PA
CBHW051516250626
47156CB00001B/107